KAYOS

KNOWS

An
Unfortunate
Lineage

VOLUME
VI

A Novel

KAYOS

KNOWS

An
Unfortunate
Lineage

VOLUME
VI

A Novel

Delaine Christine

Kayos Knows
An Unfortunate Lineage VI

ISBN-13: 978-1950563265

Book and Book Cover by D. Johnson
Model Pic by Andrey Kiselev, used with permission
Scenic Cover Image by Marina Pissarova
Interior Model Image by Badmanproduction, used with permission

Kimerah Publishing, Elkhart, IN

Printed in the United States of America.

The Prophecy

Continues...

But lo' beware the shadows will call,
tear her apart and make her fall

For within her lies a fragile heart,
but without her, we'll all be torn apart.

-Lilyandhi Blackthorne

PROLOGUE

Blackthorne Estate
near Lanarkshire, Scotland

The book was gone.

Staggering down the steps, around the banister, and into the entrance hall, Rourke Blackthorne's progression halted abruptly near the study door. His hand shook when he attempted to steady himself. Peering past the French doors into the room, his eyes found the open wooden box resting on the pedestal between the bookshelves against the East wall.

Still empty.

It hadn't been his imagination.

This was by no means a small loss.

Nearly three millennia of legible family history had been documented within the book. Their ancient lineage had been meticulously hand scribed by the Blackthorne line ever since their very first ancestor, Maxwell of Blackthorne was old enough to read and write. The story of the Blackthorne family's origin and how they were

1

linked to Major Thomas Weir of Scotland was in the book too. Along with notations of what ability each family member had been gifted with through the ages; all the way up to the present day. The shock of its loss and what that could mean for them all was only now sinking in.

After conferring with his father upon discovering its absence from its box, Rourke learned the painful truth. It had been missing for nearly thirty years now, according to him, and it had vanished around the time his own traitorous fiancée Sarah Ravena Croft had disappeared after having miscarried when she'd been beaten near to death, and just before his mother Sapphire had died.

Wanting time to research the contents of the book, his brother Rafe – against his father's wishes – had taken it with him to Colorado on his run for breeding stock thirty years before. Upon his return, he discovered it was missing from his overnight bag, though he'd sworn up and down it was on his person when he arrived back in Montana. Rourke now understood why his brother and father had stopped speaking to one another and why they had left him behind when they'd returned to Scotland after their mother Sapphire died. Rathbourne blamed the loss of it on his twin brother Rafe, thinking he had been the one to have absconded with it out of revenge for what happened to Sarah, but Rourke suspected he knew better.

Sapphire had taken it.

His mother had pilfered the book just as sure as she had sent it on to his brother whom he now suspected lived near Loveland, Colorado in the United States.

Yes, he was sure of it.

The baffling puzzle was finally starting to piece together.

Abhorred by the violence done against poor Sarah Ravena Croft, his mother had sent it on to Randulf whom

Rourke now knew to have been re-named, Bastion RavenCroft, for the RavenCroft's were kin to the Croft's; albeit distant. It had been her way of punishing them for what had happened to Sarah.

Rourke recalled vaguely now that Sapphire had befriended Sarah's mother before they had even been born. His mom had often traveled with her to visit with the woman's family in Colorado. It had never made sense at the time; her taking week-long trips with the Croft woman. Now he understood why.

She'd been visiting her son; his and Rafe's identical brother.

He might not have discovered the truth had he, his father, and recently deceased grandfather been sharing the same vision for the past month before grandfather Alestair died. It had hastened Alestair's passing, prompted Rathbourne's heart attack, and spurred Rourke's need to locate his missing brother. He'd only been digging into the past for the last few days as Rathbourne recovered from his heart attack, but in that time he had discovered the troubling book series written by an American author.

Comprised of nearly a dozen stories filled with their family names, their extensive heritage, past events – somewhat inaccurate in some cases, and current troublesome behavior of his many nieces and nephews, Rourke had been horrified to see their family secrets had been laid bare to the world within a paranormal suspense romance series. What had been most alarming was the implication that a man by the name Bastion RavenCroft, of whom he now was certain was his long-lost brother Randulf, had the Blackthorne and Weir-deVere book of lineage in his possession.

That news was what had hastened him to the pedestal where the book was to be kept within its protective confines. His lying father had supposedly been seeing to its care and maintenance ever since they had returned from Montana shortly after his mother's death.

Not true.

His father had been outed as had the entire Blackthorne family.

Yanking his wire-rimmed spectacles from his face Rourke hooked them to his shirt and rubbed the palms of his hands into his eye sockets.

What a mess.

This author, whom he'd ascertained was annoyingly utilizing a pseudonym, knew way too much.

In his mind, there were only two possibilities that made sense. Either the individual who wrote the stories had gotten ahold of the book from Bastion somehow, or...

-They were gifted just like them.

Gifted ... and quite possibly didn't even know it yet?

His stomach churned uneasily at the notion, somehow knowing that was much more likely the case. Granted, the books were listed as fictional novels but they were utilizing their real names. If the wrong people got their hands on them...

Rourke groaned, his pale blue eyes searching heavenward not so much for his Maker as he was for the spirited and spiteful minx of a mother.

"Do you have any idea of the damage you've likely caused?"

Entering the study he made a beeline for the desk and his laptop. He'd only managed to get through the first novel of the series. Learning there was a possibility the location of the Blackthorne lineage book was in question, he'd skimmed through the rest of them to determine the potential validity to the series contents. That's when he'd stopped and checked the pedestal. He figured he'd better get through the rest. Heaven only knew what secrets the blasted author was revealing, and at the request of the narrator of the story no less. Rourke somehow just knew that finding out who this Vortigern Black character was, was crucial to preventing a serious wrong. One that could devastate his entire family and potentially end their family line.

Chapter ½

Vortigern Black here.

That's right folks! I'm back, I'm back, I'm back.

Hurray, right?

I'd ask if you missed me, but I already know you do.

This time around the author is being all secretive; insisting upon writing the prologue of this story all on her own.

Phooey, I say! My fans want to hear from me. They want to know what I know and learn who I really am for I am a character within the vast An Unfortunate Lineage series.

Right?

The question is, have you figured out who I am yet?

If not, no worries folks, I'll give you another hint or two by the end of this story and believe me it's a good one.

At least, I think so.

To be honest I don't remember a lot of it. I've read through it before but was mostly skimming it so the author seems to think I missed a lot the first time around. She thinks if I'd caught it all, I wouldn't have such a carefree and blasé attitude right now.

Whatever.

What I do vaguely recall is that we're moving on to Dartanian Blackthorne in this one who, as you may remember, is the Sheriff of Loveland County and husband to Lylia, the homeschool teacher for all the Blackthorne children. Ms. Christine is being awful guarded over all the notes and versions of this here story I gave her, so I honestly can't tell you much more than that for now, but what I will do is catch you up on a few things.

When last we left the Blackthorne tale, Drinian had managed to snare Veta Rohann as his bride. It was a rough start what with all the questionable behavior going on between the two of them which was goaded along by those nasty shadows, the troublesome three. Much like what happened between Kalabernus RavenCroft and his new wife Ariana, though she was being stalked at the time by a maniac. In the end, though, things turned out all right for Veta and Drinian. The two were wed and are anxiously expecting their own brood of babes to arrive just like nearly all the rest of the triplets so far in both the RavenCroft and Blackthorne families.

By the end of the story, Drinian and Veta had returned to the ranch after their wedding to pick up her ornery cat and to see if their suspicions where their sister-in-law Lylia was concerned were true. They were worried she might have taken the journal his mother Lilyandhi had left him before she died. The very same journal that was believed to hold the prophecy she'd made. You know – the one that was supposed to somehow give Drinian some peace from those terrible shadowy creatures.

Oblivious to their concerns, and unbeknownst to most of his children, Rafe, the Blackthorne patriarch, was getting ready for his last consult trip with the CIA before his retirement. Interestingly, he was called off the case and summarily released from his long years of service with nothing more than a succinct thank you and good day.

The reader of course was left with the name Steven Adam Jameson, an anxious and edgy Rafe, a pot of 'Death Wish' coffee, and a warning from Breydon to Drinian to watch his back for it seems there were mysterious goings-on among the angels he can see. One would think that would have been a good ending point but no … not for the author who seems to love her cliffhangers. Which brings us full circle to where we are now in the Blackthorne tale and the introduction of the questionable Damien Biardon, his wife Ciara and, of all things...

-Another Dartanian.

Can you believe it – two Dartanian's? Only this one's a kid; a child who happens to be the son of the same man Rafe Blackthorne was presumably being pulled in for a consult on by the CIA.

Now, what are the odds of that?

It makes a body wonder where the author is going with this.

By now you should know the drill folks. I sure hope you're settled in and comfy somewhere cause you're in for quite a ride. Try and keep up if you can.

I'll see you at the end.

Chapter 1

"Afternoon ma'am. The name's Henley; I'm with Homeland Security."

The man produced his badge for Ciara Biardon's perusal as though finding a government agent at her front doorstep was an everyday occurrence.

Startled and oddly anxious to be in the presence of such an individual she leaned closer to the screen door which presently separated them in order to get a better look at the agent's identification. The night before the local evening news had reported that there were a couple of men who had been posing as cops in the Michiana area, so she was initially suspicious. The ID he produced though, appeared to be legitimate and the picture on it matched the gentleman in front of her.

The agent was an attractive black man with a goatee. His head was clean shaven and he was wearing expensive sunglasses, dress slacks and a leather jacket, which was odd as it was summer. His appearance seemed somewhat familiar to her for some reason but she couldn't quite place it in the instant the door opened and he greeted her.

Catching her off guard when the name he'd given finally clicked in her head, as she read it on his credentials, Ciara questioned it.

"Your name is Agent Henley?"

"Yes, ma'am. Agent Jericho Henley." He moved the ID so it was plastered to the glass pane of the screen door as though she hadn't been able to read it the first time around.

Stunned, Ciara stared back at him in dismay. It was the same name, and he was the same description of the agent she'd written about in the first manuscript of her book series. The uneasy feeling in the pit of her gut increased. She tensed noticeably.

"Is there a problem?" the man asked curiously, noticing her uneasy reaction to his name.

Blinking twice, she shook her head, giving a nervous laugh as she smiled. "No, of course not, I'm sorry. It's just … Henley. It's the last name of an ex-boyfriend I used to have." She cringed inwardly at her lack of imagination, having made up the excuse on the fly.

"Boyfriend, you say?" The agent smiled weakly back at her, causing her stomach to turn and sour. The way he looked at her was making her uneasy. "I take it things didn't work out?"

"You could say that," she said dryly. "We didn't exactly see eye to eye on things." Her heart rate increased exponentially when she suddenly realized why he seemed so familiar to her. Thinking back fifteen years before, she could almost super-impose the face of her attacker over the agents. If she didn't know better it could be the same guy but she knew that was impossible. The man who had assaulted her had a different name, had moved to Texas within days of the incident, and most importantly ... had been a white man.

"I see."

"Is there something I can help you with?" Ciara held tightly to the door for support. Her fingers gripped the knob to the point where her joints were beginning to ache from the tension.

"Yes, ma'am. I'm looking for Damien James Biardon."

"That's my husband."

"Is he home?"

"No, he's at work. What's this about?"

Evading her question, Agent Henley continued. "Mr. Biardon is currently still employed at Thoraxes Industries?"

"Agent Henley…"

"Jericho, please. Mind if I step inside?"

Instantly knowing allowing him entrance would be a huge mistake, she replied in an apologetic tone while ignoring his request. "Agent Henley, I don't mean to be rude but I actually do mind. My sons are home right now and this is not the first time someone has come looking for Damien."

"Really? Who else has been looking for your husband?"

"He's received numerous summons and court papers for one thing or another ever since we've been married." Frustrated, she stepped out onto the tiny front patio and closed both the doors behind her. Her movements forced Agent Henley to step backwards and move further down the steps.

"Can you tell me what these various court documents and summons were for?"

For some reason, Ciara found she was still a bit suspicious of the man's validity and wondered briefly if her husband was playing a practical joke on her. She knew he was aware of many of the characters she'd written about in her book. In that same instant, however, she knew somehow, that what was happening was by no means a joke. Trying to appear thoughtful, she crossed her arms in front of her. She leaned against the metal handrail, figuring it was best to simply cooperate for the moment.

"Just six months ago, the Sheriff served him with papers over a debt Damien claims isn't his. Before that, it was child support papers for a sixteen-year-old daughter they're claiming he has in Georgia; and before that, it was arrearage papers for an adopted daughter about the same age from the same state."

"What does he say about all this?" he asked while surreptitiously scanning his surroundings. Then he looked back at her, awaiting her response.

"He claims he's not the man they're looking for."

Interrupting her, Agent Henley asked coolly, "Ever think he might not be who you think he is?"

"What is that supposed to mean?" Fear enveloped her at his words, but she kept her expression placid.

"Mrs. Biardon, you never answered my question."

Ciara's eyes shifted uneasily toward the door. The agent's line of questioning was frightening her. She had written in the most recent version of her third book that the heroine's deceased husband hadn't been who he'd claimed. Determined to maintain her cool, she feigned confusion.

"Which question was that?"

"Is your husband still employed at Thoraxes Industries?"

She narrowed her gaze at the man before her. "I suspect you already know the answer to that question, so why bother asking me?"

"Ever notice anything different about … Damien?"

At the agent's obvious lack of response to her question, she posed another of her own. "Different about him … meaning what exactly?"

"Meaning anything." With a look of boredom, the man took off his sunglasses. Pulling a handkerchief from his pocket, he shrugged and began cleaning them. "Picking up on what other people were feeling, having an uncanny ability to simply know things for example or seeing auras around people. You know? That sort of thing." He was clearly trying to sound nonchalant about his inquiry.

Experiencing another tremor of fear Ciara tried desperately to keep her face from showing it. She was a good actress on most days. For as many years as she'd been married to Damien she'd learned she had to be. Forcing a harsh laugh, she rolled her eyes to the sky at what most people would deem a ridiculous question.

"The only special ability my husband has is a unique knack of managing to make me extremely angry."

"Oh? Why's that?"

"I catch him lying to me all the time. He's not very good at it." She hoped God would forgive her for the blatant lie. He was actually extremely adept at it. To the point of being maddening.

"I see."

"Agent Henley, clearly you have no intentions of telling me what this is about. It sounds to me like you really need to speak with Damien rather than with me, anyway." Ciara made it a point to emphasize his title. "So, if there's nothing else, I really do need to get back to my boys. I have things I need to get done before my daughter gets off the bus from school." Turning towards her house, she opened the screen door. The front door opened abruptly before she could reach for the handle. Seconds later her son Tanian popped his head out the door.

"Mama, can I have ice cream?" His face shone brightly with hope.

"We'll see," Ciara said quickly in response while gesturing him back into the house anxiously. At the same time her other son, Rafe came around the door. He eyed her and the man standing at the bottom of the steps outside.

"Are you okay, mama?" The boy looked uneasy and he stared at the man with a weary look in his eye.

"Yes, Honey, mama's fine. This nice man was just leaving." She barely glanced back at the agent, trying hard for the appearance of normal behavior.

"You have nice looking kids. Is Damien their daddy?" The expression on Agent Henley's face led her to believe he was more interested in her answer than what he was trying to let on.

Wishing at that moment she could respond in the negative, she replied honestly.

"Of course. Damien and I have been married now for over seven years. Listen, I'm sorry but I really do have to get to work cleaning or I won't make it down to my daughter's bus stop in time. If you need to speak with my husband, I'm sure you can locate him at his work."

"Yes, of course, Mrs. Biardon. Try and have a good day now."

With a smile and an awkward wave goodbye, she closed the door behind her, shutting him off from view.

Locking the door, Ciara applied the deadbolt for the first time in six years. Staring at the door in front of her in shock, her mind flashed back to the moment Agent Henley had produced his badge. She could visualize his name clearly printed next to his picture. He hadn't said anything to imply that she was in any danger, and yet somehow, she knew she was. Wracked with fear her arms began to shake as she spun around and peered down at her boys.

"Mama, you're all white." Rafe stared up at her with wide eyes.

"Yes, baby, I imagine I am," she whispered, afraid to speak too loudly. Irrationally she kept thinking he might still be listening.

Noise.

She needed a lot of noise.

Racing to the television, she turned it on and raised the volume.

"Mama, can I please have ice cream?" Her other son whined over the sound of the TV now blaring loudly throughout the house.

"Not now, Tanian, please! Mama needs to think." He pouted at her. She'd been sharper with him then she'd intended for her heart thumped wildly in her chest. Trying desperately to maintain control as a wave of panic seized her, she ran her hands across her face. The man was real. Agent Jericho Henley was real.

Lord, how is that possible?

Glancing at the door, she turned her attention to the bookshelf where four binders currently sat side by side next to numerous self-help books. Running her fingertips along the binding of each one, her eyes became huge and she stared at the titles she'd carefully placed on each one.

The first novel she wrote, she'd entitled 'Kayos Effect', the second, 'Total Kayos', the fourth was as yet untitled, but the third... The third was entitled 'Kayos Knows.'

Gasping loudly, one hand flew to her mouth as both hands began to shake.

"Oh, dear Lord Jesus in heaven is it true?" she whispered hoarsely. Tears swam in her eyes. *"That was a prayer. Really, Lord, I'm asking a question. Is it true?"* She turned on the spot and lifted her head to the ceiling of her mobile home, as though seeking answers from the heavens above.

Feeling sudden warmth spread from her shoulder across her chest and down her arm to her fingertips, she gasped softly. At that moment, Ciara Biardon was hit with the sudden and irrevocable revelation that everything and everyone she'd written about, was real.

- - -

Next to Ciara, the angelic presence smiled grimly, his soft grey eyes glimmering with both worry and satisfaction. The otherworldly being, in an effort to guide her through the ordeal, had been at her side since the agent had arrived upon her doorstep. The shimmering light emanating from him was warm and bright, giving his appearance an almost luminescent quality.

"Now she knows, Lord."

Seeing the woman trembling with fear and yet, an acceptance born of faith, the angel called Woreash closed his eyes and lifted his head toward the ceiling as well. He could hear the soft, soothing voice float upon the air over the muffled sounds of the woman's children and television.

Make haste. He is coming for them.

Nodding in understanding, Woreash opened his eyes and laid his hand upon her shoulder once again. "Yes, Lord. Thy will be done."

Chapter 2

Same Day
Four hours earlier.
Blackthorne Ranch
Kalispell, Montana

"Steven Adam Jameson."

Rafe stared out the balcony window at the mountainous view as he spoke. He could feel Dante's eyes on his back. He sensed, rather than saw when his son moved towards the cherry wood desk in the middle of the room.

"That name supposed to mean something to me?" Dante leaned against his father's desk, having been summoned to his office. His gaze roamed over the vast collection of Sherlock Holmes, David Eddings, Tom Clancy and, of all things, Agatha Christy novels lining his bookshelves. Shaking his head, he marveled not only at his father's tastes but his ability to read as much as he did. Both libraries, upstairs and downstairs, held a massive collection of which he was fully aware his father had read in their entirety. He was forever looking for new author collections to read.

Sighing heavily with his shoulders slumped, Rafe continued to stare out the balcony window of his study, as though looking for answers. "No, you would never have heard of him. But he is the reason why I've insisted on keeping yours and your siblings' abilities a secret all these years."

"What do you mean?" Dante eyed his dad suspiciously. His father was clearly agitated, which was unsettling. The man's normally calm demeanor was rarely if ever, cracked. "Who is this guy?" he asked, noting his father's King James Bible was out and open upon his desk. It was his favorite Bible but it was so battered and worn it was falling apart. It occurred to him a new one might work well as a Father's Day gift.

Pivoting so he could see his son, Rafe found himself facing the opposite wall with his desk rather than the one with his late wife's portrait. For the moment he was still standing in front of the balcony doorway. As tall as his son, and nearly as burly, his shirt strained at the shoulders. Bearing striking resemblances with similar features and the same crystal-clear blue eyes, one might have thought they were brothers. Even with the distinguishing salt and pepper coloring above Rafe's ears, if a person didn't personally know him, they would never know he was sixty years old.

"Steven Adam Jameson possesses the ability to discern good and evil in a person, just as your identical twin brother can." Rafe extended the folder in his hand towards his son. Surprise stretched across the younger man's face and extended to his eyes. "Years back, when he first enlisted in service, Steven's commanding officer discovered it, honed his ability and used him to facilitate his own personal little war within the bureau."

The little color left in Dante's face drained quickly at this bit of news.

"I received a call Saturday morning, as you well know. They wanted me to come back in for one last consult before retiring."

"Yes. I remember you said you were planning on heading out this morning. I take it the meeting was supposed to be over this guy?" Seeing his father begin to pace as he nodded in the affirmative, Dante inquired further while gesturing with the folder. "What happened? Breydon said you got a troubling call at breakfast and the trip was cancelled." Needing to be down at the corrals early, Dante had taken breakfast with him, in order to save on time.

"That's putting it mildly," Rafe said in contempt. "They no longer need my assistance. They thanked me for my many years of service and wished me well."

"That's good though, right? The less you're involved…"

"Dante, after over ten years of being in hiding, they managed to find that man." He pointed towards the folder in his son's hand.

Peering down at the folder in question, Dante became agitated when he saw it was clearly marked as a classified file. Upon further inspection of its exterior, it appeared to have come straight from Langley. That was alarming in and of itself. He knew such documentation was never to leave headquarters. Realizing what that must mean, his head shot up; his gaze locking with his father.

Dante's eyebrows rose in unison. "Are you serious? Did they bring him in?"

"Not yet. I doubt they intend to."

Rafe watched his son tense and peer at him in alarm.

"It gets worse. The assumed name he took, Damien James Biardon; the profile shows him as being married. He has a wife and three children."

Understanding what his father was trying to relay, he opened the file and began perusing the information quickly. "These children, we know for sure they are his? They're not adopted by chance?"

"They are not adopted."

"One of them could have his ability."

"Or all of them for all we know. But even if only one turned out to be his…"

"What do you want to do?"

"Relocate them with their mother before it's too late."

"And this Damien, slash, Steven guy?"

"I suspect that it's already too late for him." Rafe sighed heavily. "But if we can, we'll relocate him along with them. That's assuming the wife still wants anything to do with him after this. We don't know what all she knows."

"I'm assuming since you're telling me this now you already have a plan." Dante was about to lay the file back on the desk. Pausing, he finally registered what he'd just seen. Re-opening the file, he flipped through a few pictures before finding the one he was looking for. Staring down at the black and white photo curiously, he scratched his forehead in confusion.

"This photo is listed as the wife, Ciara Eve Biardon, but it's a picture of a child?"

"Caught that did you? It would seem a recent photo of her is rather elusive for some reason," Rafe said grimly, giving his son a knowing look.

"Not even from the Bureau of Motor Vehicles?"

"The state of Michigan BMV system was recently updated. Apparently, by accident, some photo records were either damaged or deleted in the process. Mrs. Biardon has apparently failed to present herself for a new photo." Then as an afterthought, he said, "She has a Facebook page but the photo she posted is a picture of a Black Baccara rose."

"Did you say Black Baccara?" Dante was floored by the coincidence. His brother Drinian had planted the same flower bush at the passing of his favorite horse fifteen years prior. It was why his new sister-in-law, Veta, had chosen to carry one the day they were wed. The sentiment behind it had been very touching.

"You heard correct."

Staring at the black and white picture of the little girl, who couldn't be more than seven or eight years old, Dante eyed it with a peculiar expression. "It might just be my imagination but the child almost appears familiar to me somehow. Why would that be? I've never been to Michigan."

"Curious. I noticed a familiarity myself and I'm not sure why. Usually, I'm good at placing faces." He gave his son a troubled look. Rafe had always prided himself upon being able to put names to faces and recall people he'd met. The fact that he'd been unable to pinpoint where he'd seen the little girl before had been extremely disturbing to him.

"This woman is nearly forty now and she's maybe eight in the photo. I would have been around the same age in order to have seen her like this and I was living on the reservation then. How would that be possible? I don't recall there ever being any white children there."

"Heaven only knows but that's not all. I'm surprised you haven't caught..."

"Dad," he exclaimed again suddenly. His face became visibly drawn and pale. Laying the file on the desk, he pulled three sheets of paper out and laid them side by side. "The names of these children..."

"Finally noticed that did you? Why do you think I'm bringing you in on this?" Rafe was showing clear signs of distress which was atypical of him. When he'd seen the children's names himself, he'd about fallen out of his chair. "I would have handled this myself otherwise. Frankly, I hate to even have to ask you to get involved, what with you having just married, and knowing that you and Alaina are expecting triplets but..."

"Don't even give it a second thought," Dante said dismissively, fully aware of the danger this could potentially pose for the entire Blackthorne family. "You're thinking this guy knows about us somehow?"

"I don't know, but I would wager he's got to know something with his kids' names being what they are. It cannot be a coincidence. This situation has my gut twisted in knots, and I don't like it. Not one bit."

Dante grimaced uneasily. The last time his father got that feeling was in January of the year two thousand. That year had ended up being a bad one for the entire family.

"We need to leave now." Rafe glanced at his watch. Seeing that it was nearly ten in the morning already he crossed to his matching cherry wood desk hutch and proceeded to shut down his computer.

Appreciating the magnitude of the situation, as well as the need for haste, Dante shoved the papers back in the folder quickly and stepped away from his father's desk. Tugging his phone from his pocket, he headed towards the study door as he spoke.

"I'll get my gear and then let Alaina know I'll be gone for a while," he said before he disappeared through the study doors. "I'll meet you out front in fifteen."

"Dante," Rafe hollered, not giving his son a chance to walk away. Seeing his son pop his head back around the door at him, he continued uneasily. "Make it ten."

Turning back around, Rafe inhaled sharply as a thought occurred to him. He realized he hadn't sought God's council on the matter. The instinct ingrained in him over years of training and experience told him the woman and children needed to be extracted immediately, but God might have another plan.

Walking swiftly back to the patio doors, he opened them and knelt down on the balcony. Raising his head to the heavens, he then bowed his head in submission as he spoke with Him.

"Lord, what is your will? What would you have me do here? Would you have me remove them from their home? I am but your humble servant; please lead me down the right path."

Sitting still in the quiet that surrounded him he listened for the voice, knowing without a doubt that this situation warranted His council. Confident he would hear from Him, Rafe stayed as he was for the moment, unconcerned by the time that passed.

Rewarded for his patience, the still muggy hot air was suddenly disturbed by a gentle breeze flowing freely about him, tickling the hair about his ears. A soft sound, like a sigh in the wind, echoed above him near the balcony railing.

Go now! Bring my children to safety.

Rafe's response was prompt and came without question.

"It will be as you say."

23

Same day.
Three hours later.
Edwardsburg, Michigan

Seeing his mark exit the Café, Steven Adam Jameson a.k.a. Damien James Biardon watched the man hobble around the side of the restaurant towards the back.

When he'd run into Ben O'Leary the night before, Steven had recognized him instantly. Over ten years before the man had helped facilitate in his identity transformation. Unfortunately, Ben had too good a memory for his taste. Apparently short on cash, the frog had threatened to expose him, if he didn't give him more money for his silence.

Broke, and having already paid the man a small fortune for his services years before, Steven had lost his temper. Punching him in the face, he had walked away, knowing instantly his mistake. Recalling the man's further threats as he'd gotten in his car and drove away, Steven had quickly come to the only conclusion he could.

He was going to have to silence Ben for good.

It occurred to him, if he'd just gone straight home as he'd told his wife he would, he might never have run into Ben last night. He'd been craving Chinese food for weeks though and had selfishly chosen to stop for dinner on his own rather than going home and eating pizza with his family.

Banging at the wheel in frustration, Steven made a careful assessment of the surrounding area to make sure no one would see him follow the man. Getting out of his car he strode with a cautious gait, quickly and quietly around the restaurant. His mind was on the task at hand, yet his focus was split. Eyes darting about him warily, he attempted to gauge whether he was being watched.

In order to facilitate the removal of this potential threat he had feigned illness at work and left early, just so he could deal with this mess. He also knew he only had a small window of opportunity in order to deal with Ben. If he did this right, no one would ever be the wiser and he could continue on living as Damien James Biardon with his wife and children.

Witnessing Ben digging in a woman's purse, which he'd clearly just stolen, Steven saw his chance. With a speed born of many years' worth of training, he grabbed Ben O'Leary suddenly from behind and reached around him. The man had no time to even make a sound for in one swift motion he'd snapped Ben's neck. Even while completing the motion an eerie sensation surged from his neck down his spine, warning of a dark presence nearby.

In the same instant, shouting erupted all around him. Five men in tactical gear converged upon him. Steven's body didn't just tense. It coiled as tightly as a twisted knot would when pulled taught by two people. Even the slightest touch of a feather would have shattered the supposed calm façade he evoked from the exterior.

"Steven Adam Jameson," the tactical leader shouted.

They held him at gunpoint.

A feeling of dread washed over him.

All he could see was black. And it was everywhere.

Like a wisp of pulsing black smoke, the darkness enshrouded their heads. His first inborn and ingrained instinct was to attack; to wage war against the evil nature within the men standing before him, to strike them down and to kill.

So that's what he did.

"You're under arrest for…"

"You will never take me alive," Steven roared. His eyes flashed with rage as spittle flew from his mouth. Out of the corner of his eye, he saw a brilliant flash of light near the back alley exit of the restaurant. In that split second he understood what it was he was seeing. Realizing what the bright light meant, he knew without a shadow of a doubt that his children's lives were at stake. He had to give them as much time as possible. His own life didn't matter anymore.

To those watching, it was as though a switch had been flipped in Steven's head. For a man who appeared to be an easy catch, having become soft around the waist, he was clearly not going to be taken down without a ferocious fight.

Peering down into the alley from a safe perch above the restaurant, Agent Jericho Henley gazed through his binoculars, as Steven Jameson engaged his men. Taking down two of the initial team members instantly, he incapacitated another while using one of the men to clobber another.

Seeing the man's skill was impressive, to say the least. Agent Henley had brought another contingent of men upon the Generals insistence but hadn't actually thought they'd be necessary until now.

"Converge. Flank him from all sides," he heard the team leader order. Agent Henley continued to watch while five more men swiftly moved in to assist.

The fight escalated and the battle below him became a brutal war zone in the alley. Becoming anxious at how much time it was taking, in order to take this man down, Agent Henley began to sweat. He watched as Jameson roared into the air then dislodged the last of the guns from the remaining tactical team members, leaving them virtually defenseless. Wiping his hand across his brow Jericho realized a decision had to be made. He had known the man wouldn't go easy but hadn't anticipated such a blood bath in the process. Clearing his throat he spoke into thin air.

"You get a shot, clean or not, take it."

No doubt people within the kitchen of the restaurant would have heard the noise by now. The last thing they needed were witnesses to this foray.

Seconds later the battle ended abruptly. Steven Adam Jameson was finally taken out by way of a sniper's shot.

Shaking his head, Jericho placed his binoculars back into his pocket. He sighed in resignation. He hated seeing a man like that cut down, rather than re-instated.

"Why do they always have to fight to the death like that?" He asked aloud to no one in particular. "What a waste. Let's bag him already and take him home," he said finally to the tactical leader while laying a light touch of his finger to his ear. "What's the casualty?"

"I got five dead and three wounded," the tactical leader came back. "One's really bad," he said between heavy shallow breaths. The fight had clearly winded him.

"Understood."

Initially, Jericho had been surprised by the request for the return of the body. He hadn't understood why until he'd been allowed classified access to the man's files. Learning of Steven's ability, the recent orders where the rest of the family was concerned made a lot more sense.

Confident the men had everything well in hand, Jericho walked swiftly to his car. His new boss had wanted to know for sure if the children were definitely Jameson's. After all, in this day and age, people were cheating left and right. Having located the wife at the house moments before the operation ensued, he already managed to ascertain that the kids were likely his.

Getting the call from the tactical leader as he left the Biardon residence, he'd learned they'd located Jameson.

Realizing he'd have to deal with him first, he'd left a man to watch the Biardon house. Now that the husband had been taken down, he could now deal with her.

Pulling out his cell phone as he got in his car, Agent Henley attempted to get a signal. Banging at the side of his phone in frustration, he stuck it out the window and waved it around, in an attempt to re-initiate a signal. Frowning at the phone, he pulled it back inside, stared down at it then threw it in the seat next to him in disgust. He had been having trouble with the blasted thing all morning and there was no reason why it shouldn't be working.

Unable to contact his guy staking out the house, he took a long drink of the iced coffee he'd left in the car, noticing most of the ice had already melted. Grunting in annoyance that the operation had taken as long as it had, Agent Henley pulled out onto the highway and headed back towards the mobile home park. The house was barely ten minutes away so it wouldn't be long before he had the wife and children in custody.

Chapter 3

Within seconds of closing the door on Agent Jericho Henley, Ciara had come to yet another revelation as well.

Everything had to go.

Now.

Every binder, notebook and scrap of paper that had to do with the Blackthorne's had to disappear from her home immediately, along with her and her children. Taking quick strides to the laundry room, Ciara grabbed the duffel bag from the hook and headed back to her bookshelf near the front door.

"Tell you what, Tanian. Mama's gonna take you all on a road trip instead. How does that sound?"

"I want ice cream," the boy cried angrily, unappeased by her attempt to pander to him. His brother gave her an anxious look.

"Part of the road trip can be getting ice cream during our stay at a hotel," Ciara exclaimed, trying hard to sound excited.

"Yeah! Ice cream *and* a hotel stay," Tanian cried.

Rafe stared at his mother in distress.

"But I'm gonna need your help if we're going to get out of here quickly because I need to grab some things first." Taking a deep breath Ciara pulled the binders from the bookshelves and tossed them in the bag in a blind panic. Whirling about, she headed for her desk and took the small black flash drive case from the top drawer. Making sure all of them were inside, she threw the case in the bag as well.

"Do me a favor; run to your rooms and grab your school bags. Pick one small toy and an item you want to sleep with that will fit in the bag. Then grab a change of clothes and pajamas."

"Okay, mama!" Tearing down the hallway, Tanian could be heard rummaging through his bedroom.

After zipping the bag up, Ciara crawled up onto her desk and stood on it. She reached for the large, three-foot squared section of paper that was taped there where she had drawn out blueprints of the Blackthorne ranch house. Carefully pulling it from the wall she dropped it to the floor. Turning to the adjacent wall, she ripped the second drawing down as well. Watching the papers fall to the floor she experienced a dizzying sensation. The feeling of Deja vu was unmistakable.

Frightened by the realization she'd written about a moment very similar to this, Ciara couldn't escape the feeling she didn't have a lot of time. The warm sensation pulsed down through her shoulder, across her chest, and along her arm once again. Peering at the clock on the wall above her television set, she noted ten minutes had already passed in a blur. Frantic now, she jumped from the desk, startling Rafe who stood watching her.

"Rafe, Honey, everything's gonna be okay." She tried to reassure him while snatching up the large roll of paper lying on her desk. Laying it on top of the other two papers on her kitchen table, she hastily rolled them all together.

"Mama, what are you doing?" He croaked, staring at her in a daze.

"I have got to get this stuff out of here." Dashing towards her son she took him carefully by the shoulders, understanding, at that moment, what must be going through his head. Rubbing his shoulders gently she smiled at him and kissed him on the forehead.

"You understand, don't you?"

"Yes, mama, I do." His face twisted as though he was about to cry.

"Little Rafe, I'm so sorry, Baby. I'm so sorry, I didn't know or understand until now. But I'm gonna get us out of here. Everything's going to be alright. God will see us to safety. You just have to have faith. Okay?"

Watching him closely, she saw him struggle to push back his fears. Nodding that he understood, little Rafe squeaked out, "Okay mama."

"Sweetie, can you be a big boy for mama and go pack a change of clothes and pajamas, too? Then help Tanian do the same. You know he'll need help; he can never stay on task."

"Okay, mama. You can count on me," he said bravely.

"Good boy."

Turning around, little Rafe sped down the hallway after his twin brother, calling out more instructions to him as he went.

"Mama says to pack clothes *and* pajamas, Tanny!"

"Oh, yeah, almost forgot. Woohoo! This is gonna be so much fun."

Returning to her own urgent task, Ciara dug through her desk drawers, managing to find a rubber band, to secure the rolled papers together. Glancing around the living room she realized there was still more she needed to pack. *Please, Lord, help me! I cannot forget anything*, she thought.

"Boys, get your shoes on too. Then let me know when you're ready." She hollered across the house as she yanked out her husband's desk chair. She knew she had to find everything she'd ever printed, even outdated copies, so she began rifling through the stack of scrap paper next to Damien's computer.

Hearing both boys respond in the affirmative, Ciara pulled all the scrap papers from the stack that had anything printed about her books on them and placed them in a separate pile. Shoving them in the bag she'd left on the table, she then crawled under her desk for her laptop bag. Thinking quickly, while still sitting on the floor, she yanked out the bottom drawer of her desk and pulled out several pads of paper on which she had all her notes. Finding two more small notebooks in her purse, she managed to squeeze the pads of paper in the duffel bag.

Running over to Damien's desk, she turned the monitor on and checked for files. Gasping aloud when she realized how much she'd saved on it, she hunted through Damien's CDs. Unable to locate the nuke disk he'd once shown her he had, she yanked out the tower and proceeded to remove the hard drive, stripping one of the screws in the process.

"No, no, no," she squealed. Her head swiveled frantically about her. *"God, please help me! I have to get this off, I cannot leave this."* Her voice raising an octave as she spoke. She looked to the ceiling, then back at the tower in her lap.

Sensing the woman's distress, the angel Woreash, who had never left her side, spoke quietly near Ciara's ear. "Do you see anything? Anything at all that might aid you in removing it?" Placing the tips of his luminous fingers against her left forearm, he touched her ever so briefly in order to gain her attention once again.

Feeling a jolting, tingling sensation in her left arm Ciara's gaze shifted from the tower briefly. Suddenly noticing a hammer laying underneath one of Damien's work boots near the desk that she hadn't seen before, she grabbed it. Smashing desperately at the tower, the hard drive broke free.

"Thank you, thank you, Lord!" She scooped it up as she stood.

Shoving the partially mutilated hard drive in one of the front pockets of the duffel bag, she unplugged her laptop from underneath Damien's desk and quickly rolled the chord up. Packing away her laptop and the chord in its bag, she set both bags next to each other on the table, along with the roll of papers. Staring at them for a moment she tried desperately to think if there was anything else she'd written that was missing.

She could be wrong. She might just be paranoid. But if her suspicions were correct and she missed something…

God help her, she wouldn't be able to live with herself if what she wrote got into the wrong hands. Phenom's hands. The potential consequences were limitless.

Ciara rubbed her hands across her face in agitation. Having heard the smashing noises, both boys had come running back down the hall. She turned towards them briefly.

"Everything's okay," she assured them quickly. "Little Rafe, we're gonna go pick Lily up from school. Can you and Tanian get a bag for her and…"

"Pack clothes for her too? I'm on it, mama. Let's go, Tanny. I'll tell you what we gotta grab."

"Thank you, little Rafe. Make sure you both grab a couple of pairs of underwear for her," she called out to them, for they'd already disappeared into their sister's room. Her heart was in her throat and she felt like she were about to have a panic attack.

"Are you sure you haven't missed something?" The angel Woreash gestured calmly toward the bottom of her desk. "Perhaps something still in the drawer?"

Out of the corner of her eye, for some reason, the bottom desk drawer caught her attention. It was still partially open from when she'd dug into it moments before. Stepping towards it curiously, she knelt down and peered into the drawer. There was something else. What was it?

"What have I missed, Lord?" she queried, her brow furrowing in concentration.

Reaching in, she rummaged through the items in the drawer. Seeing a thick manila envelope and her drawing pad, she gasped and yanked them out. Clasping them to her chest, she inhaled sharply. The envelope had her very first draft of the first book in it, and she'd drawn pictures of some of the Blackthorne family members in her drawing pad. If there happened to be any actual resemblance….

"Thank you, Lord," she said softly on a relieved sigh. *All in one.*

The voice, almost a whisper, seemed to echo off the thin walls of the mobile home, gaining the angel's attention once again. Instantly, understanding dawned upon him. No further explanation was required.

"Might it be prudent to condense everything into one bag?" Woreash spoke urgently next to her, all the while watching her look around the room. She appeared to be searching for something. Bending down suddenly the woman could be seen shaking her head as she began

34

shoving the items in her hand into the same bag. The duffel bag was already full, so fitting the manila envelope and drawing pad inside was a struggle, but she managed to do it.

Somehow she knew she had to fit everything in one bag. Picking up the roll of papers, she pulled off the rubber band. Laying them on the table, she flattened them and folded them a couple of times, squeezing them in the front zipper pocket of the duffel bag.

Grabbing the keys to the lockbox, she quickly dumped its entire contents into her purse. Seeing the envelope with her inheritance money from her grandma, she tucked it in the front pocket of her jeans, wanting to make sure she didn't lose it.

Go, now! Hurry my child!

This time, the whisper reverberating around the room was abrupt and unyielding.

Experiencing a sudden sensation of urgency, Ciara hefted the bag over her shoulder along with the laptop and picked up her purse.

"You don't have to nudge me twice, Lord."

Glancing up at the clock on the wall, she was astonished to see it had taken her nearly thirty minutes to get everything packed. She still hadn't grabbed clothes of her own.

"Boys! We have to go! Now!" With difficulty, she tried to keep the hysteria from her voice as she hollered. There was no time to grab clothes of her own. She wasn't sure how, but she knew she'd run out of time.

Turning towards the door, the boys could be heard running from their sister's bedroom. "We're ready," they said in unison, holding tightly to their bags. They handed off their sisters bag to their mother.

"Good. Hold on a moment. Mama's gonna take a quick look outside first. Then, we're going to race to the vehicle as fast as we can. Whoever gets in and locked in first, will get the biggest ice cream later."

"This is so much fun." Tanian beamed over at his brother, who stood intently watching his mother for further instruction. Though older by only six minutes, little Rafe understood better the seriousness of the situation.

Cracking the door open, Ciara peered out quickly to see if there were any unusual cars or people outside. Not seeing anyone, she quickly opened the door and herded the boys out. Slamming the door shut behind her, she didn't even bother to lock it.

As the boys raced to the vehicle and got buckled in, she tossed everything in the back. Peering around to see if anyone was watching, she forced a smile and hopped in. Putting the vehicle in gear, she backed quickly out of the drive and opted to take the back way out of the mobile home park.

Unknown to her, the angel Woreash had taken up a seat next to her in her vehicle. Aware of the presence of the two men close by, the otherworldly being lifted his gaze up through the roof of the vehicle. He sent off a message to his counterpart in the skies above, then silently urged on the woman next to him. The demons were close at hand. It was important to stay one step ahead of them or all would fail. The humans could fall into the wrong hands, which would be disastrous.

"Guess what mommy, I was first." Tanian bounced in his seat with excitement, completely oblivious to their plight. "I get the biggest ice cream!"

Woreash smiled almost sadly back at the boy. The pure innocence he saw in Tanian's face was refreshing. The angel knew the childlike innocence would one day be lost as he grew older and wiser to the ways of the world. The thought saddened him.

"Good job, Tanian," Ciara said brightly, forcing another smile as she spoke. Peering through her rear-view mirror at little Rafe, she could see him staring in a daze out the window and worried about how this was all affecting him. She'd based the little boy in her book off of her son, which meant that he might well already know if something had happened to his daddy; her husband.

Fighting back tears, Ciara realized she had no idea where she was going after she picked up her daughter from school. All she knew was that she was panicking and with good reason. She'd written about Agent Henley in her first novel but she didn't know him and had never met him before. When he showed up on her doorstep, she would have thought he'd have been looking for *her*. But instead, he asked for Damien, which felt to her, like a bad sign somehow.

"Lord, what's happening?" Ciara prayed softly. She drove along taking appropriate turns where needed. *"I'm not going crazy, am I? What I've been writing about; the Blackthorne family. It's actually real isn't it? They're real. This is what I've been sensing was coming, isn't it?"* Placing one hand near her neck, she held tightly to the cross hanging there, gaining comfort. Blinking back tears, she tried to calm herself by breathing deeply. At the same time, Woreash attempted to ease her distress with his hand. It hovered within a hairs breath of her right arm.

"The presence of Agent Jericho Henley at my house... I understand now. It means everything is real but what changed, Lord?"

Cocking a brow at her query the angel's gaze shifted over her. "Indeed, what changed? I think you know; you just don't recall it yet." Watching her closely, Woreash sensed her mind was racing through possibilities and was worried that the abrupt culmination of events would be too much for her mind to handle all at once. The gift was very strong in her, possibly even too strong. Laying a hand against her forehead Woreash attempted to ease the flow of thoughts so she might be able to piece them together more coherently.

Taking a deep breath Ciara shifted in her seat then exhaled uneasily. Allowing her racing thoughts to settle in her mind she furrowed her brow in concentration. In the third novel she was writing, her story had been about a female character who was an author. The author in her story didn't realize she was writing about herself within her own novel series. The story she had been depicting was of a woman, who it turned out, had the gift of Knowing but didn't realize it.

Shaking her head in dismay and wonder Ciara somehow just knew that she was the author she had been writing about in her own novel, just like the woman in her story who was writing about herself and hadn't known it. It would also follow to reason that she, like the character in her own book, had the gift of "Knowing." Trying to get her head around that, she rubbed at her aching forehead.

Thinking about what she'd written in the last version of her story, she recalled the CIA had not gotten tipped off to the husband's true identity in the story, until after a conversation the author had with a friend in a restaurant. She wrote that the woman had spoken of a drug lord named Kobi Radford who was a character from the very first book. He was the man that was intent upon locating and killing Alaina Blackthorne and her children. One of Kobi's henchmen overheard the conversation at the restaurant and called the drug lord, in order to find out what he wanted him to do about her. Since Kobi's phone had been tapped by the CIA, Agent Henley had come looking for the author in order to bring her in for questioning. That was when the CIA and Agent Henley discovered the author's husband wasn't really…

Gasping, her train of thought halted abruptly. Ciara suddenly knew why Agent Henley was looking for her husband.

Damien wasn't who he claimed to be.

They were looking for him now because of his past and his ability. What she couldn't figure out was how the CIA had learned about his true identity. Real life wasn't following what she had last written. What had changed?

Tears welled in her eyes as she began to cry. Her heart ached for the man she'd thought was her husband.

"Lord, please. Tell me I didn't do or say something that got him killed?" She whispered into her hand as she began to sob quietly.

"No. You did nothing, sweet Ciara," Woreash said next to her. "Steven made his own choices."

The pain of realizing she'd been living with, and born children of, a man she wasn't really married to broke her heart and the fact that Agent Henley had asked if Damien was her son's father filled her with dread. Why had he wanted to know that?

Suspecting she might already know his reasons, but not wanting to believe it or think about it, she decided she needed to determine how best to evade Agent Henley. She had a strong feeling he was bound to come looking for her again; if he wasn't already following her.

Scoffing out loud, Ciara whimpered in distress. Who was she kidding? She wasn't Damien. He had been the one who'd worked undercover and was accustomed to subterfuge; not her. If someone were following her, she'd have no idea.

Biting at her knuckle, she came upon the entrance to her daughter's elementary school. It occurred to her that she needed to come up with an excuse for pulling Lily out early on her last day. Once she grabbed her daughter, she now knew where she was meant to go; Kalispell, Montana. For it was where Ciara had written the author in her story had gone upon being discovered.

"Lord, help me find my way to the Blackthorne family I've written of in my novels. They need to know about me and what I've written. I must warn them before innocent lives are destroyed."

Hearing the song 'Something in the Water' by Carrie Underwood come on the radio, she couldn't help but feel it was a message somehow of the many drastic changes to come. But would she truly become stronger for it, or would she instead orphan her children?

Glancing in her rearview mirror, Ciara turned into her daughter's school and pulled right up to the front doors. She didn't notice anyone following her so far, but that didn't mean anything. Debating on the practicality of leaving the boys in the vehicle, she decided, in the end, she had to leave them with the SUV or Tanian would blow it for her in the office. He was such an innocent. He would never understand why she might have to lie.

"Stay here and stay locked in. I'll be back out with Lily in just a minute." Bolting from the vehicle, she ran towards the school doors. Entering the offices in a frantic state, she skidded to a halt at the receptionist desk, alarming the woman seated there.

"Can I help you?"

"Doctors appointment; Lily Biardon. I completely forgot and we're gonna be late," she exclaimed hastily, careening towards the door that led into the school hallways.

The receptionist hollered when she tried to escape through the door. Cringing inwardly, Ciara gritted her teeth and spun around to face her. She saw the woman at the desk was pointing to the counter next to her.

"You have to sign her out first, even on the last day."

"Oh, yes, of course." She walked briskly towards the desk.

"I'll call her teacher's room and have her sent down to the office."

"I'm in such a hurry, you have no idea. Can I just go get her?"

"It's really better this way; less upsetting for the other students." The receptionist rang the room.

Ciara finished signing her name. Becoming distressed at the amount of time that was elapsing, she tapped anxiously on the desk. What could possibly be taking her daughter so long?

Several minutes passed in silence before Lily finally appeared at the office door.

"Mama? What's going on?"

"You have a Doctor appointment, Honey. Mama forgot all about it." She took hold of her daughter's hand and dragged her towards the door. "Let's go or we're going to be late."

Rushing through the doors alongside her, while holding tightly to her school bag, Lily stared up at her mother looking awfully confused. "What doctor appointment? Why do I have to go to the doctor?"

Trying to rush her daughter along towards the vehicle, Ciara expelled a huge sigh of relief at seeing it still sitting there. It was untouched, with her boys still safely buckled in.

"I'll explain later."

"You lied to them. Why did you do that?" Lily stopped several paces from the vehicle. "Tell the truth, mama, where are we going?"

"We're taking a road trip, baby girl," she said in exasperation while gesturing toward the vehicle. Gritting her teeth, she spoke forcefully. "Just get in the vehicle. I will explain everything later. Right now we need to go."

Urging her daughter into the SUV, she made sure she was buckled in before running around the vehicle to the driver's side. Hopping in, it occurred to her, she couldn't remember where she'd put her keys when she got out. Checking her pockets, then the hook on her pants, she realized she must have dropped them when she got up from her seat.

After glancing around inside the vehicle first, she turned in her seat with her back facing the front windshield. Her head was bent down toward the cushions of the seat. Her eyes flitted around the cracks in a frenzy. Finding the keys wedged in the cushions, she exclaimed in relief. Turning back around, she put them in the ignition as a very tall, broad man with tanned skin, black hair, brown eyes and a scar above his brow stepped in front of the SUV. The man had effectively cut off her path.

She froze in place, staring back at the man before her. Was it possible? Could it really be who she thought it was?

The unreality of what was happening overwhelmed her.

A hysterical giggle bubbled to the surface as she stared back at the extremely handsome man who was blocking her path. It occurred to her he was exactly as she had imagined; had dreamed even. With the exception of his eyes.

"Going somewhere, Mrs. Biardon?" came a voice to her left.

Ciara cried out in surprise at the sight of another man coming up next to her unexpectedly. Heart pounding in her chest, she squealed in shock and dismay, reeling from the sight of the second figure as her hand flew to her heart. A sensation akin to Déjà vu swept over her once more. She stared back at the man, gaping in awe and wonder, shivering the closer he leaned toward her. The oddly familiar scent of his aftershave assaulting her senses was almost dizzying.

At that moment, Ciara realized instantly and without a shred of doubt who it was that was standing next to her in flesh, blood, and living color. It was the patriarch of the Blackthorne clan himself, Rafe Blackthorne.

Chapter 4

A little earlier.

Arriving in Michigan, Rafe and Dante, having taken up their assumed names once again, had procured a vehicle then headed towards the mobile home park where the Biardon family kept their home. Noting the unmarked car with a man watching the house, Rafe pulled out his cell phone. Placing a quick call to the local police department in order to report a suspicious vehicle in the area, they watched anxiously. Ten minutes later a police cruiser pulled into the park.

Rafe's suspicions were realized when the man in the vehicle, having been spooked at the sight of the police car, started his engine and drove quickly down the lane turning out of sight.

"This is off books," Dante said grimly, his eyes narrowing.

"Yup, so it would seem. The cruiser disappears, we go in."

"Got it."

The cruiser drove painfully slow down the lane. Observing movement at the Biardon residence, Rafe noticed the doors to the mobile home open. Two boys and a short, full figured woman with flowing long red hair ran for the dark blue, Jeep Cherokee parked in the drive. The woman's head was tilted down initially so they could not see her face. Her beautiful hair swung out behind her and around her shoulders as she ran.

"That's just great! Is the cop gone yet?" Rafe frowned. Leaning forward, he glanced in the direction the patrol car had gone. He was getting an unsettling feeling. It was as though he should know this woman somehow.

"Not yet. He's taking his sweet time being an idiot."

They watched in aggravation as the Jeep pulled quickly away from the house in question and sped off in the opposite direction of the police car.

"That woman appears to be in an awful hurry." Dante gestured towards the sport utility vehicle now turning right onto a back road, which appeared to lead out of the park.

"It would seem we may have arrived too late." Rafe's frown turned into a scowl. "Follow her. Let's see where she's going. She's missing a kid."

Nodding his head in silent agreement, Dante stayed with her. She drove several miles then pulled into what appeared to be an elementary school. As the woman exited the vehicle, she brushed her extraordinarily long wavy hair away from her face and over her shoulders. Her worried and seemingly distracted gaze shifted in their direction but seemed to move past their vehicle, giving them a direct view of her for the first time. Eyes bulging in surprise, both men exhaled sharply as though having been punched in the gut. They each sat gaping at her in shock, then exchanged glances in alarm.

Rafe felt almost giddy at the sight of her. "She looks just like Lylia," he exclaimed with a short laugh.

"Only about fifty pounds heavier," Dante muttered dryly in agreement, imagining what Lylia's reaction would be to learning she had her very own doppelganger. "What are we thinking here?" He tapped on the wheel, watching in amazement as the woman raced toward the school clearly in a panic. His mind was racing over the possible implications of her nearly identical appearance to his sister-in-law. Lylia's origins were unclear. She didn't know who her real parents were for she had been switched at birth. Was it possible this woman was related somehow? A twin sister maybe?

Shaking his head in dismay, Rafe watched Ciara Biardon disappear through the school doors. He struggled to maintain his composure. A nagging sensation was formulating in the back of his mind, as though a latent memory were attempting to surface and become a full-blown recollection.

"Is it my imagination, or does that woman look frightened?" Concerned, Rafe turned towards his son while trying to shake off the unsettling sensation for the moment. The last thing he needed right now was a distraction from the current situation.

"I'd say that's an understatement."

"If she comes out with her kid, we know she's running scared for some reason." Rafe gazed down at the message pinging him on his cell phone. "Because according to the chatter, Steven Adam Jameson was shot to death less than an hour ago. They were supposedly attempting to bring him in."

"There's no way she could know that yet, so what would have her running scared?" Dante's eyes surreptitiously took stock of their surroundings. Turning towards his father, he couldn't help but pose another question. "Do we have any idea how, after over ten years, they managed to locate him?"

"From what I gathered from my guy at the agency, they'd gotten a tip from a source who'd run into Damien by pure happenstance yesterday. The squealer had apparently aided Mr. Jameson in gaining his new identity years before and was currently strapped."

"I get it. He was looking for a payout one way or another."

"Right." Rafe continued to stare at the school doors then glanced behind him. "No way of knowing for sure, but I'm betting our Mr. Jameson likely told him off, then realized the predicament he was in."

"Let me guess, they got him as he was going after the nark?"

"Exactly." Hearing Dante's sharp inhalation, Rafe swiveled around in time to see the red-headed woman dragging her daughter to the vehicle. She appeared to be arguing with her.

"Ready for this?" Rafe inquired. The woman put her daughter in the vehicle, then ran around to the driver's side and got in.

"Let's do it."

Pulling the Dodge Durango up behind the Jeep Cherokee, they both quickly exited the vehicle. Without so much as a look back, the woman slammed the driver side door shut when she got in her vehicle.

"Better hurry," Rafe said crisply, not wanting to give her a chance to drive-off before they could stop her. Noting her frantic movements in her seat as he walked up beside the SUV, he realized she must have been struggling to find her keys. He signaled to his son and Dante stepped in front of her vehicle in order to block her path.

"Going somewhere, Mrs. Biardon?" Rafe asked.

Hearing her startled cry as she looked out at Dante, then over at him, Rafe found himself mesmerized a second too long by the woman's midnight blue eyes. There was a spark of light about them that he didn't often see in most people. Regaining his senses, he noted the look of shock and fear on her face. It was unmistakable. Between her reaction and the nearly identical appearance she shared with his daughter-in-law, he nearly lost his cool facade.

"Don't be afraid, my name is David Shephard…"

"Did you say, David Shephard?" Ciara asked, cutting him off in alarm. She gaped at him openly. That was the alias she had written in her novel that Rafe Blackthorne used when working with the CIA.

Eyeing her curiously, he replied, "Yes ma'am. David Shephard. Please, don't be alarmed. I'm with…"

"Oh, no. No, no, no! You cannot be here," she said urgently, her voice low and scared. Her eyes widened.

"I beg your pardon?" He gave her a quizzical look.

Peering around her frantically, she opened her door, forcing him to step back. Standing within inches of him after shutting her door, she peered up at him as though attempting to discern the true color of his eyes. A look of astonishment came over her when she saw he was wearing contacts. She clasped her hands over her mouth while trying to squelch the startled cry fixing to escape from her throat.

"Mrs. Biardon, are you quite all right?" Rafe was becoming uneasy at the look she was giving him.

"No, I am not," she said quickly, sounding terrified. Then she whispered, "You're here to get me out of here, aren't you? Me and my kids?" Even as she spoke Dante was stepping around to the other side of the vehicle.

Cocking his head to one side, Rafe watched her eyes dart wildly around the school grounds. He answered her just as quietly.

"Yes, actually, if you'd come…"

Ciara pushed at his chest suddenly, interrupting him. "Please tell me you only brought the one son and not your other three," she exclaimed.

Becoming spooked, he struggled to sequester his emotions and leave his expression blank. "My partner is here to aid in your extraction."

Dante opened the side door in order to get the kids.

"Franclin Kastle?" She hissed at Rafe, catching him off guard for a brief second.

"How did you know my name?" Dante called through the vehicle at her in dismay, having heard what she'd said.

"This isn't the time or the place for these questions," Rafe insisted darkly, taking hold of the woman's arm with a tight grip. "Let's go. Now!" The sensation that they were running out of time hit him like a blow to the chest, instilling within him an urgent desire to get them all out of there with haste.

"Yes, yes. Children let's go! Out of the vehicle now!"

"But mama you just said a minute ago…"

"Not now, Lily," Ciara said sharply. She stepped around Rafe and yanked open the door, accidentally banging it against his side. "Quickly. All of you out and into the vehicle behind us." She grabbed the clicker from her pocket and opened the back end.

"Leave it," Dante hollered, sensing both his father's and Ciara's sudden urgency yet not understanding why. He proceeded to help the kids hop down from inside.

Taking hold of her arm, Rafe began pulling her towards the Durango.

Wriggling from his grasp, she ran the few steps to the back end of the SUV, while yelling in a panic, "Get them buckled in, Rafe, please! I have to grab those two bags!" she cried desperately.

Losing his composure at her usage of his real name, he glanced towards his son with a look of incredulity. "Why?" He forced her to turn and look at him.

"Because *he* was *here*," she whispered harshly with a shaky voice. "Jericho Henley was at my home. If he gets hold of what's in these bags…"

Seeing the terror in her eyes, he didn't waste another second.

"Yes, Lord, I'm on it," Rafe mumbled under his breath. Feeling a heavy pulsing sensation grip his chest, he moved swiftly. Grabbing hold of the two bags in question with one hand, he physically lifted her from the ground by the waist with the other. Hauling his precious cargo to the vehicle, he dumped the bags in the back end then hefted her forcefully into the seat next to her children.

"Buckle up." He slammed the door shut as Dante got in on the passenger side. Getting into the driver's seat, he tore out of the school parking lot, not bothering with his own seat belt.

Intent upon the road, Dante's head swiveled around several times, attempting to see if they had anyone tailing them.

"Are we clear, David?" he asked his dad finally, turning towards him in his seat.

"I'm not sure yet, I'll let you know," Rafe said in an undertone.

"No point in calling him David. I know who you both really are," Ciara said from the back seat. Her fearful expression alighted with a soft knowing smile.

"Do not react," Rafe growled at his son. He glared at the woman through the rear-view mirror then returned his attention to the road.

"But you've come undercover. So there shouldn't be bugs in this vehicle like there were when Dante pulled Astraia from the safe house," she said aloud while gazing around the inside of the SUV. "Or, I guess actually, its Alaina now, isn't it?" Ciara observed as the two men in front of her flinched at the same time. Hand grasping the safety handle above his head she watched as Dante snapped it off. Whirling around in his seat, his eyes narrowed upon her with malice. Growling deep in his throat, he slammed his hand against the dashboard in front of him, causing her and her children to jump in fear.

Clamping her hand over her mouth, Ciara gasped. Somehow knowing in that instant, that they had no idea who she really was to them, what she was capable of, and what she had in her bags, her face took on a ghostly pallor. Tears welled in her eyes as her protective instincts took over.

"Stop it! You're scaring my children." Her eyes darted towards little Rafe. She could see his face was white and he'd begun to cry.

"Cool it." Rafe placed a hand on his own son's arm in order to get him under control. "You'll get your answers soon enough." Peering through his rear-view mirror again, he could see the little blonde headed boy appeared ill.

"Mrs. Biardon, what is wrong with your son? Does he require medicine?" he asked in concern.

Not answering, Ciara leaned towards her daughter instead. "Lily, switch with your brother please, quickly."

"Why? What's going on? Who are they? They're so big!" The little girl appeared more in awe over the men in front of her then she was concerned for her brother at that moment.

"Lilyandhi Biardon, you switch with your brother right now. I will explain everything later," she said forcefully. Reaching over she unhooked her daughter's seat belt.

"Okay," Lily sulked. Getting up from her seat, she moved towards her brother near the door. "Here, Rafe, switch with me."

"I want to sit next to mommy too, and when do I get my ice cream?" Tanian pouted.

"Dartanian, just shush, please. Come here, little Rafe." Ciara gestured towards her son, who was attempting to wobble towards her from his seat. His whole body was shaking. "Make sure you get strapped back in, Lily."

Pulling her son towards her, after buckling him in next to her, she wrapped him in her arms.

"Mama, mama…" Little Rafe began to cry as he clung to her.

"It's okay, I'm here. We're safe now."

Unaccustomed to being ignored Rafe spoke up in an attempt to gain her attention. "Mrs. Biardon does your son need…"

"What he needs is for all of this not to be real. But that isn't going to happen," she said while trying to comfort her son.

"Daddy, mama… My daddy…" The boy sobbed.

"I know. I'm so sorry, baby boy." Her voice caught as she stroked his face while trying to squelch a sob of her own. Her eyes began to well with tears again but she forced them back. She didn't have time for grief just yet. That would have to wait.

Dante turned in his seat so he could look back towards Ciara and the boy called Rafe. Brow furrowing in concern, he cleared his throat and softened his expression before speaking.

"Can you tell us what is happening with your son?" he asked kindly.

Her eyes darted towards her other two children, then she looked at him in distress. She knew the men needed some answers but needed to be careful what all she said in such close proximity of her kids.

Choosing her words carefully, she finally responded. "Some know, but others ... see." Kissing her son's forehead tentatively, she listened as he continued to cry.

In the driver's seat, Rafe winced openly. "How long have you known?"

"What time is it?" she asked, wiping tears from the corners of her eyes.

Glancing at the clock on the dashboard, Rafe replied, "It's 1:48 pm Michigan time. Why?"

"I'd say about forty-five minutes." There was a catch in her voice.

Swearing, he grimaced making a hasty decision. "Plans have changed. This is no longer an extraction and relocation."

Turning towards his father, Dante had a bad feeling he knew what the woman meant by what she'd just said. "What's plan B?"

Rafe's gaze locked on the road before him as he drove. Anxiety and anticipation waged a war within his gut. Finally, he spoke. "We take them home."

Chapter 5

Pulling into a small county airport five miles south of the Michigan border, Rafe let everyone out in front of the hanger which currently held his plane, then parked the vehicle near a different one. With both bags in hand, he walked back towards his private jet. Breathing deeply of the already hot and muggy Indiana air, he talked with God.

"What is going on, Lord? This woman you have sent me to save looks identical to Lylia. Does that mean what I think it does?" His heart thudded anxiously at the thought.

"From all appearances, her child has the gift of Sight and she had been unaware of it until now; and how is it she knows who we are?"

Wanting and needing answers, Rafe expelled an uneasy breath as he mounted the stairs of his plane. He knew he might not get those answers until he managed to get her back to the ranch, where they could speak in private without the children's tender ears being present.

Deep in thought, he frowned while entering the Blackthorne family's private jet. He was disturbed at the notion of what the boy might have seen. Wondering whether the child had tipped his mother off that something was wrong, or if Agent Henley had said something that had spooked her, he eyed the boy curiously.

"My bags! We have both of my bags?" Ciara asked in earnest bringing him out of his reverie. "We cannot afford to leave them behind like Alaina's trash bag of clothes."

Having already secured her children in seats, Dante had just come up from the floor, when she spoke. Whipping his head around, he stared at her darkly and gave her a ferocious glare.

"What is it about these bags that have you so agitated?" Rafe gestured for his son to stay quiet. Shrugging the bags in question off of his shoulder, he extended them towards her. He, like Dante, was also becoming quite unsettled by her knowledge of his son and Alaina. Closing the hatch on the plane he flicked the switch on the intercom, letting his pilot, Marshall, know he was ready to depart.

Dropping to the floor with the bags, Ciara heaved a huge sigh of relief. She had been so on edge during the drive from her home to the airport; she hadn't even bothered to investigate her current surroundings until now. It was just as she imagined it would be. Right down to the navy-blue trim on the velvety ivory couch that stretched a good portion of the inside of the plane.

Fidgeting with the zipper on her duffel bag, she debated on whether or not to show them what was in the bag just yet. Staring up at Rafe, now towering over her, his fists on hips as she huddled on the floor, her breathing became heavy and erratic. Feeling the plane taxiing down the runway she figured now was probably as good a time as any.

"Please, keep in mind, Rafe. I had no idea, okay? I really didn't know." She was struggling to keep from crying in distress. A tear trickled down her cheek as she watched him bend down in front of her.

"How is it you know my name? Did your husband tell you?" His voice was soft; his mannerism and expression curious.

Laughing nervously, Ciara placed a shaky hand over her mouth. She smiled weakly.

"No, Damien had no clue. He knew I was writing stories but he had no idea who you were. He had a gift, like your son Dartanian, but I..."

"Wait just a minute." Rafe interrupted her, becoming both overwhelmed and alarmed by everything she seemed to know about them. "Ciara, how is it you know about that, me, and my family if he did not tell you?"

"Because I ... I just know." There was a long pause. She stared Rafe directly in the eye. Seeing a glint of understanding emerge there, she nodded her head in distress. "But I didn't know, honestly, I didn't."

"You're not making any sense." Dante glowered at her.

"Knowing. You have the gift of Knowing," Rafe said evenly, startling his son. "How long have you..."

"I'm so sorry, Rafe. I didn't know."

"You didn't know what?" He asked in confusion, tiring of the repetitive response, yet trying to stay calm, and sound understanding. "That you had this gift?"

Nodding, she began to cry and her hands shook mercilessly. "Yes, and I've been writing. Since January of last year," she hiccupped. "I've been writing stories about all of you," she explained on a wail, pointing anxiously towards the bag with a shaking finger.

Shocked to his core, Rafe's insides went cold.

Grabbing for the duffel bag, he opened the bag and hastily pulled out the binders. Staring down at them in horror at seeing his family name printed across one of the cover inserts, he looked back at Ciara in wonder.

"Has this been published yet?" Rafe asked in alarm, sounding strangled.

"No. No, I hadn't the chance to…"

"Who's seen these?" His voice was crisp and void of emotion, as he quickly cut her off, having regained his senses.

"Damien read part of the first one but I think we all know he's not a concern anymore." She whispered softly, so her children wouldn't hear.

"He could have been before?" Dante's voice was barely a whisper as well.

"Oh, yes. If he knew about all of you and that you were real … he would have tipped them off in a heartbeat, just to save his own skin, as well as his children."

"Who else?" Having clearly figured out from her expression and mannerisms, that Damien wasn't the only one aware of what she'd written, Rafe crossed his arms and waited for her answer.

"A friend of mine named, Kathy. She read a few chapters of book one for me but I don't think it was enough to become an issue." She tried to assure him. "And I was telling my friend, Rachel, a little bit about you this morning."

"What specifically?"

Eyeing Rafe with trepidation, Ciara winced. "About your parents, Rathbourne and Saphire, and how they had emigrated from Scotland with family money and…"

Coming up off the floor unexpectedly, Rafe growled in frustration. He pointed at the binders in his hands. "Did you put that in here?"

Covering her face with her hands, she peered back up at him through her fingers, her face turning bright red. Moaning, she responded as though she were in pain.

"Oh, Rafe, I put everything about you and all six of your children and their spouses in them."

"Everything? Meaning what exactly?" He stared back at her in dismay, needing to hear it for himself. He already suspected he knew what she meant.

"Meaning the abilities you've all been gifted with by God, as well as … certain events."

Glancing from her to the binders, down to the duffel bag, and back up again, Rafe was flabbergasted. "From what time period does it start?"

Cringing, she glanced furtively towards Dante. "Depends on what you mean."

"Why?"

"Because it spans time," she explained weakly. "In book one, I tell about an incident from fifteen years ago that Alaina had when she was assaulted in her home." Frowning, she appeared thoughtful a moment. "Or, I guess, that part is actually my story, but she was assaulted that year. I just don't have those details. For some reason, I found myself describing my own unfortunate encounter, as though it were hers. But I do have about Dante finding out about Elizabeth in there. You know, when you broke your dad's desk."

Both men stared at her in shock.

Stunned, Rafe ran his hands through his hair in agitation while trying desperately to take it all in. Setting the binders on a nearby table he glanced towards the children sitting quietly on the couch. The girl and Tanian had turned around in their seats and were staring intently out the window. The boy called Rafe, however, was watching them with a strange look on his face.

"You have movies stored in here somewhere." It was more of a statement than a question. She glanced around the plane then crawled towards her son, taking him about the shoulders. "If you raise the TV up from the table for them and maybe pop some popcorn if you have it, then it will distract them when they get bored. It will help little Rafe too. He needs something to distract him from the images in his head right now. It worked anyway in a couple of versions of book three that I wrote."

"How many versions are there?" Rafe strode toward the cabinet on the wall. "How many books have you written? Just those four?" Opening the doors, he stared blankly at the movies there, unsure what to pick for them.

"I think you have Ironman. If not that, then any superhero cartoon will do. Tanian's like you, he loves Superman." She laughed nervously, catching the strange look Rafe exchanged with his son.

"That… is just plain eerie." Dante's eyes widened both at her uncanny knowledge and the coincidence. Superman also happened to be his brother, Dartanian's favorite as well.

"We'll get them settled first, then we need to talk while I peruse these books of yours." Pursing his lips, Rafe noted they did, in fact, have the first season of an animated Ironman in the cabinet. Grabbing it out, he pulled the first disk from its case and raised the TV. The children marveled over its sudden appearance. Seeing little Rafe's lack of reaction he noted the boy had tilted his head to one side in a way that expressed interest. Crawling onto the floor in front of the TV screen, he sat Indian style as he watched the blank screen, as though waiting.

Kneeling down next to him, Rafe gently placed a comforting hand on the boy's shoulder. "Would you like to watch Ironman?" He watched the boy's face closely.

Peering up at him with the same midnight blue eyes as his mothers, the boy simply nodded his head, then turned back and stared at the screen, as though waiting patiently. Concerned he might be going into shock, he gestured towards Dante to get him the blanket lying nearby. Taking it from him, Rafe wrapped it snuggly around the boy and started the DVD player.

"Are you okay son? Do you need anything else?" He briefly sat next to him wanting to make sure he was going to be okay. "Would you like your mama to sit with you a while?"

Little Rafe shook his head bravely and stared at the tv. "I know you two need to talk to her and there *is* a lot she needs to tell you. My brother and sister are with me right now, and besides … like the pastor said, 'God doesn't give us anything we can't handle.'"

Smiling down at him, Rafe laid his hand gently on his head and caressed his hair for a moment. "Out of the mouths of babes. Good boy. I think you'll be fine." Clearly, God had a place in the boy's life already. Pleased to see that, he got up and moved away to give the other two kids more room.

Having found a bag of popcorn in the pantry, as well as a bag of chips and apple juice boxes, Dante handed them to the children now huddling together on the floor.

Still sitting on the couch near where little Rafe had just been, Ciara tried to regroup and get her bearings as the men saw to her children. They were all content on the floor at the moment. Even little Rafe seemed to be bearing up under the weight of what he'd learned.

Taking a calming breath of her own, she ventured shyly over to them. They were both now standing near the table that currently held the binders filled with the first of her novels.

"Thank you, for bringing us to safety."

"It was nothing," Rafe said.

"On the contrary, it was everything to me." She glanced at her children, becoming extremely emotional. "*They* are everything to me."

Deferring his head towards her, Rafe spoke. "I do understand."

She took another deep breath. Where to start? No better place, she supposed then where she'd started. "You'll want to start with The Beginning."

"Sorry?"

"An Unfortunate Lineage: The Beginning. Though I suddenly can't help but wonder if Kayos Effect wouldn't have been better? Hhmmm. It's the first book about the Blackthorne's in the series. It's the one about Dante and Alaina and how they met."

"Is it really?" Both men spoke at the same time, exchanging uneasy glances.

Nodding, she proceeded to explain.

"The idea was to write a seven-book series about two different families that could branch out and become more if there was interest. At one point I'd even thought to do children's books. Three of the novels were meant to revolve around your triplets, telling one couple's story at a time. There'd be one about Dante and Alaina, and another about, Drinian and Veta."

"You skipped my third son."

"Yes, I know. Intentionally so." Ciara inhaled uneasily as she lifted the binder entitled Choices so they could see.

"He's the one who gave me the most trouble." She ran a shaky hand across its cover.

"Why? What do you mean?"

"Because this isn't the only version. It's just the first of six." She flicked a section of her long hair back over her shoulder. It occurred to her, that what she'd said wasn't true. "No, wait, eight!" When she'd first started the book originally it had been with the intent of making it solely about Dartanian. It wasn't until she'd gotten further into book one that she'd changed her mind.

Seeing Rafe watching her intently, she fidgeted where she stood. "There were two others before this copy. In here, is how I originally saw the story progressing. But it kept changing in my head. After I completed the third revision I started over again. As I was writing the fourth the title came to me."

"An Unfortunate Lineage," Dante read aloud. One eyebrow slowly rose toward his father who frowned, pursed his lips, and shook his head. The man's guarded look wasn't without reason. Dante wondered if the woman knew how truly accurate the series title was. The Blackthorne family line originated with the Weir-deVere's of Scotland. The origins of their line had been secretly guarded within an extensive book of Lineage for over seventeen hundred years that he was aware of. The book sadly had disappeared fifty-seven years before around the time his dad's brother Randulf had died.

"Choices." Rafe finished reading the title. He eyed the binder cautiously knowing full well where his son's mind had gone. His own brows rose in question as he peered over at Ciara.

"Yup, though I get the feeling now that my titles are wrong somehow. Kayos Knows would work so much better; and that's Kayos with a K, of course."

"Why a K?" Dante asked.

"I don't know."

"You don't know why it'd be spelled with a K, but you know for sure it should be?" he asked again.

"As I said, I don't know. I just know."

"Okaaaay." Dante's eyes nearly drew back into his head. Her logic made no sense, yet he noted his father was oddly smirking over the exchange.

"I didn't understand before, but now…" Her voice trailed off, her eyes fixating upon Rafe. A soft, oh, escaped her lips, as she looked upon him as though entranced. Inhaling deeply, she blinked and stared down at the binder. "I think I keep writing it over and over again because God gave mankind free will."

Dante stared at her in confusion at first, but his father looked upon her as though he were formulating a thought. Seconds later a soft sound of understanding escaped his parted lips.

"I see. Like a pebble in a stream… Every time someone makes a choice it's having a rippling effect which is changing the course of events. Ciara, are we living through the events in this story right now? Is that what I'm getting from you here?" Rafe asked.

"It appears so, yes."

"You said you started this series in January of last year?"

She nodded her head.

"But you have four books here, already." He noted the binder for book four didn't appear to be as thick as the rest. Knowing they were currently living through events of book three Rafe was startled to see she'd already been working on book four. It implied her awareness of the potential future.

"Yes, but those are only what I've printed so far, not my finished works. Book one does happen to be my final completed version but book two and three are not." She gestured towards the binders in question. "Book two and three are the secular versions I wrote, before deciding to write a more Christian oriented series. Or rather…" Confusion suddenly riddled her features and she gave the appearance her head was beginning to ache. "You know what? I'm not sure I have these in the right order. Book one should be two, book two is four, and I'm pretty sure Choices – or, yes, I think I like Kayos Knows much better – but I'm sure now it's actually meant to be book six. There should be stories in between these I think."

Dante stared at her in alarm. "Ciara, where's the finished product?"

"It's all there in the bag," she assured them. "I have everything saved on flash drives which are in a case in there, though, there might be some on the laptop," she admitted finally with a sheepish grin. "That's why I insisted on dragging it along. I tore the hard drive from Damien's tower. It's in there too. I'm pretty sure I got everything, though, I almost missed grabbing my original copy of book one and my drawing pad." she said on a side note. "Book four – which I guess is actually seven – isn't finished yet, as you can see. It's just started really, and probably the most mind-boggling and amusing of the set so far." She sighed and smiled wistfully while brushing strands of her pretty hair away from her face once again. "That chaotic woman in it has such charisma." She laughed at her own internal joke.

Rolling his eyes in amusement, Rafe could see she was heading off on a tangent. "Regardless of order, you've managed to finish three of the books and you're in the middle of the last one now?" He scratched his head in confusion. "How is that a seven-book series if you've only written three and a half of them so far? And why write them out of order?"

"Actually, all seven are started in one form or another, but as I said, they're saved on my flash drives in the case in the bag," Ciara admitted, cringing at the startled looks on their faces, as they exchanged glances. She imagined it was a rare day when either of the two men was dumbfounded as they were now.

"You said 'The Beginning' is about how Alaina and I met?" Dante opened the binder before him.

"Oh, I'm re-naming that one Kayos Effect."

Dante's eyes widened briefly before staring down at the cover page. "Where exactly does it start?" He could tell her mind was whirling a thousand miles a minute and he was having trouble keeping up.

"April nineteenth of this year at the grocery store," she said eliciting sharp looks from both men. "Though, there is a flashback in the Prologue from fifteen years before to that date. Now this one about Drinian and Veta; 'Angels and Demons' – no, no. I don't like that … Total Kayos, that's it – well, it starts on May 17th of this year the day before Dante arrived home." Lifting the binder in question, she laid it in Dante's hand.

A sound, something akin to the wind blowing through a tunnel, rushed into Ciara's left ear quite suddenly.

Stop!

Batting at her ear as she flinched, her mind on the book in Rafe's hand, she continued to speak.

"That one though – it says Choices on the cover but it's actually Kayos Knows – well, anyways, as I said it's the one that's been giving me some trouble." She rubbed at her forehead. Pausing briefly in thought, Ciara was more aware this time when the noise hit her ear once again.

Stop! Enough!

Head jerking, she batted at her ear again, appearing startled this time. "Wait, what?"

Narrowing his gaze upon her, Rafe found her behavior curious. "Is something wrong?"

"Well, I just… That was weird. What was that?" Eyes squinting, she glanced around then stared at Rafe.

"What was what?" Dante asked peering around the interior of the plane as well, then back at Ciara.

Hearing the sound once again, understanding finally dawned on her and her eyes widened in surprise.

No more. Sleep.

"Oh, okay."

Perplexed, Rafe watched the woman before him in amazement as it occurred to him what must be happening to her. One minute, Ciara was staring back at him, and in the next instant, she closed her eyes but they didn't open again.

"Catch her," little Rafe called from across the plane. He continued to stare at the TV screen, watching Ironman intently as he ate chips.

In the next instant, Ciara crumbled before them. Standing the closest, Rafe's arms shot out and took hold of her before she could fall to the floor.

"Wow, Lord. You really know how to put an extra beat in a man's heart." Rafe gazed up at the roof of the plane above him, relief washing over him for having caught her in time. Lifting her up with ease, he cradled her in his arms. She was heavy but still manageable. Her beautiful long strawberry blonde tresses, hung in tangles over his forearm as he held her protectively there.

"Little Rafe. Did you see that coming?" Dante asked the boy in astonishment.

"Uh, huh."

"Is mama okay?" Tanian asked in a soft, worried tone. His lip quivered slightly as he spoke.

"She'll be okay, Tanny," Little Rafe said.

"Yeah. It's just too much for mama at once." Lily dug into her popcorn bag voraciously, while at the same time holding a hand to her chest. "She needs rest. You'll see Tanny, just look at mama real hard like you do sometimes and you'll see it. Besides, my feet aren't tingling when I'm next to mama. It only happened when I was standing near daddy last night."

Watching as the little boy called Tanian turned and looked at his mother, he fixed her with a furrowed brow and eyed her, turning his head as he did so. Then suddenly, nodding his head as though satisfied, he glanced back at the TV and sipped at his juice box.

"Yup, she's still all white as bright as the light," he murmured into his straw. "Daddy was blacker than black this morning though," he said suddenly with a shiver. "Where is daddy anyway? Did he already go to God?" He looked at his brother sounding instantly sad.

"I'm sorry, Tanny." Little Rafe nodded sadly himself. Heaving a heavy sigh, he exchanged looks with his sister and went on. "Lily was right. He's already gone." Glancing quickly over at Rafe, he met his gaze then looked back at Tanian. Patting his brother's knee, as he was starting to cry, he continued. "Just enjoy the plane ride and movie; and wait until you see the playroom mama wrote about, Tanny. We'll really have a blast then."

"Did you actually see it happen?" Lily asked tentatively, her eyes misting with tears.

Little Rafe shook his head then answered, his voice tremulous as he spoke. "God's not cruel. He wouldn't do that to me. I dreamed about it though. When I saw the man at the house today, I knew it was about to happen."

Nodding their heads sadly in understanding, Lily and Tanian turned their attention back to their snack and the TV. A silent mutual agreement that they needed to not think on it for a while seemed to pass among them.

"Whoa," Dante said softly under his breath. He stared openly at the children.

"Get used to it. You have three of your own coming." Rafe strode toward the couch and laid Ciara upon it. "It would seem those children are already aware of their father's fate; were aware something might happen in advance even," he said quietly, trying to keep his voice down. He gestured towards Dante to do the same.

"The girl, Lily, with the tingling feet. Possibly death omens?"

"So it would seem."

"Why do I get the feeling we just barely dodged a torpedo?" Dante watched his father grab a blanket and cover Ciara, tucking it in around her for warmth. Noticing him smiling down at her, Dante eyed him curiously. His behavior towards her seemed almost familiar.

Standing, Rafe looked intently upon the woman now sleeping soundly before him. He'd never met another like him other than his late wife, Lilyandhi, and even *she* didn't have the gift as strong as what this woman seemed to.

Observing her as he was, he noted she had freckles on her cheeks. Trying to recall if Lylia had them as well, he was pretty sure they might be unique to Ciara alone. Finding the strawberry blonde coloring much more flattering to her complexion, than the bleach blonde Lylia wore, he suspected Ciara might dye her hair as well.

"They are not entirely identical I'd say. Lylia does not have freckles."

"You think it possible they may be related somehow?" Dante wondered aloud.

"Anything is possible at this point. Maybe Ciara can shed some light on that when she wakes. If she could I've no doubt Lylia would be grateful."

"Until then, it looks like we've got a lot of reading to do," Dante said dryly, beginning to flip through pages.

Hearing a soft swooshing sound, like air upon the wings of a plane, Rafe listened intently.

Only kayos effect beginning.

Shaking his head, as he grabbed up three of the binders, Rafe quickly put them away. "No, *I* have a lot of reading to do. By all means, hang on to that one. See what it says. But anything beyond book one will need to be for my eyes only."

Pausing in his reading, Dante lifted his head, staring in front of him momentarily. Frowning, he glanced at his father and sighed as he turned back to his reading.

"So it would seem." He'd heard a voice of his own. "It would appear you're the only one meant to know. I know we're not supposed to question, but I cannot help but wonder why."

"I would imagine I'll find out as I read," he said mildly.

Checking on the children to make sure they were still occupied and didn't need anything, Rafe opened the laptop bag and proceeded to boot up Ciara's computer. Finding the flash drive case in the bag, he started going through files trying to determine which ones were the most recent from the originals. Locating a file which appeared to be the final version of book one, he began reading.

After running through the prologue, Rafe marveled at the accuracy in the events she'd described of the day Dante's first wife Elizabeth had died. Recalling Ciara had said the story she'd written from fifteen years before of Alaina had actually been hers, he winced as he gazed over at her. Disturbed by the cruel nature of man, he wondered briefly at how it had affected her and why it seemed all the women in their lives had to have been abused in such a way.

Sighing heavily, he continued on in his reading. Being a speed reader, he managed to get pretty far.

"Dante, the scene at Alaina's house in Florida..." Rafe's voice was uneasy.

"Eerily accurate," Dante said quietly, his tone just as unsettled as his father. He shifted in his chair while turning another page. "I've always known they had to be real. How could they not be with what Drinian has said he's seen? Breydon too, for that matter. But knowing now, what Ciara is capable of, then seeing the battle being waged, written as it is here in black and white, and at that moment... Dad, if it truly happened as she wrote, then Alaina might have died were it not for the angel protecting her with his wings."

Not saying a word, Rafe simply watched his sons face, as he compartmentalized what he'd just read. "Even we, gifted as we are, have no true concept of the kind of power God has over our lives. There's no way for man to know the true accounting of the battle waged between the angels and demons that night."

"True, but even if a small portion of this is accurate..." Pausing Dante tapped on the table with his knuckle. "What has become very clear to me is how truly important it must be to God that mankind have our own say in our lives. Why else would He send his angels to fight for our right to choose?"

Rafe contemplated his son's words before replying.

"Why else indeed?"

Chapter 6

Waking, Ciara's eyes fluttered open as she gazed at the fire in the hearth. The flames were low, licking at the wood as they danced, their heat filling the room with a warm glow. Feeling safe and content to stay cocooned in the soft flannel blanket, her eyes shifted to the couch across the room from her.

With only a coffee table between them, she could see her two boys sleeping peacefully together cuddled up in blankets. Her gaze moved to another couch in front of the fireplace where her daughter lay with her hand curled loosely around a small Raggedy Ann doll. Mouth parted slightly, she snored softly as she slept.

Sensing movement nearby, she peered sleepily towards the large man sitting next to her in a plush chair. Ankle propped on one knee, Rafe sat with an iPad in his lap, reading as he sipped at a drink in his hand.

Legs and arms feeling weak and weighted down, as was often the case when waking from a deep sleep, Ciara was inclined to continue sleeping. Sensing that the hour was late she wondered what had awakened her in the first place. Hearing a soft whooshing sound near her left ear, this time she was ready for it and understood better what was happening.

Guardian. Protector.

"Yes, Lord, so I see."

Blinking sleepily, she watched Rafe shift and lean forward in his chair towards her. Seeing her eyes flitting open and closed, he set the iPad on the coffee table in front of him and bent down before her.

"Don't be afraid, Ciara. You're safe in my home and your children are here with you." His voice was deep; gentle and reassuring. It lulled her into a sense of security.

The soft sound swished by her ear once again, tickling her, causing her to shiver slightly.

A choice must be made.

"Yes, of course." She whispered, not realizing she was speaking aloud. Tired, so tired. If only to sleep.

Feeling a large, strong hand brush gently against her cheek, she moaned softly. She was vaguely aware that the blanket was being tucked up around her neck.

"Go back to sleep, Honey. You have nothing to fear here tonight," Rafe said quietly near her ear.

Head feeling heavy, she gazed briefly at him one more time before closing her deep blue eyes. Sighing softly, a contented smile stretched across her face, and she drifted back off to sleep.

Rafe watched her for a while, hoping when she woke she had felt safe. Brow furrowing in thought, he rested his hand against her side, trying hard not to worry that she'd been sleeping for so long. Glancing at the clock on the mantel, Rafe noted it was after midnight. She'd been out since she'd fallen unconscious on the plane.

When the plane had landed in Kalispell, he'd initially been worried for the children when he realized he couldn't wake her. Discovering all three children had fallen asleep, Dante and Rafe had carried them all to the awaiting vehicle. Still all asleep when they'd arrived at The Blackthorne Horse Ranch, they'd caused quite a stir when they'd carried the unconscious children in the house. Coming back out for Ciara last, Rafe met Megorah at the front door when he was bringing her in.

Her reaction to the woman, now lying before him, had been curious, but he hadn't the time to gauge it as Lylia had arrived in the entryway at the same moment. Since the family had been unaware of the nature of their travel plans, the sight of Lylia's doppelganger was extremely alarming to everyone.

After situating Ciara and her children on couches in the front living room, they'd all convened in the kitchen. Reheating leftovers from dinner, both Dante and Rafe sat with the family, explaining what they knew so far about the woman and children sleeping in the living room. The news of what had transpired and what Ciara was capable of had been unsettling to everyone.

Noticing several of his children and their spouses gazing upon the bag Ciara had managed to extricate from her home, Rafe decided it was high time he hid it. Taking everything to the hidden room next to his bedroom, he transferred all the files from the flash drives and her computer onto his iPad. When he'd returned downstairs, it was to find Dartanian and Lylia intently watching Ciara and the children from the kitchen through the divider.

"That could be me," he'd overheard Lylia say in wonder, pointing towards Ciara. "Those children, and the girl, Dartanian, she could be mine. She looks like I did as a child, and the hair, Dart. It's the same." Lylia had spoken with such envy as she'd pointed to her own head.

Rafe's attention hadn't wavered from them as they watched Ciara and the children like hawks circling their prey. Finding their behavior disturbing, he made himself a drink and went into the living room. Somehow knowing his presence in the living room tonight was essential; he had started a fire and had taken up a place next to the woman in a chair. Some of what he'd read so far in book one had left a chill within him that he couldn't quite dispel.

Moving back to his chair, Rafe took a sip of his third hot apple cider for the night then returned to his iPad. He was almost finished with book one, with only a few chapters left to go. Lifting his mug to his lips once again, he halted abruptly, nearly sloshing the warm liquid down his front. Alarmed by what he just read, he hoped for Lylia's sake, it wasn't true. Clenching his jaw, he set his mug down and peered over at Ciara on the couch.

Grimacing, Rafe somehow knew at that moment, that she was likely privy to other such secrets like the one he'd just read. Understanding now why the Lord did not want Dante reading further than book one, Rafe hoped that his son hadn't managed to get this far yet. Regardless, he would need to deal with the matter first thing in the morning.

- - -

The next morning, as the Blackthorne family awoke, converging on the kitchen for breakfast, it was to find Rafe already sitting at the bar stool in the kitchen. Awake since dawn, having fallen asleep in the chair in the living room, he'd already started a pot of coffee and had opted to help out Alaina, by taking care of breakfast since it was her turn.

Pans of scrambled eggs, hash brown casserole, sausage, bacon and biscuits, were already in the oven to keep warm.

Greeting each one as they came in, Rafe noticed with interest that Dartanian and Lylia had arrived by way of the living room. Opting to wait to eat until Ciara woke up; Rafe watched his family as they assisted their children with breakfast. Enjoying the camaraderie amongst his children and their spouses, he observed that they seemed more tense than usual for some reason; the laughter more forced.

Since his grandchildren usually finished eating before their parents they left the kitchen, meandering off to the playroom. Rafe sensed, more than saw, when Lylia stood to leave. Putting her dishes in the sink she headed towards the hallway, her four-inch heels clicking noisily on the tile floor.

"Lylia," Rafe called quietly, halting her before she could leave. Glancing up at her, he could see her turn towards him. "Have you seen Drinian's missing journal?"

Startled by the unexpected question, Lylia blinked and stared back at him, feigning confusion. "No, sorry. I told you I haven't." She then disappeared quickly down the hallway.

Everyone halted as Rafe turned towards his youngest son, staring at him intently. Exchanging looks with his father, Breydon stood and headed towards the coffee maker. Turning back, suddenly angry, he slammed his coffee mug on the counter and glared at his brother.

"Why is your wife lying, Dart?" Breydon challenged.

"What are you talking about?"

"Lylia. She's lying, and I want to know why. Are you guys hanging on to Drinian's journal for some reason?"

Appearing confused, Dartanian stared at his breakfast, as though he'd just lost his appetite. Scratching at the back of his neck he turned towards the hallway where his wife had just disappeared. It occurred to him then, that he hadn't noticed the white light about her lately when he'd look at her. Was it possible she was keeping something from him? Shaking his head at the notion, he scoffed. Sometimes he wasn't able to discern anything. It didn't necessarily mean she was doing anything questionable.

"First of all, I don't appreciate the accusation. Second, what reason could either of us possibly have to keep Drinian's journal from him?"

"That's a legitimate question. It could have an interesting answer," Rafe said absently as he continued to read while drinking his coffee. "You might want to ponder on that awhile." He gave Dartanian a quelling look.

Noting his coffee mug was nearly empty, Rafe handed it over to Breydon, who had moved to the coffee pot. Filling both their mugs, he passed one back to his dad as Dante called across the kitchen towards him.

"Brey, can you grab the Aspirin from the cabinet while you're there?" Dante asked, sensing his wife was struggling again this morning.

"Again?" Chase inquired, his gaze roaming over Alaina with concern. "You've been getting those every day for a couple of weeks now."

At that same moment, a very sleepy-eyed Ciara shuffled her way into the kitchen from the living room, her presence halting everything and everyone. Appearing rumpled with a long crease on her right cheek from the couch pillows, she seemed a bit out of sorts. Yawning while dragging her feet, she blinked several times, staring around the room at everyone as she spoke.

"That's probably because she needs her glasses. You really should have told Dante you left them behind,

Alaina." Ciara paused when she saw Rafe scowling at Dartanian. Her mouth formed into a silent, 'oh,' as her eyes widened in alarm. The urge to flee was overpowering.

Face flushing with heat at the sight of Dartanian's handsome chiseled features so much like his father's – only younger – Ciara's breath caught in her throat. Her steps faltered near the doorway. She peered surreptitiously towards Rafe then turned slightly towards Dartanian, who was glancing back and forth between her and the hallway in confusion. She looked longingly towards the hot brewed coffee and platters of food as everyone stared at her in silence. Wincing, she rubbed at her growling belly.

"I'll only say this once, Dart." Ciara's voice shook as she spoke directly to him. "I won't compromise on my beliefs or morals." Intentionally, avoiding both his and his father's gaze, she fled through the kitchen, and out onto the patio disappearing when her feet hit the lawn. She was both desperate and anxious to see her mountains once again, after such a long time, and this seemed the most appropriate opportunity.

"What in the world was that all about?" Dartanian asked, staring towards the patio where Ciara had gone. Starting to feel like he was being ganged up on, he tossed his napkin on the table and stood. Heading towards the door leading to the living room, he was halted by Royce.

"They're still sleeping you know."

"Your point?"

"Go out another way," Rafe ordered, his tone brooking no quarrel.

Stomping out of the house through the patio doors, Dartanian grumbled the whole way, acting anything but his full forty years.

"What in the world is going on here?" Megorah's eyes widening in distress as she watched her brother go. She sensed an inordinate amount of turmoil within her brother, as well as everyone else present, including Ciara.

"What made you think to ask, Dad?" Drinian asked. Both his and Chase's attention were drawn to the Blackthorne patriarch who placed his iPad on the counter. Finding Ciara's behavior toward his brother curious, he was otherwise distracted by Breydon's reaction to Lylia over the journal. He'd suspected for some time that his sister-in-law might have taken the book but hadn't been able to prove it until now.

"It occurred to me that when she was asked about it, Breydon was conveniently not present," Rafe said truthfully as he shrugged. Wanting to avoid any suspicion that the notion had come from Ciara's books, he carefully worded his response so that he didn't lie.

Grabbing a mug from the cupboard Rafe poured another cup then stared at it briefly. "I've no idea how she likes it," he mumbled while scratching his head. Hearing someone attempting to sneak in through the patio door off the living room, he made a harrumphing noise as he grinned, suspecting he knew who it was. Moving with both cups towards the kitchen door off the living room, he kicked the door open loudly, then strode purposefully through it.

Yelping with a start at the loud, unexpected noise, Ciara flung her arms out wildly, accidentally knocking over the lamp on a nearby stand in the process. She barely heard him say, "Cream or sugar?" as she tripped on the carpet. Finding herself in an un-ladylike position, bent over the chair near the fireplace, with her bottom in the air, she groaned in distress.

Rafe couldn't help but chuckle at the look upon her face as she thrashed wildly, trying madly to roll over, only to slide down the back of the chair with a thump. She landed with her back against the bottom cushion.

Staring up at him, with her hand over her heart, Ciara covered her eyes in mortification. Her long tresses of hair – already tangled – splayed out about her head like an angels cap.

"Black, please unless I have a stomachache. Then I put mint and sugar in it," she said finally.

"Really?"

"Yes. It seems it's a common…" With a loud gasp, she halted in what she was saying. She pressed her lips firmly together, in an attempt to try and keep herself from speaking.

"You were saying?" Rafe's expression masked the mirth he felt. She looked like she was about to burst with the knowledge of things, she shouldn't know. Understanding the feeling all too well, he bent over and held out the coffee as a peace offering.

"Forgive an old man his moment of humor. I heard you sneaking in."

"Rafe Blackthorne, you intentionally frightened me for no good reason," she cried out in dismay. "And you're not that old. Why you don't look a day over fifty."

"You flatter me."

"No, if I were going to flatter you I'd say how good you look in those jeans." Squealing suddenly, Ciara clamped her hand over her mouth in mortification. "Oh, what is wrong with me? My mouth runneth over!"

Stepping back, Rafe chuckled heartily as his ears turned pink. Eyes sparkling, he set the mugs down on the stand. Setting the lamp back in its place, he then reached for her hand.

Not thinking, she reached out towards him in order to accept his assistance, then suddenly brought her hand back towards her chest again. Holding it tightly there, she shook her head.

"Take my hand. I'll help you up."

She pursed her lips, refusing to speak.

Eyeing her curiously, Rafe inquired, "Ciara, are you refusing my hand?"

Rolling off the chair, she landed in a tangled mess. Crawling up off the floor of her own accord, she backed away from him as she held her hand.

"Why won't you take my hand?" Rafe scowled, annoyed by what he deemed silly behavior.

"How far have you read?" She answered with a question.

Irritated that she hadn't answered him, he said proudly, "I finished book one already."

"Keep reading."

Stunned by her complete lack of reaction, he glared at her. Most people were impressed by the fact he could read so quickly. Her book was by no means short. Or, for that matter, easy to read. She had an extreme lack of punctuation usage.

"Are you kidding me?" He practically roared.

"Do I look like I'm kidding to you?" She snapped back, only little self-conscious. His entire family was staring at them from the kitchen, through the divider.

"Woman, just tell me…"

"No," she said quickly, her tone sharp. "Keep reading."

"Why? Does it have something to do with what you said to Dart a minute ago?"

Paling noticeably, taking several deep breaths in a row, Ciara finally blurted out, "Some things you just have to learn for yourself."

Staring at her in shock, Rafe knew exactly where she'd gotten that. "Are you seriously going to throw my own fathers words back at me?"

"Yes!" she said defiantly. "Keep reading."

Hearing her son groaning behind her, she sighed with relief, as she knelt down next to him. "Thank you, Lord, for mercy!"

Scowling, he found his temper flaring over her evasive response. "Mercy my a..."

"Don't you finish that," she snapped crossly while caressing little Rafe's shoulders.

Rubbing his eyes Little Rafe peered up at her then looked around the room.

"Wow, we're here," he exclaimed suddenly, hopping up from the couch. "Lily," he shouted, as he crossed to the couch in front of the fireplace. Yanking off her blanket, his sister grabbed for it back to no avail.

"Rafe, stop it! I wanna sleep." Lily wined loudly causing Royce, Megorah and Crisalya to peer sharply into the living room in surprise.

"Lilyandhi, we're here," the boy exclaimed, gaining everyone's startled attention in the kitchen. The boy pointed around the living room.

Seeing where they were, Lily's eyes widened and she emitted an ear-piercing scream, forcing Rafe and Ciara to cover their ears. Wincing from the sound, they both watched as the children ran to their brother, who was just sitting up on the couch having been awakened by the screaming. Rubbing his eyes too, he groaned as they bounced before him with exuberant energy.

"Let's go! Let's go, Tanny," Little Rafe cried, his face beaming happily.

"What? Leave me alone, I wanna sleep," Tanian said irritably. He flopped back on the couch, smiled

82

contentedly, and rolled over, tucking the blanket around himself.

"Dartanian! Don't you wanna see the playroom mama drew? Don't you wanna see what's in it?" Lily cried, pulling his blanket off of him. By now the entire household was gaping openly at the children through the partition wall as they talked excitedly of the playroom.

"Oh, my gosh! Oh my gosh! The playroom!" Tanian hollered suddenly, coming up off the couch faster than the three of them combined. "Where is it, Rafe?"

"Follow me. I know where," Little Rafe hollered back. They ran from the living room, ignoring their mother who was trying unsuccessfully to get them to quiet down. "Going this way it'll be the living room, then entryway, downstairs study, the library with the laundry and dining room across the hall. Then, next to the library is the…"

"The playroom," they all cried together. They disappeared around the stairs, giggling as they went.

"Lord, help me." Rafe murmured in dismay, at the sheer amount of noise coming from the three children. He was awful grateful, at that moment, that his kids were all grown. At least with grandchildren, he could send them all back to their homes.

"More like, 'Lord help Lylia.' Just wait until they reach…"

The ear-splitting sound, of three children screaming through the house, stopped her instantly. Cringing, she grimaced at Rafe apologetically.

"Looks like I better go check on them." Ciara laughed nervously. She came up off the floor and started backing towards the stairs leading to the entryway.

Rafe gave her a dangerous look. "Ciara Eve Biardon, what are you not telling me?"

Going on the defensive, rather than answering his question, she stood her ground. Shoulders back, she placed her hands on her full hips and glared almost defiantly back at him.

"I am not your child. You do not use three names with me."

"Ciara," Rafe ground out. "What are you not telling me?"

Smacking her hand against her forehead, she replied, "The sheer vastness, of what I haven't told you yet would bring you to your knees." Her eyes darted toward Crisalya, then Royce. She didn't even have to be introduced to them yet to know who they were for they both looked back at her anxiously upon her furtive knowing gaze. "That being said, I might of, sort of, drawn out blueprints of your house," she offered up finally, figuring she'd better start there.

Dumbfounded, Rafe stared. "What?"

"If you let me get my bag, I can show you." She anxiously gestured towards the divider where his family stood watching. "But you might want to wait until they aren't present, cause…"

Pacing, Rafe stopped. "Cause why?" He gave her a suspicious look.

Seeing the look on her face, he somehow knew she was aware of his hidden rooms and passages. Growling deep in his throat, his hands balled into fists.

"How was I supposed to know this place was real?" She exclaimed defensively at the sight of his glowering countenance. "This whole time I thought I was just making it up in my head." Her arms flailed wildly about her.

"My study. Now!" Rafe headed towards the entryway, his long legs strolling past her. He pointed towards the stairs and gestured with his arm. The t-shirt he wore drew tight across his broad chest as he turned toward her in an attempt to goad her on.

"Well now, that's a bit unrealistic, don't you think?" Arms crossing across her chest she continued to stand where she was, refusing to move.

"Excuse me?"

Sighing in frustration at the man's sheer lack of sense, she gave him a stern look. "We just arrived last night and woke this morning. My kids need me. They haven't eaten since yesterday, and frankly, neither have I," she said, trying to keep from being snappish. Staring at him desperately, she continued. "I need coffee, Rafe, and Steven…"

"I've Got you covered." Rafe ran back for their mugs and headed quickly towards the stairs. "Let's go."

Stamping her feet angrily, Ciara lost her temper. "*Your* children may be adults; m*ine* aren't. They still need me, and frankly, unless you want me peeing on your leather chairs in your study, you will let me see to necessities … and have breakfast," she said vehemently, both startling and shocking Rafe. "Just because you brought me to safety does not mean you have ownership over me. You are not my husband."

"And thank God for that," Rafe said in exasperation, tired of her tirade. "Heaven only knows, how Steven Adam Jameson ever put up with being married to you for nearly eight years." The words slipped out of his mouth before he realized what he said.

Inhaling sharply, Ciara looked at him as though she'd been slapped.

"Yes, let's thank God for that," she said quietly. Her eyes stung instantly with welling tears. "Of course, turns out I never was actually married to *Steven*, now was I?" Her voice sounded tortured. Walking away, she followed after her children, figuring to hit the restroom along the way.

Seeing, the hurt expression on her face as she fled the room towards the entryway, Rafe growled in frustration and punched at the air. Glancing towards the kitchen where his children and their spouses were gaping at him openly, he groaned.

"What are you looking at?"

"Was that really necessary?" Royce spoke up first, sounding cross. He tossed a hand towel at the counter angrily. "Since when do you talk like that to a woman?"

"She's maddening, Royce. Worse than Lylia," he said, becoming irate. "And she knows stuff about us, I'd wager, that none of us is going to want her to know."

"But she's not God. She isn't all knowing, so she doesn't know everything," Veta said angrily, having been appalled and surprised by what he'd said to Ciara about her husband.

"Yes, and from the sounds of it, she knows things like you do." Hialey piped in. "From the way you and Dante talked last night, she didn't even know what she was doing until now. Like she said."

"It must be so overwhelming to learn something you thought was imagined is real," Alaina said quietly, silencing everyone as she shook her head. She had gained their attention. "She drew this house, wrote of the people living inside it; and her children's names," she exclaimed in dismay. "Why, I couldn't even imagine what she must be going through right now at finding herself standing within these walls."

"I can," Megorah said, causing heads to turn. "I can sense her roiling emotions. You know as well as I do, don't you dad? Cause you went through this sort of thing growing up. Knowing things without any idea how you'd come to find out about it."

Rafe sighed heavily. "Yes, I know I screwed up, okay? What I said was said in anger; I didn't mean it. It was uncalled for and I will apologize," he said emphatically. Grabbing up his iPad from the counter in the kitchen, he moved towards the kitchen stairs. "That said, from the looks of things, I have some reading to do. So, if you all will excuse me."

"Rafe, do you want a plate?" Royce called after him.

"No, I'll eat when she eats."

"Dad, her children's names," Breydon said trying to catch him before he disappeared. He'd never seen his dad argue with a woman like that before. It was kind of fun to see. The exchange had tickled him.

Wincing, Rafe realized he'd forgotten to mention about that. "Yes, I know. It was one of the reasons I thought to go after her in the first place. They'll have to be changed, so don't get used to them; all of them, Ciara included."

Seeing Dante looking at him, as though itching to get something off his chest, Rafe took a few steps back into the kitchen. "What is it, Dante? You look like your gonna burst."

"Steven Adam Jameson. Ciara Eve Biardon." Dante enunciated the middle names carefully. "Adam and Eve."

Shaking his head in exasperation, Rafe rolled his eyes. "Yes, it would seem even God has a sense of humor; and a rather poor one at that, if you ask me." Taking up his coffee mug, he headed on upstairs to his study.

Everyone stood momentarily, staring after him.

Incapable of handling the silence any longer, Hialey's voice could be heard suddenly piping into the air of the kitchen.

"Hhhmm. Anybody else find it interesting, that Ciara; a woman who could be Lylia's twin, named her kids after Rafe, Lilyandhi, and … out of all of you, Dartanian?" she asked as she crossed her arms over her chest and leaned back in her chair. "Wait a minute. Breydon?" Hialey whipped her head around suddenly and gazed, wide-eyed, at her husband in dismay. "Didn't you tell me once that Dartanian's middle name was Adam?"

Her words elicited a flurry of raised brows and curious, questioning glances, leaving an almost tangible weight in the air over its potential meaning.

Chapter 7

A few minutes ago.

Stomping out of the kitchen, Dartanian headed off towards the garage, nearly running into Ciara in the yard along the way. Normally in tune with his surroundings, he'd missed seeing her attempting to run past him toward the patio near the living room. Staring at the ground as he walked, not paying attention to where he was going, he bumped her shoulder in her haste to speed past him. He heard her cry out in surprise as she landed awkwardly on the ground.

"Sorry, didn't see you." Dartanian hastily reached for her as he grumbled. Seeing her glance up at him, he was confused by the frightened look on her face, so he softened his tone. "Take my hand and I'll help you up."

"No!" Ciara knocked his hand away with her wrist. Looking completely rattled she attempted to crawl up off the ground on her own. "No, don't touch me, Dart."

Irritated, he gave her a quelling look. It was the second time in so much as three weeks that a woman had nervously refused his touch. For that matter, even his own wife had been recently reticent at his close proximity. Frustrated and having very little patience due to the lack of intimacy with his own wife, Dartanian grabbed her by the arms forcefully and lifted her up from the ground against her wishes. The unexpected motion had apparently jarred her enough to knock the wind out of her.

Finding herself suddenly on her feet Ciara stared nervously, almost fearfully up at him, his height dwarfing her. A carbon copy of his brother, Dante, but for the lack of scar upon his brow, Dartanian's vast size and close proximity were both intimidating and exhilarating. Unable to stop herself, Ciara's breathing became erratic as he held her in place.

"You're married, Dart. Just remember that." Her teeth chattered as she spoke. She continued to stare at him anxiously.

Dartanian scoffed. The expression on his face was one of confusion at her statement. "I am well aware of that. I don't need a reminder."

"Are you sure about that?" She blushed, her gaze shifting to his very large hands, which were now roaming up her arms. Instead of pushing her away, he'd unconsciously pulled her in closer

His eyes flitted from his hands down her front to her feet. Taking a shaky breath in order to regain control of his senses, he grasped at her arms lightly then promptly shoved her away.

They stared at each other briefly, as though sizing each other up.

Exhaling in exasperation, Dartanian finally turned away. It might be high time to go find his wife. The sensation she'd evoked within him at her nearness was disturbing. He was more aware now of Ciara's presence than what he cared to be. He could even sense her movements as she trudged quickly away from him towards the patio.

Standing motionless, he gazed down toward the Stallion barn and corrals. He was suddenly reminded, for some inexplicable reason, of the night they'd found Megorah there fifteen years prior. Unsure why the thought had popped in his head he grimaced at the memory, allowing his thoughts to shift instead, back to the woman who had disappeared into the house.

When Ciara had first entered the kitchen he'd been startled by the intensity of the bright white light surrounding her entire frame. Normally, when he saw the light around a person it extended from one shoulder to the next around a person's head. Attracted to the light, he had found himself unusually drawn to her, as a result, moments ago.

Debating on whether to just head on into the Sheriff's Department and avoid the house entirely today, he realized he couldn't do that just yet. There was a mystery to solve where Drinian's journal was concerned and he was determined to find out if it was true.

Agitated by the notion his own wife might have his brother's journal hidden somewhere, he walked leisurely around the exterior of the house, taking his time. Not wanting his mind muddled by the exchange moments before, he attempted to clear his head of all thought. He gazed down toward the horse corrals and Appaloosa barn where the ranch hands were working the horses. Watching the foreman struggling along with another young hand with his father's new thoroughbred Stallion, Dartanian shook his head. He couldn't fathom why his father had even bothered with that one. It was too temperamental and its spirit appeared damaged even from where he stood.

Passing the movie theater room, he re-entered his father's home through the pool room. Spanning the length of the pool, he could smell the chlorinated water and feel the thick moisture-laden air sucking into his pours. The wedged heels of his boots thumped loudly against the smooth aqua blue tile on the pool room floor as he walked; the sound echoing within its walls.

Reaching the doors to the hallway he halted anxiously at the sight of Ciara standing near the playroom doors. Resting an arm against the door handle, Dartanian could hear her speaking briefly with her children in the playroom, as he stood on the other side of the door.

"I'm betting, you guys are going to have all the time in the world to play in here today," he heard her say. Her voice was soft yet clearly agitated. "But right now, let's get to the kitchen and get something to eat."

"Mommy," Lilyandhi wined, "we want to play here instead."

"Yeah," Little Rafe cried, as he and Dartanian grabbed each other's arms, and began twirling each other around the expansive playroom, giggling happily as they went.

"We have snacks in here. They're welcome to play with the others as they eat," he could hear his niece, Katana say.

"I appreciate that you're trying to help, Katana," Ciara said on an exasperated sigh. "But I need them to listen to me and your suggestion isn't helping, unfortunately. It's hindering me from getting them to do what they need to do." She watched as her children continued to play, rather than listen.

Not liking her tone with Katana, he swung open the pool room door abruptly, startling Ciara. He crossed the hall swiftly and entered the playroom.

"I'm sure they'll be fine where they are," Dartanian drawled, leaning against the door jamb. "Katana, honey, why don't you get them all a couple of juice boxes with some raisins and pretzels." He grinned at the three children who were now dancing about the room singing happily. He hadn't realized they had awakened and was glad to see they were in good spirits under the circumstances. He suspected reality would eventually hit them hard when they realized their father was gone for good.

Gazing at Dartanian uneasily, Ciara became suddenly very anxious once again and spoke sharply to her children. "No. All three of you, I want you in that kitchen now."

Surprised by her harsh tone, Dartanian became cross with her. "That's no way to talk to children."

"Must I remind you that you are not their father?" Ciara's eyes narrowed upon him. "I have three children, as opposed to your one, so my household must be run differently than yours, especially with strong-willed twin boys. I will thank you not to tell me how to talk to my children, especially since you don't know that two of them are hypoglycemic."

Banging his head against the door jamb in understanding, as she guided her three groaning children out of the playroom and down the hallway, he grimaced at Katana.

"She's right, of course," he said, catching her gaze. "Children with hypoglycemia would go more than a little nuts if they don't eat regularly. Raisins and pretzels wouldn't have been sufficient. They need a healthy combination of protein and carbohydrates," he explained to his niece. "I don't see Lylia. Where is she?" He was surprised she wasn't already in the playroom.

"She headed upstairs for a bit. Said she'd be back down."

"Thanks." Turning around, he walked past the dining room on his left, then turned left towards the stairwell near the kitchen. Noting Ciara already had her children at the table near the partition wall with plates of eggs, sausage, wheat toast and fruit, he turned toward the stairs.

"Which one of the Blackthorne twins is that?" he heard the little girl ask out of the blue.

Munching on a piece of sausage, the blonde headed little boy grabbed for a piece of toast distractedly, then glanced his way. Catching his eye before taking the first step, Dartanian noted the boy shiver lightly and give him a weary look.

"That one's Dartanian, Tanny. Dante is the one with the scar."

"He has my name, Rafe," the other boy exclaimed, staring openly.

Looking upon the boy in surprise, he halted in his ascent. Gazing now in rapt attention toward the children he missed seeing Ciara turn from the fridge and stop abruptly at the sight of him. Clearly, in her own little world, she had not overheard what her kids were talking about.

"You named your son Dartanian?" His eyes shifted towards her incredulously. It had been one thing when he found out his brother Drinian's new wife, Veta, had a cat she'd also named Drinian. But learning that his wife's doppelganger had named her son Dartanian was a little unnerving.

Swallowing hard, she simply stood there holding the carton of milk precariously in her hand.

Little Rafe's attention shifted from his mother near the fridge to the man standing near the stairwell. "Yeah, and my brother is just like you. But mama named me Rafe though," the little boy said in a haughty tone. "Because, I was born first and that's all you need to remember, Dartanian." The boy spoke firmly, fixing him with a steely glare.

"That's not true, and stop being mean." Lily banged her fork on the table. "I'm seven and I'm two years older than you. Mama named me Lilyandhi before she ever gave you the name Rafe." She stuck her tongue out at her brother then smiled openly at the good-looking man near the stairs.

"That's only 'cause you're a girl. You can't name a girl, Rafe," the little boy said matter-of-factly.

Floored by the children's names, having not been present when they woke, he gazed in particular at the boy called, Tanny, whose attention had moved back to his breakfast. "What does your son mean by, the boy is just like me?" His gut twisted, for he had a sneaky suspicion he already knew.

Shoulders, slumping as though in defeat, Ciara carried the milk carton to the counter and began pouring glasses of milk for each of her kids. "He's not like you," she said adamantly, looking cross. "He takes after his dad. Damien could..." She paused, taking a deep breath as her eyes misted over. "Or rather, Steven could see what you see."

"He could discern good from evil?" He asked quietly in an undertone. He stepped from the stairwell, moving closer to her so they could each hear better.

Nodding, Ciara's hand stilled over the milk carton, her gaze shifting towards her children uneasily. "I think it's why Agent Henley was after Steven and, by extension us, when he found out they were his kids."

Confused Dartanian inquired, "I don't understand. Who's Agent Henley?"

"Agent Jericho Henley; he works for the CIA," Ciara said in answer.

"What possible reason would someone from the CIA want with your children?"

"Not the CIA." Rafe corrected his son from the stairwell, surprising them both. Tired of reading, and in need of a break, he'd come down for more coffee, hoping to get Ciara to just tell him what was in the books she wrote. Sidling up next to his son, he took the cups of milk from the counter and passed them off to the children at the table who were hastily trying to finish eating. Returning to the island counter, he poured himself another cup of coffee and continued in hushed tones, so as not to disturb the children.

"And Henley is no longer with Central Intelligence. He's been working for someone else for a while now." Rafe's expression was dark.

His father's frank candor at the discussion they were having caught Dartanian off guard. Normally, he never talked of such things in front of them and with a stranger present at that.

"There are some within the military who would covet them," Rafe continued, tilting his head ever so slightly toward the children.

"You're serious?" Seeing him nod in affirmation, Dartanian was incredulous. "But why?"

"He doesn't know, does he, Rafe?" Ciara asked tentatively. "But Dante does, because you told him before you came to get us?"

Pausing at the cabinet, Rafe glanced back at her curiously then grabbed a small brown bottle from within. "Yes, Dante knows now. I suppose it's time Dart knows as well," he said as almost an after-thought. "Dart, your gift, in particular, is the reason why I've insisted over these many years, that we keep all your abilities a secret. Ciara?" Deferring his head toward her, he prompted her to explain.

Getting the message, she took up where he left off. "Steven once told me that shortly after he enlisted, one of his commanders discovered what he was capable of while in training. That's when they separated him into a special unit and trained him differently from the rest. Using practices on him normally used to break down individuals working black ops, they turned him into a one-man killing machine."

This news took Dartanian by surprise, leaving him wondering if the same had been done to his twin brother. Sensing his concern Rafe quickly eased his mind on the matter.

"Dante went through regular training. His ability effectively protected him from ever being discovered, for he was always one step ahead of them. What Steven Jameson went through, however, was slightly different. They basically stripped him of his internal moral compass."

Bobbing her head up and down in agreement, Ciara sipped at her coffee first then spoke. "According to Steven, because of his ability, he got really good at it," she said softly, her voice almost a whisper as she was becoming choked up. "I mean, really good at it. Whereas you, as a Sheriff, use your ability in order to help people, they trained him to hone his skill in order to kill, and he'd do it without compunction. Honestly, I get the feeling God never intended or wanted gifts of discernment to be utilized in such a dark manner, but I digress. Either way, in the end, they screwed up."

"What do you mean?" Dartanian asked.

"Ciara, if you know. If Steven told you, I would urge you not to repeat it." Rafe stated vigorously, his crystal-clear blue eyes boring into hers as he spoke.

Shaking her head she replied sadly. "I don't know. Really," she insisted. "He never would say, specifically, what had happened. All he'd tell me was that his last operation went bad. He was the only survivor and he'd been compromised, whatever that means." She shifted her gaze in a cagey fashion between the two men. "What I do know, is he was seriously messed up afterwards. There were demons inside him he just couldn't get out."

"Figuratively or literally?" Rafe wanted to know, wondering if she wrote of the angelic warfare within her books for a reason.

"Quite possibly both. He was always fighting with himself. The nightmares he had were horrible, and Damien… I'm sorry, Steven, was adamant that if he ever snapped, I was to take the kids and run, because he suffered from P.T.S.D." Ciara shook her head in frustration, having had to correct herself once again. "Of course, he tells me all this after we've had three kids and been married for over seven years. That is, living together for seven years. We were never really married, I guess." Her eyes became sad and downcast, her face awash with the hurt of betrayal from the man she'd known as her husband.

Troubled by the egregious wrong committed against the woman before him, Rafe's expression softened. "You *were* married, Ciara…"

"Don't sugar coat it for me, Rafe." She'd become testy. "He did the same thing to me that my so-called ex-husband did. Just like Alaina's ex-husband, Manuel, Raul was never actually divorced from his wife in Mexico." Seeing Rafe wince, as he gave her a meaningful look, she paused, realizing what she'd said. Nobody at the ranch knew Alaina had been married before to a Hispanic, let alone what his real name had been. Eyes widening in alarm, she cringed and spoke quickly. "Forget I said that. The point here is that each time I thought I was married, I really wasn't."

Licking his lips, Dartanian attempted to exchange a furtive look with Rafe, but his father simply ignored him. Deciding it was probably best just to let this bit of news go, he shrugged his shoulders and let out a half-hearted chuckle.

"Legally speaking you were married to Damien Biardon though," Dartanian offered in the end, thinking he was helping.

"Great, so I was married to a dead man. But I was never actually married to Steven whom I … lived with and had children with." The hurt was clear in her voice. Unable to mask the catch in her throat, she felt heat flood her cheeks as both men looked at her and exchanged uncomfortable glances. "Is your stomach upset?" she asked Rafe suddenly, intentionally changing the subject. She'd just realized what he'd grabbed from the cabinet, poured in his coffee, and was now putting away.

Giving them both a questioning look, Dartanian watched his father stirring sugar in his coffee, which he only ever did when he added mint.

"You getting sick, dad?"

"No, my stomach is just upset. I think it likely because I haven't eaten yet." Rafe gazed at Ciara, appearing slightly irritated, and leaned back against the counter.

"Why haven't you eaten yet?"

"I've been waiting on her."

"Oh, good grief." Rolling her eyes, Ciara grabbed two plates from a nearby cabinet and began filling them with what was left in the pans on the stove.

"Tell me there are some potatoes left," Rafe said desperately.

Grimacing, she cast a furtive glance back at him and shook her head. Watching him bow his head in distress, she sighed in resignation.

"Yeah, I know. Hash brown potatoes are the best part of breakfast as far as I'm concerned. Sorry." Setting a plate, piled high with eggs, the remaining sausage links and patties on the counter, she puttered around, grabbing a fork from the nearby silverware drawer and salsa and shredded cheddar cheese from the fridge. After adding cheese and salsa to the eggs she placed the fork on the plate and handed it over to Rafe with a napkin.

Staring down at the plate, only mildly surprised, Rafe quirked an eyebrow at her in amusement. "You seem to know your way around my kitchen pretty well, do you?"

"She also appears to know what you like." Dartanian pointed toward the plate, then his dad.

"That's nothing significant. I also know *you* make a real mean lasagna and that it happens to be your favorite," she said, addressing Dartanian. "Additionally, you're not terribly fond of strawberry buttercream frosting and you happen to be allergic to curry."

Smirking at his sons raised eyebrows Rafe took a seat at the counter then bent his head toward her curiously. "You're not eating?

Standing on the opposite side of the counter across from the two men, now seated before her, she laid a plate in front of herself as well. "No, I'm eating," she insisted.

Seeing her plate had barely one scrambled egg, a half piece of toast and one small broken sausage on it, Rafe scowled. "That's not eating. It's barely enough for a cat to survive on."

Wondering how the woman could be overweight and eat so little, Dartanian stared at her curiously. "Do you always eat like that?"

Heaving a long-suffering sigh, Ciara's eyes burned with embarrassment as she shrugged and looked away. "I eat whatever is left and available." Sensing they were bothered by her statement, she glanced surreptitiously between the two men. Becoming distressed by the awkward silence, she decided it was high time to fill the void with answers. "Rafe, why did you and Dante come to get me and my kids?" She nibbled on her piece of sausage, savoring the taste for it was really good.

"Okay, I'll bite. The trip was prompted by a call I received Saturday morning," Rafe said honestly, leaving his response intentionally vague for a reason.

"I see. They wanted you to come in…" she paused, her gaze shifting to Dartanian. "For one last consult?"

Nodding, Rafe tilted his head and halted his son from speaking with a raised hand. He wanted to know how much she already knew and what she could figure out on her own.

Hearing her kids scrambling from the table, Ciara stood on tiptoes, craning her neck around Rafe, to see if they'd actually finished. Apparently happy with how well they'd eaten, she gestured that they could go play even as they begged for permission. Taking their dishes from them, she brought them to the sink next to her as they ran out of the kitchen back to the playroom. She began clearing the scraps from their plates into the disposal as she sighed heavily. Her expression became pained and her brow crinkled in the same cute way Lylia's did.

"They'd been looking for him. Harder more recently, for some reason, than normal, hadn't they? Am I right to presume, they were requesting your assistance in locating him?"

"Yes." Rafe watched her expression closely.

"But something happened. Someone he knew from his past saw him, didn't they? Sunday night sometime maybe?"

"From what I gather, yes."

Lips trembling, a surge of emotion flooded her, causing her eyes to redden with tears. Wiping at the tears with shaky hands, Ciara inhaled a trembling breath.

"I knew. The moment it happened I knew. He was supposed to come home for dinner Sunday night and eat pizza with us. But he broke his promise, chose to eat out and come home later instead." Blinking back the moisture in her eyes, her face contorted in anguish, as she flung the last plate toward the sink angrily. The sound of the shattering plate filled the air, along with her strangled and frustrated cry.

If he'd just come home, she thought, while clenching her fists. None of it might ever have happened. They wouldn't have come looking because Steven wouldn't have blown his cover and been found, which meant their children would have been safe. And the people who wanted to now use her children for dark purposes might never have learned of their existence.

That was the thing about choice, she thought angrily, as she apologized to Rafe, feeling guilty over the broken plate. People never paid attention to how their choices might affect those around them; the people they claimed to love the most.

Now, as a direct result of his decision, she found herself standing in the middle of the Blackthorne family kitchen, seven days earlier than she would have anticipated, had her story progressed as it should have. Ciara knew now, one way or the other, she was inevitably meant to lose her husband for it was his time. The question had only ever been how it occurred. Whether killed in an accident as she'd originally foreseen, or shot in their bed, killed while on the run, or taken down by nearly a dozen men in an alley, Damien Biardon, aka Steven Adam Jameson had been on God's list. There was no way he could run from it because when God says it's your time the only question left, at that moment, is how you affected those around you when you died.

Ciara knew, as her wounded gaze met the Romani eyes of the men before her that Steven's choice had affected her life and the events that were meant to transpire. What she did not know, however, was whether those effects were going to be good or bad. Shifting her gaze around the room in agitation she wondered at whether there were demons present even now, trying to thwart the rightful progression of God's will. That possibility was not only overwhelming to her but unnerving. No longer knowing what part of the story she had originally written still applied to the people within the house where she now stood, she also wondered how events from other versions of her stories she'd written fit in.

Rafe and Dartanian watched her, their mutual unease born of the shattered, confused, and frightened expression plastered across the woman's face in front of them. Exchanging glances with his son, Rafe had the sudden and unnerving feeling that he urgently needed to know what was running through her head.

"Ciara, what do you know?" He coaxed her softly, almost urgently.

Feeling a tickling sensation next to her ear, Ciara's shoulder nudged up unexpectedly and she batted at her ear with her right hand. Taking a deep breath she allowed the turmoil within to ease at the Lord's prompting. Closing her eyes on a sigh she exhaled slowly, taking a bite of her food as she listened.

He must read.

She heard the soft voice upon the air at her ear and yet cringed at the words, suspecting she knew full well the response she was about to get.

"Won't listen," she said aloud almost sadly, winning herself perplexed stares from both Rafe and Dartanian.

Don't tell. Must read. Learn for themselves.

"Keep reading," she said finally, her gaze shifting nervously away as she peered out the patio doors while a single teardrop, dripped from her left eye.

Frowning at her, Rafe glared at her initially. "Something is about to happen, isn't it? Something big. And it affects my family. You know what it is, don't you? It's why God prompted me to go get you and bring you home."

Face drawn tight, Ciara turned towards Rafe, then looked upon Dartanian as her lips pursed. Swallowing hard she replied simply. "A choice must be made."

"What choice?" Dartanian inquired. "By whom?"

A puff of air, like a warm breath against her ear, sent a tingling sensation down her spine.

No! He must keep reading. Learn for himself.

Closing her eyes, she cringed openly then looked back at them through her lashes. "Rafe, if you'll just keep reading…"

Shoving away from the counter in frustration, he stood abruptly, tired of her refusal to tell him what she knew. "I'm done reading. You will tell me what you know. I won't tolerate subterfuge in my own home."

"Good to know." There was distress in her eyes as she gazed meaningfully at Dartanian. "Please, Rafe. Everything you need to know is within the pages of those novels."

"Good, which means you can just tell me…"

"No, you have to read…"

"I don't *have* to do anything." Shaking his head in refusal, Rafe's nostrils flared. "Until you tell me what I need to know, you will be a guest in my home. That said, my family is staying here for the summer months and there are no more bedrooms available."

"Rafe, please…"

"Your children," he continued, raising his voice in order to gain her attention; he dictated the terms of her presence within his home. "They may stay in rooms with other children of their choice."

"Rafe, don't…" Her voice sounded tortured.

"There is a warm place in front of my hearth, in whichever room you choose to lay." He didn't like that he had to be so firm with her, for it looked to him as though he were crushing her spirit. Grabbing up his cup of coffee, he headed towards the patio door, only to stop suddenly without turning around. "Oh, and Ciara. I trust you do understand that you will not be able to leave this house and the surrounding grounds without a new identity. Though I am willing to help you with your identity transformation, I will not do so until you tell me what I need to know."

Realizing his father had effectively made her a prisoner within the Blackthorne Ranch house, Dartanian gazed between the two of them uneasily.

"You know what? That's okay. I already know my name." Temper flaring, she glared back at him impudently.

"Oh, really?" Rafe ground out in a mocking tone. He turned towards her, his eyes narrowing to slits. "I don't suppose you're willing to tell me that, at least? You know, so everyone around here knows what to call you." He seethed quietly. Flinging his arms wide, he spilled coffee on his hand and the floor in the process.

Tell him.

The voice near her ear startled her this time, as it came without a soft breeze or a brush of air gliding by.

"Seriously?" She mumbled under her breath. Her eyes darted around the room anxiously. She was still growing accustomed to the voice.

Tell him the name I have given you.

The voice prompted her to speak her name, as though coaxing a child to play a game who desired only to play alone.

"RavenCroft," she whispered finally, exhaling anxiously.

"Wait. What did you say?" Rafe asked incredulously. Spinning around, he strode back towards her in three quick strides.

Backing up against the cabinets as he neared her, Ciara reached behind her, resting her hands on the countertop for support as he leaned into her. Both alarmed and thoughtful, he was no longer angry.

"Ina ... Inara RavenCroft," she said softly in a small voice, meeting his gaze shyly. Her imploring eyes had become deep, midnight blue saucers, with a sheen of tears that made them sparkle unnaturally.

Blinking twice, as though in shock, having just registered what she'd said, Rafe inhaled sharply. He experienced a slight tremor of excitement from within him.

"Did you say... *Inara* RavenCroft?" He asked hopefully. A faint memory from many years past was wheedling its way to the forefront of his mind as he waited with bated breath for her response.

"Yes." Her shimmering eyes locked with his, then darted towards Dartanian anxiously

The memory was very clear to him now as he tilted his head towards her thoughtfully then gazed just as curiously over at his son. Closing his eyes momentarily, Rafe allowed what little of the memory he could recall to re-play in his mind. It was as clear as if he were reliving it at that moment. Nodding his head in understanding and resolve he calmly wiped his damp hand on his jeans as he gave her a calculating look. Then, taking a deep breath in anticipation, he insisted this time, as he extended his hand towards her once again.

"Give me your hand."

Rafe saw it then, a slight movement of her hand, as if wanting to reach out to him for the lifeline he was giving her, but too afraid to for some reason.

"No.," she said tremulously.

Her response troubled him. Frowning at her with concern, his eyes crinkled lightly in the corners, belaying his age.

"Then take Dartanian's hand," he said evenly and without emotion. He gestured towards his son, struggling to keep from showing his disappointment.

Balling her hands into fists, she shoved one into her mouth and shook her head, as though in denial. Peering around the kitchen frantically she stifled a sob. "No, Rafe, please. I can't. I just can't."

She knew full well what God wanted of her and wanted so desperately to be able to please Him. The dilemma she faced now seemed almost surreal.

"Well now. I'd say you weren't kidding when you said a choice needed to be made, now were you?" Rafe asked mildly. His eyes roamed her face as though sizing her up. Harrumphing softly, twin creases appeared upon his brow and his expression thinned, as though what he saw was lacking, or wanting in some way.

"Dartanian, when you look upon, Inara," he began quietly, using Ciara's new name. "What do you see?"

Baffled by his father's behavior and inquiry, Dartanian stared at him briefly. Then moving his gaze over to the woman before him, he gave her a similar quick perusal. Shrugging in an attempt to feign indifference, he was careful with his response, sensing he was being tested in some way.

"It's as though her entire form is encased in a bright white inviting light."

Shaking her head as though distraught, Inara peered over at Dartanian out of the corner of her eye, a wounded expression upon her face.

"I see. I'm to understand that's all you see when you look at her?" Seeing his son nod in agreement he probed further. "Is that unusual in any way from what you normally see when you look at a woman? Lylia for example?"

"Yes, usually the light or darkness is simply encasing the head from one shoulder to the next."

Watching the two men uneasily, Ciara cleared her throat as though to speak, but instead, Rafe beat her to it.

"Interesting. Very interesting indeed. I must think on this awhile."

Lost in his own thought process, Rafe walked away towards the patio once again, banging through the doors as he went.

Chapter 8

Finding the entire exchange very odd Dartanian disappeared up the stairs near the kitchen, as he had initially intended before becoming distracted in the kitchen. Heading straight for his room, he didn't bother knocking as he entered. He realized he probably should have when he saw Lylia's startled expression at his presence.

She was sitting curled up on the bed with an old worn book in her hand. She stared back at him with a guilty expression and he realized what he was seeing.

"Is that the journal Drinian's been looking for?" His tone was dangerous.

Seeing her face switch from guilt to fear within a matter of seconds, he gaped at her openly. "He's been absolutely frantic looking for that and you've had it all this time?"

"I know I'm sorry. I needed answers."

"Answers to what exactly?"

Gesturing urgently for him to sit down next to her she laid the journal out in front of her and began searching for the page she needed. She was determined to evade his question for the moment.

"It's good that you're here because I have to show you something. I just found it a few minutes ago. I won't lie. I was considering getting rid of this book until now. I get the feeling none of your family fully understands what's been going on."

"What are you talking about? And you still haven't answered my question." He both looked and sounded confused.

"If I hadn't gotten my hands on this, we would have never known what was about to happen. This would have never been discovered in time." Locating the page she wanted she stuck a long, manicured nail at the edge of the page near the binding. Finding the separation she slid her nail across the top of the page gently and began to pull the page apart, effectively separating it into two pages.

Dartanian looked at the page in shock then glanced at Lylia. "How did you discover that?" Distracted from his inquiries over the journal by the recent discovery, he reached for the book.

"Purely by accident. I was drinking my lemonade." She indicated the damp glass next to her. "I was reading when I got to that page and took a drink. A water droplet fell from the glass onto the corner of the page. It began to curl as it was drying."

"Mom's written something here. No, wait a minute … that's Breydon's handwriting." He looked at it more closely, taking special note of its date. He realized his brother must have written something down for their mother when he last saw her on the day she died. "It looks like a poem. It's very faint but I think I can make it out." He was intrigued by the discovery.

"If you can't, I can. It's about the prophecy she made," she said with excitement.

Pursing his lips, Dartanian narrowed his gaze at his wife then proceeded to read.

"A prophecy was made this day;
a healing path is on the way.

Two of mirror image there will be,
crossing their paths in time you will see

Dartanian's brows furrowed with interest. His mother had clearly relayed this after she had made the missing prophecy. Pausing briefly, he realized the reference of two of mirror image could very well mean his own wife and Ciara. He began to pace the room as he continued to read aloud

"A choice to make - one right one wrong.
We will know for sure before long.

Two years from now it must begin
or the millennium will see much sin."

"What year was it you were shot?"

Halting where he stood at the end of the bed, he stared at his wife. Realizing what she was saying, he dropped the book to his side.

"The year two thousand." His eyes grew wide with understanding of the implication. "Lylia, the millennium. That was the worst year of my family's lives!"

Lylia anxiously curled her legs up towards her bed. "I know, you told me about some of it. Dante's wife Elizabeth was killed in April, Drinian had that accident in May that killed his horse Rohn and…"

"I was shot in June checking on a lead to that drug case. It nearly killed me."

"Yes, on June sixteenth, right? Wait a minute. What's today's date?"

"The ninth," he said off-handedly. "And yes, it was the sixteenth of June when I was shot. I'll never forget that day."

The date in question was only seven days away. She stared up at him as he knelt next to her. "It's the one and only time I'll admit to being grateful that Dante has that connection with you and can discern thoughts. If it hadn't been for him you'd…"

"-Be dead." He stared down at his mother's journal.

"The millennium saw many sins." Lylia gazed at the wedding ring on her hand with a troubled expression.

Dartanian's expression darkened. "You can say that again. A month later Breydon and his girlfriend at the time nearly died from that mushroom poisoning incident. The month after that we found Megorah raped in the barn. The only one not affected that year was Crisalya."

Startled by this revelation, her eyes opened wide. "Wait a minute… I thought that all happened several years later."

"You're remembering it wrong. I told you this. We were all still living at home at the time." Tilting his head thoughtfully he frowned and pursed his lips. The look on his face at that moment reminded her of her father-in-law. "Although, now that I think on it, we did have to go get her from the Howard's cattle ranch about a month after Meg was found. She'd had a scare of some sort while walking to the cabin near the divide in the woods and had sprained her ankle really bad. It took her a few months to recover from that as I recall." Seeing a funny look cross his wife's face, he gave her a curious look.

"What is it?

In the back of her mind, Lylia suddenly realized there had to be so much more to the original prophecy Dartanian's mother had made. It occurred to her she knew what the significance was to some of the other numbers she had found in the journal Lilyandhi had given Dartanian before she died. She brushed it off, for the time being, figuring she'd get into it later.

Sensing Dartanian was still waiting for a response she said finally. "I think I just made a connection of sorts, but we can get into that later. This is more important right now." She gestured for him to continue reading.

"Fifteen years we must then wait.
If not start then twill be too late."

"Okay, I get the part about fifteen years. It makes a kind of sense, I guess, as we're currently in the year 2015, but, too late for what?"

"I don't know,"

Turning his attention back to the journal he read on.

"Through waxen hair no gift doth breed
for surely lacking the strength of seed."

Dartanian stared back at his wife in alarm. Seeing her sad eyes looking back at him, he cleared his throat and took a deep breath.

"You think this refers to you?"

Face falling in despair, Lylia choked back a sob. "I've never been able to give you children of your own. We had to go to a sperm bank to have Kayla. I think you may have made the wrong choice in me. It would seem we were never meant to be married. But I do think you are meant to be able to have children. This poem is how I know it's not meant to be me." Seeing his disbelieving look, she pointed toward the journal. "Keep reading, you'll understand in a minute."

Eyeing her skeptically he did as asked.

> *"Another shall come on the last of day.*
> *A writer's word shows another way."*

He gaped openly at his wife. "That has to be Ciara, or rather, I guess her name's Inara now. This isn't just a poem it's a prophecy. Mom made more than one prophecy!"

Unable to control her tears any longer, Lylia began to cry softly. She spoke between ragged breaths. "So it would seem, keep reading."

Dartanian's brow furrowed, deliberating over the poems meaning. Getting up he began to pace as he read, shaking his hand absent-mindedly in the air. The mannerism was somewhat reminiscent of her father-in-law as well, who often behaved similarly when working through an issue or theory.

> *"For through fiery hair of silver and gold,*
> *and eyes of night filled with silver mists of old.*
>
> *A seed shall lie within her womb.*
> *Three times blessed we can presume."*

Dropping the journal on the bed suddenly, as though it had burned him, Dartanian stared wide-eyed down at it. Running his hands through his hair frantically, he breathed heavily and began to pace again, his mind on overdrive.

"Lylia … Lylia… Three times blessed, Lylia. That means… that has to mean…"

He rambled repetitively in dismay. A mixture of joy and anguish overwhelmed him at what he was learning.

Crying heavily, she cringed and turned away. "Triplets, I know. She'll give you triplets just like Dante and Drinian. If you were to … be intimate with her by the end of the day on June 16th." She wept bitterly.

"Wait… What?" He looked both alarmed and horrified at the notion.

"Lilyandhi's prophecy is within the pages of this journal. I discovered it but Alaina was already figuring it out when I came across her passed out that day. I just happened to finish it. See?"

Tossing the notebook lying on her nightstand next to him on the bed, she opened it and flipped through the pages. Tapping at the paper, she pointed to a bunch of numbers on the page.

2000_4-19//15//2015_(30)^(4-19=2)(5-18=3)(6-16=1?I)

At first glance, he didn't see what she was referring to. As he took a closer look at the numbers, then began reading through the notes, it became much clearer.

"Alaina was right. We're living through this prophecy now." His excitement was clearly mounting at what he was learning. "Something significant happened to all three of us boys, each within thirty days of each other."

(2000_4-19) Prophecy begins with this date(?)

April 19, 2000 – (4-19=2) Dante's wife killed in an accident

May 18, 2000 – (5-18=3) Drinian's horse Rohn killed, Nearly gets killed as well.

June 16, 2000 – (6-16=1?I) Dartanian shot and nearly killed

"In keeping with that, something significant happened on those same very dates of that year to the women now currently in the Blackthorne men's lives." She sounded utterly dejected and forlorn.

April 19, 2000 – (4-19=2) Alaina assaulted and raped
May 18, 2000 – (5-18=3) Veta gang-raped at college
June 16, 2000 – (6-16=1?I) Lylia (?) (I – unknown variable)

"Everyone, that is except…"
"-Except you." Understanding dawned on him as he finished reading the remaining notes his wife had written out.

Fifteen years later - on the same date of the year 2015
April 19, 2015 - Dante and Alaina conceive triplets
May 18, 2015 - Drinian and Veta conceive triplets
June 16, 2015 - Dartanian and Lylia (?) (Possibly meant to have triplets as well?)

"You honestly believe that I…"
"You picked the wrong woman," she said bitterly, slowly rising from the bed. Sniffling, she grabbed for a

tissue from the box and wiped her nose. "I'll just bet Ciara's here to take my place."

Grimacing noticeably at the notion, Dartanian shook his head in denial. "No, not necessarily."

"Yes. You're meant to be with her, not me."

"Now look, this says right here, 'fiery hair of silver and gold.' She's a redhead."

Rolling her eyes Lylia leaned against the patio door and stared out across the vast mountain range. The view was extraordinary here. She'd always loved it. It was even better from their house near The Bluff but she knew she could never live there again after the divorce. In order to fulfill the prophecy and for Dartanian to have children, that's what would have to happen, and quickly.

"Dart, honey, think about it. The strawberry blonde is not natural. Her own daughter has the same hair as me so I'm willing to bet she dyes it. Her hair is probably just like mine was as well. You know; the golden blonde with that awful grey color. It's why I've always dyed it light blonde cause it was so ugly." She made a face, recalling all the teasing she used to get. It was like she had an old person's hair at age ten. "If you want children it looks like God will grant them to you, but only if you're with her instead of me."

Peering back down at the pad of paper, he continued reading through the notes then peered at his mother's journal noting there was still more to the prophetic poem.

They stared at each other, neither saying a word for the longest time. When Dartanian finally spoke next, it was with true regret in his voice.

"I don't know that I can do that to you. This, us, it couldn't possibly have been a mistake. I love you too much." The emotion in his voice was raw and filled with pain.

"Unless … something is going to happen to her," she said softly, frowning in concern.

Repeating her questioning words Dartanian stared at her in confusion.

"Finish reading. I'll… I'll explain everything once you finish." Tears stung her eyes as her hand became shaky upon her mouth.

Picking the journal up from the bed, he continued.

"An artist and a poet she will be;
her gift to know, her child's to see.

A dove brought forth shall burst to fly
when she sends a gift through the nigh.'

For during a time of memory
its gift of peace shall set her free."

"See now, that's the part I don't understand." Lylia interrupted, sounding perplexed. "But the rest, speaks for itself."

After reading the last of the prophetic poem, Dartanian thought he understood what she meant.

"But lo' beware the shadows will call,
tear her apart and make her fall.

For within her lies a fragile heart
but without her, it'll all be torn apart."

Their eyes met across their bed.

Taking a deep breath Lylia spoke first. "I knew when I read this a little bit ago there was significance somehow, but I had no idea how much so until just now." She strode toward the patio door once again. Touching her trembling fingers to her own brow, she spoke in a murmur, "For through fiery hair of silver and gold…but lo' beware the shadows will call." Turning towards her husband unexpectedly she spoke urgently. "Don't you see, Dart? Both Rafe and Dante said it was a really close call getting her out of Michigan before they got to her."

"The part about the shadows. You believe the demons were trying to take her out of the equation when my dad and brother showed up and thwarted them." He already knew what her answer would be. Seeing her nod, he stared down at the journal in his hands. "Yes, it would seem to make sense. In which case I'm surprised she escaped at all, though with God, anything *is* possible. It would clearly stand to reason he had angels protecting her."

"I think the demons are trying to stop you from having these children with her for some reason. You know, the troublesome three that are always giving Drinian such a hard time. For all we know, you were supposed to have met her twenty years ago. 'Crossing paths in time. A choice to make, one right one wrong'. Don't you see? You and her together; it's pivotal somehow to the prophecy."

Bothered a great deal by the last four words of the poem Dartanian re-read them, murmuring the words aloud softly. "This reference to tearing her apart and making her fall. Lylia, is it possible? Do you think she's in real danger?" The thought troubled him deeply. Inara had looked anxious and afraid in the kitchen moments before. Her mannerisms had reminded him of Drinian when he was seeing demons and attempting to bat them away.

"I'm afraid she might be. We're only seven days away from the fifteen-year anniversary of the day you were shot and nearly killed. I cannot help but wonder if they went after her now." Her lips trembled; a mixture of emotions roiling within. Fighting back the tears, she came and knelt on the bed near her husband.

"I know what it's like to want something and not be able to have it. I love you so much, Dartanian Blackthorne, and I don't want to lose you, but I know I can't be selfish. I sense there is something more to this prophecy of your mother's - specifically the one with the numbers. It feels as though it's the beginning of something extremely important to God. Clearly, the Lord has a plan for you. So far two of these events have come to pass." She pointed toward the notes on the pad of paper for emphasis. "And now, she's here. Like a light in your darkest hour, Ciara…"

"It's Inara now. According to her, Inara RavenCroft is her name."

"Ciara … Inara. Either way, she's here, right now in this home, brought to you by your own father. If you truly want children of your own, I'll give you what you need to accomplish that," she paused taking a shaky breath. "I'll consent to a divorce."

"Stop." Voice booming, Dartanian held up his hand to halt her from speaking further. His crystal blue eyes flashed with anger and pain. "Just don't. I won't accept that that is our fate. This has to be a mistake."

"Listen to me, please. I…"

"No." He emphatically shook his head. "Not another word on the subject; and don't you dare go anywhere." His eyes narrowed dangerously upon her. He knew full well, thinking herself a martyr, that she'd take off with Kayla. Grabbing up the journal and pad of paper, he tucked them close to his side and disappeared from the room.

Running into Drinian in the hallway near his brother's old bedroom, he barely glanced at him, as he attempted to walk past.

"Is Lylia in your room?" Drinian asked as he attempted to step past him.

"Leave her alone, Drin. Not now," he growled, continuing at a steady pace down the hallway towards the front of the house.

"Wait just a minute," Drinian scowled at his brother, following close behind him. "If she has my journal then I have a right to confront her."

"She *had* your journal, but not anymore." He shook the journal in question and pad of paper in front of him, then plastered it to his side protectively.

Drinian seethed, turning on Dart angrily. "So she did have it."

Hearing the commotion in the hallway, Dante stepped out of his bedroom to find Drinian chasing Dartanian. He managed to halt him on the upstairs landing where he proceeded to aggressively shove at Dart's shoulder. Sensing trouble was brewing, he hurried towards them hoping to ward off a fight.

"What's going on?" Seeing the journal and pad of paper in Dart's arms, Dante's own brow furrowed angrily. Knowing at least one of them needed to keep a cool head, he tempered it. "Is that what I think it is?"

"Lylia had it this whole time," Drinian growled.

"Is that true? She's had it all this time?" He kept his tone even, though his gaze bore into his brother's eyes.

"Whether she did or didn't, what's it to you anyway?" Dartanian was desperate now to get out of the house and away from prying eyes so he could look into the journal and notes more thoroughly alone. He attempted to continue down the stairs. Drinian stopped him again by pushing at his chest. The movement merely served to stoke his temper further.

"I'd say since my wife has been worrying herself crazy thinking she'd lost Drinian's prized journal in the first place, that it might just be more than a little something to me," Dante said. "Why did Lylia take it in the first place?"

Aggravated, Dartanian's patience was waning thin. Shouting, he knocked Drinian's hands away from the book. "Let it alone for now. I need time to think."

Temper flaring, Drinian's scowl became fierce. "Give me my journal, Dart!"

"No. I need to think. I need to…"

"Return it to me at once," Drinian roared, his voice booming throughout the house.

The sound reverberated into the kitchen, where Breydon was grabbing a snack. He had returned home early from a meeting. Hearing the commotion in the entryway, he stepped into the living room where he could hear and see better. Taking another bite of his roast beef sandwich, he licked horseradish from his lips, as he watched his older brothers fighting over the journal that had been missing.

"I see you finally found it. Lylia have it like dad thought?" Breydon called across the room, moving closer toward them.

Managing to finally make it down some of the stairs, Dartanian tried to step onto the bottom landing only to feel himself being yanked back by his shirt. Turning back, with his left arm he shoved at his brother angrily. Face coloring in frustration his crystal eyes flared with an almost luminescent quality.

"Knock it off, Drin! You think this is just about you?" He shouted, waving the journal in the air once again, panic surging within him as his voice rose. "It's not! It affects more than just you and Breydon."

Fed up Drinian grabbed for the journal once again, managing to snatch it from him.

Growling fiercely, Dartanian reared back and punched him in response. Snatching the journal back, he stuck it out in front of him as Drinian came up off the floor, lunging for him. His face was livid with fury.

"No, Drin, stop!" Dante hollered, stepping into the fray just in time to haul his brother back and away. As big as Drin was, he was the only one capable of keeping him down, if necessary, and only because of his speed and agility from the training he'd received.

"It doesn't belong to him," Drinian exclaimed, both distressed and furious that it was being kept from him. "What do you want with it anyway?"

"What do I want? I'd just as soon have nothing to do with it! But because of this blasted thing, my wife wants a divorce," Dartanian shouted back, his face filled with anguish and rage of his own. His eyes bore into his brother. "And I just might have to give it to her." His gaze flitted between Drinian and Breydon."

Drinian stopped struggling. Exchanging stunned looks with Breydon, they both turned back to Dartanian, looking completely flummoxed.

"But, why?" Breydon inquired.

"Ask Inara RavenCroft. She seems to know everything. I'd be willing to bet she knew what was in here too." Dartanian shook the journal in the air.

Confused, Drinian scratched at his temple absent-mindedly. "Who's Inara RavenCroft?"

Dante watched as his twin brother slapped the book against his leg and strode from the entryway out onto the front patio. "Well now, *that* Drinian would be *the* question of the day."

"Ciara," Dante said in understanding, as the angel at his side kindly bestowed the news. His response won him a surprised glance from Drinian.

"What?"

"Like Abram and Sarai of the Bible, God gave her a new name." Dante closed his eyes, concentrating hard on what he was being told. He wanted to be sure he got everything that was being shared with him the first time.

"I see." Noting that his brother was in a quiet repose, Drinian coaxed him gently. "Dante, what is going on?"

"I don't know for sure. I don't know. But something is definitely up." Twin creases could be seen on his brow. He stood next to them, staring out the front doors where Dartanian had just disappeared. It was rare when he could sense his brother's emotions but being identical Blackthorne twins they were linked. Therefore on occasion, they could tell when something significant was happening with the other, even from a great distance. It was how he'd known his brother had been shot fifteen years before.

"Do us all a favor and leave it alone for now."

"But he still has my journal," Drinian said with heat.

Raising his hand in the same way their father did when trying to gain their attention, Dante curbed any further discussion with a simple gesture.

"Trust me, Drin. You *will* get it back but you must drop it for now."

"What are you sensing?" Breydon asked as he continued to eat his sandwich. His appetite had clearly not been hampered.

"I'm gathering he feels his world is literally falling apart around him." Deciding it was best to simply leave it at that, he glanced between his two brothers then turned and walked back up to his room. What he didn't tell them was what Dartanian's last thought had been as he left.

"If I don't give her a divorce, Drinian and Breydon will never find peace."

The words kept flitting through Dante's head, haunting him.

Chapter 9

They stood together, man and horse, staring out over the expansive Rocky Mountain vista from Eagles Peak. Picking up a rock at his foot, Rafe drew back then flung it out over the outcropping watching as it sailed down towards the trails below him.

He had always loved the view from this place. The quiet solitude suited him on days when he wrestled with difficult decisions. It gave him a chance to talk to God and reflect on what He wanted of him. Finding himself in the middle of one of his greater dilemmas since fifteen years past, he had sought solace in his manual labor of the day for a time, but not even that was enough to distract him.

After attempting for hours to break the stubborn Stallion he'd been foolish enough to purchase, he came here. When he'd seen the Stallion the first time, Rafe sensed within the creature the same demons his own son struggled with. Believing – hoping even – that he could make a difference and aid the magnificent black beauty in finding some peace, he had generously offered to take him off of widow Havish's hands.

The monstrous beast was the reason her late husband had been killed. Thinking he could break him on his own without any assistance or, for that matter, training, Ragland Havish had mounted the horse before it was ready for a rider on its back. It's presence within her barn walls and on her land was a constant reminder of her loss. She couldn't handle him anymore, nor afford to keep him anyway.

The stallion had a long way to go before he'd be ready to ride, but that wasn't what had him so distracted now. Closing his eyes in distress, Rafe gave up his worries and troubles to God, knowing He would ease his anxiety and fears.

He supposed he should have known who Inara really was when he first learned of the similarities between her and Lylia. Wincing at the memory of their discussion that morning he realized he'd been a bit rough with her when they'd spoke. He felt guilty for it. Reflecting further, it occurred to him that Dartanian had not called him on it. He found his son's lack of response bothered him a great deal, particularly considering who she might end up being to him. Like Lylia, the woman could be extremely pig-headed and stubborn. Rafe imagined, in order to survive what she had, with the ability that she had, while not even knowing she had it, Inara probably needed to be that way.

When she told them her new name, he suspected God had picked it for her, and that she knew what her presence within his home meant. Discouraged by her refusal to admit it in front of his son, it had been his hope to get her to open up and tell him herself. But she'd closed up on them, and he couldn't understand why. Wondering if it had something to do with the very recent loss of her husband, it occurred to him that it might be too much for her, too fast. It had taken years to recover from the loss of his own beloved wife, Lilyandhi. He had known her time was short, for she'd been ill for some time before she'd died. But Inara had had no real warning. It had been sudden and complicated by her gift and knowledge of his family.

Patting the horse next to him Rafe closed his eyes once again. The partial memory he had recalled earlier in the day was now playing out in his mind once again. His mouth quirked up on one side in a sardonic smile, as he recalled even more of the memory now in more detail.

"Lilyandhi Blackthorne, you little minx. You should have told me," he said softly. The prospect of what was to come lighted a spark of excitement within him, that hadn't been there in a long time. Worried at whether they were all ready for this, if he was ready for this, he sighed and raised his work-weary eyes to the sky above him.

The sun wouldn't set for hours from now. By the look of the sky, it was nearing the dinner hour. He tarried on, however, not wanting yet to leave the quiet solitude of his master's presence. In the privacy of this sacred place, Rafe finally allowed tears of joy and regret to spill from his eyes for the first time. Only here in this spot would he allow himself the freedom to express himself in this way. He knew full well his presence would need to evoke strength and competence in the next several weeks to come, so he prepared himself mentally in order to return to his home tonight.

"Thank you, God," he called out while choking on a strangled laugh. "Thank you for this … opportunity; to be a part of your grand plan. Whatever that might be. Though, I'm not sure these old bones are as capable as they used to be."

There have been many like you, who were older.

The familiar voice floated upon the wind. Laughing aloud Rafe shook his head.

"Things were different then. Times were different. People often lived much longer."

And yet, man has not changed.

Nodding his agreement, Rafe said, "You're right, of course."

I am God.

Harrumphing softly, he found humor in the Lord's words.

"I have to ask, Adam and Eve. Was that really necessary? I would have figured it out, without the parallel."

A deep rumble sounded in the distant clear skies, as though announcing a coming rainstorm. Though Rafe suspected it was more likely God laughing at him.

In the beginning, there was Adam and Eve.

The smooth serene voice spoke clear and concise, as though right next to his ear. Spinning about, he blinked at the sound so close to him.

"Sometimes, it's as though you're standing right next to me," he said finally on a sigh. His heart was calm once again, as though God himself had reached in with a gentle hand and massaged it back into its peaceful state.

I am always by your side. You should know that by now. And where there is a beginning, there is always an Adam and an Eve.

"Yes, Lord, I suppose so, though her name has changed. I presume at your bidding?"

I name all my children. It is mankind who corrupts the given name.

"We do indeed," he said on a troubled sigh. After a moment he queried further, knowing full well the Lord would know to whom he was referring. "What does she need Lord?"

Patience.

Kindness.

And above all ... understanding.

Brow furrowing in confusion, he inquired further. "What about love?"

Rafe Blackthorne, the voice chastised. Even in its soft, gentle state sounding cross or annoyed. *You already know the answer.*

Smiling to himself, as though holding an internal secret, he nodded as his mouth curved into a contented smile. His anxiety over the delicate and tenuous situation he had within his household right now, had abated somewhat.

Wiping at his watery eyes with the back of his hand, he heard his cell phone ring. Pulling it from his pocket he could see it was Dartanian. He grimaced. Coughing, he cleared his throat and spit at the ground, attempting to compose himself before answering gruffly.

"Yeah," he said.

There was a long pause on the other end of the phone. Then finally Dartanian spoke.

"We need to talk," he said simply.

"Okay."

"I have.... That is, Lylia and I, we have something you need to see," he said before going silent again.

"Yeah, okay."

Hanging up, he cringed inwardly while tucking the phone back into his pocket. Grabbing hold of the reigns he mounted his horse adjusting his seat in the saddle.

"Let's go, Nova." Turning his Appaloosa toward the trail he flicked the reins and brought his steed to a gallop. "Home, Nova," he said aloud, "quickly."

Rafe did not know for sure what to make of Inara RavenCroft. The Lord was being curiously silent with him where she was concerned. Wanting, Rafe imagined, the right choice to be made by mankind rather than Him. God was probably hoping He wouldn't have to take things into His own hands, Rafe mused thoughtfully, as he continued to gallop back to the barn.

But what he did know was that she might be their only chance at saving his two sons, and Hialey for that matter, from being tormented for life. If he was right, as he suspected he was, Inara might also be his son Dartanian's only chance at having children of his own. Wondering what it was they needed him to see, Rafe worried whether he'd be able to be the guardian and protector, he knew Inara would need in the next several days.

- - -

The smell of roast beef, homemade bread rolls baking, and what Inara suspected was baked cinnamon apples wafted through the Blackthorne ranch house toward the library where she awoke with a start.

Having been left on her own for most of the day, Inara had wandered the house, investigating many of the rooms that were open. The Blackthorne Ranch house was exactly as she imagined it. Somehow she found herself feeling at home in it even with the anxiety she couldn't completely dispel. Though still overwhelmed a bit at the discovery that everything was real, she was starting to come to terms with it, particularly after seeing the library the day before. The excitement she'd felt at the sight of the vast collection Rafe had, still hummed within her today. She could easily imagine herself wiling away many hours sitting contentedly on the twin sofa curled up in an afghan with a good book.

Checking out the pool room, she marveled at its size yet observed that it hadn't been overly done. Rafe Blackthorne had, as she'd always suspected, simple tastes. Choosing comfort and functionality over flashy or sophisticated furnishings and décor, he'd still managed to imbue a note of elegance and class within his home. It was obvious by the appearance of the foyer.

Moving on to the movie room, she turned on the lights so she could see, noting first the half circular shaped cushiony couches at the back of the room, not far from a fireplace. Making a mental note of them and the blankets already present, her gaze flitted about the room. There were two fireplaces and a set of patio doors on the exterior wall of the house, in addition to twenty-two chairs lined up within the center of the room. Looking more like a cross between a recliner and a theater chair, Inara chuckled to see there were cup holders and cubbies in the arms of the chairs for such things as food and drinks.

Turning towards the wall, which most believed housed the pantry on the other side, Inara grinned mysteriously at the sight of the enormous theater screen centered on it. Imagining that her children, Tanian in particular, would have a blast watching movies in here, she sighed sadly. Rolling her eyes at the long stretch of cabinets against the shared wall of the pool room, she could see there was a sink, refrigerator, and two microwaves.

Wondering briefly how often they actually did family movie nights, Inara decided she wasn't really in the mood to watch anything and wouldn't know how to work the system anyway. Heading back the way she came, she found herself once again in the library after checking in with her children in the playroom.

Restless, Inara's fingers had itched for her keyboard, wanting desperately to be able to tap out the words now collecting in her mind. Much like Rafe, and she imagined the rest of the household, she had so many questions now. For example, if she would continue writing would it still be their story or someone else's. The problem was, Inara no longer had her computer. Rafe had hidden it away along with her novels within one of his many secret rooms. Reflecting on how she'd spent over a year writing the first three to six novels of the An Unfortunate Lineage series in varying stages, she grimaced slightly. Any spare time she could find had been consumed by doing just that.

In the end, Inara found herself at loose ends and began perusing with voracious zeal Rafe's expansive collection of books within the library. An avid reader, as well as writer, she nearly squealed aloud in delight to discover he had a first edition original of The Brothers Grimm Collection.

Not even bothering to run back and grab a drink from the kitchen, she had sat down and begun reading. It was as she read that she overheard the argument between the Blackthorne brothers over their mother, Lilyandhi's journal. Grimacing at hearing her name exclaimed in frustration by Dartanian, she'd halted in her reading while anxiously resting her head upon the couch. Staring off into space sadly, she lost all inclination to read after that. Unable to concentrate any further, she bookmarked her spot and left it on the coffee table.

Leaning back against the cushions of the loveseat, she pulled the afghan lying across the back over her, and allowed her weary eyes to droop, then close. Her children were aware she was in the library. She'd known if they needed her, they'd come for her here. Besides, she was nowhere near as worried about them as she was herself. Yet, she'd still been able to fall into a restless sleep.

Now, however, she was fully awake and suspected she may have slept longer than she'd intended. Her belly growled ravenously at the magnificent aromas now curling in tantalizing tendrils down the hallways into the library causing her mouth to water in anticipation. Groaning, Inara realized she'd not eaten lunch before lying down. She hadn't had anything to drink since early that morning either. Stumbling from the loveseat, she bumped the coffee table as she headed for the library door. Stepping out of the library she cast a glance both directions, trying to determine which would be the shorter route.

Opting to take a right and investigate first where her children were, she noted they were no longer in the playroom. Turning around she turned down the hallway past the formal dining room, then took a left at the next hallway. She could already hear the Blackthorne, Howard, and Ryans families congregating in the kitchen for dinner. Peeking her head around the door in order to see where her children were, Inara saw they were happily chatting away at a table with Hialey and Breydon. Coming to a dead stop at the sight of Dartanian and Lylia standing together near the counter with Rafe, she gasped. The journal was being passed from Dartanian into his father's capable strong hands, as Lylia apologized profusely next to them, with tears in her eyes.

Other than Drinian, no one looked upon the scene, though Inara suspected everyone was listening intently. Megorah, Hialey and Alaina could be heard attempting to quiet their children.

"I'm sorry. I truly am," Lylia went on. "But I did discover something that Dartanian feels you need to see."

Opening the journal to a specific page, she pointed to it as Rafe spoke.

"Ah, so you did have it." Distracted with his own thoughts, it took a moment for Rafe's attention to register what it was he was seeing. "Wait a minute. What is this?" His expression and voice both belayed a hint of surprise.

"Just read it. You'll see," Dartanian insisted, looking at his wife in distress. Tears ran down her cheeks as she attempted to choke back a sob. "Lylia found it by pure accident. If she hadn't had the journal, it might not have been found at all, or in time."

"Why?" Rafe asked with a frown. "And what do you mean by, in time?"

"Because it was hidden" Lylia wiped at her nose with a tissue. "Two pages were stuck together. If you read it, you'll understand what he means."

"There *was* always one page toward the back that was thicker," Drinian said aloud. He got up from his chair and came around the table toward them. The news of the discovery had drawn everyone's attention, including his new bride, Veta. "I always wondered why. What do you see, dad? What's written there?"

Inara's breathing became heavy and erratic as she stood, unobserved near the stairwell, listening to Rafe read the poem aloud. She already knew the words on the page by rote, without even seeing it, having written them in book three and read them numerous times, over and over again, in an attempt to make sure she had them right. Halfway through the poem, she startled everyone by continuing the poem for him, without even needing to see the page.

Upon completing the poem, Inara's eyes darted first to Drinian and Breydon, then to Dartanian and Lylia. They settled finally on Rafe. Their gazes locked. She could see the muscles in his jaw twitch as he cleared his throat, then eyed Dartanian and Lylia uneasily, suspecting he was fully aware of what they were thinking.

"I take it you were aware of this?" Rafe asked her in a tight voice, already knowing the answer.

"Please, listen to me," Inara begged.

"Why?" Rafe thundered in a deadly calm tone. "Are you now, going to tell me what you have written in those stories of yours?"

Inhaling a trembling breath, Inara's words were quiet. "Rafe, you must read…"

"No, I think not," he said quickly with a pained expression. "This isn't a game, Inara."

"I never said it was." She could see the look Dartanian was giving her, as though sizing her up. Shifting back a step nervously, she felt her arms begin to shake. All eyes were upon her. Wanting so desperately to tell him everything so they would understand, so that he would understand, she blinked several times. Her head felt like it was beginning to spin.

"Listen, this is really important," she began, feeling the whoosh pass her shoulder and gently collide with her cheek.

No. He must read.

Cupping her hand around her ear she rubbed it in frustration. "But they don't understand," she exclaimed in distress. Blushing, she looked upon Dartanian then glanced quickly away in embarrassment. She tried again. "Rafe, you need to know. It's in the original copy of book three."

Experiencing another sensation of air against her opposite ear, the voice spoke again, more urgently.

No, Inara. He must read to understand.

"I know," she cried softly, fully aware she was likely making a spectacle of herself and that they thought her an idiot. "But how? How do I convince without telling?" she asked in confusion. The room seemed to spin before her.

"Inara, what are you trying to tell me?" Concern was evident in Rafe's tone. She appeared fragile, tired even, and he wondered why. He suspected she may have fallen asleep at some point during the day, as her left cheek had a dimpled pattern imprinted on it from one of the library afghans. Her apparent distress was becoming very obvious, especially to Megorah. She kept inching back towards the stairs as if prepared to flee. Her behavior led him to believe she was afraid.

"To read, Rafe. To read, please!" Inara whimpered angrily, her gaze never wavering from a spot to Dartanian's left, unable to look the man in the eye. Heat flooded her. She knew what everyone, including Dartanian and Lylia, was thinking now that the poem had been found and read. They weren't entirely wrong for God had brought her to them to help them. Knowing that Inara was having difficulty understanding why the man before her had to be so stubborn. She clenched her teeth in frustration, refusing to be weak.

Sighing in exasperation and irritation, Rafe gave her a perplexed look. "Why is it so all-fired important to read those lousy books, Inara?" He saw her flinch; a wounded look filled her eyes. Kicking himself internally for his choice of words, he laid the journal on the counter.

"Yes, *Inara*," Dartanian said quietly, a note of distaste within his tone. "Why can't you just tell us? Tell me?" One eyebrow rose arrogantly. Hand clenching at his side, he appeared tense

"Why do you read the Bible, Rafe?" Inara asked quickly. "What is the Bible's purpose, Dartanian?" She prompted, casting her gaze towards him shyly, catching Lylia's angry eyes staring back at her.

"To learn, to teach," Dartanian began as Lylia watched the dialogue from the sidelines.

"To help us prevent past wrongs from repeating themselves," Rafe cut in. "And to prevent future wrongs from..." Stopping suddenly, his stance became almost domineering as he moved unexpectedly toward her. Cocking his head, his gaze shifted over her, then flitted towards Dartanian, who was staring at her with an unnatural glint in his eye.

That worried Rafe.

"Dartanian, what do you see when you look at Inara?" Rafe asked suddenly.

Jaw clenching, Dartanian didn't answer at first. Masking his expression with indifference, he swallowed hard and finally spoke. "I told you this morning, I see a very ... pretty, bright white light." The muscles in his neck were drawn tight, his tone almost a coaxing caress.

Inhaling sharply, Rafe shifted an uneasy gaze back at Inara. "You have my attention. I'll read," he said, disturbed by the slight change in his son's response.

Nodding gratefully, she turned as though to leave.

"But, Inara," he said, his voice turning her head and halting her. "You are safe in this house. You know that right?"

"Oh, Rafe. If only that were true," she said sadly. Her gaze roamed nervously about the room.

Disturbed by her response and mannerism, Rafe grimaced and gestured for her to come into the kitchen. "You need to eat," he said sternly when he noted her reticence. "The meaning behind the poem is clear to those it applies to, regardless of what others present might be thinking. Take comfort that you are in my home and presence for now. Please." Extending his hand towards her, as any gentleman would in order to guide her to her children's table. She reached out to him, then suddenly drew back and peered over at Dartanian. Tucking her hands behind her back as she walked, she tried not to let the eyes of his family upon her grate on her nerves too much.

"Over here, Inara. Your children are sitting with us tonight," Breydon called. Taking her hand into his as she neared, he helped her into her seat next to her daughter.

"Oh, but you'll take Breydon's hand, I see," Rafe said on a low chuckle next to her ear while setting a large glass of milk next to her plate.

Eyeing the tall cup of milk hungrily, Inara wondered briefly if Rafe knew how truly appreciative she was over the glass now sitting before her. Blushing, she caught his wink as he disappeared behind her and returned moments later with a plate laden with succulent roast beef, mashed potatoes with gravy, green beans, carrots, and baked apples. Groaning at the abundance of food before her, she imagined she probably could inhale it all but would likely regret it later. She normally never ate so well.

"Yes, well, Breydon doesn't bite," she said suddenly and without thinking. She reached with anticipation towards a roll from the basket on the table. Staring down at her plate almost stupidly, she paused before buttering her roll. She blinked as her eyes widened to saucers when she realized what she'd just said. Clamping a hand over her mouth in mortification she watched as Breydon and Hialey exchanged looks and began to laugh hysterically.

Taking a seat at the counter so he could see, Rafe chortled at her words. He watched his family eat and could hear the heated discussion in the hall between Lylia and Dartanian as he buttered his roll. Sighing in resignation, he had the feeling it was going to be a long night when he heard Lylia stomping away, refusing to join the family for dinner.

Angry, Dartanian filled a couple of plates with food and attempted to follow her, only to return moments later, in a right foul mood, with his own plate. Inhaling his dinner quickly at the counter near the fridge, rather than sitting at the table with the rest of them, he threw his plate into the sink loudly and stomped from the kitchen. After catching Inara's eye, he exited through the patio door and slammed it shut loudly, startling everyone at the table.

The unexpected noise came at the most inopportune time since Inara was just taking a long drink from her tall cool glass of milk. Choking loudly, she swallowed hard and knocked over her glass. Heaving up from her chair, she smacked at her chest with her right hand. Warning shouts erupted behind her, but she was too distracted by her need for air. She didn't hear what was being said.

Stepping back in order to maintain her balance, she slid unexpectedly on the spilled milk and pitched backwards. Her body twisted awkwardly as she fell and she smacked her forehead on the chair as she went down. She lay for a second, motionless, too stunned by the pain rocketing through her head. Body twitching slightly, she rolled over the rest of the way on all fours. Trying to get back up, she sensed the dizziness even before it came upon her. Touching her hand to her brow she could feel the warm sticky blood on her fingertips before she even pulled them away. Staring down at her hand with foggy eyes, Inara could hear the startled cries and fearful voices of her children as they asked her if she was all right. Throat and chest still hurting from gagging on the milk, she tried to speak after swallowing hard once again.

"Hate to say I told you so," she said in a thick voice. Head bobbing, Inara lost consciousness while still wobbling on her hands and knees. She would have slid the rest of the way to the floor had Breydon not caught her about the shoulders before she fell.

"Give her to me, Breydon," Rafe said anxiously, worried at the blood on her forehead. "Little Rafe, Tanny, your mama's gonna be fine," he said calmly. He knelt with Inara to the floor and rolled her over across his knee so he could inspect her head better.

"Oh, no! Mama's bleeding," Lily said.

"It's okay, Honey." Hialey reached across the table and patted her arm in an attempt to sooth her. "It doesn't look too bad. Does it Rafe?" She hoped she was telling the truth.

"No, but I suspect she might be out for a bit."

"It looks like that could use a couple of stitches though," Chase said, having knelt down next to her. Probing the cut with his fingers, as well as a clinical eye, he turned to Rafe. "If I do it quickly before she wakes," he prompted.

"Yes, of course." Picking Inara up with surprising ease considering her weight and his age, Rafe carried her to the living room. Chase followed with a clean napkin in hand, waiting patiently as Rafe laid her on the couch near the fireplace.

"Meg, would you…"

"Get your bag? Yes, I'm on my way," Megorah disappeared into the hall.

In less than ten minutes, Chase had her cut cleaned up, stitched and bandaged, before Inara even stirred.

Chapter 10

Waking several hours later to a splitting headache Inara groaned and rolled to her side. Seeing a pair of long, jean-clad legs propped up on an ottoman nearby she realized someone was sitting in the chair next to her. Glancing out the window of the living room she discovered the sun had set but didn't see her children on the couches nearby as she had the first night. Not too worried at their absence, Inara suspected she knew where they would be. She'd written of a similar instance occurring in book three. Inara also knew full well of the kindness of the adult Blackthorne children where kids were concerned.

A fire crackled lightly in the hearth once again, giving Inara cause to believe the person who'd made it simply liked the glow and feel of it. The need to warm the room with its glowing embers was unnecessary as it was the middle of June and decidedly warm outside. Inara smiled almost wistfully through the pain in her head. She was experiencing a feeling of Deja Vue at waking in the same spot she had the night before. The sense of security was present once again, though this time she sensed, for some reason, she should be uneasy regardless of the presence at her side.

Leaning forward in his chair Rafe peered down at the head bobbing up from the couch. Noting his place where he was reading he lay his iPad down on the stand next to him and stood. Kneeling down next to her Rafe caught Inara's eye.

Flinching slightly as his hand reached for her forehead she saw his face register a wounded expression at her response. Sighing outwardly Inara apologized.

"No need to say sorry." He shook his head as though shrugging it off as nothing. "You took a nasty bump to your head when you fell."

"So it would seem. The pain in my head would agree," she said wryly. "You know? We really gotta stop meeting like this," she said playfully, in an attempt to make amends as he peered under her bandage.

Chuckling softly, his kind pale blue eyes met hers. They seemed to glow in the darkened room. "Your boys opted to sleep in with Aiden; Cris's son. And Lily, it would seem, has made quite a little friend in Alaina's daughter, Sayleena."

Nodding Inara instantly wished she hadn't moved her head. "Somehow I knew that's where they'd be."

Making a non-committal sound in the back of his throat Rafe rested his hands on the couch next to her. "I'll get you something for your headache. Stay here and don't move too much. Do you want anything else while I'm up?"

Stomach growling loudly, Inara's face flushed. "Food?" she asked in a small voice. "A tall glass of milk would be nice too if it's not too much trouble. That is, if there is enough, of course."

Coming up from the floor, Rafe pulled himself up to his full height and stretched while yawning. "Milk got you in this state in the first place," he said, his tone dry.

Eyes anxiously roaming around the room Inara said quietly on another long-suffering sigh. "I think we both know it wasn't the milk." She met his gaze evenly. "Would I be right?"

"According to two of my sons, and Veta, you might well be," Rafe answered after a moment, concern evident in his expression. Inhaling deeply he ran a hand across his face in agitation then told her to stay put. Disappearing through the kitchen door, Inara could hear him opening the partition between the kitchen and the living room. She could almost feel when his eyes were upon her, checking to be sure she was still okay as he puttered around his kitchen.

Guardian. Protector.

The voice came upon her this time without a sound, yet somehow she knew it was coming. Smiling weakly she answered on a whisper.

"Yes, Lord. I know."

Being difficult. Very difficult.

The voice said, causing her to chuckle softly.

"Yes, Lord. He is."

Was not referring to him.

Scowling into the fire, she became testy in response.

"The woman is not always the one being difficult."

Sure about that?

"I don't understand. You don't want me to tell them the stories and yet you're saying I am being difficult. How? What am I doing wrong?"

Wasn't referring to you.

Rolling onto her back, Inara stared at the ceiling, deep in thought. Then suddenly understanding dawned upon her.

"Oh, I see."

"What do you see, Inara?" Rafe strolled into the living room with a tray in hand.

Glancing his direction, Inara saw the glass of milk on the tray and sat up too fast. Grimacing in pain, her hand flew to her forehead and she moaned softly.

"Take it easy there. You'll make yourself pass out again." He handed her the headache medicine after setting the tray down on the coffee table in front of her.

Inara grabbed for the milk anxiously. Trying not to be so obviously desperate, she initially started with only a sip in order to wash down the pills. But the moment the creamy white liquid touched her tongue she couldn't stop herself from guzzling half the glass before his very eyes. Setting the glass down she wiped awkwardly at her mouth, realizing he'd been watching her intently.

"You seem to like milk."

"Yes, sorry. I don't get it very much. So this is a real treat for me." Seeing his questioning look she explained. "There was never enough. I always made sure the kids got it."

Rafe could tell she was embarrassed. He wanted to put her at ease but realized grimly, that he needed to put her in her place where this sort of thing was concerned. Otherwise, she could wind up really hurting herself in the future.

"You will need to stop doing that. Especially now, don't you think?"

Catching the serious look in his eye she felt her cheeks flush with heat as he stared intently at her. Getting his meaning, she replied, "I suppose you're right."

"Good. Whether you're in my house or ... my children's, you will not go without. Now, please eat and don't be embarrassed. I'll be in the chair reading."

Nodding amiably, she thanked him gratefully and began to eat.

"I'd like to ask a question," Inara said tentatively while forking a piece of roast beef. "But I'm afraid you might take my reasons for asking the wrong way."

Having taken his place back in his chair, Rafe laid his iPad back in his lap then he peered at her curiously. "Go ahead," he prompted.

"Where is Dartanian sleeping tonight?" She intentionally avoided his gaze. Not hearing a response, she finally glanced his way and could see a hint of annoyance in his gaze at her query.

Taking his iPad back up in his hand, he attempted to return to his reading. "I locked him in my bedroom for the night, if you must know."

Twiddling with her fork in her hand nervously, Inara inquired, "Do you really think that's wise?"

"I locked all my closet doors if that's what you're wondering. He won't discover anything he shouldn't." Rafe knew full well she was referencing the passages that led to his hidden rooms.

"You're not worried about ... you know ... the extra door in the bathroom?"

Glaring at her, his pale blue eyes became steely. "I'm not too sure I like that you're privy to the secrets in my house," he said in response. "It's hidden well enough. I suspect he won't find it."

"Right, sorry." Seeing him gesturing towards her, she realized he was trying to prompt her to eat, so she continued.

"Rafe."

"Yes, Inara."

"Why did you lock him in your room?"

"I have a recently widowed woman under my roof, a Blackthorne son presently being denied his husbandly rights, and a second prophecy made by my late wife, of which, is both illuminating and alarming in its content. I think we both know full well the tenuous situation we have here."

"But Rafe," Inara frowned, knowing full well of the Blackthorne lines aggressive tendencies when being denied, for she'd written of them. "Your single and there is more Blackthorne in you than your son."

"I'm sixty years old, Inara and my wife passed many years ago. I haven't been affected by such temptations since I lost Lilyandhi. So I think it's safe to say you are safe with me," he said dryly. "Don't you think?"

Face flaming in embarrassment, Inara swallowed hard as she struggled to choke back a sob. Tears threatened to pool in her eyes as she stared down at the tasty meal on her plate, quickly losing her appetite.

Sensing he unintentionally might have hurt her feelings somehow, he also noted she was suddenly picking at her food. Scowling, he worried she hadn't been eating enough since she'd arrived. "Inara, don't lose your appetite now. You need to eat," he urged.

Huffing at his words, Inara frowned irritably. "Oh, yes. We must make sure she's ready for it. Wouldn't want..."

"Don't finish that," Rafe barked, his temper flaring. Setting his Ipad aside he could tell he wasn't going to get any further in his reading until they had this conversation out. "Inara, you are not the only one with the gift of 'Knowing'."

"I'm well aware of what your capable of, Rafe," she shot back.

"Good. Then you're also aware of Proverbs 3:5 where God tells us to trust in the Lord with all our hearts and to never rely upon what we *think* we know," he said emphatically.

Huffing again softly, she mumbled under her breath. "I suspect I know more than what you might think."

Exasperated Rafe replied, "We each are being given separate pieces of the puzzle. Though you may think you have all the answers, you would be wrong. That chapter does go on to say in verse six that if we remember the Lord in everything we do, then he will show us the right way."

Inhaling sharply as tears threatened at her eyes once again, she struggled to reign in her tumultuous emotions. "I'm already painfully aware of what the way is." Hearing him scoff she frowned at what she deemed an all-knowing attitude of his own while glaring at him impudently. "Isn't there also something in that verse about never allowing ourselves to think that we are wiser than what we are?" she shot back, having trouble remembering the verses for her memory, she suspected, wasn't as good as Rafe's, regardless of his age.

"Yes, that's in verse seven of the same chapter. It continues by saying to simply obey the Lord and refuse to do wrong," he concluded while giving her a meaningful look.

Inara shoved at her food with her fork in aggravation. "Obey and refuse to do wrong? Rafe Blackthorne, *I* am not the one who is being difficult here. I think you know full well what my choice has been from the beginning."

"Which is to follow God's plan wherever it may lead you. I understand. It's highly commendable and I am ever so grateful to you for that," he said patiently, forcing his

149

voice to stay calm. "That said, we each have our roles in this. Are you clear on yours?"

"Well gee, now I am," she retorted. Shoving her fork in her roast beef, she took a big bite and stared at him with a mulish expression. Gagging suddenly, having taken a larger bite then she intended, Rafe came up off the chair and was behind her in two quick strides. Grabbing her around the waist with one arm as he pulled her up, he thumped her on the back with the other, effectively forcing the food from her throat.

Sighing heavily in relief, he leaned his head against her shoulder momentarily, his panic subsiding.

"I really wish you would stop doing that."

"You and me both," she said in a hoarse voice, her hands shaking. Her knees began to buckle on her. "But it's not all my fault, you know."

"I know." His eyes shifted about the room. "It's one of the reasons why I am here. Are you okay?" he asked kindly, laying his large hand gently upon her shoulder, hoping to ease her discomfort. Feeling her shiver under his hand, he reached for the blanket on the back of the couch and wrapped it around her shoulders. Returning to the chair after she was settled, he took up his iPad again in order to read. For a time it was quiet aside from the sounds of Inara's utensils tapping lightly against her plate as she ate.

"Inara, I have to ask," Rafe said finally, clearing his throat. "You know, just so we're thorough, of course." He paused.

"But of course."

"Are you?"

"Am I what?"

"An artist and a poet. I ask because you reference a little girl drawing a portrait here at age six and I wondered if you knew whether or not the girl in question is you or..."

"Or?"

"Someone else." Shrugging, he pointed towards his iPad.

"Have you not been through my bag yet?"

"Do I need to go through your bag for that answer?" One eyebrow raised, he looked at her inquisitively, a hint of annoyance in his mannerism.

Flustered, Inara rubbed at her knees nervously. "I can tell you, at least, that I used to paint, though I haven't done so for years," she said reluctantly.

"Paint you say? Any good at it?"

"Nothing exceptional I'd say. Not like the artist who displays his works at the Sheriff's Department or Royce's coffee house. What accounts for good to one might well be shabby comparatively to another. Art is extremely subjective as you well know." She gave him a look out of the corner of her eye. "That said, I liked painting."

"Liked, past tense. Why did you stop?"

Evading his question, Inara's brow furrowed suddenly. "Wait a minute. Which book are you reading right now?"

"It's entitled, 'Choices second final copy.' Why?"

"Oh, wow. Done with book two are you?" Seeing him giving her a mild expression she continued. "You do read fast. Well, you should probably start with the first one I wrote and completed." She took a deep uneasy breath as she scraped the remains of her mashed potatoes from her plate and into her mouth. Recalling some of the content within that particular story version, she winced outwardly.

"Which one is that? You appear to have numerous copies of book three in here. It's extremely confusing." The way he spoke, he almost sounded annoyed again. Was he always so annoyed by everything, she wondered? Or was it just her?

Harrumphing softly, she said in response, "Try being me. I've started this story over again more than half a dozen times." She took a bite of her fried apples, groaning with pleasure as they melded in her mouth. "

"You said as much on the plane," he said, sounding grumpy. He shook his iPad before her eyes.

"Yes, I did, and it turns out the variables were ever changing due, in large part, to the fact the people within it are real." Inara vented. Her tone was testy again but her hands were shaking now and she dropped her silverware loudly on her plate in frustration. "Now, I have a new one playing out in my head. It's shifting so much I cannot keep up, and I no longer have an outlet for it." Holding her hands together, as though attempting to stop them from trembling, she continued. "In answer to your question, I think the file is called 'Choices first final copy.' But now that I think about it, the one you really need to read is probably Choices Dreaming."

"Dreaming you say? All right, well, I *will* eventually get to them all. Why entitle it Choices anyway?" He sighed wearily.

"It seems kind of poignant, don't you think?" She heard him snort softly into his hand. His eyes continued to roam the iPad screen.

"You're not … you're not going to switch to the one I suggested?" she asked, sounding worried.

"No, I'll finish this first and get to the rest as I'm able."

"You're a pretty quick read," Inara observed, thinking frantically. It was really important that he read that particular one soon. "How long do you think it will take to get to that one?" she asked tentatively, trying to seem simply curious rather than panicky.

Staring her down, he paused in his reading, "Without interruptions, much quicker than I currently am," he said dryly.

"Fair point. Gotcha."

"That said, I do need to sleep eventually, and I have other responsibilities around the ranch. Plus, I must deal with the necessary name changes for you and your children." He pressed on, lifting the notepad lying next to him up, so she could see. "Or, nothing can happen on June sixteenth. Especially if your story here is right, for it seems in order for the prophecy to be complete, the couple must be married. So names must be corrected by then."

Blushing profusely Inara turned her head away from him as she spoke. "Any ideas on…"

"Inara, one thing at a time, please. I too have much in my head and on my plate."

Swallowing hard, Inara couldn't help the catch in her throat nor the tears that threatened at her eyes. "Right, order of importance and everything."

"Inara," Rafe said softly, giving her a perplexed look, not sure what he'd said that had managed to upset her this time.

"Think nothing of it, Rafe. I do understand my place, after all." She set her silverware down and rested her arms across her belly. Closing her eyes she grimaced. Her stomach rumbled obnoxiously from being overly filled. Not having eaten most of the day, she made the same mistake she always did by eating too much. Hiccupping softly she missed seeing Rafe watching her with worry.

"Is everything all right?"

"I'm just really full," she said with a pained expression, not bothering to open her eyes. Suddenly feeling drowsy all over again, she marveled at the abundant need for sleep since she'd been at the ranch and wondered about it.

"Inara, one last question; I can tell you appear to be quite drowsy," he observed while frowning down at the iPad in his hand. Glancing back up at her, he could see her leaning back on the couch. She was curling up within the blanket once again, looking very tired and in desperate need of further sleep.

"By all means, ask away," she said amidst a yawn.

"When you write poetry, does it lack punctuation as much as your novels do?" he asked irately. Not getting a response, he peered over at her, only to see she'd instantly fallen asleep. Pursing his lips, he got up once again and adjusted the blanket over her so she'd be more comfortable.

"At least this time, you let her get something to eat before knocking her out, Lord," Rafe said, staring heavenward.

The fire flamed in the hearth, as a soft clucking noise could be heard filling the air.

Chapter 11

Early morning. Around sunrise.
Wednesday, June 10, 2015

Wake up!

Heart thumping wildly, Inara flopped over on the couch, her eyes opening wide at the abrupt wake-up call. Groaning into her pillow, she moaned softly as her gaze caught the faint light of the sunrise, wafting its way through the window blinds.

Inara stretched then yawned contentedly. She had slept the rest of the night through quite peacefully. Suspecting she was likely meant to be getting up for some reason, she pushed back her blanket and went in search of coffee, only to find that Rafe had nodded off in the chair next to her as he was reading. A little self-conscious about having slept alone in the same room with the Blackthorne patriarch, she stood momentarily just staring at him, unsure of what to do. Making a decision she set his iPad on the stand next to him then nervously held out the blanket she'd used, hoping not to disturb him when she covered him. Tiptoeing from the living room, she moved to the kitchen with a relieved sigh and started a pot of coffee.

Tapping her fingers on the counter impatiently she waited for the pot to brew. She was extremely grateful when it finally finished percolating. Pouring herself a mug, it occurred to her it was day three since her last shower. She really needed new clothes. The children had been able to borrow things from the other kids in the house easily enough but she was still wearing what she arrived in. Taking a few sips of her coffee she wandered through the quiet halls and on to the laundry room. Feeling a bit guilty about going through the clothes there, she eventually found a large, royal blue Colts T-shirt, as well as a black house robe and fresh clean towels. Hoping the party who owned the items wouldn't be too upset at her borrowing them, she locked the door, stripped down and threw on the robe.

Tossing her clothes in the wash along with other clothes she found in a basket nearby, she started the machine. Then grabbing up the towel and washcloth she found, she headed down to the pool area in order to shower. Finding bottles of shampoo, conditioner and soap under the sink in the women's bath, Inara took a rigorous shower then hastily dried off, anxious to be covered in the T-shirt and house robe quickly. At one point in the story of one of her novels she'd written, every member of the household, Blackthorne or otherwise, had seen her naked. She was not terribly inclined toward living that particular experience in real life.

Not finding any kind of hairbrush or pick, Inara towel dried her hair, exclaiming in exasperation after peering in the mirror. Her waist length wavy locks were a tangled mess. Attempting to brush through her hair with her fingers, she noted it hadn't really done any good. Distressed that everyone would be seeing her in such a state, she banged her head against the mirror in frustration.

"Really, Lord, I'm a mess. He deserves so much better than me. Someone slender and well put together, like Lylia."

Trying hard, at that moment, not to think about Damien she hung the towel on the hook and continued to stare into the mirror in misery.

"I wasn't even able to give my so-called husband a proper funeral, Lord." Her face contorted in pain at the thought. Giving in to a few precious moments of weeping over the loss of Damien, Inara realized after several minutes, it wasn't going to get her anywhere. Pulling herself together, she shook out her arms and legs briefly, then wiped the tears away. She'd find a way later to give herself and the children time to grieve. Right now she suspected there was much to be done.

Heading back down the hall to the laundry room, she was happy to see her load of laundry had stopped. Switching it to the dryer, she started it up and headed back down to the kitchen, rather than the living room. Unsure when exactly everyone began to rise, she noted the time and realized it might be still a bit early.

Topping off her mug since it was cooling, she then headed past the board on the kitchen wall, only to stop abruptly. Seeing both Rafe and Dartanian's name was on the board for breakfast that morning, she peered into the living room, knowing full well Rafe wouldn't wake in time. Suspecting Dartanian might have other things on his mind than breakfast duty, it occurred to her this might well be why the Lord had awakened her.

Peering around the vast kitchen, Inara debated what she wanted to do. Knowing how much her own children enjoyed breakfast sandwiches and her homemade banana bread, she started searching for ingredients. She was well aware many of the Blackthorne family members were big eaters so both would likely be needed. Grabbing three mixing bowls first, she made a double batch of quick bread batter in each bowl with the cinnamon applesauce jars she found in the fridge since she couldn't find any bananas. Adding chopped nuts and allspice instead of cinnamon to the batter, she divided it evenly amongst six bread loaf pans. She had them in the oven quicker than she would have thought. Setting the timer, Inara started the other two coffee pots anticipating people would likely be heading down within the next half hour.

Clearing up her mess quickly, she grabbed more items from the fridge and pantry. Inara began making breakfast sandwiches, the same way she always did, only on a much greater scale than what was her norm. A half hour later, after scrambling three dozen eggs with butter, frying sausage and bacon, and toasting an enormous amount of bread, Inara started pulling the sandwiches together, topping them with cheese. Finding it odd she hadn't seen anybody yet, as the hour was past seven, she began to wonder why no one was up. Thinking Chase and Dante, in particular, might want to take coffee with them, she pulled several thermoses from the cupboards and set them near the coffee pots.

After peeling and cutting mangos, oranges, peaches and strawberries, Inara pulled the blenders away from the wall and began tossing fruit and yogurt in them. Seeing the time was nearing quarter till eight, Inara became anxious as the timer went off for the cinnamon apple bread. Pulling the loaves from the oven, she allowed the loaves to cool a few minutes before slicing them up. At the last minute, she decided to start packaging them up in plastic wrap and tin foil along with the breakfast sandwiches, although she didn't know why. Completing that task, she lay the wrapped cinnamon bread in a pan on the counter and put the breakfast sandwiches back in the oven, in order to keep them warm.

She was starting to worry she'd gone to all the effort for nothing.

Realizing she'd never started the blenders, she turned all four of them on at once. A sudden loud banging noise erupted behind her, causing her to shriek with fright. Hand on her wildly thumping heart; she turned to find Rafe standing in the kitchen doorway near the living room, staring in at her in dismay.

"Inara, is that really the time?"

"If you mean nearly eight, then yes."

Rubbing his eyes, he peered at the board in the kitchen in horror. "It's my day for breakfast and I have nothing started. They're never going to let me live this down." He groaned.

"It's Dartanian's day too if you notice, and where is he? Besides I have some…"

"Wait a minute," Rafe interrupted, looking around the kitchen in confusion. "Where is everybody? They should all be down here by now."

"I don't know." She was just as perplexed. She shrugged and turned off the blenders, suspecting that was what had woke him. No sooner had the words come out of her mouth, then the sound of thundering feet could be heard on the kitchen stairwell. Voices, all exclaiming in dismay at the late hour and inevitably harried morning, carried down into the kitchen as bodies began racing into the kitchen.

"Late!" Hialey screeched, tucking her navy-blue work shirt into her black leggings as Breydon flew past her. "I got a delivery coming early."

"You're late? I have to be in court in an hour, and I still need to swing by the office." Breydon hastily donned his suit jacket.

Behind them came Chase and Megorah, along with Dante and Royce. "I don't have time Meg. I have to go." Chase hollered as he slipped into his shoes.

"You have to eat *something*," Megorah exclaimed. She peered around the kitchen while attempting to brush out her hair.

"You too, Brey," Hialey said suddenly, eliciting a growl from her husband. Pointing towards him she glared. "You know how you get if you don't. You cannot afford to upset judge Morris again, or you'll lose this case."

"What food? What breakfast?" Breydon nearly hollered, pointing towards the kitchen tables irritably. "Do you see any food on these tables? Whoever's turn it was screwed up! There *is* no breakfast. Besides, I have no time."

As Breydon had been hollering, more thundering feet could be heard coming down the stairs and into the kitchen. Popping his head into the room, Drinian called out in distress, upon hearing Breydon's pronouncement.

"No breakfast! Are you kidding me?" He cried as Veta and Alaina followed close behind.

"Wait! Calm down, everyone!" Inara yelled above the noise and general commotion of people shoving on shoes last minute and arguing with their spouse. Getting their attention, she pointed toward the counter near the sink, then pulled open the oven door and struggled to remove the heavy pan laden with food.

"There is breakfast. You're all running late so just grab what you need and go!" Inara reached for more thermos cups and lids and began pouring mugs of coffee and smoothies.

"What's this?" Drinian asked, reaching for one of the foil wrapped packages lying in the pan she'd pulled from the oven.

"Breakfast sandwiches. Some are egg and sausage with cheese and some are with bacon instead, although I really couldn't tell you which one is which now," Inara said.

"Doesn't matter, it's food," Breydon exclaimed gratefully in relief. He swooped in and grabbed two, then the thermos of coffee she'd handed him after adding sugar and French vanilla creamer. Turning around toward the table, he dumped the sandwiches in his bag. "I can eat them on the way," he said quickly while moving hastily toward the door.

"Breydon, wait!" Inara called after him as she plucked up two packages from the pan on the counter. Tossing them toward Hialey who was closer, she gestured for her to hand them to Breydon. Throwing the packages on to Breydon, he caught them in one hand, looked at them for a second then ran past his dad out the kitchen door through the living room.

"What was that?" Hialey asked, turning back towards Inara as she placed a smoothie in her hand.

"Apple cinnamon nut bread."

"Yum, I'll take one of everything," Hialey said eagerly. Inara procured what was needed and passed them on. "Coffee too please."

"You're so small," Inara exclaimed, quickly adding French vanilla creamer and sugar to her thermos as well. "How can you eat and drink all that?" She asked as Hialey too headed hastily toward the kitchen door.

"High metabolism," Hialey called, sipping at the smoothie. "Oh, this is good." she could be heard to say while running for the front door herself.

Within minutes everyone's hands were reaching into the pans, filching food and grabbing up the coffee and smoothies. As the blenders emptied, Inara filled them up quickly with the ingredients still lying on the counter. Ten minutes later nearly the entire kitchen had emptied of most of the adults, as they disappeared to their prospective jobs leaving behind the children in their wake. Tending to each one as they came down, Inara made sure they each got what they wanted and needed, with Rafe and Megorah's help.

As the noise died down and the children began disappearing to the playroom, Rafe finally had a chance to grab a much-needed cup of coffee after making a couple more pots in order to cover the rest of the morning. He liked to have some available for the ladies who came to clean for him on Wednesdays. Pouring himself a mug of straight black java, as well as the same for Inara, he handed off a mug to her and leaned against the counter.

Watching Inara hand Katana a smoothie and sandwich, he could see Meg's daughter was confused.

"Lylia never showed for breakfast. I suspect she probably needs to eat too," Inara said in answer.

Smiling sweetly, Katana allowed the children to drag her along. "I'll be sure to tell her you sent it on for her."

"Oh, heavens no," she exclaimed anxiously, causing the girl to stop and look back curiously. "Don't do that child! She might think I'm trying to poison her or something."

"Why would you do that?" Katana asked.

"Just tell her 'they' sent it on from the kitchen for her. Trust me. It's better this way, honey."

Katana simply shrugged. "Okay."

Thinking Inara's gesture was thoughtful, considering the situation with her and Dartanian, Rafe eyed her with renewed admiration.

"So, Inara," Rafe said finally, taking a sip of coffee. He looked at her gratefully. "Nice save this morning."

"It was no biggie."

"I notice all the breakfast sandwiches are gone." He sounded despondent while staring longingly at the empty pans on the counter.

"Yes, under the circumstances they went awful quick didn't they?" Reaching for the oven door, she bent down and grabbed a small pan from inside. "But I did save a couple for you," she told him while tossing a couple of sandwiches on the counter towards him.

"Save any for me?" came a deep voice from the hallway. Strolling towards her, freshly shaven and dressed in his Sheriff's uniform, Dartanian fixed her with an even gaze. His crystal-clear blue eyes were seemingly more vibrant than usual as he gazed upon her. The expression on his face was cautious and yet curious, even interested. Peering down at the two remaining sandwiches in front of her, he came to stand next to her, his gaze roaming over her makeup-free face. Picking them up, he grabbed a thermos. "Thanks. I appreciate it." He gave her a wide almost flirtatious smile in gratitude. Moving away toward the coffee pot to pour himself a cup, he stopped suddenly.

Turning back, Dartanian stared down at her. Setting the sandwiches back in front of him, he reached out and pulled at the shoulder of the robe she was wearing. Jaw clenching, his eyes became hard. He stared angrily at her, then over at his dad.

"Really?" he exclaimed in disgust.

Rafe raised an eyebrow at him and took another drink of his coffee, not saying a word. He was leaning nonchalantly against the counter with his feet crossed as though he hadn't a care in the world.

Grabbing up his thermos after pouring himself a mug of straight black coffee, Dartanian snatched up the sandwiches angrily. "I *will* be talking to you later, Inara." He made only a slight effort at softening his tone. Striding from the room, he banged through the doors as he went.

"So much for breakfast," Inara grumbled unhappily, watching her sandwiches disappear. It hadn't occurred to her until just then, that Dartanian hadn't graced them with his presence yet. "And what was that about anyway?" She stared down at the robe.

Concluding that she hadn't been saving any for his son, Rafe handed one of his sandwich packages off to Inara. "I suspect he was probably upset because you were wearing *my* Bears robe with *his* favorite Colts t-shirt." He tipped his mug towards her while backing away toward the patio doors.

Gasping audibly, Inara's hands flew to her mouth in dismay.

Shrugging, an amused grin played upon his face. "I was wondering when someone was going to notice. It was probably just as well Lylia didn't show. She gave Dart the shirt for his birthday."

Absolutely mortified, Inara watched Rafe disappear through the patio doors, her sandwich dangling precariously in her hand.

Chapter 12

Once finally overcoming the shock of learning she'd been publicly wearing Rafe's robe with Dartanian's t-shirt, Inara fled to the laundry in hopes of discovering her clothes would be clean. It was Wednesday so the cleaning staff had arrived and had already pulled the load from the dryer. Gratefully regaining her clothing from them she disappeared to the bathroom closest to the library under the upstairs landing and changed back. Returning the shirt and robe to the laundry, she asked that they wash them again for her, before returning them to their respective rooms.

Returning to the kitchen, Inara picked her wrapped sandwich up off the floor where she dropped it. She was about to attempt to eat it when one of the cleaning ladies appeared at her side. Extending an envelope toward her the woman appeared nervous.

"Ma'am? Is this yours?"

Staring at it momentarily, Inara's mind went blank. It took her a second to realize the envelope in question was, in fact, hers. Gasping in dismay her eyes flew open and she banged herself in the head with her hand.

"Oh, my goodness! Thank you so much. Yes!" Opening the envelope in front of the woman she noted it still had everything in it. "What's your name?" Inara took a closer look at the woman standing at her side. She appeared tired already and she was just starting her work for the day. Her hazel eyes squinted and there were bags under them. The woman appeared to be in her mid-thirties but she had the feeling she might be younger. Though tidy in appearance, she seemed a bit frazzled.

"Abigail, Ma'am. I promise it's all there. I didn't take any." The cleaning lady appeared anxious.

"I know." Gratefully producing two fifty-dollar bills, Inara startled Abigail when she folded them and tucked the money into the woman's hand.

"I didn't return it to gain anything by it. The money is yours." The woman attempted to push the money back into Inara's hand even as she eyed it in distress. It was obvious to her that there was definitely a need there.

"I do realize and appreciate that, but sometimes honesty *should* be rewarded, especially when someone else's need is greater than our own. I completely spaced that I had even placed it in the robe. You could have just as easily taken the whole thousand dollars and no one in this house would have been the wiser. Besides, somehow I just know you need it more than me right now." Not knowing the woman's story Inara took it on faith that God would see to her and her own children's needs one way or another. Recognizing that a person must learn to earn what they have and not have it handed to them, she gratefully gave the woman ten percent of what she had.

Glancing down in surprise at the hundred dollars in her hand Abigail peered back up at Inara in astonishment.

"You're giving me a hundred dollars because I returned the envelope you didn't know was missing?"

"Yes. Proverbs 28:6 tells us it's 'better to be poor and honest than rich and dishonest.' In the long run, God's rewards are so much greater when you give thankfully; even in your own hour of need. Don't you think? Now go, I suspect you have a long day ahead of you." Inara smiled knowingly.

Tearing up at the generosity, Abigail exclaimed in delight as she backed away. "Thank you! Thank you so much! You have no idea how much this helps right now."

Briefly watching her walk away, Inara peered down at the remaining money in the envelope thoughtfully. Nine hundred dollars was all she had left in the world and she suspected she knew exactly what needed to be done with it. Forgetting about her breakfast sitting on the counter once again, she traipsed up the stairs towards Rafe's study. Knocking lightly on the door she waited patiently but there was no answer. Remembering she'd seen him leave to head down to the Stallion corral, she knocked harder once more for good measure, and then let herself in.

Moving quickly and quietly into his study, she found a pen lying on his desk and wrote on the envelope. Pulling three hundred dollars out, she left the remaining six hundred in the envelope, taped it closed and left it, writing side up, on Rafe's desk. Turning to leave, feeling a little like she was trespassing, she halted at the sight of the painting on his wall.

"So, you're Lilyandhi," Inara said softly. She took in the young woman's high cheekbones, long dark hair, and pale blue eyes. The artist who had painted her had portrayed her as being very beautiful. No taller than herself, the pure-blooded Indian woman before her was easily fifty pounds smaller than Inara and was wearing her wedding dress. Sick with envy at the sight of her, and knowing she shouldn't be, Inara swallowed hard and turned to leave only to find her way barred by Dante.

"S…sorry," she stammered. "I was just leaving."

"What were you doing in here?" Dante asked suspiciously.

"I forgot to give Rafe something yesterday. I was just leaving it on his desk." She pointed nervously towards Rafe's desk at the envelope she'd left him. She was feeling more and more like an intruder in the Blackthorne home. Then, gesturing at the painting before her as a distraction, she went on. "Your mom, she was a very beautiful woman."

"Yes, she was." Dante glanced at the portrait briefly then back at Inara curiously, as though trying to figure her out. "But then pictures and portraits especially can be deceiving sometimes. An artist's eye is subjective after all."

Walking slowly towards the study door, Inara turned slightly, confused a little by Dante's statement. "What do you mean by, a portrait can be deceiving?"

"You don't know, do you?" he peered suddenly at the portrait of his mom once again then back at Inara. He looked as if he'd just been given some internal insight.

"What don't I…"

"It figures I'd find both of you here." Rafe scowled. He entered his study, effectively cutting off the line of inquiry. Removing his Stetson from his head, he tossed it on the sofa, strolled around his desk and took a seat. Seeing the envelope, he lifted it in his hands and eyed it curiously. Peering over at Inara, he gave her a questioning and almost annoyed look.

Rolling her eyes in frustration, she said, "It's about to become an issue, I think. Just wait, you'll see," she said quickly while drawing an embarrassed sigh. "At some point, Rafe, you have to at least let me out to a store for clothes."

"My grandchildren have plenty of clothes they can lend out for right now." Rafe barely looked up from his desk but set the envelope in his drawer for the time being. He suspected he already knew what was in it and was unhappy about its contents being given to him.

"Maybe so, but I'm going to need clothes eventually unless you expect me to walk around in the same thing for seven days."

"Seven days?" Dante asked. Was there significance to the time frame, he wondered?

"What's wrong with what you had on this morning?" Rafe said, trying to be funny. Seeing Inara shoot him a warning look, he waved his hand as a white flag. "I get it Inara, but it's going to have to wait."

"Right, order of importance and all," Inara said in a flat tone, gaining Dante's attention. Seeing her wounded expression, he wondered at it.

"I'm sure Alaina has some clothing she could loan you."

Shaking her head miserably she placed both palms of her hands to her forehead in distress. "Thanks but no, Dante. We've been through this before. Her sweatpants will be okay, though snug but her shirts will be…"

"Will be what?" Rafe asked distractedly while digging in his desk, looking for something.

Wrapping her arms across her chest protectively, Inara hugged herself. "Inappropriate in front of everyone to say the least," she said shyly, not missing the look on Rafe's face and the cagey glance her way before he could squelch it. She couldn't help but wonder if he was messing with her intentionally.

"When have we been through this before?" Dante asked slowly, gaining her attention as twin creases carved a questioning look on his forehead.

"You know. Before, when..." Stopping, she became distressed. "Wait, no. You're right. That was version three of book three, no, wait ... version four. The one where everybody kept seeing me naked."

"Excuse me?" Dante's head swiveled towards her in dismay.

"What did you say?" Rafe exclaimed in shock.

"Oh, never mind." Inara shook her head while fidgeting. Her face flushed crimson with heat. "Just ... skip that one in your reading, Rafe, please. It bears no real significance anymore. At least, I don't think it does. It just happens to be highly disturbing." Feeling suddenly very warm and desperate to flee, she turned to leave.

"So, I'm to skip version three of book three?" Rafe called after her, forcing her to stop and turn back. In the back of his mind, he made a mental note to find the file in question she was just referring to. It seemed prudent to read it, if for no other reason, then to determine how to prevent the events leading up to his household potentially seeing her naked.

Arms flailing around her and smacking against her sides, Inara blinked once, then responded. "No, version four."

"And what's the file called again? Because, you know, there's over half a dozen of them and I'd hate to skip the wrong one." He was intentionally giving her a hard time.

Scratching at the back of her head and across the nape of her neck, she stretched her shoulders anxiously. Inara became thoughtful in her exasperation. "Well, I believe it's called, Choices Dreaming."

"Inara."

"Yes?"

"You told me last night that was the one I needed to read. Are you telling me now to skip it?" He was mildly irritated now. Sitting back in his chair, he really looked at the red-headed mess before him. Troubled by the confusion he was seeing, he pursed his lips as he waited, his eyes twinkling.

"No… Wait…um, yes." Her brow furrowed in confusion. "I mean, there are two files listed that way but one is with a roman numeral."

"Okay, so which one am I reading, Inara?" Rafe asked calmly, becoming exasperated. He rubbed his forefinger and thumb against his forehead in aggravation, while peering at his desk. "Which one is more important?"

"They're both important," she said quickly, sounding alarmed. "But the roman numeral … bears greater significance, I think," she finished softly, pausing meaningfully as she spoke.

Her words grabbed his attention and his head shot up in surprise. Fidgeting where she stood, Inara's face flamed brighter in her embarrassment and he found he actually had to force himself to keep from laughing out loud in delight.

And the look on her face was priceless.

Watching the play of emotions in her expression, Rafe additionally made a startling connection of his own at something she'd said. Hand dropping to his desk suddenly, he peered back over at her with a cautious look, his eyes hinting at a humorous light.

"Are you sure?" He sounded both flabbergasted and incredulous in one.

"Yes," Inara said slowly while swallowing hard, becoming just as agitated at the mellow timber in his voice.

"Roman numeral one … is highly significant in Choices Dreaming."

"Inara, do you have dreams? And, if so, do you write about those in your stories as well?" He quirked an eyebrow at her in a curious and playful manner. He suddenly found the titles for her files both exhilarating and yet troubling at the same time.

Inhaling sharply, her eyes grew wide as though a rabbit caught in the line of sight of a hungry mountain lion. Glancing uneasily back and forth at both men, while taking a few tentative steps back, she finally responded. "It depends," she said, her voice rising at first. Highly flustered, looking all the while as though she were ready to bolt, she paused. Seeing him waiting patiently for a response, her insides became jelly.

"On?" Rafe prompted, staring at her intently. He sensed her mind had drawn a blank for some reason.

"On the version of the story I'm writing at the time," she stammered anxiously, her voice catching.

Seeing the almost fearful look in her wide eyes, Rafe's expression became suddenly grim. What was in her stories that had her so worked up? And why wouldn't God just let her tell him?

"Okay, well… I'll leave you to it then." She figured it was way past time to go. Turning on her heels, she left the study abruptly, not wanting to intrude any further.

Watching her leave Dante whistled softly. "Wow," he said finally. "Her head is all over the place."

"You said it."

"So … are you going to read it? You know - the story where everyone sees her naked?" The humor in Dante's tone was obvious.

Rafe stared back at his son as he swiveled his chair back and forth. The grin on his face and the merriment in his eyes made it quite clear what his intentions were where that particular story was concerned.

Chuckling softly Dante glanced toward the door where Inara had just exited, his expression suddenly becoming serious. "What are we going to do with her and her kids anyway? It's not like they can stay here forever, and it's not fair to those children of hers, to be living in this environment too long when she won't be able to maintain this standard of living for them on her own."

"On the contrary, I have the distinct feeling they won't be going anywhere," Rafe said evasively, looking somewhat distracted. He twiddled his hand in the air, looking as though he were trying to remember where he'd put something.

Startled by his father's assessment, he stared at him. "Meaning?"

"Meaning she needs to start eating better." He gave his son a quick meaningful look then returned to his task.

"Dad? Are you saying what I think you are?" Dante questioned, thoroughly appalled and confused by the mere implication his father was making with his statement. Frustrated that his angelic guide wasn't giving him anything right now, he queried further. "And how do you know she's not eating?"

"Because, as any good mother would, she took care of everyone else this morning but then, became distracted and left her breakfast on the counter. Both I and Royce have noticed she hasn't been eating well, or for that matter, eating in general."

"Wait a minute. You're saying she's the one that fixed all the sandwiches and cinnamon bread this morning? Inara made breakfast? On her own?"

"Yes."

"But this morning ... whose name was on the board in the kitchen?"

"Does it matter? She covered for the person or persons after all." Rafe leaned back in his chair briefly. He stared back up at his son intently. "Pretty interesting turn of events, wouldn't you say?"

Dante suddenly gaped at his father, perplexed. He appeared as though completely at a loss for words. "But, I thought it was Dart's turn? Does that mean..."

"His turn, my turn. Does it really matter?" Sitting up, Rafe folded his hands on top of each other on his desk, giving his son a peculiar look. He was beginning to wonder when Dante would finally pick up on what he was trying to tell him. Taking a more direct route he asked, "You have seen the notepad with Alaina and Lylia's notes, right?"

Sensing his father was attempting to pass on a message or hint at something Dante's attention was piqued. "Yes, I have. We all made copies of it." He pulled a paper from his front pocket and unfolded it.

"Seeing the numbers and now knowing the order, do you recall as well the poetic prophecy your mother wrote?"

"I believe so. Why?"

"For through fiery hair of silver and gold ... a seed shall lie within her womb, three times blessed we can presume." He repeated some of the words as he leaned back in his chair again and rested his head against the back cushion. A slow worried smile played at his lips.

"Whoa, wait just a minute. Dad!" Dante exclaimed without warning, finally making the connection. "But I thought..."

"Shush. Don't tell anyone. Just let them figure it out. We'll see how this plays out." Rafe's brow furrowed playfully.

"But the sixteenth is Tuesday. That's, what? Six days away? How are we going to get them together in that short time frame? It's impossible under the circumstances!" Dante vented understanding Inara's comment about wearing the same clothes for seven days better now. Clearly agitated, he began pacing the room. "And does Inara understand what her role is?"

"I'd say she probably understands what it is that God wants of her better than the rest of us do from the looks of these," he answered wryly. Rafe rolled his eyes heavenward and shook his iPad towards his son. "As you well know, nothing is impossible where God is concerned. Besides, it's not up to us. They'll figure it out I'm sure." He indicated the door Inara had just exited through.

"But what about Lylia...?"

"Dante, you need to trust me."

"But Sunday..."

"Between Breydon and me, we'll take care of the necessary details. Have patience."

Looking at his father with both skepticism and unease Dante cleared his throat. The look on his father's face led him to believe he was having way too much fun with this situation. Though serious, it was obvious he was also tickled to death about what was to come. It was a look he hadn't seen in his father's eye in some time.

"You do realize how many babies this means are going to be around here?" Dante sounded suddenly horrified at the realization himself.

Groaning Rafe frowned and swiveled in his chair. "Oh, no, no no! Two of my sons have houses of their own," he said firmly. "Mark my words; I will not have all those babies in my house at once. Besides, there's a bigger concern here." Rafe grinned openly.

"And that would be?" He marveled at his father's relative calm over the situation.

"The vast amount of diapers the Blackthorne family is about to go through."

"Diapers," Dante said automatically, trying to recover from the news his father had just given him. He appeared shell shocked. "Right, diapers." Mumbling as he turned and walked away Rafe overheard his next words before he exited his study. "Stock in diapers. That's what I need; and a four-year supply of earplugs."

Thinking his son's idea a good one, Rafe swiveled in his chair once again and turned toward the notepad lying on the desk behind him, near his computer. Grabbing a pen he added to his list as he spoke aloud.

"Buy stock in diapers and earplugs." Pausing, he grinned thoughtfully and continued. "Baby wipes too. Oh, and baby lotion." He stared down at the pad, sure that he was missing something.

Chapter 13

The awkward air within the kitchen at dinner time was almost tangible. Everyone took extreme measures at being polite. Managing to avoid each other for most of the day Lylia, Dartanian and Inara were in the kitchen and, by pure coincidence, sitting relatively close to each other during the meal. Making small talk initially, Hialey and Veta attempted to pull Inara into the conversation.

"What's your favorite part of the house now that you've seen it?" Hialey prompted, hoping to keep the conversation light. Her gaze flitted anxiously between Lylia, Inara, and Dartanian.

"I'd say the library downstairs." Inara smiled slowly. "If I sit in the one corner of the room nearest the playroom, the light from the door hits the book just right, at sunset. It's very cozy."

"Good, I'll meet you there after dinner." Dartanian won himself a glare from his wife. "We'll talk then." He calmly ignored the look from Lylia as he attempted to engage Inara.

"No, I don't think so." Inara's eyes flew open in alarm. Fidgeting, she tucked a strand of hair behind her ear nervously.

"Why not?" Dartanian growled.

"Because I really don't think that it's wise right now," she said in a formal tone. With a nervous laugh, she cast a wary sideways glance through her lashes at Lylia, who could be seen sulking next to Veta across the table from her.

"We need to talk." Dartanian scowled next to Inara, his temper flaring further. Pulling a piece of paper from his pocket, he waggled it in the air in front of her.

"No, we really don't," she said firmly becoming increasingly uncomfortable at everyone's eyes suddenly on her. Heat infused her face at the sight of the prophetic numbers and poem listed on the paper. She became agitated. Bumping his hand out of the way with the back of her wrist she continued, as she turned her attention back to Hialey, trying to ignore Dartanian further. "But it is my favorite room. I discovered Rafe has a First Edition of Brothers Grimm Fairy Tales in there."

"Have you had a chance to read any of it?" Veta asked, trying to help move the conversation along.

"Of course not, she's been too busy spinning her web," Lylia said bitterly, loud enough for all to hear. Her words caused Megorah and Crisalya to exchange glances in sympathy.

"I think maybe you and I should really talk, Lylia," Inara said quietly with an uneasy look her way. The whole situation was becoming more than a little uncomfortable for her. Grateful her children were sitting at the other table with the other kids, she was glad to hear them happily eating away, as though nothing was wrong.

"I don't need to hear anything you have to say," Lylia said while shooting a look over at her husband. He sat with his arm draped possessively around the back of Inara's chair. Turned towards her in his seat, he almost appeared as if he were attempting to woo Inara. "And don't worry, I'll be out of your way soon enough," she declared on a huff.

The couple exchanged heated looks. Lylia's expression appeared hurt and dumbfounded as if to say, "The least you could do is wait until it's over." Dartanian, on the other hand, looked blatantly right back at his wife as if to say, "What do you expect? You keep pushing me away?"

Appalled at their behavior and worried about the distress Inara was experiencing at the attention, Megorah cleared her throat. She tried to pull her from the battalion of words and emotions.

"So, Inara. You say you've been reading Brothers Grimm?" Megorah probed further, sensing the conversation was quickly getting out of hand. Bothered by her brother's mannerism towards Inara, she could see out of the corner of her eye that her dad wasn't any more pleased then Lylia was. Taking note of his hawk-like gaze she'd also observed he'd sat at the head of the table this time, rather than taking his normal seat at the counter.

"Yes, I do love fairy tales." Inara was grateful for the distraction. She attempted to take a bite of food. Several long strands of her hair got caught on her hand and fork and she nervously tucked the long tresses once again behind her ear in frustration. Her messy waves were hindering her ability to eat.

Frowning slightly, it occurred to Megorah as she watched Inara that she might want to loan her a few hair ties or clips until she managed to get some of her own.

Taking another quick bite of the beef, noodles, and mashed potatoes from her plate, Inara sighed softly while closing her eyes on a wave of pleasure. The food was scrumptious but she'd been having difficulty getting a chance to eat much of it.

"Cinderella, in particular, happens to be my favorite," she went on to explain, while blushing profusely, causing the freckles on her cheeks to become more pronounced. "Though, I wish it wasn't so violent and that the girl…"

Snorting loudly, Lylia scoffed as she interrupted, "Cinderella? And I suppose you liken yourself to her, and me to one of the homely, contriving step-sisters?"

Shaking her head Inara wiped her mouth with a napkin. "Now why would I think that? Besides, that would imply we're related in some way, which we are not."

Catching her emphatic response, Lylia's head jerked towards the woman, who looked so similar to her. Eyes narrowing upon her, she countered, "How do you know? Aside from you being twice my size, we could be twins; and it's much more likely the other way around where Cinderella's concerned, wouldn't you say? Not that apparently it seems to matter any, but I guarantee you there won't be a happily ever after in this case. We all know he only wants you for one thing."

Face flaming brightly Inara felt heat surge up her neck and into her face. Her eyes moistened as the table went quiet at the insult. The comment, though said offhandedly, had been hurtful none the less, and her hands began to shake.

"I think that's quite enough," Rafe said heatedly from the other end of the table. He glared down towards Lylia with a dark expression on his face. Seeing the hurt in Inara's eyes, he was additionally upset to see Dartanian hadn't chastised or corrected his wife at all.

Catching her father-in-law's steely gaze, Lylia faltered. Realizing what she'd said, she cringed as wounded tears of her own filled her eyes.

"I hadn't intended to be cruel I was just..."

"No, it's okay. You're simply speaking an honest truth. That said, I accept your attempt at a compliment," Inara said gracefully. Struggling to keep from losing her temper, she managed to maintain her cool. She peered over at the blonde headed bombshell across the table, who was perfectly made up and coifed. She was irritated by the blatant hostility and embarrassed by Lylia's choice of words.

"Wait a minute, what?" Lylia stared blankly back at Inara, startled at the unexpected turn while gaining curious confused stares from those around her.

"In the original Brothers Grimm stories, the step-sisters were actually described as being quite beautiful. Though their hearts were dark and their temperaments were hateful," Inara explained. "And I think it rather unlikely that I could be described as having either of those attributes, particularly since I am a Christian. After all, I've invited Jesus Christ into my life, I have deigned that I will always follow Him, and I've asked Him to forgive me of my sins. You know. Because no one, whether man or woman, is without sin after all. Of course, I'm stereotyping here but as a general rule most Christians aren't dark-hearted and hateful because even when they fail they're still trying to live by God's word."

Giving the woman before her an assessing look, Inara noted that Lylia's reaction to her words seemed contrary to her normal nature. Instead of becoming defensive and stand-offish, she'd recoiled from her words as though she'd been slapped. Sighing sadly, realizing what that meant, Inara's expression softened in understanding and she continued quietly.

"That is, in fact, what it takes to be a Christian, right?" Inara inquired. "But Cinderella was very beautiful as well and since, aside for the weight, as you said, we look alike, it would follow to reason that you think I am beautiful." Inara finished. Avoiding everyone's gaze she proceeded to fork another bite of beef and noodles. Noting the woman's silence and her pursed pained expression she continued. "And, honestly, I don't know what you're complaining about anyways, Lylia. You have *your* prince charming. So you tell me. What do you need to do in order to keep him? For that matter, is there anything, perchance, you need to tell him?" She gave her a quiet, calculating stare, as though she were attempting to send her a silent message.

From the other end of the table, both Royce and Rafe shot looks down her way. One appeared mildly amused at the statement; the other was curious.

"This is more like a nightmare than any fairytale." Lylia tossed her napkin on the table in distress. Her face flamed as red as Inara's. Flustered, and clearly agitated, her eyes began to water. "You know Dart, you could have saved us all this trouble - your brothers included - if you'd just told me about your gifts before we got married," Lylia cried angrily, tossing her fork on the table in disgust.

His expression darkening, Dartanian looked at his wife incredulously. "We've been through this enough! I'm tired of re-opening the same old wound. I made a promise, Lylia, to my brothers and sisters and in this family keeping your word matters a great deal. Kind of like when you take vows," he spat back. Flicking his hand towards Inara next to him, he continued. "Besides, I had no way of knowing…"

"Oh, my gosh," Inara exclaimed loudly and without warning, gaining everyone's attention. Hands outstretched and shaking in front of her, she stood abruptly and leaned away from the table as though ready to take flight. "How could I have forgotten?" She exclaimed while banging at her forehead with one hand.

"Inara? What's wrong?" Megorah's face registered concern as she exchanged looks with her father. She could sense an inordinate amount of anxiety coming from her but suspected it had nothing to do with Dart and Lylia at the moment.

Smacking at her head again in dismay, Inara let out a strangled laugh. "What day is today?"

"Wednesday," Drinian said. Skewering a bite of beef and noodles, he gazed up at her from his seat curiously.

"That's right! It was supposed to happen Wednesday morning." Inara's face was animated as she looked toward Veta. "No, wait! Wednesday morning." Suddenly looking worried and confused she started shaking her head. "No, no, no! It was supposed to happen this morning. Why didn't it?"

"What are you going on about?" Dartanian was perplexed by her behavior and becoming cross at having been interrupted.

"Wait a minute, everyone woke up late this morning. That never happened before." Inara said in confusion.

Baffled, everyone exchanged glances as Rafe eyed her thoughtfully.

"So?" Dante prompted, his eyes narrowing upon her.

"So, that meant Chase didn't go for his early morning run, which meant he didn't grab the newspaper from the drive on the way back. And Lylia!"

"What?" Lylia banged her hands on the table before her angrily and glared back at her.

"You never called."

"I was supposed to call you? Why on earth would I call you?" Lylia asked in disgust, looking at the woman as if she needed a strait jacket.

"No, not me. Dart." Becoming cross, Inara pointed in his direction. "You called your *husband* because you found them on your way out this morning. But you never went out, did you? You've been in all day." Scooting her chair back, she vigorously scratched at her head with her fingertips, causing her long messy waves to tangle further. Pacing the kitchen floor she began murmuring unintelligibly to herself. "But wouldn't they have found it when they drove out?"

"Is she okay?" Crisalya asked, her fork poised near her mouth. She watched the woman before her pace back and forth in a daze.

"Did she finally flip her lid?" Hialey piped.

"Wouldn't be surprised if she did." Breydon ventured, catching his father's eye before clearing his throat.

"Stop it, stop it," Inara said to herself in frustration as she continued to bang at her head. Getting up from his chair, Rafe came up behind her. Grabbing at her wrist, he effectively halted her from hitting herself further.

"There's no need to keep hitting yourself. You're liable to give yourself brain damage." Rafe was struggling to keep his face sober, but his eyes belayed the humor he was experiencing at her distress, knowing full well what she was likely going through.

"Oh, Rafe," Inara said seriously, almost desperately, as she gazed up into his handsome features which were so similar to his sons. Noting his eyes crinkling more than usual, she sensed he found her frustration funny somehow. "I think we both know I'm already there," she said with a conspiratorial whisper. "Does anybody have a newspaper?" she asked suddenly over Rafe's chuckle.

Reaching for his briefcase Breydon opened it and pulled out a paper as he spoke. "I have one with my briefcase. I just haven't had time to read it ... yet."

Snatching it from his hands before he finished speaking, she hastily unfolded the paper. "Yes! Yes, it's here! Right on the front page!" She banged at the paper loudly. "But where are they?" Dropping the paper on the floor, Inara tore from the kitchen with a determined look and disappeared into the living room, her eyes lighting with excitement as she ran. Her hair flew out behind her, nearly catching between the door and door jamb when it banged shut.

Reaching down Rafe picked up the newspaper and opened it to the front page. His eyebrows rose in surprise as he glanced over at Veta.

"Dear All I Have Left, by Thief with a Conscience," Rafe read aloud. Seeing Veta's shocked expression, he realized she was just as unaware as everyone else of the article, so he continued to read.

> *"It was by pure chance I saw your article.*
> *Had I not seen it I would have never known*
> *of your plight."*

Rafe paused, his gaze settling on his new daughter-in-law, Veta. When Drinian's new wife had first arrived in Whitefish, Montana her U-Haul had been stolen. Among the many belongings that had been taken were three memory boxes of her deceased children. Taking Lylia up on a piece of advice she'd given her, Veta had placed an article in the newspaper, asking the thief in question if they would be willing to return them to her without fear of reprisal.

Peering back down at the paper, Rafe proceeded to read the thief's response.

> *"When I saw the memory boxes in the U-Haul*
> *I thought, at the time the person they belonged*
> *to would miss them, though I had no idea*
> *how much. Thinking only of myself and my*
> *own family's needs, it never occurred to me the*
> *pain I might cause for taking them.*
>
> *Though a thief by circumstance, I am one who*
> *is merely trying to get by. Being a parent of four*
> *children of my own, I can't even imagine what it*
> *must have been like for you to lose yours so suddenly.*
> *I am truly sorry for any additional pain I may have*
> *caused you. I can only hope the return of your*
> *cherished treasures will help ease that pain."*

Hearing Veta gasp, Rafe paused in his reading. Glancing over at her once again, he watched as Veta turned toward Drinian. Her hand flew to her mouth as tears started welling in her eyes. The possibility that she might actually be getting them back, he could see, was overwhelming her. Rafe's voice softened as he continued reading the article.

> *"I was pleased to see you've experienced a recent*
> *joy when I saw the announcement of your marriage*
> *to Drinian Blackthorne in Monday's paper. May*
> *your recent union, and the return of your missing*
> *treasure be a sign of happier times to come."*

Setting the paper down on the table next to her, Rafe stepped back and eyed her carefully.

"Veta, it would seem you are getting your memory boxes back." Rafe smiled as the room fell quiet.

Staring down at the paper, Veta picked it up with a shaky hand and glanced through the article. Looking up at Rafe, then back at her husband in confusion, she stood on shaky legs.

"I don't understand." Veta stood with the paper dangling in her hand. She peered towards the living room where Inara had disappeared. "If they returned them then, as Inara said, where are they?"

"Maybe they left them at the newspaper. It's kind of been your go-between after all," Hialey said.

"You know, you could be right," Breydon said, turning towards his wife.

"Good thought, but she'd be wrong. Come, everyone! Come see!" Inara exclaimed with a bright smile. Her strawberry blonde head had popped in through the kitchen doors. Then suddenly releasing the door it swiveled back and forth as she ran through the living room toward the front of the house once again. Following after her, she could be seen seconds later opening the front door. Peering out at the mound next to the door, she pulled the blanket off and found four large packages that had been wrapped in white and silver wedding paper.

"Everyone walked past them not even realizing it because the person covered them with a blanket," Inara called as Veta and Drinian sped toward the front doors.

Stepping out onto the front porch Veta reached to grab one up. Taking her shoulder and pulling her out of the way, Chase shook his head.

"No, we'll get them for you," he said quickly while picking one up.

"With you being pregnant with triplets you have no business carrying anything heavy right now," Rafe said coming up behind her. Between Rafe, Drinian and Dartanian they carried the other three presents into the house and set them on the coffee table in front of the fireplace.

Veta began unwrapping them excitedly.

Megorah noticed the paper was slightly wrinkled, as though having been re-used. "They must have been dropped off sometime early this morning. If we hadn't been in such a hurry when heading out we might have noticed them when we all left."

"What I'm wondering, is what's in the fourth one?" Hialey's excitement was clear on her face.

Drinian was about to start on the second package when Veta opened the lid of the first box and gasped. Clutching at her shirt with her hand over her mouth tears spilled from her eyes as she wept openly.

They all watched as Veta, with trembling hands, pulled a pale pink box from the tissue paper within and hugged it to her chest. Smiling happily with tears dripping down her face, she set it on the table and tapped on its lid, which held a picture of a newborn baby swaddled in a white and pink blanket.

"That's your daughter, Sarah, isn't it?" Drinian's voice was overcome with emotion. He stared down at the picture, then back up at his wife. Seeing her nod her head, he began ripping excitedly at the paper on the other two packages that were the same size. Once opened he carefully lifted out from each package two more boxes, one green and one blue, both covered in animal patterns. Each had baby pictures in the lid.

"Veta! You got your memory boxes back," Lylia cried in delight. Leaning over the couch, she hugged her exuberantly. Staring down at the baby pictures on the tops of each box she smiled, her eyes misting over. "Oh, they were so beautiful!"

Trailing her hands across each lid lovingly Veta tilted her head and she smiled down at them. Glancing up at Meg and Crisalya happily another tear fell from her eye onto her hand.

"Yes. Yes, they were," she said softly.

Megorah's daughter, Katana, ducked her head into the living room from the kitchen as Veta spoke. She was trying to see what was going on without being too obvious. Seeing everyone exclaiming over the returned memory boxes Katana continued to watch from a distance, a smile playing on her face.

"Open the fourth one." Megorah urged, pointing at the box. She seemed to be just as curious as everyone else.

Puzzled by the fourth package as well, Veta leaned forward and took it from Dartanian. Before ripping at the paper, she noticed an envelope attached to it. Opening the envelope she read it aloud.

"Dear All I Have Left,
I came across this in the U-Haul as well.
It appeared to be handmade so I thought,
perchance, it might hold sentimental value
to you also.

Yours Truly,
Thief with a Conscience"

"Oh, my! Could it be?" Eyes widening in surprise as her heart leaped in her chest with hope, she tore at the wrapping paper.

"What is it Veta?" Megorah could sense her sister-in-law's anxious state.

Struggling to open the box that had been taped shut, she gave her husband a pleading look. Reaching over Drinian ripped at the box, opening the flaps for her with ease. Getting up from the couch, she reached down into the box and squealed in delight. Pulling out the quilt within, she allowed it to cascade out over the table. Holding it tightly in her arms relief flooded her. She wept openly.

"This was made by my adopted grandmother before she died. She was the only family I knew of, that I had left." The quilt, though mostly white, had a boxy royal blue edging with a few patches of color interspersed among the wedding ring pattern sewn into it with intricate stitches.

"It's beautiful Veta. It reminds me of the one my grandmother made me." Alaina glanced sadly toward her husband.

Dante could tell by the look his wife gave him that she was somewhat envious. She'd had to leave everything behind when he'd taken her from her home over a month ago.

"You should go through the boxes and make sure everything's in them," Royce suggested when he saw her hands inching towards them as though desperate to investigate their contents.

Most stayed and watched for a short time, as she began pulling items from the boxes and passing them around. After a while it became obvious that it was becoming a personal moment between her and Drinian, so the family respectfully began gradually wandering back into the kitchen.

Inara had stood in the background as well, watching it all unfold just as she'd written it from the moment the boxes had been found on the porch. Seeing her standing near the kitchen doorway as he was heading back in to finish dinner, Dartanian caught her eye.

"If it hadn't been for you, those boxes might well have not been found for a while. Most of us usually tend to leave for the garage through the kitchen patio." Dartanian explained. He walked cautiously towards her.

Shrugging it off as nothing, Inara spoke. "Lylia was supposed to find them and bring them up to the door." She leaned her head against the door jamb thoughtfully. "Then, Chase would have had one up on everyone, when he came in with the newspaper and realized the mound he'd passed on the way back in from running was the boxes."

Chuckling, Dart nudged her playfully under the chin. She stared with a dreamy smile up into his handsome face which was so much like his fathers. "That's how you imagined it, did you?" Speaking softly, he leaned in towards her. His voice became low and seductive as he spoke. "What else might you have imagined?" He asked quietly next to her ear. His eyes sparkled knowingly.

Shivering and feeling somewhat penned in where she stood, Inara glanced toward the living room and saw Lylia standing near the couch watching them closely. A tremor ran through her when she witnessed the determined set to Lylia's jaw.

"No, Lylia, don't," she said with a pained whisper.

"Breydon, grab your plate and briefcase," Lylia said abruptly, having made a decision. Shoulders back, she walked proudly into the kitchen, taking up her plate, cup and silverware.

"What? Why?" Breydon called back through the partition from the living room near the fireplace.

"Follow me to the formal dining room. We need to talk." The slight quiver in her voice belayed the indifferent facade she was attempting to create.

Not liking the look he saw in Lylia's eye, Breydon sighed heavily. He strode into the kitchen and took up his own plate and cup.

"Breydon... don't," Hialey urged next to him. Placing her hand on his arm, she looked at him in distress, suspecting she knew full well why Lylia wanted to speak with him alone. He was a lawyer after all. Though prosecuting attorney for the county, he could still handle divorce papers if need be.

Shaking his head at her, Breydon pulled away, looking towards his brother and Inara. "It's inevitable." His attention was soon distracted by the two squabbling in the kitchen doorway.

"Let go of me," Inara said forcefully, feeling Dartanian's hand on her arm again.

"We need to ... discuss things." He said firmly, gritting his teeth at the sight of his wife heading down the hallway and out of sight. "Stop putting me off, Inara. Everyone knows why you're here and time is getting away from us."

"They do, eh? Or do they just think they know?" Inara shook his hand off her arm as Breydon disappeared as well.

The scene had gained Rafe's attention. Scowling, his hands balled into fists at the sight of his married son hovering over the recently widowed, Inara.

"I might just have a solution that would make everyone happy." Dartanian didn't bother keeping his voice down.

"Everyone, Dart?" Inara asked as she trembled. The hurt she was experiencing at the unspoken suggestion he was making was obvious. "Or just you and Lylia?"

"Either way, we need to talk. Let's go."

"No."

"Why?" He snarled back at her in frustration.

"Because what you think you know may not be right and what you're considering suggesting is wrong. Either way, you're still a married man." Her voice was showing clear signs of distress.

Yanking out the paper again from his front pocket, Dartanian practically shoved it in her face as he growled. "It's all right here, Inara, in black and white. I know what the prophecy says. I'm painfully aware of what God has ordained to happen here."

"You have no clue…"

"Then enlighten me," Dartanian shouted, his face becoming florid while backing Inara into the kitchen against the fridge. "Because the way I see it, there's only one solution to this."

"Dartanian Adam Blackthorne, that's enough. Back away from her." Rafe bellowed across the kitchen, startling the children. The anger seething within threatened to overrun him at the sight of Inara being bullied by his son. He knew he'd taught him better than that. Clearly, the stress of the situation was getting to him.

Dartanian glared over at his father, not moving an inch from where he stood. "That's right. I'm an Adam and she's an Eve," he said as though staking some sort of ridiculous claim.

Sensing Rafe quickly moving towards them, Inara whispered tremulously next to Dartanian. "Yes, but I'm not the only Eve you know." Then more loudly she spoke, "Look at the numbers, Dart. Both new and old. Look really hard at the order and you'll see God's will more clearly." Inara urged as she felt the tickling sensation at her ear.

Pulling away from her, he stared at her momentarily, confused by what she was saying. Watching, as she rubbed at her ear in agitation, he experienced an overwhelming sensation flow through him. He could not decipher its meaning. Feeling drawn to her for some reason, at that moment, and as a result intent upon her, he was taken by surprise when his father stepped in front of her protectively. Catching the dangerous glint in his dad's eye, he threw his hands up in the air and stalked away angrily.

"Old numbers, new numbers. What is that supposed to mean? And what does it matter anyway?" He exclaimed as he went, disappearing around the corner. The need to feel release from the pent-up frustration within had become unbearable.

"It matters a great deal." Inara felt the tickling sensation at her ear once again. She shivered. Knowing full well she'd be hearing the voice soon, she sighed heavily, suspecting she also knew what was about to happen.

"Old and new numbers matter," Royce repeated thoughtfully. "Do they now?" He asked while pulling a paper from his pants pocket. Gazing upon it intently, he managed to gain the attention of several at the table. "Hhmm. Old versus new?" After staring at them a moment, he turned his attention to the poem and re-read it aloud. Then, thumping at the table he laughed. Turning towards, Rafe, he asked, "Seriously?"

Gaining no other response than a raised eyebrow from Rafe, as Inara's cheeks flooded with heat, Royce stood and took his dishes to the sink, grinning and shaking his head.

"Wait a minute, what?" Hialey implored, hating she was a few steps behind. She watched everyone hastily pulling their own respective papers out.

Blinking several times, Inara gazed around the room then at Rafe as the sound passed her ear.

They've learned enough for now. Sleep, my child.

The voice was firm and unyielding. Overcome with a sudden desire to lie down, Inara stared at her barely eaten dinner plate and milk glass longingly, then over at her children at the kid's table in distress. Seeing little Rafe smile and wave happily, she watched his legs swing back and forth under the table as though she were almost in a daze.

"We'll be okay, momma. Father's watching over us," little Rafe said then called out, "Catch her Royce!"

Inara didn't even get a chance to speak. Eyes closing, her body slumped next to Royce before Rafe could spin around in order to grab onto her. Grasping Inara about the waste, Royce caught her before she slid too far. The warning, though brief, had been just enough in order to allow him to catch her in time before she fell and hit her head on the floor.

"Thanks for the warning," Rafe grumbled under his breath. "Hand her over Royce."

"I can probably manage if you want me to carry her to the front living room." There was a devilish look in Royce's eye.

Giving him a stern look Rafe chastised him. "You're married; I'm not. It's more appropriate this way. Besides, I figure I better give her a change of scenery for tonight."

His expression one of mild indifference, Rafe lifted Inara up into his arms. It was starting to become a habit. Her long reddish blonde tresses tangled over his forearm once again as he proceeded to carry her from the kitchen and down the hall.

"Where is dad going with her?" Crisalya wondered aloud. Her head swiveled from the hallway where he'd disappeared. Then her gaze moved back into the front living room.

"She did say a little bit ago she really loves the library. He's probably taking her there," Veta said.

"Nah. I'm betting the movie room." Royce began clearing the counters from dinner. Several children skittered off to the playroom with Inara's brood. Royce found it curious that Inara's children seemed completely nonplussed by their mother's unconscious state and couldn't help but wonder if the children knew something they didn't.

"How do you figure he's taking her there?" Hialey asked.

"It has both a couch and a fireplace," Royce said with a shrug, watching Lily wave at him and smile gratefully. He got the feeling she enjoyed the dinner he'd prepared, which pleased him.

"I still don't get it. What is it you're seeing Royce?" Chase wiped his mouth with his napkin and stared down at his paper.

"There is an order after all." Royce bobbed his head toward Drinian and Dante as he continued to clean. "Figure that out and the rest will come to you, you'll see." he chuckled knowingly.

Exchanging wide-eyed glances, Megorah and Drinian grabbed up their own papers once again and began perusing them.

"Okay, there's the date; four, nineteen with a three." Megorah read aloud.

"Then the date; five, eighteen with a two." Chase followed after.

"And then presumably the date six, sixteen, one with a question mark and the letter I," Veta said, reading off the rest, having just returned to the table. She appeared stumped.

2000_4-19//15//2015_(30)^(4-19=3)(5-18=2)(6-16=1?I)

"Right, I get the dates now. April 19th is about Dante and Alaina, May 18th is about Drinian and Veta, and June 16th is about Dartanian," Hialey said offhandedly, not commenting on who should be listed with him. Pausing for a gulp of milk, she then went on. "But what's the three got to do with you," she asked, gesturing towards Dante, "the two got to do with you," she continued in irritation, pointing at Drinian, "and the one with the question mark and letter I got to do with him?" she finished while pointing down the hallway where Dartanian and Rafe had gone.

Most of the Blackthorne children and their spouses stared in varying states of confusion in the direction Hialey had been waiving her arm. Suddenly, Megorah's head shot up and peered towards Drinian, catching his eye. They both turned towards Dante who stood suddenly, taking up his dirty dishes in hand.

"Yup. I figured it out earlier today," Dante gave them both a knowing look.

"How did we not see this before?" Megorah gasped, staring at her paper.

"See what?" Hialey asked in frustration.

"But the house. Dad was leaving it to you, Dante." Crisalya said, catching his eye, having just figured it out as well. She knew how badly he wanted the house too. But she also now understood that her father had intended it for someone else.

"I know. Alaina, honey, when you're done we should talk. I'll be upstairs." Turning away sadly, he headed up the staircase as his wife watched him go with a troubled expression.

"Why? Would someone please just tell me what's going on? Cause I'm apparently too stupid to figure this out," Hialey exclaimed.

"Dante's not the eldest like we all originally thought. He's the third born and Drinian came second." Chase held up three fingers, then two. "Dartanian, it would seem, was born first," he said while removing a finger, leaving only one left in the air.

Chapter 14

Chase watched his wife and Crisalya frown and exchange disturbed looks.

"Whoa," Hialey said quietly. "I know Breydon said Rafe wanted the house to go to the eldest. So, Dante moves out and Dart moves back in?" Toying with the remnants of food on her plate, she became thoughtful. "Well, at least he'll have someplace to go. Alaina, you and Dante could move into Dart's place on The Bluff, unless of course, you want to buy a place of your own."

"If it's a third the size of this place, then I'm fine with that," Alaina said quietly in response.

"Not necessarily, Hialey." Drinian stood and took up both his and Veta's plates. Carrying them around the island to the counter, he placed them into the sink. Resting his hands on the counter, he stared back out at his sister-in-law. "After all, Lylia and Kayla will need a place."

Wrinkling her nose in disgust, Hialey fumed. "Right. Dante moves out and Dart moves in but with Inara instead. Not Lylia." She scratched the back of her head in agitation.

Getting up from her seat, she walked around the counter and plopped her dishes in the sink next to Drinian who also scratched at his head. Looking up at his towering frame she frowned.

"I don't know, Drin. Somehow that just doesn't seem right. Do you really believe Dart made the wrong choice? I mean, think about it," Hialey continued, appearing extremely bothered by the whole situation. "When exactly would he have had a chance to meet Inara anyway? Besides, he and Lylia really do fit so well together; even when they argue!"

"Who says he wasn't supposed to meet Inara now?" Drinian countered. "Dad disappeared Monday with Dante after his meeting was cancelled. Then suddenly they show up with her and her children in tow. I have to think God had him bring her home for a reason. And why else would she look like Lylia, if he wasn't meant to have chosen her instead."

"Hhhmm. Guess you have a point." Hialey frowned. Sighing heavily, she turned toward the hallway. Feeling at a loss for what to do next, since Breydon was meeting with Lylia, she decided to head toward the playroom and spend some time with her boys. They'd been especially difficult as of late. She hoped giving them more time with her might help.

- - -

The hour was late and Dartanian was restless. Feigning off partaking in evening devotions with his siblings and in-laws, he'd left the house. He wandered for a while along one of the many trails which led up towards the woods. After a while, the sun had set and his mind was racing with notions and ideas. Feeling anxious, jittery even, he turned about abruptly in the trail and headed quickly back the way he'd come.

Deciding it was high time to get some answers, Dartanian went in search of Inara the moment he reached the house. Entering through the playroom, he cut a swift path down the hall past the dining room, the library, and the laundry room, and stepped around the landing near the base of the stairs. Figuring he'd see her sleeping on the couch near the fireplace, he was irritated to find his father instead. Rafe was sitting in a chair nearby where Inara usually lay. He was gazing intently at his iPad. The fire glowed brightly in the hearth next to him as if it had been burning for a while.

"Where is she?" He asked brusquely as he entered the living room, scowling over at his father.

Not bothering to raise his head in greeting, Rafe kept his eyes downcast on the iPad screen he was reading from. "If you're looking for your wife, then she is upstairs in your bedroom."

"I know where Lylia is." His lips thinned as he snapped. "What I don't know is where Inara is."

Setting his iPad in his lap while peering up at his son, Rafe expelled a heavy breath. "Now, why are you looking for her?"

"I think we both know full well why, and why do you and Inara have to be so cryptic all the time anyway? Why can't you just spit it out and tell us all what's going on and what is supposed to happen here." He sounded testy.

"First of all, neither one of us ever said we knew everything. Only God can know everything; and second, because sometimes you have to learn some things for yourself." Rafe threw his own fathers words at his son. Inara had been kind enough to throw them at him when she'd arrived. "Besides when you're looking for answers

God's about as good a place as any to start with. Don't you think?"

"What is that supposed to mean?"

"Read." Rafe managed to elicit a disgusted snort from his son. "Try Genesis, chapter three," he continued as Dartanian turned toward the kitchen and flung out his arms wildly, completely agitated.

"And how exactly do you expect me to do that?"

"By applying the most well-known concept taught to man through the ages." He gazed over at his son in annoyance. Seeing Dartanian shrugging toward him, as though awaiting him to continue giving him the answers, he was clearly incapable of gaining for himself, Rafe frowned. Placing his hands in front of him he put them together then spread them open. "Try opening 'The Book.'" His sarcasm was evident as he gave him the visual.

Too tightly wound to prevent it, Dartanian exploded at his father. "How do you expect me to read my Bible when Lylia's locked me out of our room?" His father came up out of his chair, with surprising speed for a sixty-year-old. Dartanian lowered his voice immediately, realizing his mistake. "My Bible is in my bedroom," he exclaimed in a quieter tone, sounding uncharacteristically petulant even to himself.

Eyes glowing with a fire of their own now, Rafe pointed towards the entryway angrily. "There are two libraries with over two dozen Bibles in varying forms between the two of them." Seeing the glazed, almost dazed look in his son's eyes, which had turned a gleaming sapphire blue, he noted the perspiration upon his brow, as well as the tension in his arms and shoulders. His son was so tightly wound, he was ready to snap.

Shaking his head in amazement, Rafe marveled at how his sons could become so dense, while they were in a state such as Dartanian was currently in now. He hoped for everyone's sake, that one way or another, the necessary choices would be made soon.

Scratching his head, Dartanian peered around him as though looking for something. "Right, of course." Swearing suddenly, he clenched his fists, punching at the air around him. He growled and began pacing the room in a frenzy. "Urgh! If I could just … if only Lylia would just... But Inara…" He chuckled darkly while shaking his index finger towards his father. His eyes seemed to shimmer even more at the mere mention of her. "Now when I find her, I'm gonna…"

"You leave Inara alone. She is not your wife," Rafe said forcefully, not liking the look in his son's eye.

"I know that, Dad. But the prophecy… If she and I could make an arrangement of sorts, then everyone could have…"

"Don't you finish that," Rafe roared. His eyes bore into his sons fiercely. "The mere suggestion is not only inappropriate under the circumstances but sinful."

Crumbling into a nearby chair, Dartanian slouched in the cushions of his seat then flung his head back in distress. Running his hands through his hair and gazed sheepishly over at his father. His expression showed the clear desperation he was experiencing.

"It's this dang Blackthorne blood in me. I can't help it, Dad. I need…" He said emphatically, shaking his hands before him.

Scoffing loudly, Rafe peered down upon his son in disgust. "It's got nothing to do with the Blackthorne bloodline and everything to do with being human."

Dartanian looked upon his father with a doubtful expression. "Even you have to admit there's a history in our family of having an insatiable desire for intimacy. I remember the stories you used to tell us, about how Grandpa Rathbourne used to chase Grandma Saphire through the house. And even Uncle Rourke…"

Shushing him, Rafe's visage darkened noticeably. "That poor excuse for a brother isn't worth mentioning. Besides his problem wasn't with intimacy, it was the fact that he was a reprobate and a cur." His voice rose as he spoke. "And, of course, there's history. Every family has its own internal battle with one, if not several of the seven deadly sins. They've been passed down since the beginning of Adam and Eve and aren't likely to disappear anytime soon."

Agitated, Rafe began to pace in front of his son. "That's all I've heard from you kids since you all hit puberty; one excuse after another…

…It's not my fault.

…I couldn't help myself.

…It's in my blood after all.

Oh, but Breydon's, his was always my personal favorite…

…It feels so good, dad. I just can't get enough of it."

Exclaiming with righteous indignation, Rafe waved his hands in the air. "Of course it does! I'd posit to say it's just one of many reasons why God created the sanctity of marriage in the first place because once you've had it, you want more."

Laughing sardonically Dartanian's head bobbed up and down in misery. "You can say that again."

"God knew that better than any of us. He gave us an outlet for the lust within the arms of our spouses."

"Easy for you to say. You're not the one currently being denied. These dang prophecies have everything all screwed up." Dartanian rolled his eyes in annoyance.

"These prophecies have nothing to do with what's wrong between the two of you," Rafe said emphatically. "If you can't get through to Lylia, then, in the end, you must make a choice."

"Make a choice?" His heart thudded to a halt at what that might mean. Then out of the blue, he exclaimed loudly, not bothering to mask his aggravation. "Sure they do! The prophecies are at the very core of our problem! I got one telling me the only chance I've got for children is on June sixteenth, and another telling me I've chosen the wrong woman. Because of both, Lylia now won't have anything to do with me and the temptation. This need … it's driving me mad, and it's getting worse."

Rafe raised his head to the heavens and his eyes rolled back in his head. "Daft, Lord! My children, they are all daft!" He decided it was high time his forty-year-old son re-learn the same lesson he'd been taught so very long ago. "I'd think, you being the Sheriff of this county, born with the gift of discerning good and evil, seeing what you do in your patrol car all day long, that you would have a better understanding and grasp of temptation and addiction. They go hand and hand with sin."

Catching his son rolling his own eyes as he groaned miserably in his chair, Rafe halted in front of him and pointed at his arm. "What? Do you think having certain blood determines our addictions? No! It's got nothing to do with that and everything to do with mankind's inability to overcome their own selfish desires. It says so in the Bible if you'd just read it more. As for Lylia cutting you off, why don't you ask yourself, why she really did so in the first place."

Looking at his father in bewilderment initially, it took Dartanian a moment to realize what he was saying. His weary eyes blinked rapidly and darted about frantically.

They didn't find out about the poem in the book until after Inara had arrived. But Lylia had cut him off prior to that, knowing full well from the journal she'd taken of Drinian's, what that might mean for them.

"I don't understand, Lylia's always wanted children before," Dartanian said in confusion as twin creases furrowed his brow.

"Yes, and so have you."

"Before the poem was found there wasn't any question as to whether it was her or not. So, why…?"

"Why wasn't she jumping for joy?" Rafe finished for him. "This is your chance for the two of you to have children together." He softened his voice from its harsh tenure from moments before.

Dartanian sat, staring into the fire, his eyes reflecting the light from the flames. Deep in thought, he narrowed his gaze at the pieces of wood within it, watching them burn brightly as the flames licked repeatedly at the wood. Then suddenly shaking his head in distress he allowed it to drop, bouncing in place as he moaned.

"It doesn't matter why anymore," he said glumly. He began repeating words from the poem. "Two of mirror image there'll be, crossing paths in time. Through waxen hair no gift doth breed. For truly lacking the strength of seed. A choice to make, one right, one wrong," he repeated irritably. "Dad, the poem says…"

"Oh, forget the poem your mom wrote. That's just like you youngsters today, all presuming everything's always got to be about you! Dartanian Blackthorne, do you love your wife?" Rafe exclaimed in frustration.

"Yes," he responded promptly, feeling like he'd just missed something in what his dad had said.

"When you asked her to marry you, did you want to marry her?"

"Of course I did. I wouldn't have waited for her for three years hoping Dante would return home if I didn't."

"And are you currently married to her?" Rafe questioned further, already knowing the answer of course.

"Yes, but dad!" Dartanian halted his father with a raised hand, trying to get his attention. "According to this prophecy, my only chances of having children is by way of Inara. Am I right, or am I right?"

"The prophecy says that, does it?" Rafe mused, staring at his son thoughtfully. "And which one exactly would you be referring too?" Amid his sarcasm, he almost sounded amused. "Dart, what does your gut tell you? What do you see when you look at Inara?"

Flummoxed by his father's repetitive question, Dartanian's shoulders drooped further as he sighed. "What do I see? She's not here, how can I tell you what I see?" he gestured wildly in front of him. "I don't know what I see," he continued to exclaim in exasperation, gaining a quick irritated glance from his father. "Lately, I can be in a room in this house, or on the grounds of this property even and all I'll see is darkness around everyone. Makes no sense. There are good Christian people working for us and living in this house. But, when she's present when she enters the room, I see the light again, regardless of where I am. There, are you satisfied?" Dartanian glowered. "I don't know what that means but what I can tell you, what I sense in my gut and know without a shadow of a doubt, is that my only chance at children is by way of Inara."

Smiling grimly, Rafe said simply, "Then so shall it be. Go, find a Bible."

"What? Wait a minute, why?"

"Read. Genesis chapter three." Picking up his Ipad, Rafe strolled slowly toward the kitchen.

"What in the world does Genesis have to do with any of this?"

"It is the beginning of everything, after all, son. You will see. And pay close attention to verse twenty." Rafe called, all the while waving his free hand in the air above him. He walked away with his Ipad and disappeared into the kitchen.

"Oh, for the love of might!" Dartanian growled, punching at the air once again. Standing, he stalked through the house to the lower library. Finding it empty, he searched the shelves till he found a Good News Bible. It wasn't his preferred version but it would do till he could get a hold of his King James Bible in the morning.

Taking a seat, he pulled on the chord of the lamp on the end table next to him. Blinking in the harsh light he opened the Bible to the front. Delving through the first nineteen verses, he didn't see anything different about the creation of man and woman than what he already knew. Reaching verse twenty, he read it aloud:

"Adam named his wife Eve because she was the mother of all human beings. Genesis 3:20."

Thoroughly mystified, Dartanian scowled. His father had to have gotten the verse wrong.

Then suddenly, as if being placed there by the hand of God, a faint memory shimmered to the forefront of his mind. Anxious, Dartanian leapt to his feet, realizing instantly he had to go home to The Bluff immediately. Dropping the Bible, he sped out of the room, down the hall of the house and out through the front entrance, not caring that he was wearing his pajama bottoms with a sleeveless tank. Leaping barefoot down the steps of the porch, he took the distance between the porch to the garage at a dead run. Punching his code into the keypad he waited impatiently as the garage door opened so he could get inside. Attempting to duck through the opening before the door had raised completely he nearly banged his head on it.

Grabbing a pair of keys from the pegboard on the wall near his sport utility vehicle, he got in it and backed out of the garage. He tore down the Blackthorne ranch drive, his mind on overdrive.

God, is it possible? Dartanian prayed anxiously, his heart racing in his chest. He drove recklessly down the county roads towards his house near The Bluff. Reaching it in record time, his tires squealed to a halt in front of the double garage doors closest the entrance of his home. Leaving his car door wide open and lights still on, he let himself into his home and ran straight for his study. Pulling his Living Life portrait away from the wall in his office, he opened the safe hidden there.

Reaching inside, he dug through the varying papers and documents within, trying desperately to find what he was looking for. Locating the envelope, yellowed by age, that he'd managed to procure from the nurse who'd been present at Lylia's birth, he dumped its contents on his desk. Turning the birth certificate over so he could see the name for himself, he let out an excited cry of relief as he laughed.

Chapter 15

His father had known this whole time, Dartanian realized.

Rafe had known because he was the one who had assisted him in correcting Lylia's original birth certificate for him. Recalling Inara's words from earlier in the day when she'd whispered them to him in the kitchen, he chuckled and shook his head.

"Eve V. Doe." Dartanian read aloud. Smiling, he was overcome with emotion.

Lylia's origins had been in question from the moment he'd met her. She'd learned in her late teens after an accident she was in, that she couldn't be her parents' child because her blood work didn't match. So, when they began dating, Lylia had asked him if he'd be able to find out for her anything more about her biological parents. Unable to come up with anything for years, it wasn't until around the time of Breydon and Hialey's wedding that he'd found the nurse who'd been present at her birth.

That's when they learned she'd been switched at birth intentionally and given to Lylia's parents, the Minnosa's, in place of the baby they had lost the same day. The doctor had given her the name, Baby Doe since Lylia's actual birth mother had died after giving birth and had been unable to choose a name, or for that matter, give her own.

Dartanian's wife had been crushed to learn that she didn't even have a real name given by her biological mother. Wanting to be able to do something for her, Dartanian had enlisted his father's assistance in correcting her birth certificate.

Sitting down in his desk chair, he leaned back, resting his head against the cushion of the tall leather-backed chair. He could still recall in great detail, the conversation they'd had over her name choice.

"Everything's taken care of," his father had said when they had entered his study and sat in the chairs across from him that day. "All we need now is a name."

"Really? You can actually fix it so I have a real name?" Lylia was delighted. Her midnight blue eyes had sparkled with unshed tears at the news.

Rafe had smiled easily, catching his sons' eye with a mysterious glimmer. "More than that. Once this process is completed this birth certificate will be linked to the rest of your life. All I need now is a name to list on it. I can put Lylia Doe if you wish."

"It's the only name I've ever known so that's fine with me. I wouldn't even know what name I'd want it to be anyways. But could you add a V for the middle initial?"

"Certainly," Rafe said amiably.

"No," Dartanian interjected, gaining his wife's startled attention. "Put the V as the middle name if you want, honey. It is on the lace handkerchief the nurse gave us, after all, so it makes sense to include it. What I mean is, it's not right; you having to name yourself. A child should be given a name by someone who loves them. I'm not a parent, obviously, but I do love you with all my heart. Will you allow me to give you a name?"

He recalled at that moment he'd had an urgent, unmistakable desire to name her himself for some reason.

"What? *You* want to name me? I suppose you see me as an Eden or an Eve maybe?" she'd joked, surprising him.

"Why not? My middle name is Adam after all, and the Adam of the Bible did name his wife."

Laughing softly Lylia had smiled shyly, in embarrassment. "Does that make me your Eve then? Is that it? You wish to name me Eve?"

"Yes." Dartanian had said firmly, startling both his father and Lylia.

"All right, then Eve it shall be, but I have to ask, out of all of the names in the world, why that one?" she'd asked curiously.

"Because, just as the original Eve was the mother of mankind, you shall be the mother of my many children," he'd replied with mirth in his eyes, causing her to blush and laugh.

"We'll just have to see about that," she'd said while gazing wistfully out the balcony doors of the study. A soft, secretive smile had played at her lips then, and he'd wondered about it at the time. Later on, he found out she'd thought she might be pregnant again, but it had been a false alarm.

Choking back a relieved sob as he held the birth certificate in his hand against his chest, a tear threatened at the corner of his eyes.

"Thank you, God, for this." Dartanian prayed aloud in the quiet solitude of his office study. "I know now, you've always meant her for me, for you gave me the name to give to her, didn't you? But what does this mean Lord? The prophetic poem mom wrote. How does it apply here? I still don't understand. If you've always meant Lylia for me, then why is Inara here? What choice needs to be made? If you're trying to ascertain my heart's desire, you know it will always be Lylia. Next to you, God, she is my heart, my life."

Pulling the folded paper from his pajama bottom pocket, he unfolded and stared down upon the page, re-reading the poem he'd copied from the journal. Mumbling to himself about old and new numbers, his gaze shifted between the prophetic numbers and the poem, he tried to see what it was that Royce had apparently figured out.

His brother-in-law was the owner of a coffee house.

Dartanian was a Sheriff.

If Royce could figure out what it all meant, then he sure should be able to.

The poem he was certain was about both Inara and Lylia, or Inara wouldn't be responding the way she was with him. Grunting in agitation, he tapped on the desk while mulling over in his head what he knew.

Two prophecies.

Which came first?

The numeric one or the poem?

He presumed the numeric one had from the way the poem was written. The question was whether they were actually related or not.

Thoughts started randomly popping in his head. He pondered this notion. The numeric prophecy being fulfilled would somehow relieve his brothers of their torment, but what if there was something else going on here. What if there really was more to the story?

It occurred to Dartanian, at that moment, that an all-knowing entity such as God would likely not allow the direction of His will, His grand plan, to be halted or harmed by the actions or poor choices of man. Knowing mankind as God did, it would be entirely plausible He'd create a contingency. But in this case, what would it be?

"A seed shall lie within her womb, three times blessed we can presume..." Dartanian read aloud. Then suddenly he shot up from his chair, the kernel of a thought festering in his mind growing to a full-blown notion. "Whoa, seriously, Lord? Does this mean what I think it does?" He cringed, suddenly extremely embarrassed by his behavior toward Inara earlier in the day. Raising his head to the heavens, he spoke while shaking the paper in his hand.

Floating nearby, the heads of the angels, Woreash and Maleeka, drooped in annoyance and frustration. Even in the absence of the demon's presence, they'd managed to fail in their attempts to get through to the man before them.

"Oh, good grief," Woreash vented.

Maleeka turned towards his counterpart. His eyes lit with fury. "Really?" He exclaimed, then turned back to watch Dartanian drop the creased paper on his desk. "How could we not be any clearer?" The angel fumed when the man before them spoke again.

"Inara's already pregnant, isn't she? You sent her here to us for protection. Didn't you, Lord?"

The angels groaned.

"Rafe's right," Maleeka said.

"So it would seem," Woreash replied grimly.

"They're daft; all of them."

"Yes, every last one." Woreash agreed

"You do realize that all of Rafe's children and their spouses have come to an incorrect conclusion," Maleeka stated, sounding almost irate as his blue eyes flashed.

"Royce figured it out," the older angel corrected.

"Yes, but Royce isn't a Blackthorne. He's a Howard now isn't he?" Maleeka pointed out in a huff.

Sighing heavily, Woreash responded, "Fair point. But his father Misham Howard is a very perceptive man."

"And Rafe Blackthorne isn't?"

"Not all things are inherited," Woreash argued.

"Clearly."

"A writer's word shows another way. That's why she's insisting that dad read her stories." Dartanian went on, unaware of the banter between the divine entities nearby. His excitement mounted. "There's something within them that's crucial to the prophecy being fulfilled and to Lylia and I having children."

Sighing in exasperation, both angels fumed. "Well, he got part of it right anyway."

"You know God is probably up there laughing at us right now."

"No doubt," Woreash said quickly. "Humans. Their minds simply cannot grasp the magnanimous plan God has laid out for them." Huffing indignantly both angels disappeared in a flash of light. It was time they became more aggressive. If they didn't they would fail in their task and it was crucial they didn't fail.

Chapter 16

Turning restlessly in her sleep Inara shivered and moaned.

Her heart pounded in her chest.

She slept fitfully, writhing on the couch in fear.

Hands clenching the sheets, her legs pulled taught then spread wide, as though being yanked apart. Her body arched and she cried out in distress, terrified. Somewhere between the state of sleeping and waking, her eyelids flickered rapidly.

Body shaking, her eyes widened within her dream, and she saw him standing before her. Tall and dark, his features were cast in shadows.

The dream wasn't the same one she usually had. It was starting different for it was as though he was not alone this time. As a mirror reflects one's image, so did they seem to reflect each other. Coming from opposite corners of the room they stood before her in all their glory. They both looked the same, brown hair, brown eyes, yellowing teeth. But the one on the right had a darkness about him; a violence about him that she feared. It snarled at her as she stared back at him in startled surprise.

The two men turned toward each other. Their hands raised; fingers straight and prone, as they met each other halfway, spanning the distance between them. Hands flat, they hovered within an inch of each other. They stared back at each other with placid expressions on their faces, though the man to the right began to grin almost evilly. Their voices echoed each other when they spoke.

"Which one will it be?" she heard them say. Then they turned to look at her. The small room was dark and somehow familiar. The light from the lantern on the table cast shadows upon their faces. She lay, tied down to the cot in the corner of the tiny room.

Her heart constricted in her chest. She could hear it pounding in her ears. Pain wrenched at both her heart and her left cheek where he had struck her. It wasn't supposed to happen this way. This wasn't how she'd written it, what changed and why?

Staring down at herself anxiously, she saw the man had stripped her of her jeans. All she had left was her ripped t-shirt and underwear. Looking back up at the men before her she found herself crying out for help but they simply looked at her, unmoving.

"Please, somebody help me! God help me please!"

Simultaneously they moved towards her, as though they were stalking her like prey. Kneeling on the bed on either side of her, they crawled forward, each reaching out to her as they sidled up over her. Facing them, she couldn't understand why no one had come to help her. Why the door hadn't flung open. Her hero should have come rushing in to save her by now.

"What do you want from me?" A wave of anxiety and fear overwhelmed her as she sobbed.

Speaking in unison they responded. "Only three."

"Three what?"

Grinning darkly, the two men began merging together, their body's slipping and sliding within each other, becoming one man. The new figure before her was the same, yet clearly not for his eyes, once brown, had now turned black and ominous. They shimmered brightly and the whites of his eyes had disappeared.

Understanding dawned on her. She shrieked at the man's sudden advance on her. Pouncing upon her it snarled before her, its eyes now glowing red. The otherworldly being - not man but more creature - clasped its gnarled hands about her throat.

Angry, Inara cried out once again, only this time she was smart and used His name. "Jesus! Jesus!" She croaked, struggling to speak, struggling to breathe through the fear.

The figure growled before her, its scaly hands dislodging from her neck upon her cries. It advanced upon her once again, attempting to attack her but she deflected its blows with her arms and began to sing in her terror.

"Jesus loves me this I know,

for the Bible tells me so.

Little ones to Him belong.

They are weak but He is strong.

Yes, Jesus loves me! Yes, Jesus loves me…"

Inara continued to sing the age-old song, her voice becoming stronger and clearer, seemingly instilling terror within the being before her. Leaping away from her, the figure cried out in agony. It clasped its gnarled hands over its ears and its eyes glowed angrily with malice, with hate.

The fear that had been so ever present but moments before had now abated. In its place was a warmth, a bright light sensation hovering within her chest. It ignited into a white-hot light which exploded within the confines of the small room she was in, filling it from one corner to the next.

Soft squalling cries like a baby exploded within her ears, waking her abruptly with a start. Blinking rapidly, Inara turned upon the couch. Rolling to her side, she grabbed at her chest. Heart still pounding with a rough rhythm, she was grateful for the waking as the dream had become quite disturbing before its end, compared to the many times before.

Usually, when she dreamed of him it was scary, but never quite so frightening and she suspected she knew why. Shaking her head, in an attempt to clear it, she sat up quickly pulling her blankets with her for cover, though the gesture was unnecessary as she was fully clothed.

Having awakened from her dream drenched in sweat, her shirt was now stuck to her back and it clung to her sides. Inara's jeans were damp and her messy, tangled hair was plastered to her head. Peeling the shirt from her back and sides, her gaze darted about the movie room anxiously from where she lay on the couch.

Rolling her eyes with unease, Inara moaned as she crept from the couch, turning to look at the cushions and blankets in frustration. Realizing it would all have to be washed, she began ripping the blankets off and dumped them on the floor next to the couch. Satisfied for the moment, Inara determined a shower was due under the circumstances. She walked with unsteady legs towards the closest pool room doors.

Still shaken by the dream, but grateful to God for the protection and waking her, she rested a hand against the pool door. Unable to get it to budge initially, she realized it needed the hex lock key dangling on a nearby chain on the wall near the door. Of course, Inara thought, they keep it locked at night because of the children.

Managing to unlock the door, she made a mental note to relock it when she finished cleaning up. Stepping onto the tiled floor of the pool room, her bare feet slapped noisily against the floor, sounding hollow in the vast expanse of the pool room. The moisture from the pool water made the air seem thicker. Inhaling deeply of the moisture-laden air it felt heavy in her chest, making it seem slightly harder to breathe. She headed toward the bathroom she'd been using much of the week. Inara was still thinking about the nightmare and desperate to feel the shower water upon her head for it itched. Eyes closing upon a yawn, she rubbed at her arms as a chilling sensation washed over her, causing her to shiver violently.

With her eyes closed as she stretched her neck and scratched at her head Inara was unaware of a shadow hovering above the pool nearby. It lapped at the water, swishing it back and forth gleefully as if waiting for just the right moment. Demons can't kill but they can sure torment, torture and at times, even cause a person pain and harm. Reaching down the demon suddenly splashed at the water forcefully. Inara missed seeing the water slosh out from the pool over the tiling before her. In her groggy state, her uneven walking pattern caused her to venture too close to the side of the pool. Foot slipping on the wet tile, Inara was surprised to find herself ricocheting backwards. In the instant she slipped she'd had the thought her head was about to hit the tiled floor. Instead, she felt herself flying further through the air than what she should as though she were being carried upon the air.

Splashing into the water instead, Inara was startled to be engulfed by the icy water. Though at room temperature, it felt about twenty degrees less, having just come from a sweaty warm couch and blankets. The shock of falling into the pool caused her mouth to open as she cried out in surprise. Gagging, she accidentally inhaled some of the water. Her eyes, nose and lungs burned from the chlorine as she struggled to upright herself in the pool. Confused and disoriented, she began to panic.

The water swirled around her as though she'd been caught within a whirlpool. Frantically, she kicked out with her arms and legs haphazardly. Squealing in desperation Inara flailed in the water having lost all sense of which direction was up or down. The muffled crashing sound of something else nearby vaguely caught her ears. Seconds later an arm snaked around her waist, yanking her towards the surface and much-needed oxygen. Gasping, her head finally surged above the water. Inara coughed and spluttered, having inhaled a little more of the chlorinated liquid than what she'd thought. Blinking to try and clear her cloudy vision, she twisted in the water as someone deftly pulled her from within the pool. Doors could be heard flinging open from both sides of the pool room as she felt herself being lifted into someone's strong arms.

Heaving her from the pool, he laid her wet and dripping on the tile floor, as he gained his own ragged breath back. The icy chill he'd felt when he'd attempted to pull Inara from the pool, reaffirmed his suspicions that something had aided her in her foray into the pool. Turning back towards her as he lay next to her on the pool floor, their gazes locked.

Startled to see who it was who had pulled her from the pool, she flinched and scooted away. Several pairs of slipper clad and bare feet padded towards her from the pool room doors.

"Inara, are you all right?" Veta exclaimed, kneeling down next to her in her nightgown and robe. Her black hair was tousled from sleep but she looked sensational as usual, even with her worried expression and no makeup.

Peering up at Veta with envy at how she could look so good after having just awakened, Inara struggled to speak. Her throat still burned but she managed to croak out that she was okay. Noting Veta's wide-eyed gaze, she watched Crisalya come around and kneel down before her. Inara glanced down at herself horrified to see that her shirt had ripped and was gaping open, exposing her scarred belly. Trying to cover herself with the ripped shirt, she shoved the pieces together and attempted to come up off the floor.

"Stay put Inara," Rafe ordered from the doorway of the pool room. His son gained his footing and pulled himself up to his full height. He could see that Dartanian's eyes held concern for her as he dripped on the floor next to her.

"Dad's right, stay down. Let Chase check you out." Glancing towards his dad, Dartanian explained in a serious tone. "I think she inhaled water."

Rafe nodded in understanding when he heard Inara cough violently. Worry reflected in his own eyes, Rafe watched while Crisalya turned Inara so she faced the floor. Spitting up water, Inara gasped at the painful burning sensation rocketing through her chest, lungs and throat.

"Whoa, that was close. What happened!" Hialey exclaimed.

Inara hurled onto the tile floor again as Hialey spoke. Water spewed from her mouth at Chase's urging as he rubbed at her back. Having knelt down next to her, the good doctor was already performing a thorough inspection of her condition.

Arms wrapped tightly about her waist in order to maintain cover with her torn shirt, Inara felt herself being laid down finally on the floor. Her tired gaze flitted from Dartanian standing above her, over to Rafe, still poised within the doorway. Face screwing up in distress she could only imagine how absolutely dreadful she looked with her wet and tangled hair strewn about her.

"Thank you," Inara said gratefully, her lips trembling as she spoke. She returned her gaze back to Dartanian.

The chatter around the room was that everyone had awakened to Inara's screams through the house as she'd dreamed. Having come to investigate the source of her cries most of the Blackthorne, Howard and Ryans' family had found their way to the pool room and were now watching the scene play out before them.

Shaking his head as he grimaced then grinned, Dartanian replied as his family looked on. "Think nothing of it. I wouldn't want anything to happen to those three babies of yours after all." He pointed toward her belly.

Tensing where she lay, Inara gaped up at the man, still somewhat dazed by her ordeal. "Dart, did you say…?"

"No need to be embarrassed, Inara. You needn't keep this secret any longer. I know you're pregnant."

Eyes flashing, with almost a wolfish expression Dartanian turned and walked away, avoiding his family's stunned gaze as he went.

Chapter 17

Unable to sleep well after nearly drowning in the pool, Inara had spent much of the night curled up on the twin couch in the library reading. Dozing off briefly around sunrise she woke an hour later at her sons prodding hand.

"Mama, are you okay?" Little Rafe asked anxiously. His eyes were puffy and red. Clearly, he'd been crying.

Pulling him towards her into a fierce embrace, she'd hugged him as she'd responded. "Yes, baby boy. I'm so sorry Rafe. You were sleeping. It never occurred to me you might have seen. Do you want to talk about it?"

Shaking his head, he pulled at her arm and gestured with his head toward the doorway where Lily and Tanian stood quietly. Smiling brightly at them Inara motioned for them to come closer so she could hug them both. Giggling as they smiled, they sped toward her, assaulting her where she sat on the loveseat. Buried under her children's tangled arms and legs, Inara could feel their warm bodies and smell their rancid morning breath. Delighting in both equally even as her nose crinkled at the smell she laughed in spite of herself. Grateful for their presence when she awoke, her eyes misted with tears as they giggled happily at her.

After several minutes of cuddling Inara could hear Tanian's tummy rumbling and she laughed again while tickling his belly. He erupted in ecstatic giggles. "What say we get you guys some breakfast?" She attempted to stand haphazardly.

Pulling at her arms, little Rafe and Lily guided their mom from the library, while Tanian ran ahead of them. Arriving in the kitchen her smile quickly faded when everyone stopped what they were doing and stared. The children raced to the kid's table near the patio, oblivious to the awkward silence. Eagerly grabbing pieces of fruit and breakfast sandwiches from the platter sitting on the table, they began to eat voraciously.

Getting up from his chair instantly upon her arrival, Dartanian took hold of Inara's arm and dragged her anxiously towards the chair. At the same time, Lylia left through the front living room in a huff, glaring back at her husband angrily with hurt filled eyes before she disappeared.

"Sit, I'll get you something to eat. Royce, Cris, what does she need?" Dartanian asked the couple sitting nearby.

Peering over his coffee mug with an almost clinical stare, Royce murmured while rolling his eyes. "What doesn't she need?" Nodding his head toward Crisalya she stood and rounded the table, heading for the counter laden with breakfast trays filled with food. Grabbing a plate, Crisalya proceeded to fill it from the trays.

Face flushing, Inara had a strong feeling she knew what Royce had meant. Since her arrival, Inara noticed Royce and Crisalya had the habit of plating her meals for her, insisting that she needed it all. She knew her eating habits for the past five years had been horrible. Her body had been deprived of nutritious, balanced meals for so long that Inara could only imagine what they must see when they looked at her.

Expressing her appreciation as Crisalya placed the plate before her, she gazed upon it with a tired look in her eye. It all looked really good but she knew she'd struggle to eat everything.

Rafe was sitting at the table near the patio with the children as he read the morning paper. She noticed his mouth pull tight when she glanced his way. He folded the newspaper and handed it off to Breydon who strolled by him. Rafe crossed his forearms and rested them on the table.

"Do you want to talk about last night?" He asked.

Inara had just taken a bite of her food so she covered her mouth self-consciously with her hand in order to answer while chewing.

"Not particularly."

She frowned when he continued to stare at her. Inara glanced down at her plate and then over at Hialey. Her gaze roamed past Breydon to Dartanian at the end of the table. Sensing, rather than seeing Rafe stand, her gaze moved back to him.

"What day is today?" Inara asked, watching him grab the coffee thermos from the table. He looked like he was heading out already which was suddenly making her anxious for some reason. When she entered the kitchen she'd noticed Dartanian wasn't wearing his Sheriff's uniform this morning, choosing instead running pants and a t-shirt. That led her to believe Dartanian might be planning to stay home for the day.

"It would be Friday," Veta said kindly.

"Rafe, where are you in your reading?"

Sighing heavily, Rafe stopped in the patio doorway and rested a hand upon the doorjamb as he turned back to look at her. "I have a rather stubborn Stallion to break Inara. I have the sense that it cannot wait much longer or it could become problematic. Why do you ask?"

"Have you gotten to the file Choices Dreaming, Roman numeral one yet?"

"No, I'm still on version four of Choices." He grinned widely. What he'd read so far had not only been disturbing in its nature but also highly amusing. Between a towel dropping open in the hallway, a son walking in on her after a shower, a ripped shirt falling away coming out of a pool and a son-in-law catching her without a shirt while changing, pretty much everyone had seen Inara undressed at one point or another in her story. All seemingly innocuous situations and yet the events leading up to the moment in question were exceedingly amusing.

Gasping Inara swallowed hard. Her eyes flew open wide in dismay. "But I told you not to bother with that one!"

"Seemed prudent to know how best to prevent my entire household from seeing you naked." There was a glimmer in his eye. Taking a sip of his coffee, he noted that he'd managed to gain everyone's attention. He chuckled.

Her face flamed for what felt like the hundredth time since she'd entered the Blackthorne ranch house. "I see." She fumbled with her fork and napkin. Dropping the fork on the floor she bent down only to bang her head on the table hard on the way up. Rubbing at the sore spot on her head Inara realized she wasn't getting any prompting sensations against saying anything to him about the stories. Making a hasty decision, as her eyes darted back and forth before her, she halted Rafe by calling out to him as he attempted to exit the kitchen onto the patio.

Peering back over his shoulder, Rafe noticed Her troubled expression.

"Yes?"

"Where are you going? Right now, that is?" She noticed he was wearing his cowboy boots, jeans, and a tight navy-blue t-shirt. A red bandana was poking out of his back pocket, and he was carrying his Stetson hat in his other hand.

Curious by her sudden desire to know where he was going Rafe pivoted where he stood until he faced her. "I'll be working with my foreman in the Stallion corrals attempting to break that black Stallion I got in. Why the sudden interest?"

Their conversation had everyone listening intently.

"N-no reason really I j-just…" Anxiety built within her, but once again she wasn't being swayed to stop by the voice as she had been in the past several days.

"Inara?" Rafe prompted again, becoming concerned. Her face had become ashen and her hands were trembling.

Bucking up her courage she adjusted in her seat. "You might want to detour to the Arabian barn first. I think you'll find your foreman, Steven Simms there."

"Why will I find my foreman in the Arabian barn when he's supposed to be tending to the stallions?" Rafe was trying to hold his temper in check. He had a bad feeling he already knew why Simms was in his Arabian barn.

Exhaling slowly Inara stared back at him, her expression calm, though her fidgeting mannerisms gave away her anxiety. She scratched hard at the itch on her head near the back of her ears before responding.

"Because he's stealing from you."

Rafe swore loudly, his gaze narrowing upon her. "I would have seen…"

"No, last week, with the wedding … and everything, you missed something."

For the moment the kitchen was quiet other than the sounds of the children talking as they ate. Everyone stared at her, allowing what she'd said to sink in. So far, she'd been right about everything she'd told them. Alaina had, in fact, needed glasses and Veta's memory boxes had been on the porch.

"If you don't believe me check the camera footage near the mess hall from yesterday around noon. I'm pretty sure you'll overhear Simms taking a call on his cell from a competing ranch in Canada." Her words caused a flurry of activity as the Blackthorne men stood abruptly and moved towards the sink to dump their plates.

Hearing the sudden clank and clatter of dishes hitting the sink, she peered across the counter at the four men standing there. Relieved of their dishes, they now stood side by side, from all appearances, readying themselves for a confrontation.

Swearing again in frustration, Rafe paced back and forth in front of the patio doors. His nostrils flared and the sounds erupting from his throat were guttural; like a bull preparing for a fight.

"He should be arrested this time if that's really true." Dartanian crossed his arms across his chest, his gaze moving between Inara and his dad.

Stopping suddenly in his pacing, after running a hand through his salt and pepper hair, Rafe pointed towards his sons.

"No. Go on with your business. This ends now. Simms is my problem, I will deal with it," Rafe insisted.

Wincing, Dante had a strong feeling he knew what his father meant. "Are you sure about that? He's been with us an awfully long time."

"Yes, now go. All of you. Be on about your business." Turning once again toward the patio kitchen doors, Rafe was nearly out the door this time when Inara's voice halted him once again.

"Rafe, please!" Inara called, sounding not only distressed but scared.

Startled by the strangled sound of her voice his head jerked back towards her. He could see anxiety and fear in her eyes

"Simms. He could b-become a p-problem for m-me," she spluttered out in a rush, hoping she'd made the right decision to say something. Knowing somehow that God was giving her a choice, she hoped she had made the right one by telling him.

Understanding finally dawned on him. The situation with Simms was the reason why she'd been so adamant about him reading her stories. Suspecting something was about to happen that could affect her adversely if he didn't handle it properly, Rafe grimaced. Deferring his head towards her, he stepped out of the kitchen onto the patio, disappearing as he hit the lawn.

Inara stared after him nervously. She could feel everyone's eyes upon her. It was more than a bit unnerving. Taking a deep breath Inara scratched at her head vigorously. Seeing Hialey's almond brown eyes darting towards her, then suddenly away, Inara became thoughtful. Figuring now was just as good a time as any, she blinked a few times then spoke again after clearing her throat.

"Hialey, you need to tell Breydon."

Confused, Hialey paused with her fork in mid-air. "What are you talking about?"

"There's something you did long ago that you haven't told him yet - the day you turned eighteen. What do you need to tell him?"

The tiny woman stared back at Inara with a blank expression, completely oblivious to what she was referring to. Then, without warning, comprehension dawned on her. She gaped with incredulity.

"No!" Hialey shouted, her temper flaring. Her reaction startled the children, and they all turned to look at her.

"Listen to me," Inara said.

"No, *you* listen to *me*. I don't know what you think you know, but whatever you think you know, you better know better than to tell anyone what you know."

Thumping her hand on the table to gain her attention, Inara became cross. "My presence here today is living proof that making a poor choice in a moment of indecision and fear can affect your future course of events. This is going to become an issue soon."

"Inara, what choice did you make?" Royce asked suddenly, having caught the meaning behind her words. Reminded of the phrase in the poem about crossing paths in time, he suddenly couldn't help but wonder if Inara had been in Montana once before.

Fidgeting uncomfortably, Inara glanced his way and attempted to shrug it off. "It's neither the point nor the time to explain that. As I said, this is going to become an issue." Her fingers flexed in her lap and Inara had the sudden urge to want to be sitting in front of her laptop, tapping away at the keypad feverishly.

"There is no need or reason for this to become an issue at all." Hialey's eyes narrowed on Inara.

"Knock it off," Inara fumed. "Galatians 6:7 states that we are not to be deceived: God is not mocked: for whatsoever a man soweth, that shall he also reap, Hialey."

"Meaning?" Hialey shot back heatedly.

"It means that vindictive nature of yours is about to come back and bite you in the bottom. And whether you like it or not, Breydon has a right to know what really happened and what kind of danger..."

Placing her hands on her ears Hialey shook her head childishly and began humming, cutting Inara off. Closing her eyes in an attempt to ignore Inara's stern expression, she stood to leave.

"Hialey, what don't I know?" Breydon hollered crossly, gaining his wife's attention. He was more than a little annoyed to learn she'd been keeping something from him all these years and still was. And it was very obvious to him that Inara was speaking the truth.

Sticking her tongue out at him impudently Hialey turned towards her sons instead, ignoring him. Shaking her head toward the front room at them, the boys stood, wiping their mouths on their napkins. Following closely behind her, Cody and Seth sniggered together and pushed at each other as they left the kitchen. Hialey's hands still covered her ears so she couldn't hear Breydon calling after her as she went.

"Inara, tell me what's going on." Breydon insisted.

"I can't." Inara sighed, filled with regret. "Particularly in this case and in present company. It wouldn't be appropriate and frankly, it's not my place." She directed her gaze towards the children's table meaningfully.

Turning back to her breakfast, she tried to ignore everyone's curious attention while she ate. Lifting her mug to her lips, she realized it was filled with lemon-scented tea rather than coffee. Sighing in exasperation she got up and emptied its contents into the sink. She needed her coffee in the mornings for as long as she could get it. Moving toward the coffee maker Crisalya halted her.

"What are you doing? You shouldn't be drinking that right now."

Inara gave the woman a hard look. "I think we both know full well that I can have coffee right now."

Giving Inara a once over Crisalya's perplexed gaze shifted to Dartanian who was still eating at the table then back to Inara. "I don't understand. After what Dartanian said last night, I thought maybe…" Her voice trailing off, she proceeded to pour Inara a full mug.

Crisalya watched in further confusion as Inara poured French vanilla creamer and a lot of sugar into her coffee mug. "I thought you drank your coffee black."

"I always drink the same thing as the couple I'm currently writing about at the time for some reason," she said without thinking. Seeing Crisalya's confusion by her statement Inara stared down at her mug blankly. A sound emitted from her, as her mouth formed a soft oh, and she continued to stare at the mug. It occurred to her then, that her desire to drink the same as what Breydon and Hialey did in their coffee, must mean that their story was beginning sooner than she had written it would.

"What are you talking about?"

Shrugging, Inara winced, having a strong feeling she knew what was about to happen at Hialey's shop today. "Nothing. I'm sure she'll handle it just fine." She hoped Crisalya would drop it. It also occurred to her in that same instant that it was Friday.

Giggling suddenly, Inara's face brightened with excitement. In every version of book three in her stories, she'd taken her first ride on a horse within four days of arriving back in Montana for the first time. Excitement building within her at the idea of being out of the house, surrounded by her mountains and riding on the back of a horse made her giddy. Glancing at the clock on the wall, Inara figured she could be done with breakfast in about ten minutes if she hurried. It had been nearly ten minutes already so she imagined Rafe would have taken care of the foreman by then. It would be safe for her to go down to the corrals to see the horses.

Sitting back down at the table she smiled brightly while sloshing her coffee on the table nervously in anticipation. Sopping it up with her napkin, she apologized to Dartanian for getting some on his hand.

"No biggie." At the sight of Inara's sparkling bright blue eyes gleaming over at him, Dartanian gave her a quizzical look as his insides quivered for reasons he couldn't fathom. "Why Inara, if I didn't know better I'd say you were fairly beaming at me. What's got you all hot and bothered." His tone teasing as he winked.

Giving him an impish grin, she giggled again.

"No reason."

Digging into her breakfast, she ate quickly. She'd dreamed all her life of riding on a horse surrounded by the mountains of Montana. Inara couldn't wait for her first ride.

Chapter 18

Pulling his cell phone from his pocket Rafe tapped at the screen as he stood in his yard. Linking to his computer footage of the Arabian barn in the house he reverted back to the day before about a half hour before noon. Watching the footage of his foreman coming out of the mess hall Rafe turned up the volume on his phone when he saw the man answer his cell. Listening in on the conversation, Rafe's temper raged at hearing his own foreman, Steven Simms, speak of previous sales in the past week to the Heartland Horse ranch out of Alberta, Canada. Turning off his phone he inhaled deeply and kicked angrily at the ground. Dirt caught on the toe of his boot and it flew up in the air becoming a torrential downpour of dry dusty powder, like a sandstorm in the desert.

Walking down towards the corrals, Rafe tried to calm down as he watched a few of the ranch hands exercising a couple of Mustangs and an Appaloosa. Nearing the corral he noticed one of the mares was looking quite cumbersome. Perplexed at why it was being ridden he inquired of its foaling date when he arrived at the fence.

"She's about to pop any time, Sir," the young handler responded.

Annoyed, Rafe gestured for him to get off the horse. "You need to get down then and walk her. Don't ride her."

"She won't let me walk her, Sir."

"Then just let her alone. It means she'll likely be delivering soon. Don't ever ride them when they're this close."

"Yes, Sir." The young man looked properly chastised. Swinging down off the horse, the ranch hand nodded towards him. Not recognizing the young man, Rafe wondered if he was new.

"What's your name son? I don't think I've met you yet."

"Brauman, Sir." The handler extended his hand in greeting after pulling off his glove. "Your foreman Simms, he hired me a couple of weeks ago. He's had me working on fixing fencing near the north field until now."

"What's your first name?"

Grinning, Brauman flashed his almond brown eyes at him. "That *is* my first name but my last is Yakerson." Pulling his black Stetson from his head, he ran his free hand through his short brown hair now plastered to his brow. He was a good-looking lad in his early twenties with a lean build. Though slender he appeared to be strong.

"I see." He recalled now that the name had come across his desk a month ago for a background check. "You might as well take her back to the barn for now Brauman."

"Yes, Sir." The young handler attempted to lead the mare back towards the opposite barn. Making a mental note to have Dante come down and check on the mare in an hour, he watched Teddy directing another handler.

"Where's Simms?" Glancing around, not seeing his foreman, he knew Inara was likely right about where the man was currently at but was hoping that she was wrong. Simms had been with them for twenty-five years and had been loyal to a fault until recently. It had only been in the past year or so, that he had begun having problems with him. This wouldn't be the first time he'd caught him stealing from him, but as Simms had been with them for many years Rafe had given him a second chance. He'd been warned at the time, however, that it would be his last.

"In the barn with the Arabian's. I think he's got one in the breeding stall right now," Teddy came up beside Rafe on a black mustang.

"Does he now? Which one?" Reaching out he ran his hand along Black Betsy's hindquarters. "She's healing up nicely."

Looking at him in surprise Teddy pulled off his hat and wiped his brow with his bandana while looking down on Rafe. The heat of the day was clearly already getting to the man.

"I think its Mocktail. I didn't realize you were aware Black Betsy had been hurt." Teddy looked at his boss curiously. Rafe was a hard man to read sometimes but the ranch hand got the feeling something was up.

"For the most part, I know all and see all, Teddy. That's something to keep in mind when you work for me." He wished he hadn't missed most recent events, for usually, his statement was true. "What do you think of the new hand Simms hired?"

"He's a nice young man; polite. He's got a lot of learning to do but he's good with the horses," Teddy said thoughtfully, scratching his chin.

"Do you want to keep him on when Simms leaves?"

Staring at him in surprise Teddy looked alarmed. "Simms is leaving us, Sir?"

Not answering Rafe gave the man a calculating look then turned on his heel. Heading towards the Arabian barn, he sidled up against the door. Walking past the stall where Mocktail, his champion black Arabian Stallion should be, he noticed the horse was missing. Eyes narrowing angrily, he crept quietly towards the end of the barn to the breeding stall.

Just two weeks prior he'd told his foreman he didn't want Mocktail up on the mount or in the breeding stalls again anytime soon. He'd been running through barn footage at that time and noticed Simms had several of his Arabians in the breeding stalls pretty regularly, collecting semen samples on his own.

Normally, it was at the very least a two-man job, especially when collecting from an Arabian Stallion because it can be extremely dangerous due to the unpredictability of a half-ton of aroused horseflesh. The excited animal would commonly walk on its hind legs approaching the dummy mare, rearing up to ten feet high at the withers. It was why Rafe had developed a new technique which would manually collect Mocktail into an AV with all four feet on the ground, making the collection far safer to both the stallion and the handler. But Rafe still insisted on there being two handlers involved as it was still dangerous and Simms knew that.

Rafe suspected after further investigation into the matter, he'd find there would be no record of the recent sales he'd overheard discussed over the phone. He didn't even need to confer with Dante to know that no recent breeding sales had been approved either, for he'd seen the look on his son's face moments before in the kitchen. Rafe already had proof of Simms' admission of theft with the footage of the phone conversation. He imagined he'd also likely catch Simms on camera exchanging money for vials after handling several collections. It's how he'd caught him before. Clearly, Simms was selling his pure-bred semen to competing horse ranches again and pocketing the money.

Creeping quietly towards the breeding stall Rafe could see Mocktail had already been up on the mount and Simms was in the stall with him. Obviously unaware of Rafe's presence, the man continued to make his collection.

"What do you think you are doing?"

Startled, Simms jumped visibly. "I was … I'm just collecting for breeding."

"I told you two weeks ago; I don't want Mocktail being collected." Rafe's voice was deathly quiet as he spoke. Glowering at the man angrily he continued, "You know what? Get out! You're fired, Simms. I want you off my property now and you can forget your stuff. I'll send it to you."

"Now see here, Rafe," Simms flared. Nearly ten years younger than the Blackthorne patriarch he hadn't aged near as well, as there were obvious wrinkles near his eyes and his teeth were yellow from excessive drinking and smoking. Pulling off his rubber gloves, he tossed them in the trash.

"I've been with you for twenty-five years!"

"That's the only thing keeping me from filing charges against you! I got you dead to rights on footage admitting to selling my prize Arabian stallion seed, to of all places, the Heartland Horse Ranch. My competitor!" Thinking that having the man arrested might prove Inara's undoing somehow, he'd made the decision on his walk down to the corrals to fire Simms and throw him off his property.

Unable to deny Rafe's accusation Simms sniffed noisily, turning his head away. Looking back at his longtime employer, he shifted uneasily and then strode out of the stall.

"Look, Rafe, I need this job now more than ever. I made some bets I cannot repay. You can't fire me over this right now."

Simms began to sweat profusely. He'd already promised several vials to a dealer up north in Canada who'd paid half up front. If he couldn't cover the order he was a dead man because they weren't the sort of men you re-nigged on and he'd spent the money already.

"I can and have." He grabbed Simms by the arm and began dragging him from the barn. "I've had this conversation with you before Simms, about your gambling issue. I've been understanding to a fault. But now you're stealing from me and my family again and that is *not* acceptable."

Shrugging out of his grasp once they'd reached the exterior of the barn Steven Simms scowled at Rafe and turned on him suddenly. Their aggressive stances caught the attention of Teddy and the nearby ranch hands.

Simms swore angrily as he yelled. "You can't do this to me! I've worked my butt off for you for the past twenty-five years!"

"And I've paid you very well for it! Better than any foreman around these parts, and this is how you repay me? By stealing?" Out of the corner of his eye, Rafe could see Inara strolling lazily toward them from the house. Unaware of what was going down, she appeared deep in thought. Turning his attention back to Simms, he growled dangerously as his nostrils flared.

"Get off my land now or I'll throw you off." Hoisting his shoulders in a domineering fashion he stepped toward the foreman aggressively.

Well aware of his bosses physical capabilities, as he'd seen him throw a ranch hand off the property once before, Steven Simms stepped back anxiously. Kicking at the ground angrily, he turned away to head towards his truck when he saw the woman with waist length red hair, walking towards them. Eyes narrowing in confusion at the sight of a woman who looked like the Sheriff's wife but clearly wasn't, he turned back suddenly.

"You'll regret this Blackthorne! Mark my words." He gestured wildly toward Rafe as he shouted. It was slight, but Simms observed his former employer's furtive glance in the redhead's direction. Scoffing darkly, his eyes shifted back to the woman. Who was she?

Hearing the man shouting, Inara glanced toward him uneasily, recognizing him instantly from her nightmares. Her face went white and a shiver ran down her spine. She could see him staring at her and she didn't like the look in his eye. Wild and crazy like a man with nothing to lose. Eyes widening in alarm she finished the length of the yard quickly, reaching Rafe and the ranch hands in seconds. She thought she'd waited long enough to come out to the corrals to see the horses but she'd been wrong. Rafe had clearly picked up on the look as well for he drew her into him protectively. Continuing to watch Simms as he left, he waited until the man peeled away dragging up dirt as he went.

"Teddy, Mocktail is in the breeding stall. Put him back where he belongs. I'm gonna want to talk to you in a little while too. Come see me up at the house after dinner, will you?"

"Yes, Sir," Teddy said promptly.

Turning on Inara, Rafe scowled. "I thought I told you to stay in the house when you arrived."

241

"You did, I'm sorry. I just wanted to see the horses, and you can't keep me cooped up forever. A person needs to stretch their legs after all. Besides, I thought he'd be gone by now."

"Well, he wasn't now was he?" He ground out; his voice harsher than he'd meant.

Inara glanced away towards the mountains, her eyes appearing haunted and hurt. He expelled an uneasy breath and softened his tone when he saw he'd frightened her.

"I need you to do something for me, Inara." He glanced down at her, then his gaze shifted back in the direction where Simms had driven away. "Don't go walking alone for the next few days. Stay up at the house and don't leave it otherwise."

Nodding anxiously in ascent, he could tell by the look on her face that she'd been rattled by what the man said. Confident he wouldn't have to worry about her disobeying him this time, he proceeded to head toward the corrals. Hearing Inara calling timidly after him, he turned back to see what she needed.

"I'm sorry... I know you're terribly busy but I've never ridden a horse before and was wondering if I might get a chance," she said shyly, noticing they'd gained the attention of the men in the corral.

There was disappointment and confusion in her tone and Rafe couldn't understand why. "Are you sure that's wise?" He smirked, his crystal blue eyes sparkling with mischief.

Confused, Inara just stared at him.

"You know. What with you being pregnant with triplets and all," he called loudly as he began backing away.

Hands balling into fists at her sides Inara huffed, her eyes shooting daggers at him. "I ain't pregnant, Rafe Blackthorne, and you know that full well!"

"Well, now there's no need to be shouting, little lady." Rafe teased back as he drawled. He was enjoying how her face seemed to puff up in indignation.

"Little lady?" Inara ground out. "Why you …. you! Oh, forget it!"

"Inara, darling," he called back in a mocking plaintive fashion, gaining her attention. He stretched his arms wide and shrugged. "But I thought you said you wanted a ride?"

Her eyes flew open, knowing full well he was messing with her and angry for it.

"We both know I am by no means little, nor have I ever been accused of being a lady; and I sure as spit ain't your darling! I'd ride with Dartanian before I'd ever ride with you!" Hair swinging wildly, she whipped around and stalked away, back towards the house all the while scratching at the back of her head vigorously.

Watching her fume away angrily, Rafe shook his head and chuckled, hoping he hadn't taken it too far; he'd thought he might have seen a bit of hurt in her eyes. But it was important to him that she stay up at the house for the next few days until he was certain the situation with Simms was under control. Promising himself he'd apologize later, he turned back towards the corral. He noted the ranch hands glancing away quickly, where before they'd been eyeing him curiously.

"All right men. Let's get that stallion broke," he called, sensing Inara was gaining more of their attention now as she walked away than what he was. It was the hair of course. Inara's thick lustrous main fell loose down her arms to her elbows in messy waves, which curled at the

243

ends. Long and beautiful like his daughter Megorah's, the strawberry blonde coloring could easily grab any man's attention in the golden light of the Montana sky. The fact that she looked like Lylia, whether heavier or not, probably wasn't helping. Both were beautiful women as far as Rafe was concerned.

"I'll go let the monster out of its stall," he called back over his shoulder. He headed into the stallion barn from the side entrance where the corral fencing butted up against it on either side. Several ranch hands followed, having been motioned to do so in order to assist.

The rest of the ranch hands watched with admiration as the woman strolled away scratching at her head. Her movements caused her hair to fly out all around her.

Seeing the look on Rafe's face as he'd stepped into the corral, David shook his head and smiled.

"What's the look for?" Brauman asked, riding up next to him on a palomino.

"Mr. Blackthorne, I think, might be soft on that little lady." David nodded towards the direction of the house where the woman was headed.

"Mr. Blackthorne is protective of women in general. He's well known for it too." Teddy was having a hard time imagining his employer to be sweet on any woman. The man was too proper for such things. Pulling off his hat again, he patted it against his side while wiping sweat from his brow with a bandana. The heat was getting to him earlier in the day then he liked.

"Who is she? Is she related to the Sheriff's wife? They look alike." David asked, curiosity getting the better of him.

"I couldn't tell you for sure, but I'd say that's a fair guess considering the likeness. But for the hair, they could be twins." Leaning forward, Teddy grabbed his rope and began looping it to make a lasso.

"Her hair is mighty beautiful, that's for sure. I would hate to see something happen to it." Brauman's gaze shifted towards the house. His face was placid but his words and tone implied real concern.

Giving Brauman a funny look, David nodded toward the woman in question, who was quickly nearing the ranch house. "She looks a little younger than Mr. Blackthorne." He dismounted next to them and proceeded to pull the saddle from the Appaloosa they had been working with.

Teddy snorted. "If she's about the same age as Lylia, which is what she looks to be, then try twenty years younger."

Both men turned toward him in surprise. "How old is Mr. Blackthorne exactly, if you don't mind me asking?" Brauman asked curiously.

"That man turned sixty years old in March." Teddy sniggered at Brauman's startled expression and watched as the young man looked again towards the house.

"Hhmm. I'd of thought Simms over there was older than him; I know for a fact he's fifty. He told me himself when I was hired," Brauman said.

Glancing up at the young man, Teddy saw his eyes narrowing in the opposite direction where Steven Simms had driven off. Both he and David turned in the direction he was looking and witnessed the man who'd just been fired sitting with his truck idling, eyeing the Blackthorne house as the woman entered the kitchen from the patio deck. Realizing he'd been discovered he sped off quickly. Teddy got an uneasy feeling in his gut at the sight of Simms on Blackthorne property so soon after having just being fired for stealing.

He tilted his hat toward the handler. "Good eye young man. You see him again you let me know. That goes for you too David," Teddy said evenly. Nickering at his horse he prodded his stallion in motion. "And David, be sure to spread the word to the others too. Our old foreman might just become a problem."

Removing the blanket from the appaloosa's back, he grabbed the reigns and guided the horse back into the barn in order to make way for the stallion.

"Will do."

Chapter 19

Returning to the house terribly disappointed and in a foul mood, as a result, Inara slammed the patio door behind her after she entered. Mumbling under her breath in agitation as her heart skipped painfully in her chest, she crossed the kitchen with her head down, not paying attention to where she was going. Finding her way barred as her face smacked into a man's chest, she shivered when she realized it was Dartanian.

"Problem?" One eyebrow of his rose. Taking a bite of the bacon he'd procured from the frying pan but moments ago, he was grateful he hadn't had his coffee mug in hand.

Inara took a few steps back and looked up. "That man is a pain. An absolute pain! Now, where is your wife anyway? She's got to stop avoiding me; I need to talk to her." Continuing to scratch rigorously at her head Inara suddenly fumed. "And why is my head itching so badly? It's been like this since I arrived here. What are you people putting in your water anyway?"

Eyeing her closely Dartanian stepped toward her, narrowing his gaze upon her head as she kept scratching. Having exceptionally good vision, he could see something tiny moving near her brow. He reached out and plucked something from her hair between two fingers. Looking down at it, then back at Inara, he spoke with a straight face.

"It's much more likely due to the lice in your hair."

Megorah's head swiveled towards him from the breakfast table in alarm. She backed away towards the partition wall anxiously, eliciting a curious stare from her husband nearby, who had been relaxing on his morning off with a newspaper.

"That's not funny. In the thirty-nine years, I've been alive, I've never had lice." Inara said crossly, not paying attention to his outstretched arm. Scratching wildly at her head with both hands, she growled in frustration.

"Dart, are you serious?" Crisalya exclaimed from the kitchen counter, looking horrified. Placing the dishes she'd pulled from the dishwasher into the cabinets above her, she turned to face him.

"Yup, serious as a heart attack," Dartanian said, sounding pained. He'd planned on trying to convince Lylia to go on a picnic with him and their daughter Kayla today, in order to try and sway her his way. He suspected there wasn't much chance of that happening now.

Setting down his bacon on the platter next to him on the counter Dartanian reached toward Inara's head with his other hand. "That would be another," he said grimly while plucking another louse from her hair.

The sound of chairs scooting quickly back could be heard throughout the kitchen. "Do you realize what this means?" Megorah looked horror struck as she watched Crisalya gesture toward the children still in the kitchen to quickly finish eating. She gazed upon Inara in dismay then caught her sister's eye.

"Why I... How could I possibly have lice?" Inara asked, looking both baffled and disbelieving.

"We've never had that problem here so you must have brought it with you when you came." Dante grimaced as he poured coffee into his thermos. Distracted, he missed seeing Alaina's head swivel quickly toward Megorah's eldest daughter, Katana. Knowing full well his brother was serious, as he had the best eyes out of all of them, it occurred to him that they might need help clearing the lice infestation from the house. The little buggers breed fast so he knew they could be everywhere by now.

"I did not, and I do not have lice!" Inara declared heatedly as she turned toward Dante, then swiveled back toward Dartanian. She sounded as though she were ready to panic. "Really Lord, are you kidding me with this? And after everything else!" Pulling a swatch of her long tresses off of her shoulder, she irrationally ran a hand down the length of it, knowing all the while that if she had them, they'd be near her scalp. Imagining she saw a bug the size of a gnat drop from her head to her hand, she flinched violently and gave a startled cry.

"No, no, no! I can't have lice," Inara cried in distress, spinning around as she swatted at her long hair.

"What did you do?" Megorah wailed loudly, gaining Inara's attention. They stared at each other. Inara's face was filled with shock, Megorah's with anger and resentment. "How could you bring that into this house?"

"It's not like I did it intentionally," Inara declared with a wounded expression.

"Intentional or not it's here now," Megorah hollered back.

"Calm down, Meg. Where has she been?" Drinian asked, thinking everyone was getting worked up for no reason. It was just a bug after all; a nuisance for sure but nothing to get hysterical over. His new wife Veta, on the other hand, seemed to think otherwise, however, as her first reaction was to grab at her hair in dismay. She stood quickly next to him, pulling her black hair back over her shoulders.

"She's been everywhere, Drin!" Megorah exploded. "I swear if that stuff gets in my hair because of you," she hissed at Inara while swooping her long hair back and balling it up in her hands, as if for protection. "I'll *never* forgive you if it does."

"Meg!" Chase said crossly, appalled at his wife's unusual behavior.

"That's a horrible thing to say. It's just lice." Alaina quietly watched as Inara turned where she stood, becoming more and more agitated as she pulled at her hair. She seemed near hysterics. Having been through the ordeal with her own daughter over a year before, Alaina was sympathetic to the woman's plight. She imagined having lice in hair as hers was going to be a bear to deal with.

"Just lice. Do any of you have any idea what that could do to me with my hair as long as it is?" Megorah's crystal blue eyes flashed in a panic. Feeling an inordinate amount of anxiety, and something else for which she couldn't understand, she stared over at Inara in distress.

Stomping her feet, Inara's temper flared. She glared at Megorah. "I think *I* might have a pretty good idea." She stretched her long hair out with both hands for emphasis, annoyed that Megorah was forgetting their hair was of similar length, if not color.

"After everything my father and brother did for you, bringing you to safety, sharing our home, food, clothing and you bring lice here?" Megorah hollered, her eyes narrowing to a scowl. She was suddenly starting to understand the emotion churning within her and didn't like it one bit. Megorah had begun picking up on it the moment Inara had returned and run into Dartanian.

"Meg that's enough," Dante said firmly, irritated and surprised by his sister's reaction to a few bugs. Even without the angel next to him telling him so, he could see Inara was becoming hysterical. Tears were welling in her eyes.

Inara pranced in place while staring wide-eyed down at her hair in her hands.

"No, it's not enough," Megorah argued. "She's staying here free of charge and…"

"For your information," Inara interrupted, "I actually *have* given Rafe money for staying here." She'd known the statement would come; it had just been a matter of time. It was why she'd given the money to him in the first place. She had known she would eventually need the ammunition, to be able to use for her defense, when the inevitable accusations began. She just hadn't known at the time, when or how it would happen as things had changed in the story too much.

Breydon's head turned toward her in surprise. "You have?"

"Yes, six hundred dollars," Inara said, effectively silencing everyone.

"Well, that's just…" Megorah struggled to find words. "It's actually not that much when you consider three kids and an adult…"

"Meg, what on earth is with you?" Chase gave his wife a stern look. Her behavior was peculiar. She'd never before baulked at helping someone before without reimbursement when there was an obvious need. If anything he felt they all should be extremely grateful to Inara, for she had gone through great lengths to protect them, by bringing all her stories with her when she came.

"It's more than you guys give him for staying here at the ranch," Inara said angrily, attempting to defend herself while visibly upset. The morning was most definitely not turning out as she had thought. She'd hoped to be on the back of a horse by now surrounded by her mountains, rather than dealing with lice and defending herself against Rafe's children; and she was still unsettled at having been seen by Steven Simms.

"This is our home. We don't need to pay dad to stay here." Giving a short laugh, Crisalya smiled as though she were humoring Inara, then leaned against the counter with a piece of toast dangling in her hand.

Glancing over at his wife, Royce scowled at her. He stood poised with a spatula in hand over the stove. Trying to get a head start on the evening meal before heading out to the Coffee Haven, he now suddenly wished he'd already left. Disappointed by his wife's opinion on the situation, he figured he'd correct her later on in private, rather than publicly.

"No, this used to be your home. You're all adults now." Inara corrected her before Royce had the chance. "It's your father's house, not yours. You all have your own houses now. You only come to stay here for the summer months and during Christmastime, I'd wager."

"So, what's your point? We grew up here. You didn't. This isn't your home," Dartanian said, becoming testy at her words.

"Which means you really shouldn't get used to it," Megorah snapped, giving her a meaningful look.

Face appearing as though she'd been slapped Inara inhaled a deep breath, struggling to keep her emotions under control. "My point is, even when my family would visit our cousins in Minnesota for the holidays, my parents would try and give my uncle money in order to help contribute to the Christmas meal and breakfasts they'd provide. They'd also bring things to share. Nobody here does that. Seriously, do you people really have no comprehension what it takes for your father to run this house? Especially when you're here?" She asked incredulously, still frantically staring at her hair.

"So what? He's rich." Breydon shrugged as he stood. He hadn't missed the look on Inara's face and he wondered at it. Peering over at his twin sister he had the feeling her uncharacteristic behavior might have something to do with how their house guest was feeling right now.

"Just because a person has money doesn't mean you should take advantage of them, even when they are your dad. Every time you all come home you bring your whole family, kids and all. Water, gas, electric; it all spikes during those times." Inara harrumphed softly as her eyes wildly roamed her hair. "Shoot the food bill alone I would imagine skyrockets twelve times over. Yet the expectation is that Rafe should always take care of everything, isn't it? All because he's your dad and you used to live here." Wailing suddenly as Dartanian presented her with another louse he'd just pulled from her hair, her eyes brimmed with tears.

"You know what? I think you need to leave." Megorah said firmly while pressing against the wall. She had figured it out. No longer confused by the woman's emotions before her, Megorah wanted her out of her presence.

"Meg, stop it. She has nowhere to go yet." Veta pointed out, appalled at Megorah's attitude and confused by it.

Drinian nodded in agreement, "And she's pregnant too, so…"

"I'm not pregnant," Inara shouted in exasperation.

Ignoring her denials the conversation persisted. "I didn't mean for her to leave the house," Megorah corrected. Inara's denial of her pregnancy solidified her suspicions on what was going on. "I just meant she needed to go somewhere other than the kitchen with that stuff. You know - away from me." She groaned loudly, turning towards her sister. "Do you realize how much cleaning this means?"

Fed up and in tears, Inara fled the kitchen for the pool room, embarrassed at her situation and desperate to get away from Megorah's knowing eyes.

"Yes, Meg, but we'll all deal with it," Royce said in a firm tone. Turning off the stove, he grabbed a nearby towel from the counter and wiped at his hands. He suspected he might have a pretty good idea why Megorah was acting the way she was and it irritated him. They were all adults after all, capable of making their own choices.

Out of the corner of his eye, Royce watched as Megorah's daughter, Katana, quietly slipped from the kitchen. He became cross, for she appeared to be scratching at her head as she went.

"Poor thing. Why did you have to be so harsh, Meg? She looked like she was about to cry. I guess I better go help her. She won't be able to get through all that hair herself." Disappearing down the hall, she headed to the playroom first to make sure her children were settled with Lylia.

The men watched as the rest of the women fled the kitchen in search of their bathrooms, in order to check their hair. Sighing heavily, Breydon grabbed his cell phone. "I better call and warn, Hialey. I have to go into the office briefly for something but I'll be back to help shortly. I expect you all are going to need it."

"I'll run into town for treatment in order to get rid of the lice. I expect we'll go through a lot." Dartanian followed after his brother, disappearing into the living room.

Walking quickly toward the partition, Royce opened it and hollered after Dartanian. "Count heads and bring enough for everyone. I suspect it has probably been in the house longer then what the women think."

"Got it!" Dartanian hollered back as he twirled his keys in the air. His Sheriff's cruiser was parked in the front of the house. He figured he'd just take that instead of the car in the garage since it was already out.

Closing the partition wall Royce exchanged looks with Chase, Dante, and Drinian then headed towards the stairs. "I'll be back down. I need to check on something."

"You noticed her disappear quickly too, did you?" Drinian asked, suspecting he knew full well where Royce was going. Seeing his brother-in-law nod, he waved him on, figuring he could take care of it.

"You know guys, Inara's not entirely wrong about what she said." Chase set his coffee on the counter near the sink.

"What? You mean about how we're not helping out when we visit?" It occurred to Drinian that Inara might have a point; particularly since he tended to eat three and four times as much as everyone else.

Nodding, Chase continued. "I've actually thought the same thing on occasion."

"I know. It occurred to me recently as well." Dante said, recalling the most recent grocery delivery he'd signed for when it arrived. The receipt had been as long as he was tall, and the grand total absurdly high.

Chapter 20

Irritated by the events of the morning and not looking forward to Lylia's reaction at finding out there was lice in the house, Dartanian pulled his cruiser up in front of the local pharmaceutical store. By his count, there would be twenty-six kits to get. So far he'd bought out three stores and was looking potentially to buy out another since he still needed seven more.

Distracted as he was coming out of the store, he was not on his guard like he normally was, and he missed seeing the figure crouched near the back end of the vehicle parked next to him.

Clicking to unlock his cruiser, Dartanian deposited his bags with the others in the back seat. Closing the back door he opened the driver's side door and slid inside. Placing his keys in the ignition he started the vehicle just as someone hastily opened his front passenger door.

Hopping in quickly and slamming the door behind him, the Hispanic man with brown hair, eyes, and a goatee pressed his Colt 45, up into Dartanian's neck and jawline.

Dartanian inhaled sharply and tensed, noting the man had it cocked and ready to shoot.

"Your reaction time's off bud," the man said, his voice thick with a Hispanic accent. "I couldn't believe my eyes when I saw you going into that last store; and what's with all the lice treatment back there anyway, you got an epidemic somewhere or something?"

Tensing, and feeling stupid for getting caught off guard, Dartanian stared the man down, his natural discerning instincts kicking in. He could see a haze circling the man's head from shoulder to shoulder. It pulsed between white and black, lending him to believe he might be able to convince the man to stand down.

"You really don't want to do this," he said calmly. "This is a really bad idea. Why don't you put that gun down and we'll talk?"

"I'm fully aware of what you're capable of, so I think I'll keep this handy if you don't mind." The man shook the gun before him. "Besides, it would seem your undercover persona might be able to help me out of a jamb I'm in."

"I'm not sure exactly what you're talking about, but you have to know that holding a gun on a Sheriff really isn't wise, right?" He kept his hands on his thighs, not interested in making any sudden movements – yet.

"Ah, well, you forget we worked together for over a year on a job. I've seen what you can do to a guy. Exactly how did you get this gig anyway? And so quickly? Sheriff, huh? The big cheese himself."

Shaking his head slightly Dartanian eyed the man closely. "I don't know you, buddy, you got the wrong…"

"Hey, what's with your eyes anyway?" The man screwed up his face as he stared closely at the man before him. He knew it had to be Franc but something about the guy seemed off somehow. "How did you get rid of that scar of yours, Franc? You have yourself an operation or something?"

Hearing the man refer to him as Franc and mention a scar, it dawned on Dartanian instantly who he thought he was. Closing his eyes he banged his head against his headrest, swearing internally at having to be an identical twin. His brother, Dante, had been going by the alias Franclin Kastle when he'd arrived home with Alaina. Realizing he needed to determine who this guy was before going any further, he decided to play along.

"Something like that," he said mildly in an undertone. "Why are you here anyway?"

"Chance," Ricardo said quickly. "Pure chance. I happened to be passing through and saw you coming out of that last store."

"I see. How exactly do you think I can help you? What with me being Sheriff of Breckenridge County and all?" Dartanian inquired cautiously.

"Oh. Well, you know how we agreed to disappear after that last job we did?" Ricardo asked. Seeing Dartanian nod cautiously, he continued while scratching at his goatee with the tip of his gun. "Well, it would seem I took the wrong vehicle from the wrong person while picking up the little lady in Chicago. Seriously, what were the odds it would wind up being one belonging to Kobi Radford's henchman? Filled with drugs it was. No worries though, I destroyed it all so that drug lord won't get a bit of it back."

The man laughed mirthlessly, appearing somewhat miserable.

"Right, what were the odds?" Dartanian replied on a morose chuckle, groaning internally.

"Man, they have been chasing me and the little lady ever since, showing up out of the blue everywhere we go.

If it was just me and her I wouldn't worry so much, but you know, with the baby..." Ricardo's voice trailed off at the lack of reaction from Dartanian. "You know, little Javier," he prompted while furrowing his brow in confusion. The man before him acted as though he didn't have any idea what he was talking about.

"I see, so you're just trying to get to the next state are you?" Dartanian prompted, sensing the man next to him might have been one of Dante's partners with the CIA at one point.

"I'm thinking Canada actually, but I need to lay low for a bit, you know?"

"Of course, a safe place for the lady and all." He avoided using the term wife since he didn't know what the situation was with her and this guy. "Where are they now?"

"I got them hidden," was all Ricardo said. "Now don't worry. I ain't here to bust your undercover or nothing. I just need a little help." Waving his gun toward the vehicle's ignition, he prompted Dartanian to move the Sheriff's cruiser as if to drive him somewhere.

Slowly moving his hands towards the wheel so the man next to him knew what his intentions were, he shifted the vehicle in gear. Dartanian had a feeling he knew exactly where they were hiding.

"So, in other words, they're at the Howard's Motel?"

"What makes you say that?" Ricardo tensed noticeably. The man was horrible at subterfuge. No wonder the men after them kept finding him.

Shaking his head Dartanian chuckled humorlessly. "It's where everyone goes in this town when they are hiding." Putting the vehicle in motion, he pulled away from the building. "Let's go get them then. I wouldn't want anything to happen to little Javier after all. So what am I calling you now?"

"Francesco Castillo, but I'm thinking I'm gonna have to change it again. I'm sure you can help me with that too." Ricardo said in answer, eyeing him carefully.

"Francesco Castillo. Are you kidding me?" He cringed at the man's vast stupidity, wondering if all CIA agents were really that dumb.

"Seemed funny somehow at the time. Figured it was better than Toni Starck, you know?" Ricardo sniggered then sat watching him as though waiting for a response. Becoming thoughtful, he scratched at his goatee with his free hand this time. He'd thought maybe Franc might be related somehow to one of his last partners. The similarities were definitely there, but apparently, there hadn't been anything to his suspicions after all. Simply a coincidence he guessed. Turning his attention toward the window, he watched the roads carefully, recognizing the direction they were going. They'd be at the motel soon.

"So, you never answered me. How did you get this gig?"

"You wouldn't believe me if I told you," Dartanian said in response. Moments later they were pulling into the motel in front of Ricardo's room. "Am I waiting here or what?"

"What's wrong with you, man? Of course, you're coming with me." Ricardo gave him a funny look. "Maria's gotta meet you before she'll go with you. You know how it is with women in these cases. They need to feel secure and all."

Sliding his gun into his back pocket, Ricardo got out and stood by the vehicle waiting for Dartanian to exit from the driver's side. Shoulders slumping in irritation he cursed his brother internally and got out. When he saw Dante next, he just might clobber him.

- - -

Back at the ranch house, Alaina was still trying to convince Inara to come out of the restroom in the pool room. Deciding to try one last time she knocked on the door again.

"Inara, it can happen to anyone. There's no need to be embarrassed. If you won't come out then why don't you let me in, at least, so we can talk?" She asked, calling through the door.

Cracking the door open a bit, Inara peered back out at her. "I honestly didn't know, Alaina. I never asked to be such a burden to anyone. I never wrote this scenario out so I had no idea it was even a possibility."

"You're not a burden, and rationally speaking you can't possibly know everything that's going to happen."

"You can say that again." Her tone was despondent. She looked so sad and disappointed that Alaina wondered if she might have missed something.

"If it's any consolation I don't believe the lice started with you. I get the feeling it may have already been present before you got here." With the ability to be able to know thoughts as the result of an angel ever present at her side, Alaina had figured out what had happened. She hadn't noticed Katana escaping from the kitchen but she had been told by the angel what she'd been thinking when she'd left in such a hurry. Disappointed that the girl hadn't said anything to her mother, Alaina at least understood why, having seen Megorah's reaction to Inara.

"I can help you brush it out," she offered, breaking the silence, hoping to assuage her distress.

"Who are you trying to kid here?" Inara flung open the door and pointed at her hair. "It's going to take a team of people and the entire night in order to comb this mess out. I don't even have a comb! Or hairbrush for that matter!"

Seeing Inara was struggling to fight back tears, Alaina sighed, knowing full well she might be right. Though beautiful even in its messy state, she could see the mass of tangles, spanning from the past several days. Gazing upon the woman before her, she also noted Inara appeared small, almost fragile even for the first time since she'd arrived; whereas before she'd seemed the opposite. The stress of the past several days had taken a toll on her. She could see it in her face.

It occurred to Alaina, as she watched Inara fidget anxiously before her, that she hadn't been able to brush or comb her hair out since she'd arrived because no one had lent her either one.

"Do you even have a toothbrush?" Alaina asked suddenly. Seeing Inara's lip trembling, she watched her shrug it off as if it were no big deal.

"Let's just say you don't want to get too close." She laughed nervously. "I have what I need, that's all that matters." She held her hand up to keep Alaina from speaking. "And I'm not being pathetic, I'm being real. There's a roof over my head and my children are safe, there's more food than I can eat on the table, clothes on my back, and money in my back pocket in case of emergency. It's not much but more than most have."

Realizing how thoughtless they had all been, Alaina took careful stock of the woman standing in front of her. Inara was still wearing the same jeans she'd had on when she had arrived and the oversized t-shirt was one her husband had lent Inara the night before when she'd fallen into the pool and torn her own.

The lack of makeup and inability to groom her hair had left her in kind of a frumpy state. She looked tired - very tired. Remembering that stressed and drawn feeling well from when she'd been taken from her own home and her life had been uprooted, Alaina took hold of Inara's hand.

"You forget, I've been where you are. I understand better than the rest what you're going through right now."

"I know. Our stories are very similar." She dropped to the tiled floor of the bathroom. Leaning against the wall she curled her legs up against herself.

Alaina knelt down in front of her. "Yes. Honestly, I would have thought you would look like me rather than Lylia for that reason."

"Yes, well, that would make things much less complicated I suppose," Inara mumbled. "You know, it's funny. I have a sudden craving for coffee with honey," she said out of the blue. Her eyes seemed to glaze over and she stared at the wall as though transfixed. Her mouth formed into a silent "oh" and she exhaled softly as she spoke. "Oh, no! That *cannot* be good."

Perplexed, Alaina watched Inara's face turn as white as the towel behind her. Tapping on her leg, in order to try and get her attention, she prodded her for answers.

"Inara, what's wrong?"

"Please tell me you have your cell phone on you," Inara demanded, sounding distressed.

"Of course." Alaina pulled it from her pocket. "Dante insists that I keep it on me at all times. I'm not even two months pregnant yet and he's already worried about me going into labor," she smiled dreamily, clearly pleased by his concern.

"Trust me, in your case that is a good habit to keep. Do you have Rafe's number?" Inara snatched the phone away from her, then began urgently swiping through the contact list on Alaina's phone.

"All the family is on there." She frowned at the woman, getting the feeling there might be something wrong.

Finding the number, Inara dialed it and waited impatiently for him to answer. She had to warn Rafe before it was too late, or the next hour could play out very badly for everyone.

Chapter 21

Rafe stood in the center of the corral staring down the Stallion.

They watched each other.

He could see the distrustful glint in his beautiful black eyes.

Unblinking, he nickered at the horse while holding the rope loosely in his hand. So far they'd only been able to get the Stallion to allow the halter and bridle. He kept refusing the saddle.

The horse pawed at the ground with one hoof, as if marking an imaginary line between them that he wasn't allowed to cross. Chuckling softly Rafe smiled. He sensed the horse would be ready soon; might even be able to get a blanket on his back by the end of the day. Several of the ranch hands watched from the fencing, wanting to learn his technique for breaking horses. Amused by their desire to learn from him, he felt it wasn't so much that he was breaking them down as it was getting the horses permission. The only way a man got on the back of a horse was if it allowed them to. And for that to happen there had to be a measure of trust between them.

In this case, Rafe sensed the Stallion needed to know he had no intentions of ruling over him but partnering with him instead as companions, friends. The bond between a man and a horse could be quite strong if the relationship was born on trust. That had been proven to him long ago with Drinian and his horse Rohn. Bought for, and given to his son when he had been ten years old, they had been inseparable. That is, until the day the horse had died fifteen years before, in that fateful accident that nearly killed his son. He suspected his son might have died that day if the horse hadn't responded the way it did. Rohn had acted as though she were attempting to protect him from the demons that day. That had been what had ended her life, saving his.

Seeing the same look in this Stallion's eyes as he'd seen in Rohn when he first got her, Rafe suspected he knew its internal battle. Nickering softly at the horse, he slowly reached into his denim pocket and pulled out the sugar cubes. He extended his hand towards the horse. The Stallion snorted and tossed his head as if to say he couldn't be bribed. Chuckling again, he put the cubes back. He already knew the horse's true weakness. Reaching into his back pocket with his other hand he pulled out the carrot. Offering it instead, he watched, his eyes squinting in the bright light of the sun as the horse slowly meandered towards him. Sniffing the carrot first, the horse nuzzled it then opened its mouth, whinnying as it chomped happily on the carrot.

Beaming from ear to ear, Rafe patted the horse's muzzle affectionately. It would be a good breeding horse, but he suspected he knew what he really needed to do for him, and where he belonged.

"So, you got a name for him yet?" Teddy called from the fence.

Nodding, Rafe replied, "This one, gentleman, will be called Redemption."

"I would have thought, Demon would be more appropriate." David glowered at the horse.

"Ah, you're just mad 'cause he kicked you coming out of his stall yesterday morning," Teddy said dryly, sniggering at the man.

"My leg still hurts too!" David could see his boss chuckling him. "I don't suppose I get injury pay for that?" He called crossly across the corral.

Laughing, Rafe called back, "Nope, but I did request that Hank make you up that apple cobbler you love so much, for lunch today."

Whooping loudly, David dropped from the fence and limped toward the mess hall.

"He does realize lunch isn't for another four hours, right?" Brauman asked, watching the man hobble toward the hall.

The ranch hands all laughed as Rafe responded, "Yup. I suspect he's likely going to attempt to get a taste of the filling before it's baked." Feeling his phone vibrate in his pocket, he patted the Stallion one last time and stepped away. Striding toward the corral fence, he pulled the phone from his pocket. Noting it was Alaina he frowned, wondering why she'd be calling him.

"Yeah, Alaina. What's up?" Answering the call, he pulled himself up onto the fence rail and sat, kicking his legs around to the other side. There was silence on the other end. "Hello?" He prompted, poised where he sat.

"Rafe, its Inara."

His eyebrows lifted in surprise. "Well, hello Inara. To what do I owe this pleasure of your voice?" Rafe's voice dropped an octave.

"We're about to get an unexpected visitor." She sounded anxious.

Anxiety coiled unexpectedly in his gut. "Who?"

"That depends on who you ask." Inara grimaced as she spoke, really wishing she didn't have to be the bearer of bad news. "Formerly known as Agent Ricardo Pegueros of the CIA - he is now calling himself..." Inara's voice trailed off. She exhaled into the phone, almost afraid to tell him while watching Alaina's face register shock and fear.

"Yes?" He prompted her again, wondering why a former agent was about to pop up in their lives.

"Francesco Castillo."

A lead weight dropped in his gut. He somehow just knew it had something to do with Dante and Alaina. Dropping from the fence he strode away from the corral quickly so the ranch hands couldn't overhear.

"Are you kidding me with this?"

"I only wish I was."

"He's coming here? To the ranch?" Rafe asked incredulously. He had enough to deal with already - now this?

"Yes, but I don't think it was originally the plan if it's any consolation."

"Why do you say that?"

"Because originally Dartanian never went into town this morning."

"I see. And this man, who presumably knows Dante, is gonna run into Dart?"

"I believe so, yes."

"And do we know why Dart went into town if he wasn't meant to originally?" There was a pause on the other end of the phone as Inara cringed and scratched at her head in misery. She hated knowing that she was about to ruin the man's day.

"Because…"

"Because why, Inara?" He ground out.

"Because I have lice," she said in a small voice. "He went into town to get a bunch of lice treatment for everyone." She rushed on, covering her mouth upon finishing in distress.

"Did you say you have lice?" He asked with a short laugh, wanting to clarify what he'd heard. He most definitely had not anticipated her saying that. Scratching at his head, he realized what he was doing. Pulling his hand away he stared at it in dismay. What had initially seemed amusing had instantly become not so funny anymore.

"I'm sorry, Rafe. I'm so sorry." Inara practically wailed into the phone.

Shaking his head in order to clear it, he sighed heavily while trying to think. "Inara, do you know if Dart is okay?"

"I believe so but that's not your biggest worry right now."

"Why? What do you know that I don't?"

"I know who the people are that are chasing him, his wife, and son," she said quickly.

Groaning into the phone, he rubbed at his forehead in distress. "Okay, so he's not alone. How old is this kid? And who's chasing him and why?"

"About twenty months now." She could hear Rafe swear into the phone. "And, oh, you're really not going to like this Rafe, but Kobi Radford's men are the ones who are after him." Proceeding to explain why she then sat listening intently at the stunned silence on the other end of the phone. Suddenly, she could hear Rafe swearing like a drunkard in a bar.

"Rafe?" Inara called into the phone, trying to get his attention. "Listen it gets worse."

"Gee, Inara I cannot imagine how this could possibly get any worse! You got any idea who Kobi Radford is?"

"Oh, yes. Unfortunately, I know all too well. You know that." She managed to garner silence from him once again. Cringing, she leaned her head against the bathroom wall, while continuing to scratch at it. "What you don't know yet, is that he's the one after Alaina and her kid's."

"What? You mean the henchman who is after this Francesco?"

"No. Kobi Radford. You don't know, cause as the rule goes, the less everyone knows the better, right? That's why Dante never said anything. But Kobi's after them because Alaina's former husband is the one who shot and killed Kobi Radford's brother." This bit of news won Inara a startled look from Alaina. She cringed for she was fully aware Dante's new wife had not known that until now.

More swearing could be heard on the other end of the phone. "Alaina's husband was the one who killed Lionel Radford? Why not paint a dart board on our foreheads, Dante? Geez! That man's organization is vast! He's even found his way into Billings."

"I know," Inara cried. "Well, okay I didn't know the last part but I know the rest. It's why I'm calling to warn you. You have to get this out of your system now Rafe or you're going to blow it with Ricardo when he arrives."

Hearing him exhale into the phone, Inara breathed a heavy sigh, trying to dissuade her own anxiety. She felt horrible, for she knew it was her own fault that this was happening. If she hadn't gotten lice in her hair, Dartanian

271

would have never ventured into town today and might not have been seen by Ricardo.

"Rafe, I'm so sorry," she said meekly into the phone. Tears welled in her eyes as she bit at her fist.

Hearing her snuffling softly on the other end of the phone, Rafe closed his eyes, knowing full well she was blaming herself for what was happening. Feeling a soft breeze graze his cheek and pass his ear he sensed he was about to hear a voice on the wind.

Not her doing.

Short and brief, it gave him the knowledge he needed for the moment.

"Awe, honey, it's no one person's fault. Don't let this get to you. It's not a big deal."

"Isn't it?"

"Why don't you worry instead about the situation with Dartanian…"

"You know what?" Inara said angrily, her temper flaring. "Fine! Just forget it." Hanging up on him, she turned away from Alaina's curious gaze. Wiping away the tears now cascading down her cheeks in waves with a shaking hand, she spoke between sobs. "Can you give me a minute alone, please?"

Getting up from the floor Alaina stared down at Inara, initially confused. Feeling a warm sensation spread across her shoulder, she instantly understood the woman's pain.

"Oh, dear. I see." Deciding it might be best to give her a few minutes to compose herself Alaina stepped quietly from the bathroom out into the pool room. Her first thought was to go warn Dante what was about to happen until she heard a commotion coming from down the hallway near the kitchen. Realizing it was too late, she paused at the pool room doorway, listening to the exchange between Dartanian and Dante. Figuring it was best to let the men hash out their issues, she opted instead to go for a walk. Glancing down toward the far end of the pool, she opted to exit through the pool room doors leading out onto the back deck.

Rafe, on the other hand, was still staring down at his phone, wondering what in the world he'd said that had upset Inara so much. Clearly, she was mad for some reason but he couldn't fathom why. Growling in frustration he nearly flung his phone across the yard.

Chaos.

The word echoed in the air around him. Scoffing he rolled his eyes and raised his head to the sky above him. Dotted with white puffy clouds like billowing folds of melted marshmallow, he couldn't help but notice in his distress how beautiful the sight was.

"You think?" he said aloud, knowing he probably looked like an idiot to his ranch hands for talking to the heavens above him.

Just breathe.

Inhaling deeply, Rafe exhaled the same breath, repeating the process several times in quick succession.

"Patience and guidance, Lord. I'm going to need both today - in droves." He paced back and forth, attempting to determine the best way to handle things. Strolling back towards the corral, brow furrowed in thought, he gestured absently toward Teddy.

"Put Redemption back for now and make sure you have plenty of help doing it."

"Yes, Sir. Is everything okay Mr. Blackthorne? Anything I can help you with?" Teddy noticed his longtime employer's agitation. It was rare when the man ever showed such emotion.

Rafe tilted his head towards Teddy. "Your sister works at that cleaning service I use doesn't she?"

Resting his hands on the horn of his saddle Teddy responded with a nod. "Yup, but I believe she's off today."

"Do me a favor, will you? Give her a call and see if she'd be willing to come over and work today? Tell her I'll pay her the normal wage plus some. I have some extra cleaning needing to be done, more so than usual. And have her bring anyone else that might be off today." Rafe turned away and began heading for the house. "Oh, and Teddy," he called suddenly, spinning around.

"Yes, Sir?"

"Tell her to bring shower caps to wear."

"Uh, you say shower caps, Sir?" The man looked awful confused as he held his cell phone in hand in front of him, poised as though to make a call.

"Yes, apparently I have an epidemic of lice in my house." He shouted in annoyance, gaining raised brows from his ranch hands as he walked away.

Exchanging glances with each other Teddy and David turned and looked towards Brauman who had been standing near the gate of the corral, chewing on a piece of straw.

"Didn't he say something funny earlier about that woman's hair?" David asked under his breath as they continued to stare.

"Yup. Now how do you suppose he knew?" Teddy could see the young man grin back at them. They watched him shrug nonchalantly. Tapping the side of his boot on the gate post, Brauman then walked away without a backward glance.

Chapter 22

Dartanian pulled up to the ranch house in his Sheriff's cruiser, imagining different ways he would torture his brother once the situation had been dealt with. Having picked up Ricardo's lady friend, and his son from the hotel, they were now sitting in the back seat.

The introduction between them initially had been complicated when Dartanian realized she couldn't speak English. Knowing that Dante spoke fluent Spanish, Ricardo naturally presumed he would be able to understand Maria. Unable to speak anything more than broken Spanish at best, he'd been at a loss for what she was saying to him. When asked why he was pretending not to be able to understand her, he'd answered by saying that the Sheriff of Breckenridge County couldn't speak Spanish, so by extension, neither should he.

Ricardo had given him a funny look but had shrugged it off. Now sitting next to him in the front seat, the man stared out of the windshield in confusion as they pulled up to the house.

"Where in the world are you taking us, Franc? What is this place?"

"You saw the signage near the road didn't you?"

"Well, yeah. It said The Blackthorne Horse Ranch," Ricardo said as the woman introduced as simply Maria, exclaimed over the beautiful house in excitement.

Parking the car near the walkway up to the house Dartanian moved to get out. Feeling a hand take hold of his arm he stopped and turned back.

"Maria asked you if we're gonna be staying here. Are you gonna respond?" He asked darkly, from all appearances becoming cross.

"Sure, why not? We're short on rooms at the moment but knowing the way my dad is, no doubt he'll find a place for you all anyway." He shook his arm off as he got out of the vehicle. Popping the trunk, he grabbed half a dozen bags from within. "Help me out here, Francesco, will you? And by the way, you might want to full worn Maria that we have lice in the house."

"Lice?" Maria anxiously pulled her son protectively into her arms as she got out of the vehicle. Eyes widening in alarm she began speaking rapid-fire Spanish toward Ricardo.

Waving them on, Dartanian strolled along the walkway to the porch. "Follow me," he called while mumbling under his breath. "Sure, she knows the word lice but can't speak a hint of English."

"Uh, Franc, did you really say lice? And wait a minute…" The man was hollering now, sounding upset and confused all in one.

Turning around, Dartanian continued to walk backward towards the porch. He shook the bags in his hands for emphasis. "What is it, *Francesco*? I'm kind of in a hurry here."

Pointing towards the house Ricardo stared in awe. "Are you telling me this is your dad's house?"

In response, he shrugged his head towards the house. "What that? Yeah, for now. One day it'll go to my older brother though." Turning back around, he mounted the steps of the porch.

Dartanian let himself in, not bothering to wait for Ricardo - who was calling himself Francesco - and his woman and child. Striding quickly across the entryway towards the hallway near the kitchen, he wrestled with the bags to keep from dropping them as he walked.

"Good, you're back," Dante greeted while grabbing for the bags as his brother entered the kitchen.

"Yeah. No thanks to you, *Franc*." Dartanian growled under his breath intentionally using the wrong name. He dropped the bags on the counter rather than allowing his brother to take them from him. Striding toward the fridge he grabbed a root beer from within and pulled off its cap.

"What is your problem?"

"You know what? Why don't you ask your angel because I have more bags to get?" He didn't bother to conceal his animosity.

"Hola?" A thick male accented voice called from the entryway. "Franc, donde esta? Where'd you go? Whoa! This place is huge," Ricardo said as he crossed the entrance threshold. He was holding bags in his hands as he stared around him.

"In here, *Francesco*," Dartanian emphasized loudly. He gave his brother a dark meaningful look and took another drink of his root beer.

Dante's eyes nearly bugged out of his head at the familiar voice. Walking towards the hallway, he peered with dread around the corner just as Ricardo and Maria came into view with Javier in tow.

277

"Es muy bonita, mi amor," Maria exclaimed.

"Hey Franc, what do you want me to do with these?" Ricardo unwittingly extended the bags of lice treatment toward the real Dante as he walked towards him.

Dante's jaw clenched; a dangerous scowl fastening on Ricardo. Somehow he'd known he'd see him again, but he never imagined it would be like this; in his own home.

"What in the blazes are you doing here?" He roared, his eyes narrowing darkly upon Ricardo. "And who is this?" He gestured toward Maria and the boy, suspecting he already knew.

"What are you talking about Franc? I already introduced you to Maria, and stop yelling, or you're gonna frighten little Javier."

Chest heaving as it tightened with fear Dante's first natural instinct took over. Feeling threatened and afraid for Alaina and his children he reached swiftly around Ricardo, placing him in a choke hold effectively causing the man to drop the bags. Screaming wildly in Spanish, Maria became hysterical.

"Oy Dios, Ricardo! No me esposo! No, por favor!"

"Whoa, Dante, calm down." Drinian charged towards them from near the patio doors.

"What the heck is going on out here?" Breydon strolled into the kitchen from the movie room. He could hear the commotion over the movie he'd been trying to watch.

Turning her sons head into her shoulder, Maria continued to scream as she watched Dante take Ricardo to the ground; his face turning red through his tan. "Mi hijo esta aqui! Por favor, Senor, por favor! Oy Dios, Ricardo!"

"What are you doing here, Ricardo?" Dante shouted into the man's ear, ignoring the woman's cries. "Did you

278

tell them where I am? Did you tell them about my wife?" He growled as they struggled on the floor.

Grabbing at his arms Drinian tried desperately to pull his brother off of the man. "Stop it, Dante. Let him go, you're killing him."

"It looks like that's kind of the point," Breydon said, worried at how this was affecting the woman screaming in terror in the hallway.

Turning toward Dartanian, who was still drinking his root beer looking unconcerned, Drinian hollered at him. "Don't just stand there, help me out here Dart! You know we can't do it alone." Breydon had rushed over to help but it wasn't doing a lot of good. They needed another strong arm.

"*Fine!*" Dartanian vented, thumping his bottle on the table. "I suppose he does look like he's turning purple."

Between the three of them, they managed to yank their brother off of Ricardo. Gasping for air the man came up off the floor in a panic. Crawling backwards towards Maria he gestured for her to stay back, afraid for her and his child.

Staring wild-eyed up at the men in the hallway, Ricardo gaped at them as they held Dante back. Thinking he was seeing double he shook his head and blinked.

"What the... What's going on here?" He finally managed to choke out.

Maria slid to the floor, cradling her son in her arms as she cried.

"What are you doing here?" Dante raged, trying to get from his brothers grasp.

"This man here? Well now ... he was just passing through when he saw me." Dartanian explained for the poor shmuck hovering over his woman. "You see, he thought *I* was *you* outside one of the four drug stores I had to go to. Now being the smart man he is, he decided to pull a gun on me in my Sheriff's car." He gave his brother only a second to register what that meant before releasing his hold on him.

Dante surged forward, growling angrily at the news. He was just barely being restrained by Breydon and Drinian. "You pulled a gun on my brother? Thinking he was me?" He roared and attempted to get at Ricardo again.

"No wonder he wasn't helping you, Drin!" Breydon directed his next words toward Ricardo as he struggled to hold his brother back. "That was a pretty stupid move. You do realize he is the Sheriff of Breckenridge County, right?"

Pointing towards the two men Ricardo gaped. "But I thought you were... But you were actually *him*? Or, I mean ... you?"

"So, knowing your situation here, *Franc*," Dartanian continued harshly and with obvious sarcasm while ignoring Ricardo's blustering. "I figured I'd better find out who he was first. From what I gather - and let me see if I have this straight - the two of you used to work together for the CIA."

He circled his twin brother making the pretense of appearing thoughtful.

"I'm just guessing here but, I'd say in undercover special ops kind of work, and you got tired of it. Kind like what dad said about two months ago when you showed up here, Dante." Eyes gleaming with barely concealed anger Dartanian pointed towards him. "Now you both decided to go off grid - as they put it - and disappear. But here is the real kicker. Apparently, thinking it was funny, your buddy there decided to take up your old name, Franclin Kastle, as his new alias. Only in Spanish." He reached for his bottle while flipping a hand through the air.

"Is that why you... Are you *kidding* me?" Dante's face contorted angrily. "What are you, *stupid*?" He yelled at Ricardo, surging toward him again, barely being contained by Drinian and Breydon.

"A little help here?" Breydon called back at Dartanian.

"Nope, cause that's not all; it gets better." He paused a moment, noting the woman was still hysterical. Trying hard to remember his Spanish class from high school he finally spoke again, quickly attempting to calm the woman crumpled on the floor with his child-like broken Spanish. "Los siento, Senorita. I'm sorry. Tu y tu nino es seguro aqui en la casa. You and your son are safe here in this house." He gestured towards Ricardo. "That said, this idiot here ... well, apparently he didn't pay much attention to whose vehicle he was stealing in Chicago. Cause he - oh, and this is the funny part Dante - he stole the car of a drug lord's henchman with a whole bunch of drugs in the trunk without realizing it. They've been chasing him and his family there ever since," he finished while pointing towards Maria and the child.

With a feral growl and a strength born of pure rage, Dante surged from the floor and his brother's grasp, tackling Ricardo as he punched him.

"But don't worry *Franclin Kastle*, 'cause *Francesco Castillo* there was smart! He destroyed the drugs that belonged to that drug lord there - oh, what was his name again? Oh right! Kobi Radford!" Dartanian took a swig of his root beer again and watched with a dark glimmer in his eye as his twin brother's head spun towards him in shock. Turning back he proceeded to pummel Ricardo with renewed force.

"Are you serious with this?" Drinian asked in dismay.

Dartanian's eyes rolled heavenward. "I couldn't make this stuff up if I tried."

"Well, shoot, he deserves what he gets," Breydon said in disgust, shaking out his arms. He was relieved to not have to continue attempting to restrain his brother. There was no way they would have been able to keep it up anyway.

"Maybe, but *she* sure doesn't," Drinian said with real concern. He was worried for the woman sobbing on the floor with her crying child.

"I would agree," Rafe said from the patio doorway.

"Yeah, but dad, that guy there..."

"I am aware of the situation. I spoke with Inara not long ago and I heard everything just now. So, I'd say I understand his anger even more so than the rest of you." Walking swiftly toward the hallway where his son was still beating Ricardo, Rafe stood next to them with his arms crossing his chest. "I think that's more than enough," he said firmly.

Leaning back on his haunches, Dante breathed heavily. Wiping his brow with one hand, he stared up at him angrily. "But dad, he..."

"I *am* aware. Now expect you'll be hearing from me later on today for beating a man in front of his wife and child," he declared while gesturing toward the sobbing frightened woman on the floor. "You know better than that."

"I got your message Rafe, what did you... Whoa." Halting at the bottom of the stairs, Dr. Chase Ryans stared down upon the man crumpled and groaning on the floor. His face was swollen on one side and his lip was bloody from the beating he'd taken. "I see. That's what you need. Should I even ask?" He cautiously stepped around Dante and knelt down in front of the injured man.

"Do me a favor, Chase and patch him up if you can. I'm sure all will be explained shortly." Rafe stepped past

282

them, slowly making his way to the woman cowering in the hallway. His hands were outstretched so she'd see he meant her no harm.

"No, no, Senor! Por favor," she cried in alarm, her expression widening the closer he came. Gasping softly when she saw his face she eyed him cautiously. "Los piadoso ojos," she breathed on a sigh.

Well versed in Spanish, Rafe knew she'd just said he had Godly eyes. Smiling warmly at the woman, he extended his hand towards her.

"Los siento Senorita. You flatter me. Me llamo Rafe Blackthorne. I am the head of this house. The quarrel between my son and your husband is over. Any further issue will be dealt with in a gentlemanly manner rather than violently. You have my assurance." Speaking in Spanish and in a soothing tone, he explained to her the situation so that she would understand. Taking her hand in his, he helped her up with her son and led her into the kitchen for a glass of water and some juice for the boy. Kindly assisting her into her chair, he could tell she was grateful another person in the house spoke Spanish, as she crooned to her son in order to keep him calm.

"Tu esposo es muy estupido!" Dante declared darkly from the freezer door while shaking out his hand. Grabbing an ice pack from within, he placed it on his knuckles and leaned against the counter. "And I am truly sorry if I frightened you," he continued more gently in Spanish.

"Si, Senor," Maria said after a moment. Gazing over at Ricardo, who was being tended to on the floor in the hallway by Chase, she then peered back over at him. "Pero, el es mi esposo," she said then paused. A sad smile spread across her pretty features. "Le amo." She seemed to understand that her husband had done something seriously wrong but was expressing that she still loved him regardless.

"Of course you do," Rafe spoke once again in her language only to be abruptly cut off.

The sound of two boys running through the living room screaming about lice in their hair erupted into the relative quiet of the kitchen. Seconds later, Rafe's grandsons', Cody and Seth, sped into the kitchen. Their mother Hialey, trailed not far behind with two large containers of laundry detergent swinging in either hand as she shook them at her boys.

"Now that's enough caterwauling. We don't even know for sure you got it yet, so hush," Hialey said with heat. Peering around her she noted the Hispanic woman at the table with an adorable little boy who was sitting on her lap. Taking in Chase hovering over the battered man in the hallway, her husbands and Drinian's winded expressions, and the icepack on Dante's knuckles; she stopped mid-way through the kitchen doorway.

"All right. What did I miss?" She demanded as she thumped the laundry detergent on the counter. Placing her small hands on her tiny hips, she took up a determined stance. She really hated missing the entertaining stuff, and this had the look of being entertaining.

Chapter 23

"How is it Alaina and her kids didn't get this?"

Megorah sat at a kitchen bar stool near the counter as her husband and Crisalya attempted to comb through her hair. Wincing as Chase's lice pick tangled briefly in her hair, she expelled a relieved breath when he managed to dislodge it and continue pulling it through her hair.

"Probably because I have the habit of buying shampoo with Rosemary in it. Then I add Neem, Tea Tree, and Lavender oil to the bottles and mix it together really good. The little buggers can't stand the smell of the Neem oil, in particular, so they tend to avoid it. Plus, it's really good for your hair, so I put it in the kid's hair de-tangle spray too as a preventative measure." Scrunching her eyes together, Alaina opened them then blinked several times, wishing she had her new glasses already. Seeing the lice would be easier if she had them.

Feeling tired already from having to sit so long, Megorah rubbed at her forehead. She watched Inara's daughter, Lily, sitting impatiently near Rafe. The little girl swung her legs back and forth in front of her, as she beamed up at him with a bright smile. She was waiting to have her hair brushed through by him. He was presently working on little Rafe's hair. Megorah had been surprised at her father's insistence that he would take care of brushing out the hair of Inara's children. Little Tanian didn't seem to care one way or another, as he was in his own little world, but Lily and little Rafe had been ecstatic by her father's attention.

Inara was currently hiding in the pool room bathroom. She'd quietly accepted the box of lice treatment as it was handed into her by Alaina. After applying the treatment to her hair on her own she'd reluctantly accepted Hialey's offered help in combing through it. Tangled and in quite a disarray, it was taking a long time for her to get through it. So for the moment, she wasn't able to assist with her own children.

"All right little Rafe. I think we got what we can for now. It's time to give your sis a turn." Rafe squeezed the little boys shoulders gently and smiled down at him as he gestured toward Lily.

"Okay." Little Rafe hopped down from the kitchen chair.

"You too Tanian. There are no more." Alaina tapped the little boy on the shoulder, letting him know she was done with him.

"Yes!" Tanian exclaimed. The two boys happily sped off toward the playroom in order to find Saruman and Storman.

"I think I'll go see if I can help Hialey," Alaina told Rafe.

Casting a cautious look toward Megorah, he nodded in acknowledgement. "I'm sure your help would be appreciated. Oh, and Alaina? Please be sure to tell her there's no need to hide out in there any longer. I would like to see ... or rather, speak with her, that is." Rafe corrected himself quickly.

Frowning, Megorah huffed and turned away.

Alaina was grabbing a water bottle from the fridge before heading to the pool room when Hialey came slowly into the kitchen. Her movements were hesitant and her face was pale. She held something behind her back as though attempting to hide it.

"What's up?" Dante called across the room. She looked as though she wanted to fall through the floor. He was currently working on Katana as he stood next to Dartanian who was brushing through Lylia's hair.

"How bad is it Hialey?" Lylia asked, genuinely sounding concerned.

Drinian peered over at her. "You look like you've seen a ghost or something."

"Ouch," Veta cried out suddenly. Her hand shot up to her left ear.

"Oops. Sorry Honey." Drinian apologized, having just run the pick into her ear. Bending down he kissed his wife gently near her injury and nuzzled her.

Pausing in what he was doing, Rafe stared at her when she didn't respond. "Hialey?" He was becoming concerned by her silence and dazed expression.

Clearing her throat, she finally spoke. "I think it best to leave Inara alone for a while," she said in a hoarse voice.

"Why?" Royce asked.

Breydon looked at his wife, bemused by her unusually silent demeanor. "Speak up Honey. What's going on?"

Pulling her arm from behind her back Hialey extended the shaking hand. Within it held one of the lice combs which was currently tangled in a knotted mass of reddish blonde hair; easily a two-foot length of it dangled from the comb.

Letting loose a long whistle as several of the women gasped in horror, Rafe stepped around the counter and took the length of hair in hand. Closing his eyes he cringed internally, knowing full well how the loss of her hair was probably affecting Inara right now, after everything else that had happened.

Covering her mouth briefly, Veta exclaimed from the table near the patio porch. "What happened?" She gaped in dismay, her green eyes bulging.

Everyone else had stopped what they were doing upon seeing the long length of hair now laying across Rafe's hands rather than on the back of Inara's head. Placing it gently on the counter next to him, he slowly returned to the other side of the counter to his task. His expression was pensive.

Croaking out a response Hialey explained. "It got caught and I couldn't get it untangled. The more I worked at it the more it just seemed to get worse. It got to a point where I had no choice but to … to cut her hair."

"How long is it now?" Breydon exchanged looks with his father and brothers. They all knew full well that the loss of a woman's hair could often time be traumatizing for them. They'd seen it before with their own mother, Lilyandhi.

Hialey lifted her free hand up to her shoulders and Megorah gave a startled gasp while covering her face with her hands. Moaning softly she shook her head. "Oh, that could have been me."

"Needless to say she's more than a little bit upset right now. I mean, she understands it's no one's fault but obviously…" Voice trailing off, Hialey expelled an uneasy breath. "Well, it was really long hair after all," she finished quietly.

Lylia patted Katana's leg as the girl started to cry next to her. It had been discovered that she had been experiencing problems with the itching for the past two weeks. Since she'd been reading in the same places as what Inara had been sleeping for the past several days, Inara had likely picked it up from the blankets Katana had also curled up in.

"It's all my fault! If I'd just said something sooner." Katana snuffled softly.

"It's no one's fault." Lylia tried to reassure her. "These things just happen sometimes and we have no control over them."

"Lylia is right Honey. That said; I believe there are a couple lady's in my household who owe her apologies." Chase direct his gaze towards his daughter, then down at his wife. "Wouldn't you agree, Meg?"

Slapping her hands on the counter before her Megorah pursed her lips in aggravation. "Yes, Katana. You should apologize," she said between her teeth, unwilling to admit to any wrongdoing.

Staring at the back of his wife's head Chase narrowed his gaze on her and stopped what he was doing. When he'd awoken that morning he'd been really looking forward to his day off and spending time with his family. The last thing he'd anticipated was having to patch up a half-beaten man and having to comb through lice-infested hair. Let alone dealing with a selfish wife who couldn't see past her own nose.

"Why are you stopping?"

"You know what? I'm done," Chase said becoming testy. He placed the lice comb on the counter and started walking away.

Grabbing at her hair Megorah gave him a startled look. "Wait, what? You haven't even done the left side."

"Nope. I haven't and I'm not going to."

"Why?"

"Because you displayed some pretty horrible behavior earlier today with Inara; in front of your daughter too. It made Katana think she couldn't come to us about it as a result, which is unacceptable. Now until you can get your head around that fact and come around to the realization that you also owe Inara an apology, then I'm not touching it. No one else should either."

Megorah called after him as he walked away but disappeared up the stairwell.

Rafe eyed his eldest daughter closely. "What exactly did you say to her?" Turning his attention to Lily's hair, he was relieved to see there weren't many nits in it but up around her bangs and near her ears. Dipping the comb into the boiling water near the stove after drawing it through her pretty locks, he wondered briefly if Inara would continue to keep coloring her hair now that it was shorter. Or if she'd let the silver and gold return to it like it was in her daughter's hair for he thought it was actually quite pretty.

"Nothing worth mentioning." She refused to look at her father in the eye. Instead, she turned to her sister. "You'll still comb through it though, right?"

Fidgeting uneasily next to her, Crisalya played with the lice comb in her hand, trying to avoid her own husband's grim stare. Becoming exasperated at being placed in the middle she slammed the comb on the counter.

"Royce, I cannot just let her sit with the stuff in her hair. We have to get the lice out of the house or it's going to spread. That has to take precedence." She met his eyes with an impudent stare of her own.

From the corner of the room near the patio, Ricardo groaned next to his wife Maria, having overheard the entire conversation.

"Not that I'm sure any of you care about my opinion but she's got a fair point there." Ricardo's voice sounded muffled. He was holding a wad of tissue against his nose and an ice pack to his blackened eye.

"Ricardo has a point about Crisalya's point." A soft small voice said from the hallway. Inara padded self-consciously into the kitchen, gaining everyone's attention. Her strawberry blonde hair fell in large waves about her face. Hialey had clearly attempted to shape it by adding layers and trimming it to frame her face.

Dartanian noted her deep blue eyes appeared larger and more than a little sad. It was obvious she'd been crying and was attempting to put up a brave front, but her gaze caught on the length of hair lying on the counter. Her face screwed up in the same way Lylia's did when she'd get overly emotional, and it made Dartanian want to reach out and hold her. Hands flexing at his sides his fingers itched to touch someone. Any woman. As his own wife was closest he took Lylia about the shoulders and bent forward, kissing her on the forehead, holding her tighter than what he might normally.

"Ouch, Dart. Not so hard." Lylia said, flinching at the feel of his fingers digging into her shoulders. Staring up at him she realized he was gazing longingly at Inara and it startled her. Becoming worried at his response she realized that with the shorter hairstyle Inara reminded him more of her.

Taking hold of Dartanian's hand in order to gain his attention Lylia managed to divert his eyes from Inara back to her. "Dart, Honey - the hair, please. Can you finish?" she asked sweetly. She took hold of his other hand attempting to ground him. His gaze locked with his wife's, Dartanian shook his head, grateful for the distraction.

"You need to finish her hair, Cris." Inara said quietly, "don't just leave her sitting like that." Tentatively, she stepped toward the fridge nearest to her, which happened to be the one right next to Rafe. Catching his eye she glanced away quickly, then peered over at Dartanian with a look of disappointment on her face, as she reached for the refrigerator door handle. He'd returned to his task and she noted was no longer looking at her.

"Inara…" Rafe began only to be interrupted.

"I just came for something to drink," she said quickly. She looked pale, though her cheeks were tinged with color. Finding a bottle of water in the fridge, she closed the door. "I really need to talk to you Lylia. It's … it's important. Please come see me when you're done," she said in a hollow voice, then walked quickly away back down the hall without saying another word.

The silence that followed lasted barely a moment when Ricardo spoke once again. "Is it my imagination or does that sister of yours, Lylia, look like she's been kicked in the teeth?"

Frowning at Ricardo's assessment Rafe combed through Lily's hair one last time, not bothering to correct his error where Lylia and Inara were concerned.

"I think your good Lily," Rafe said finally. "There wasn't much there, to begin with. We'll check it again later."

Hopping down from her chair Lily beamed up at him then reached out and gave him a huge hug. Thank you…" Lily faltered, as though she were about to say something else. Smiling up at him she continued shyly while giggling.

"Thank you, Rafe." Fleeing from the room the girl headed toward the playroom.

"Inara's not my sister," Lylia said quietly after a moment, gazing up at Dartanian. "At least, I don't think she is."

Confused, Ricardo looked at Lylia then glanced furtively around the room, his gaze falling on Dante. "What in the world is going on here, Franc? And how can your sister-in-law here not know whether or not her identical twin is her sister?"

Groaning Dante bowed his head in frustration. "Just let it go, Ricardo."

"Yeah but…"

"Drop it, Ricardo." Dante scowled toward him. Seeing his brother put his lice comb down, he observed as Lylia got up and moved toward the living room. "I'd imagine Inara's in the downstairs library, Lylia," he offered, trying to gauge whether she intended to go see her as requested.

"Good for her." Lylia banged her way through the kitchen door into the living room.

Rafe and Dante exchanged looks across the kitchen, managing to gain Ricardo's quizzical gaze. Aggravated and trying hard not to show it, Rafe inhaled deeply and headed towards the stairwell, gesturing for Ricardo to follow.

"Come Ricardo and bring your pretty wife and son. Let's see what I can do for you, in order to get you somewhere safe." He repeated himself in Spanish so Maria could understand. With the most immediate issue of lice having been dealt with, he could now move on to the other problem he had. And he knew he needed to move quickly where Ricardo and his wife were concerned. The sooner he got the couple and their child out of Montana and into Canada the better. He figured the best way to accomplish

293

it was by way of the second plane his family was unaware of. Housed at another hanger in another name, he needed only to reach his other pilot and convince him to fly the couple and their child to safety.

Rafe knew the last thing he needed was Kobi Radford's henchmen finding their way into town, let alone showing up on his doorstep. Even with the relocation of Ricardo's family, Rafe was aware the henchmen would likely still find their way into town. But it was important to him that the trail ended there. Silently praying for the chaos to end soon he rubbed at his face wearily as he ascended the stairs. Rafe was starting to become overwhelmed by the many issues, which seemed to keep creeping up on him, while he was still trying to run and maintain his horse ranch.

Beaming at the handsome Blackthorne patriarch's back as he disappeared, Maria quickly followed behind him and Ricardo. She carried her son Javier with her, cooing at him softly as she went.

Chapter 24

Twenty-four hours later Inara was still attempting to pin down Lylia. The woman had managed to evade her since the day before and it was starting to wear on her nerves. Knowing full well she might not have a whole lot of time left to be able to reach Lylia, she was becoming anxious.

Learning at breakfast that Lylia had left with Kayla to go shopping, Inara hadn't been able to eat much. When lunchtime had rolled around and she hadn't returned home Inara had skipped lunch entirely, opting instead to hole up in the library and read as her anxiety grew. Her inability to get the woman to sit down and talk with her was making her more than a little nervous. She knew she was running out of time and she couldn't go looking for her in town because she still wasn't allowed off the property.

Hearing Lylia arrive home around three that afternoon, Inara had ventured out of the library in the hopes of gaining an audience with her. Finding her in the middle of a heated discussion with Dartanian over her many purchases she'd opted to wait until later to try and catch her.

Tired of worrying on the subject she'd finally sat down and prayed, giving it up to God. She knew it would happen in His time. Absorbed in her prayer, it wasn't until she'd finished that she'd become aware of her surroundings. The wonderful aromas of a dinner being prepared in the kitchen wafted down the hall into the library, prompting her to sniff with appreciation at the air.

Her stomach growled ravenously.

If she wasn't mistaken it was barbeque chicken she smelled. The scent was heavenly, lifting her mood slightly. Inara had been in a funk much of the day as the result of the previous day's disappointments and the loss of her long lustrous locks. She hadn't eaten much during the day and she woke late that morning to her children's prodding arms. The nightmares had kept her up much of the night once again.

Though hating the notion of an audience she decided the best time to speak with her might well be at dinner time. Inara placed a bookmark in the book she'd been feverishly reading since last night and laid it on the loveseat she'd been sitting on. Stretching her arms and legs, she yawned, picked the Bible back up and headed down the hallway, hoping to catch her in the kitchen. She wasn't really looking forward to making an appearance in front of everyone but recognized it was necessary under the circumstances. Inara knew she might not get another chance before bedtime. Lylia had the habit of disappearing into her room after dinner to read.

Feeling naked not having her hair flinging out about her arms and waist as she walked, Inara tried to get past it as best she could. Discovering the families were already seated and appeared to have been eating for a while she became timid. No longer worried about the loss of hair she instead felt alienated from the rest of the household. Not even her children had said anything to her about dinner having started already. She was feeling very much like an intruding outsider. Figuring she'd escape back the way she came she turned to leave only to be halted by Dante's voice.

"There's a seat open at the end of the table if you'd like to join us," he offered, gesturing towards the opposite end of the table where his father was sitting. He hadn't even realized Inara wasn't present until then and felt guilty for it. Sensing her reticence at joining them he peered down the table towards his father, wondering at why he hadn't said anything.

Glancing in the same direction Inara noticed Rafe seated at the very end. Looking her way he beckoned for her to join them but didn't say anything or seem inclined to encourage her further. To his right was an empty seat between him and Dartanian. She immediately shook her head and stammered a response.

"Thank you, no. I'm not hungry." Inara said, eliciting a concerned frown from Rafe. He suspected she was hungry and was sure he hadn't seen her at lunchtime.

"Don't be absurd. You haven't really eaten all day," Megorah confirmed, giving her an odd look. She could sense Inara's anxiety increasing and could tell she was extremely uncomfortable. Wondering why she paused in her eating and stared.

"It's quite alright." Lylia spoke up, gaining everyone's attention. Pushing away from the table she took her half-eaten plate of food in her hand and moved towards the kitchen counter and sink. "I'm done. I need to finish packing anyways."

"Why are you packing?" Dartanian asked suddenly, turning in his seat toward his wife.

"You know full well why. We talked about this earlier today. Stop trying to pretend this isn't happening. I'll be out of your way by morning. Breydon said he'd have the papers ready by Monday." Lylia's voice caught as she scraped her remaining food in the trash, rinsed her dishes, and opened the dishwasher to place them inside. Then she turned towards Inara and faced her head on. "Just do me a favor and take good care of him, all right?" Her face had been washed clear of makeup from earlier in the day and her eyes were puffy, as though she had been crying at some point. Wiping her damp hands on the back of her pants she attempted to move past Inara towards the stairwell all the while looking completely defeated.

Rolling her eyes to the heavens Inara exploded. "Oh, for the love of might! That's it! I've had it! You and I are gonna have it out right now." Grabbing hold of Lylia's arm forcefully she jerked her towards the hallway leading to the living room.

"There's nothing to say to each other."

"You may have nothing to say to me, Lylia Blackthorne, but I sure have a lot to say to you," she vented angrily, pulling her along unwillingly towards the living room. "Get in there. Now! Or we can have it out in front of everyone, including your daughter."

"You wouldn't dare…"

"Wouldn't I?" Inara gritted her teeth. "Might I remind you that in the past five days I have lost my supposed husband, been uprooted from my home and lost everything in my possession but my children. I've discovered that everything I was writing about was true, learned I'm part of a prophecy, and been assaulted by demons in an attempt to knock me unconscious, choke me, and drown me in order to scare me off. I've been accused of being pregnant with triplets, gotten lice in my hair, for the first time in my life mind you, and subsequently lost more than half my hair all because I didn't have a brush. And I'm still wearing the same clothes I had on since Monday! I have long past lost my patience with everyone here who seems to think they know what my purpose is in being here but in truth hasn't even a clue. Do you honestly think I give one iota whether you get a little bit humiliated?"

Recovering quickly from being thoroughly chastised Lylia's deep blue eyes, so similar to Inara's, darkened with animosity as she flung her arm out of her grasp.

"I've no doubt you've never once cared about what happened to me and how I felt about any of this at all," Lylia shouted. Her raised voice startled everyone, making it obvious she was losing her patience and temper. Normally a quiet woman with an easy disposition her fighting stance and flaring expression were unusual.

Inhaling deeply as her own face flamed with exasperation and righteous anger, Inara shouted back at the blonde headed woman before her. But for the color of their hair, their appearances mirrored each other aside from the freckles on Inara's face and added weight.

"Lylia Eve Minnosa-Blackthorne if I didn't love you so much I wouldn't even be here right now. You are the reason I am here in the first place." Inara shot back surprising everyone. "I'm not here for Dart. This has never been about your husband. It has always been about you," she finished crossly. Her eyes softened with pity as she looked upon the woman who could be her twin sister.

Lylia stared back at her in confusion though her eyes became wary. "What are you talking about?"

Inara moved down the hallway and into the living room, forcing Lylia to follow behind her in order to gain answers. Anxious, completely distressed, and unsure where to start; Inara pleaded out loud for assistance.

"Dear Lord Jesus please guide my words and thoughts. Help me to do this. I don't know how to do this!" The thought of failing at this task scared her. If she didn't do this right, if she screwed this up with Lylia then she knew it would ruin everything. But she knew she had to try and hoped and prayed that she was truly ready to do that which someone else had done for her.

She, Inara RavenCroft, was but one of billions of people in the world. She couldn't understand why God would set this task upon her of all people; a screw up with two failed attempts at marriage and an inability to complete anything she'd ever started.

Voicing her prayer aloud she raised her head to the ceiling above her in distress. "Why me Lord? Why'd you have to put this on me?" Tears were streaming down her cheeks and she turned to Lylia, her chest heaving with the panic she was experiencing.

Because you are ready came a voice near Inara's ear.

She had been praying about this moment since bedtime the night before. It was the first time Inara heard Gods voice until then. The weight upon her heart was great and she honestly didn't know if she was in fact ready. She was new to this herself. How could she possibly make a difference?

Not realizing she'd voiced the query aloud Inara heard the same soft voice speak near her opposite ear.

Anyone can make a difference if they choose to.

Flustered, yet believing in God's wisdom she began rambling to herself in an attempt to calm her quaking heart.

Lylia gawked at the woman pacing wildly before her. "What's the matter with you?" Inara looked slightly nuts which merely solidified Lylia's belief that she just couldn't do it. She couldn't allow herself to be like this woman.

Stopping in front of the fireplace Inara peered around the room, blinking back tears, then looked Lylia directly in the eye. "I know," she said firmly.

"You know what?" Lylia expounded loudly in exasperation. "What do you think you know?"

Shaking her head back and forth Inara returned to her pacing but kept her gaze upon her never wavering. "I know, Lylia."

Suddenly appearing anxious herself, Lylia fidgeted, eyeing the closed divider between the living room and kitchen. "I don't know what it is that you think you know, but it's got nothing to do with this and I'd appreciate it if you'd just drop it."

"I can't. You know I can't. And on the contrary, it's got everything to do with this." she exclaimed. The hand holding the Bible made a circle in the air encompassing her gesture toward the kitchen as well as the two of them. "You've seen the prophecy yourself. You know full well it's about you, and I think you now know what's supposed to happen here. So why are you fighting it? We are not so dissimilar," she asked desperately. The bright evening sunlight gleamed through the open windows as fresh air wafted into the living room. Streaks of light bounced off the lamps and couch cushions giving an almost surreal feel to the room.

"That's absurd. We're nothing alike; aside from appearances that is, and nothing bad has ever happened to me. So it can't be about me. I really don't know what you're talking about."

"That's not true and you know it."

Shaking her head in denial Lylia's face became pinched and drawn.

"Don't do that. You know full well what I am referring to. You think not voicing it aloud makes what happened to you any less real? Any less painful than what happened to me, Alaina, Veta or Megorah?" Inara's gaze narrowed on her as she moved steadily toward Lylia. "A woman doesn't have to be raped to feel the sting of betrayal from a man."

Gasping, Lylia covered her face with her hands. "Don't. Please don't do this."

"Does he even know about your former fiancée?" She pointed toward the kitchen where she knew Dartanian sat listening. "Did you ever tell him why you chose to transfer to Montana University in order to complete your senior year of College?"

The silence between them was deafening.

"Secrets, Lylia," Inara said quietly. Placing a hand to her upset belly she exhaled slowly. "They fester within us, eating at our insides; our soul, and they often times prevent us from being the person we want to be. The *Christian* we want to be," she emphasized, noting Lylia's face blanching at the statement.

Crying, Lylia stamped her feet in distress. "Stop it, please," she begged.

"It's fear, isn't it? That's what it is. I get it Lylia. I understand better than what you can possibly imagine. The fear. It's got you all tied up inside and it's making it almost impossible to let go and surrender yourself to His will."

"His will. You mean God?"

"Yes," Inara practically shouted. "Lylia, don't do what I did over twenty years ago," she exclaimed becoming desperate. She knew they could all hear her. The whole

Blackthorne family was listening intently from the kitchen and the notion of having to admit what she was about to, was twisting her up in knots. But she also knew that the only way to reach her was to voice her own pain.

"What has twenty years ago for you got to do with me now?" Lylia gave her a questioning look. Seeing the fear in her eyes, she imagined she had the same look upon her own face and latched onto it, hoping desperately to turn things around. "You were here once before weren't you?" Lylia accused, voicing her suspicions. "I was right. I told Dart as much. You were here in Montana twenty years ago and you were supposed to meet Dart then but instead…"

"No! Oh, Lylia," Inara wailed. "Yes! Okay? Yes, I was here in Montana twenty years ago and I ran into one of the Blackthorne's then, although I'm sure he has no recollection of that. He was preoccupied with other matters at the time. But that's a separate situation and has nothing to do with Dart." She paused briefly shaking her head. "No that's not true. It does … but it doesn't."

"That makes no sense. How can you say it has nothing to do with my husband? You were supposed to meet him and…"

"Okay stop!" Inara said firmly, halting anything more from Lylia's mouth with a raised hand. Taking a trembling breath, her lips shook as tears swam in her eyes. "The point is I was here, and in the end, I made a hasty decision in a moment of fear. Because of me, everything got messed up. It's my fault, don't you understand? Everything got messed up because of me and I lost my chance at happiness. I was supposed to be here but I made a choice. I could stay and fulfill that which I was brought here to see come to pass. Or I could go back home and not have to subject myself to that which I feared the most. I knew, you see, but I didn't understand at the time what that meant

303

until now. So I buried my gift deep within and pretended it wasn't there." Hiccupping loudly, she cried softly as she laid a trembling hand across her mouth. Her eyes shifted furtively toward the divider then closed in remorse.

"What did you fear the most?" Lylia asked, her curiosity getting the better of her. Somehow inside her, she knew it was the same fear she had.

"Rejection."

Eyes flashing toward the divider Lylia's face filled with emotion and brimmed with tears. Sniffling loudly her hand began to tremble as she began to shake. A soft whimper escaped her lips as her gaze shifted from the divider back to Inara.

Fumbling with her words, Lylia inquired, "If you had stayed, do you think you would have been rejected? That is, do you believe…"

"You're asking if I believe whether or not I would have been accepted for who I was at the time." Knowing full well what it was that Lylia was truly asking of her, Inara's head bowed in distress.

"Yes," Lylia said in a small voice, afraid of the answer.

"I don't know." Inara wailed, tears falling from her own eyes. "I don't have a time capsule. We make choices sometimes, allowing fear to rule us in the moment. We forget to think about what our purpose is. What greater good can come from our decisions or who can be affected or hurt by them."

Weeping openly Lylia dropped down in the chair next to her. Bent forward as though in agony she clutched one hand to her heart feeling as if it were about to burst.

"What I do know," Inara continued as she knelt down next to Lylia and took her shaking hand in hers. "Is that there is an entire family in that kitchen right now that has been affected by that decision of mine - two men in particular. If I had stayed maybe none of them would have suffered through the millennium as they did."

"There's no way of knowing that for sure," Lylia offered kindly through her tears, seeing the pain and remorse in the other woman's eyes.

"I know but that's just it. It's in the past. We can't go back. There is no way of knowing for sure. Shoot. If I'd been here like I was supposed to be, then you might never have been in this position now."

"I don't understand." Wiping at her face Lylia reached for a tissue from the nearby stand.

"Because, we would have met way back then, rather than now and we would have talked about you not being a Christian that much sooner."

Chapter 25

In the kitchen, Dartanian sat in stunned silence amongst his family. Inara's last words rang in his ears. Mouth agape his silverware dropped from his hands onto the table as he peered over at his brother Breydon in surprise. They stared at each other and for what felt like the hundredth time since she'd arrived he wanted his brother to shake his head no. To denounce the words Inara spoke as being a lie rather than truth.

Dartanian's face fell when he saw his brother exhale slowly and shift his gaze away. The undeniable truth of her words was startling. But how? How was it possible after nearly seven years of marriage that he could have not known his own wife was not a Christian?

"I don't understand," he mumbled softly, not wanting to be overheard by the women in the living room. "We attend church. She's involved with the women's ministries and she reads the Bible regularly." He turned his gaze towards his father. "Lylia even teaches the children Bible stories."

"There's more to being a Christian than simply going through the motions," Dante replied instead, gaining his brother's attention. "You know that."

"Yes but I thought... She said she was."

"Dart, did she actually tell you she was a born-again Christian? Or did you assume she was because she attended church and was going through the motions?" Drinian asked in a low voice.

After meeting his brother's gaze he stared down at the table while shaking his head. "I'm not sure. I don't recall. Did you know?" He turned towards his father, imploring him for the truth.

Giving his head a small shake Rafe clasped his hands together before him as he bowed his head. "No. I did not know that was part of her issue. Though it would explain a lot." Sighing softly he rested his brow against his fore fingertips briefly then raised his head to look around at the rest of his family. "I thought Inara was here to help Lylia surrender her fears over our family's gifts." He chose his words carefully. He could hear Lylia crying quietly from the other side of the divider and suspected from the soothing sounds Inara was making that she was trying to ease her fears.

"The important thing right now is to remember that we love her regardless and to not judge her," Veta said firmly next to Drinian. "Clearly the fact that she's a non-Christian living amongst a Christian family is distressing to her for some reason. I wonder why?"

"She was extremely afraid of our finding out," Megorah said quietly, looking troubled. "But why? She knows we'd never judge her. Doesn't she?" She shifted her gaze to her sister. Crisalya simply shrugged and shook her head.

"I guess I always just assumed she was one," Crisalya whispered in reply.

"What I don't understand is why Lylia never told Dart she'd been engaged before, and who was it that Inara saw twenty years ago?" Hialey was talking unnaturally quiet for her. She peered curiously around the table at the Blackthorne men, her gaze settling on Dartanian who shifted uncomfortably in his seat.

The fact that Lylia wasn't a Christian only bothered Hialey in that she'd wished she'd known so they could have talked about it together. What did bother her was that she had felt so embarrassed and afraid to say anything to any of them about it. Hialey began wondering if she'd said or done something over time that might have led Lylia to think she was prejudiced in some way against those who didn't believe in God. She didn't have long to wait for her answer. Moments later they could all hear Inara begin speaking again, trying to get Lylia to calm down and talk to her.

"Do you honestly think your family is going to love you any less just because you haven't surrendered your life to God?" Inara asked kindly, being sure to keep her voice gentle and nonjudgmental.

Laughing between sobs Lylia grabbed another tissue and dabbed at her nose, blowing it loudly seconds later. "This whole family - the Blackthorne's, Howard's and Ryans - they're all born again Christian's. What would they possibly want with a non-Christian in their midst?"

"Oh, Lylia. You've spent so much time in church, listening to God's word, reading about it and even teaching it."

"That's just it. I've done it all. I have," she wailed. "I try to be this person for them; for Dart, a good person and a God-fearing woman who loves the Lord."

Laying a hand against her arm Inara interrupted her. "Lylia, do you believe in God?"

"Well, yes of course I do. I wouldn't go to church if I didn't believe there was a God." Dabbing at the tears streaking down her face she could feel the heat crawling up her neck from embarrassment. "And I guess, if I were to be honest, I didn't fully understand that I wasn't one until a few nights ago at the dinner table when you said what you did. Though I had suspected."

A warm sensation filled Inara's heart lighting within her a spark of hope. "Lylia Honey, all is not lost for you've got the first requirement down all ready. Romans 10:9 says, 'That if thou shalt confess with thy mouth the Lord Jesus and shall believe in thine heart that God hath raised him from the dead, thou shalt be saved.'"

"What does that mean? Inara, you're quoting the King James Bible; I've never been able to disseminate what the verses are saying."

Thinking quickly she switched to a simpler version she'd learned as a child, hoping she was recalling it accurately. "If you confess that Jesus is Lord and believe that God raised him from death, you will be saved. So basically, to start with, you have to believe in God. As you've said you do. You're already on the right track, for that is the most fundamental requirement of becoming a Christian."

Managing to gain a half smile from Lylia and a nervous laugh, Inara grinned openly. "And just so we cover the second part of that, do you believe that Jesus is your Lord and Savior and that He died to wash away your sins?"

Blinking, Lylia laughed nervously as she shook, feeling silly and stupid to have to be asked the very questions she often asked of the children during Sunday school classes. "Yes, I've always known that. I really do believe He died on the cross in order to save me from my sins," she said almost urgently, as though desperate for those listening to believe it.

Inara beamed at her through her tears, "Well, then Honey, your more than half-way there. You've already begun the journey and you're crossing that bridge as we speak."

Fresh tears streamed down both their faces as they could be heard actually laughing together as they cried. After a moment their giggling dissipated and the mood became serious again.

"I know what's holding you back," Inara said finally. Hands trembling in her lap she stared at them momentarily before peering up at Lylia's face through her wet lashes. "I bet it's the same thing that held me up until recently."

Head jerking up Lylia gazed at Inara in surprise. "Recently? When…"

"January, of this year."

In the kitchen, Rafe's brow rose curiously at Inara's admission. Dismissing the rest of the children from the kitchen he shifted in his chair and set back, placing his napkin on the table. He was no longer hungry. Somehow he had a strong feeling the timing was significant and he could tell Royce might well be thinking along the same lines. Exchanging looks his gaze shifted down the table towards his son Dante and their eyes met.

Back in the living room Lylia appeared startled. "But I thought you were like Veta. That you'd been a Christian for a long time."

"Oh, Lylia. I was asked the questions as a child and I surrendered myself to Him then, but I had no real understanding of what it meant to be a Christian until I grew older. Especially to be a Christian with a discerning gift from God," Inara said nervously She paused momentarily, feeling drained yet somehow knowing an angelic presence was nearby urging her on, even though she couldn't see it. Taking a deep breath she continued, her lashes fluttering in the golden light of the sun shining through the windows upon her.

"The Blackthorne children were lucky. They were fortunate to have been blessed with someone in their lives who understood a little about what they were going through. There was no one else like me in my family who was capable of what I was. At least, none that would admit to it and any time I shared what I had come to know without knowing why, I simply sounded crazy to them. People would look at me funny and whisper about me. So I stopped listening to the voice at my side and I started ignoring the knowledge that came to me."

Shifting uneasily in her seat Inara tilted her head to one side as she watched the particles of dust twirling in the beams of light surrounding her. Bowing her head she toyed with the tissue between her fingers.

"So, not having the proper guidance at a crucial point in my life and not understanding that I needed to be tenaciously seeking a relationship with God by reading His word, I found myself simply going through the motions just like you. It happens to a lot of people. They become born again Christians at an early age then fall away from God for one reason or another. But it doesn't mean they cannot find their way back. In my case, well... I made a bad choice at a very pivotal point in my life." Struggling to continue she became choked up and began to cry. "Unfortunately I now know and understand that it had a rippling effect on many people's lives. Without meaning to I allowed my own fears to hurt people I loved and that's why I'm here to warn you."

"Warn me of what exactly?" Lylia asked anxiously. She avidly stared at Inara who was bathed by the light of the sun washing over her through the windows.

"Don't fall into the same trap I did. Don't allow the shadowy voices of doubt to get you to make a hasty decision. Don't allow the fear to prevent you from doing what you know in your heart and your mind is right."

"Which is?"

"Romans chapter ten, verse ten goes on to say that, 'For it is by our faith that we are put right with God; it is by our confession that we are saved', which means that you must be able to admit that you're a sinner and repent of those very sins."

Fidgeting Lylia's gaze shifted uneasily. "What if the sin in question is so painful you can't bear to admit it aloud? What if you're too embarrassed or ashamed to admit them to anyone?"

"Your problem is that you assume you have to speak them aloud and that everyone must know what they are." Inara pointed toward her with a hand fisted around a tissue of her own. "I thought the same thing. You don't have to tell the whole world of your sins. If asked, don't lie of course, but the only being who needs to hear you voice them is God."

They stared at each other, both knowing full well Inara was aware of what Lylia was worried about. "Honey, *He* already knows what our sins are," she prompted, pointing toward the ceiling.

"I know, it's just... What do I tell people when they ask?" Her gaze flitted toward the divider anxiously. "Because you know they're all going to want to know why."

"Listen to me. Absolution comes from God. Not people. That said, there is one person who I do believe does need to hear this; who deserves to hear this."

"No, no. I can't." Shaking her head violently, Lylia stood abruptly as though ready to flee. "He'll never look at me the same way again."

Standing quickly Inara called after her before she could bolt. "Are you really going to allow this to prevent you from having that which you and Dartanian both want the most?"

Skidding to a halt near the foyer, Lylia turned on her heels, staring at Inara incredulously. The full breadth of her meaning was obvious to even those sitting quietly in the kitchen, eavesdropping rather than eating.

"Are you telling me that in order for Dartanian and I to have children together that I have to tell him everything I've ever done wrong in my life?"

Sighing heavily Inara shook her head. "Awe Lylia. You don't have to share with him every single little thing you might have done since the moment of your birth. That's not what I'm saying. Sometimes there are some things that can be kept between you and God."

Relief washed across her face then disappeared mere seconds later at Inara's next statement.

"But you do need to tell him about that which applies to here and now and you know what I am referring to."

"Why?" Lylia wailed. Renewed tears washed over her. "Why does anyone need to know?"

"Since you were in college and you gave that young man that ultimatum of yours, you have viewed Christianity as something that would prevent you from having that which you wanted the most. By doing so you unwittingly damned yourself to that very fate."

"What purpose will it serve to rehash old wounds?"

Becoming exasperated with the woman's stubborn nature, so like her own, Inara balled her hands into fists and clenched her jaw. "Lylia, do you love your husband?"

"Yes, of course, I do!"

"When he asked you to marry him, did you want to marry him?"

"Yes!" Lylia shouted. "I wouldn't have waited for three years to marry that man if I didn't want to marry him. I've always known I would marry a man like him."

"And do you want to be the woman to bare his many children?" Inara countered.

"Yes!" She cried angrily. Her eyes brimmed with tears and she punched at the air for effect.

"Then I'll make this simple. You have a choice. You can tell him and gain the chance to have that which you both want. Or, you can be a coward, finish packing up and leave him as you intended to tonight."

Chapter 26

Inara's words resounded within the kitchen. The weight of them lay heavy upon all present, especially Dartanian. Sucking in a deep long breath he expelled it as he banged his hands upon the table. He shook his head as though in denial and prayed fervently.

"God no, please. No this can't be it."

The silence in the living room left those in the kitchen to wonder what was happening that they couldn't see. A few heads bowed around the table as others cast anxious gazes around them, waiting for someone to speak. Then Inara's voice came, clear and concise from the other side of the partition walls. It was gentle, soothing yet held a mixture of pain and regret of her own.

"Before you make that choice I need to ask you something. If you cannot open your heart and share with the one person in your life that you love the most the deepest darkest pain that makes your heart bleed, then how can you possibly expect to be open to the many, many blessings God has in store for you?"

"That's it, isn't it?" Lylia turned on her suddenly. Her face contorted in anguish as it lit up with understanding. "It is all me, isn't it? I am the one keeping us from having children?"

"Yes, I'm so sorry but it's true," Inara said sadly, her own downcast face sharing the woman's pain. "Our bodies and our spirits are linked while joined to this world. Our emotional state can, in fact, affect our health and by extension, in your case, the ability to bear children with him. Your own unwillingness to be open and honest with yourself and the man you love prevents you from being open to His will." Walking towards Lylia in order to extend comfort to her Lylia ducked away, looking from all appearances, as though she were about to close herself off from the world. Desperate and angry she lashed out at Inara.

"Just don't. Get away from me! You're one to talk. If it wasn't for you none of this would have ever happened in the first place." The despair Lylia felt within her was more than she thought she could bear.

Wincing at the truth in her words Inara sniffled loudly, trying to reign in her emotions. She tried not to allow her words to inflict further harm to her own heart which was already hurting.

"You're right. My choice affected many lives and caused a lot of pain but I am just as human as you, or anyone else in that room for that matter. God granted free will to us all, not just me. We all have a choice; a say in our lives. I didn't put those words and thoughts into your head fifteen years ago. Just as I didn't force Dartanian to knowingly walk into that drug deal alone fifteen years ago without any backup." The truth in what Inara said couldn't be denied.

Plopping down in the chair next to her Lylia wept bitterly. "What if I'm just too afraid?"

"Too afraid to what? To tell Dart about what really happened back then?"

Shaking her head no, she continued on a whisper. "Too afraid of the gifts God might ask me to bear," she said honestly, for the first time voicing her greatest fear. "Because I don't know that I could do what you do. You know? The knowing thoughts, like Dante and Alaina or knowing things without knowing why. Or worse yet, to see demons like Drinian and Veta." She became hysterical at the mere thought.

"First of all, Drinian's gift is exceedingly rare. Literally, one in a trillion … bajillion are gifted with it. I'd wager to guess there are likely only a handful of people capable of it currently in existence. Plus, it was never meant to be split as it is here. You've seen for yourself how differently Veta is affected by it compared to Drinian. Being able to see angels, acts as a kind of salve when seeing demons. You cannot have one without the other or it can be harmful in different ways to the person's spirit. Until Veta asked God to make Drinian invisible from the demons, he had no defense against them other than his voice. As I understand it, his voice was no longer enough for they were becoming too many. Being a God-fearing man, a Christian man, he was attracting more than he was capable of handling anymore, without the ability to see the messengers of God."

"I see. All demon, twenty-four hours a day every day…"

"Exactly. In a similar way, Breydon is afflicted, for he is not simply aware of the angels' presence but actually sees them. Imagine how overwhelming it would be if all you ever saw were angels."

"I'd never feel like I'd be able to measure up. Always afraid of making a mistake and when I did… Oh my, poor Breydon." Lylia had never thought about it in those terms before where he was concerned. Even the smallest of mistakes would seem like monumental disasters, knowing one of the angels had been present, to witness it in person.

"I would posit to say that it is one of many reasons the gift is so rare. God knows most humans are incapable of enduring the side effects but I digress. My point is, God won't give you anything He doesn't honestly believe that you can't handle."

"Are you sure about that? Because I see what this discerning gift of knowing is doing to you. You said it yourself. Suddenly one day you found out everything you thought was imagined was real. Frankly, it looks like it's making you nuts," Lylia said, sounding more than a little skeptical.

Unable to help herself Inara laughed out loud. "That's because I am nuts! Who else would stay in love with a man for over twenty years, creating a whole little world of her own within the pages of her books and then be too afraid to do anything about it once confronted with him?" She had responded without thinking and wished instantly she hadn't said anything. The look of pity and discomfort in Lylia's resulting expression left her feeling hollow and alone. "Forget what I said," she said dismissively. "Crack open that wall Lylia and look inside your heart. Break down those defenses you've created and maintained since college. Dig deep within you and determine what it is you *can* handle. Then pray about it."

Taking a tremulous breath Lylia dabbed at her nose with a tissue. Grabbing another she wiped at her face imagining she looked an absolute mess. "How do I do that? I mean, what do I have to do?"

"You don't *have* to do anything, and you don't have to make any decisions this instant or today for that matter. But I would strongly encourage you to talk with Dart. Let him help you through this and to take those last couple steps if you choose to." Inara gave Lylia a meaningful look, then she closed her eyes on a weary sigh. "He's going to love you regardless. He always has and I think deep down you've always known that."

Tell her.

Fidgeting suddenly from the words now echoing near her left ear Inara grimaced, knowing full well now what it was God wanted Lylia to know. The image had been made clear in her head. Speaking quickly she stammered out the next words in a rush.

"I would imagine it's one of the reasons why God blessed you with the man of your dreams in the first place. You really shouldn't have stopped drawing Lylia. A portrait with such great detail at such an early age; I would have thought you'd pursue art rather than teaching."

At that moment it dawned on Lylia to what Inara was referring. Instantly the image of a black and white drawing done in charcoal greys popped into Lylia's head and her eyes widened in dismay. Clamping a hand over her mouth she stared back at Inara's knowing gaze. She still had the drawing too. It was locked away in her hope chest in her bedroom at her home at The Bluff. She'd never told anyone, not even Dartanian about it, thinking he might laugh and believe her to be silly for having drawn a picture of the man of her dreams at age nine. But the image in her head had been with her long before that.

"Stop denying your own discerning gift. Everyone has at least one. They just happen to be more pronounced in some than in others - as is in the case of the Blackthorne's."

Once again the air was filled with silence. The beams of sunlight in the room shifted and spun as the hour grew later. Shadows left behind by the shifting beams of light were beginning to play in the corners of the room where they hadn't been before. The screeching sound of wooden chair legs shifting across the tiled floor in the kitchen carried across the living room. Moments later a tall towering figure appeared in the kitchen doorway. The crystal-clear blue eyes that met Lylia's were bright and clear, shimmering in the remaining sunlight filtering into the room.

Lylia's shoulders were straight and erect yet seemed to droop as Dartanian beckoned gently toward her with one outstretched arm. Seeing her tear stained face contort painfully in anguish, he called to her softly.

"Eve. My love?" he said. The hope and love shining in his eyes were unmistakable.

Lylia's eyes flew open. "Adam," she cried. Rushing toward him she was engulfed within his embrace the instant she was within an arm's length. Sobbing, she shoved her face into his shoulder as she wept openly.

Murmuring softly, Dartanian pressed his lips against his wife's forehead, not even glancing Inara's way as he sighed with relief. "For as long as I live, I could never love another. You know that, right?" His voice was filled with emotion.

Unseen by everyone in the kitchen Inara stood in the living room watching as her hand clutched at her chest. Haunted by the familiar words he'd just spoken, so similar to the ones she'd heard over twenty years before; she wept silently her face twisting in silent agony.

Feeling Lylia's head bob up and down against his shoulder Dartanian pulled her into an even closer embrace. "Come, my love, let's talk, please. Come upstairs with me?" He asked hopefully.

Shaking nervously in his arms, Lylia wiped at her eyes. "Okay."

Releasing her just enough so they could walk together side by side they turned towards the back stairs near the kitchen, oblivious to the rest of the family in the kitchen.

With light quick steps, Inara hurried across the living room and stood near the open kitchen doorway. "Dartanian?" she called to him with a strangled voice, struggling to keep from crying.

Shifting only enough so he could turn to see her, he peered around at Inara. He waited for her to speak but she simply stared at him, her deep blue irises seemed to darken before his very eyes.

"Yes, Inara. What is it?" He prompted, becoming almost uncomfortable at her intense gaze.

"Just be there and listen." She allowed her gaze to shift away sadly. "She needs to know you will still love her in every way … regardless of the decisions, she's made."

Giving her a short nod signifying that he understood, Dartanian mouthed the words "thank you" then turned away. Pulling his wife into his side they walked quietly side by side up the stairs.

Watching them disappear from view Inara stared almost longingly after them. Chest heaving in quick succession she was unable to prevent the tears from falling down her cheeks. Realizing many within the kitchen were staring at her just as intently as she had upon Dartanian, she desperately wiped at her face. Catching Megorah's eye she gave a tiny strangled laugh when she noted Rafe staring straight ahead with his back to her. Elbows on the table his chin rested on the hands he had clasped before him.

Feeling Inara's gaze upon him, Rafe turned toward her with a weary expression on his face. Worry lines creased his brow and his eyes were distant. Over twenty years, he mused, was a long time to wait he imagined. Seeing the sadness in her eyes and knowing the sorrow she must be experiencing in her heart he couldn't help but struggle over the lost time. The pain, suffering and heartache all present could have avoided fifteen years before, gnawed at his gut.

"Please forgive me. I'm so sorry. I was supposed to be here a long time ago for ... for your family," Inara said quietly, faltering over her words. Gulping down a sob a single tear escaped down her cheek, dripping onto her shirt. She looked like a lost and wounded child as she fidgeted with the tissue in her hands.

Closing his eyes on a wave of newfound understanding he replied simply, "I know."

Getting up from his chair Rafe sauntered from the kitchen, the sound of his boots thumping against the ceramic tiled floor resounded in the air until the patio door closed quietly behind him.

Chapter 27

Hiding.

Inara was getting good at it.

Disappearing within the house, unseen by everyone there.

People walked into rooms and didn't even notice her, but that was okay. She was used to feeling alone even when in a crowd of people.

Finding her children near bedtime she played with them, tumbling to the floor amongst tangling legs and arms as they tickled and hugged each other tightly. The feel of their small hands and arms embracing her centered her. Grounded her even as the empty void within seemed to fill her.

"Will you sleep well tonight mama?" Little Rafe asked. His worried tone was the only inkling that anything might be wrong among the laughter and giggles of Tanian and Lily.

"I sleep every night, Honey. Just some nights not so well," she said with a half-smile, forcing herself to be positive and upbeat for her children. "Tomorrow after church I'll take you all on a picnic. How does that sound?"

"Are we really going on a picnic mama? Outside? And we get to go to church too?" Lily squealed with delight, clapping her hands together.

Hesitating only briefly Inara responded finally, "Yes, and we will go on a picnic outside." In the back of her mind, she knew Rafe wouldn't like it but figured they'd been all cooped up long enough. One way or another she was determined to convince him.

On a whim she decided a camp out with her children in the library was past due. Explaining her plan to them, they all beamed with excitement at the idea. Heading to the front living room she was scooping up pillows and cushions from the couch when Rafe entered through the patio doors.

"What in the world are you doing?" He could see multiple cushions and pillows being crushed in her arms. She looked absurd hampered down by them.

"I was just trying to create a camp-out in the library for the kids." She hated the nervous catch in her voice. He hadn't returned to the house since dinner time, nor had Dartanian and Lylia been seen since as well.

"I'd much rather you not drag everything in here to the library." He looked cross and tired too. His jeans were riddled with dirt from the corrals

"This house is huge, Rafe. I'm all alone down here and everyone, including my children, are always upstairs at night," she said defensively, once again feeling alienated.

Seeing the firm set to his jaw Inara dropped everything where she stood and stalked off angrily. Tears stung the back of her eyes. Throwing a look back over her shoulder she yelled at him for good measure.

"You know what? Fine! This *is* your house after all, and I am nothing more than a guest within it until you've figured out where you're going to dump me." Grumbling aloud she headed back toward the library. "Even Ricardo and Maria got to stay upstairs when they were here." She continued to vent while rounding the stairs, running into her children on the way.

"Where are the pillows and cushions? Do you need help carrying them?" Tanian asked.

"No. Change of plans. You're all sleeping upstairs with your new friends again." Inara attempted to sound chipper. Inside, all she felt was trapped.

"Mama? You're not sleeping down here alone again, are you? What about your nightmares?" Little Rafe asked with concern.

"Honey, mama will be fine, really. I'm a big girl."

"But I wanted to sleep with you; to be with you," Lily said sadly, her lip trembling slightly. For some reason, she appeared to be a bit shaken.

Explaining to her children that they'd be much more comfortable tucked up in their friend's rooms than on the uncomfortable cushions and pillows on the library floor, she then sent them on upstairs. Feeling at a loss for what to do next she roamed the empty halls of the house for a while. Everyone was upstairs preparing for bed. At least, she thought they were.

She was standing at the pool room entrance, wishing she had a bathing suit in order to go swimming, when Dante appeared unexpectedly behind her.

"They're waiting for you upstairs," he said, catching her unaware.

"Sorry?"

"Your children. They're upstairs in the library waiting for you." He was holding a tray in his hands loaded with what appeared to be nearly a dozen cups with milk. Dante noted her curious gaze. "Steamed cows," he grinned. "The kids have all become addicted to them at night. Claim they can't get to sleep without one." His bright toothy smile, so like his twin brother, caught her attention. Heaving a troubled sigh she gave him a shy weak smile back.

"I used to do that for my daughter for the longest time. It was a nightly ritual." Inara followed behind him curiously as they walked upstairs. She didn't quite understand why her children were waiting for her in the upstairs library. Not having ventured to the second level of the house for the past couple days, she found herself gazing along the walls more closely than before. Her eye caught sight of a painting at the top of the stairs that she hadn't really paid much attention to before. Marveling at the intricate brush strokes she found herself mesmerized by the extraordinary mountain scenic view depicted within the painting.

"That is a beautiful painting. It's unsigned," she noted.

"Dad got that off a local artist. Come to think of it, he didn't really say who. Only commented that the artist had the habit of signing and dating the back rather than the front. He had it framed and hung before I could see who it was rendered by."

"He has a lot of paintings in this house."

Making a soft noise of ascent, as he led her down the hall toward the library, he turned toward her once they reached the doorway. "He's always been a fan of the arts. What about you? Do you have any hidden talents?"

"Aside from infuriating your father?" Inara asked, only half joking. "No. I've never been good at any one particular thing. I'm more of a dabbler, I guess." She sighed, wishing longingly to hold a paintbrush in her hand once again. Normally when she used to paint she enjoyed the flourish of a mountainous scene or more abstract imagery. The only time she'd ever created a portrait was as a child when she was eight. And that had been a crayon drawing.

"I see." Dante sensed he'd lost her in her thoughts. "Well, here you go. Grab yours for your brood." He motioned the tray filled with cups toward her. He was wearing pajama bottoms and a flannel shirt that was open in the front. Inara's gaze flitted briefly across his bare chest in appreciation, her imagination getting the better of her.

Reaching for two of the mugs shyly, as her children rushed toward her to take them, she then peered up at Dante in confusion. Seeing her questioning look he pointed into the library toward the mantel above the fireplace.

"Dad said to remind you there was a warm place near the hearth wherever you chose to lay your head." He repeated his father's words to her, which Rafe had spoken to him not but ten minutes before.

"Really?" Inara's gaze shifted down the hall. She could see the closed door of Rafe's bedroom and wondered if he had already gone off to bed or if he was hiding in one of his secret rooms.

Shrugging, he bent down so little Rafe could grab his steamed vanilla cow greedily. Thanking him happily the children disappeared with their mugs back towards the pillows on the floor as Dante placed the fourth drink in her hand.

The weight of the warm mug in her hand felt good, its creamy vanilla scented contents tempting her to drink of it. Stomach rumbling loudly, she clasped her hand against her belly in embarrassment as it growled. Her face flamed and Dante chuckled at her.

"Dad's last words to me tonight make much more sense now." He laughed, reached into his pajama pocket and pulled out a box. "He seemed to think you might need a box of these. Told me to tell you when you filch them to take them from Dart's stash rather than his," he suggested with a grin. "He also told me to tell you what you really need is hidden in the microwave. Something about your novels and absurd disgusting cravings needing to be fulfilled?" With a questioning look of his own, he backed down the hallway. Giving her a salute he walked away, turning down the hall near the stairs towards his room, he balanced the tray in one hand as he disappeared.

Staring down at the box of Junior Mints in her hand, which happened to be her all-time favorite candy, Inara's eyes flew open with excitement. Setting the steamed cow down on an end table in the library she sped quickly from the room, calling out to her children that she'd be back momentarily. Racing down the stairs she ran to the kitchen and opened the first microwave door. Not finding anything inside she checked the second, ever hopeful of what she might find. Seeing a plate within, she exclaimed with excitement while dancing in place. Noticing a small note card tucked within the three taco's on the plate she picked it up. Inara opened the card and read while heading back upstairs with her dinner in hand.

"There were four tacos. Not so disgusting after all," she read while laughing out loud.

Upstairs, hidden within the secret room between the library and his bedroom Rafe sat watching the monitor on the wall. In one corner of the monitor, he could see Inara's children having a pillow fight as they played on the floor of his library. In the opposite corner, he could see Inara race down the hallway to the stairs. Punching a button on his remote the image shifted. Seconds later he could see her dashing for the microwaves in the kitchen. Taking another bite of his food he groaned in irritation as he chewed. He could see her laughing as she read the note, and he could only imagine what she was likely thinking right now.

"Yeah, yeah. Laugh it up, lady." He grumbled softly while taking another bite of his food, in appreciation. Sighing with contentment he chuckled to himself, recalling Royce's stunned expression when he told him he was breaking his own cardinal rule. It was widely known amongst everyone who knew Rafe that he hated Mexican food with a passion. So when he had told Royce he wanted him to make up a bunch of taco's the man had almost lost it.

Agreeing to fix the disgusting things for Inara and break Rafe's own rule, Royce had dictated the terms of the rule-breaking with glee. Insisting that he and Crisalya got to partake of half of them and that his father-in-law had to at least try one, Rafe had reluctantly agreed.

Prepared to gag and throw up at the mere taste of it Rafe had been irritatingly surprised to find they were quite good. The batch Royce had prepared made a dozen. He and Crisalya were supposed to get half of them but Rafe wound up filching two of them, insisting they were needed in an experiment. There were actually supposed to be six left for Inara but he'd wound up swiping three more before setting them in the microwave for her. He figured she didn't need to know that, though he suspected even with his note somehow she probably already did.

Chapter 28

Sunday morning brought overcast skies and grey clouds which only served to hamper Inara's diminishing mood. Much to her irritation, Rafe had insisted she still was unable to leave the house. Not having had the time yet to devote to creating her new identification, background, and story; what with having to deal with Ricardo and Maria's situation, he had argued that bringing her to the same church Dartanian and Lylia attended would be a disaster.

"How do you figure that?" Inara had countered.

"And where exactly are we supposed to tell everyone you came from?" Rafe responded irately.

"That's nothing compared to having to explain why she looks like Lylia." Breydon piped in. Peering into one of the mirrors in the entryway he adjusted his tie.

Coming up behind him Hialey leaped up onto her husband's back, her blue skirts hiking up to her hips as she circled him with her legs.

"Hialey, you little squirrel." Reaching behind him with one arm Breydon grabbed her by the waist and pulled her around to his front. "You are intentionally trying to hamper my progression."

"Yup. Is it working?" She grinned back up at him. Her almond eyes sparkled with mischief. She was forever attempting new and inventive ways to make him late to anything.

He responded with a resounding laugh. "And you wonder where your sons get it from?"

Whacking him with her purse, Hialey stuck her tongue out at him.

"Okay, you two." Dante glowered. It was like watching a couple of teenagers whenever the two of them were in a room. Turning his attention back to Inara, he placed his hands on his hips for good measure, as he watched his father and her argue.

"Why not just tell them I'm her long-lost evil twin sister?" Inara grinned. Seeing the face Rafe made at her suggestion, she smirked, knowing full well why he'd been disturbed by the notion. Then, becoming cross at his stubbornness she continued to argue her case. "Rafe, please, I promised my children they'd get to go to church today. We've all been cooped up in this house all week."

"We get it, Inara. We do." Dante jumped in, attempting to save his dad further argument. He noticed Inara had spent extra time on her hair that morning and appeared to have borrowed someone's makeup. Recognizing the soft suede brown dress she was wearing as one he'd bought for Alaina, he also noted it seemed to fit her better somehow.

"I'm sorry but dad's right. We can't be too careful with your situation right now; especially where you're concerned," Dante said.

"Why? Because of Ricardo showing up?" Inara asked, trying to understand. "I thought they were already long gone?"

"They are," Rafe assured her. "But that's not the point." When he had come downstairs from his room and caught sight of Inara all dressed up and ready for church he had wanted to kick himself. He had forgotten to take the time to talk with her about the issue of attending church that morning. With his desperate need to get the stallion broke last night, the time had gotten away from him, unfortunately.

"People are going to see you and instantly have all kinds of questions." Breydon surmised as Drinian joined them with Veta in tow. "The sort of questions we are not prepared yet to answer."

"The children would be easy enough to explain away," Veta offered. "Wouldn't you say? We can tell people they're friends of the family. It wouldn't be untrue."

"I would agree," Drinian said while sliding his feet into his specially made, size seventeen, dress shoes.

"Yes, but you Inara are a whole other matter," Megorah said in an aloof manner. "You need to stay here. You cannot go to church with us as a family."

"Megorah, stop it," Chase ordered, giving his wife a stern look. Her tone when she spoke made it sound as though Inara was unwelcome, and he was getting fed up with her attitude. He couldn't understand it.

Megorah became defensive as she brushed lint from her skirts. "I just mean, we have no real way of explaining her away."

Troubled by the exchange between Chase and his eldest daughter, Rafe frowned. They appeared to be fighting a lot lately. "I truly am sorry, Inara," he said with real regret, genuinely feeling bad for the lone woman pleading her case before him. She was all dressed up with nowhere to go, and she looked really pretty too. Catching a glance at her bare feet he struggled to keep from chuckling as his eyes twinkled.

"We can take the kids for you." Alaina padded into the entryway from the living room. Stopping, she tipped her head to one side and gave Inara an appraising look. "Wow, Inara. You look even better in that dress then I do." Not realizing the situation was still being ironed out where she was concerned, Alaina felt a bit guilty for having encouraged Inara by loaning the dress.

Caving in, to the inevitable disappointment Inara gazed up at Rafe. The forlorn look in her eyes was evident.

"I could stay and keep you company if you'd like," Rafe offered without thinking.

Jerking his head towards his father, Drinian gave him a funny look. "No you can't," he said forcefully.

"And what makes you think I can't?" he responded harsher than intended.

Stepping around his father Dante patted his shoulder as he went. "You're supposed to be locking up the church afterwards this month. Remember?"

Scowling, Rafe ran his hand through his hair. "He's right, I completely forgot. I'm sorry. There's just too much in my head."

"It's okay. It was a nice gesture anyway," Inara said in a quiet tiny voice.

Calling for Inara's children, Rafe beckoned for them to hurry down the stairs.

"No worries, Inara. I promise I'll take good care of them." Rafe urged the three kids out the door ahead of them. "The house is locked down, alright? I really don't want you leaving it but you can go anywhere you want inside."

"Anywhere?" Inara queried mischievously.

He gave her a severe look. "Anywhere within reason. Just be sure you stay inside until we get back. Can I trust you to keep to your word?"

Sighing heavily at his anxious gaze she nodded in agreement. "I promise. I won't step outside."

The door closed behind Rafe, the lock clicking in place as he left. Pressing her forehead against the window panel in the door, Inara watched as they all drove away without her.

Have patience.

The voice echoed in the empty entryway.

"Yes, Lord," Inara replied miserably. "I shall try."

Staring down at herself she gazed upon her bare feet on the floor. "In hindsight, having to explain attending church barefooted would have been difficult," she said aloud.

Contemplating on what she wanted to do while they were gone, she determined quickly that attempting to mess with the theater system was probably not a good idea. She had never been very good at figuring such things out. Wondering briefly on how Dartanian and Lylia were doing, she recalled hearing when she awoke, that they headed into church early. Hoping that was a good sign, she strolled past the downstairs library, not terribly inclined towards reading since she had been doing a lot of that lately.

Her fingers itched once again for the keyboard of her computer. Feeling a bit mischievous she made her way to the upstairs library. Figuring out how to enter Rafe's secret room behind his closet she located her laptop bag. Taking a brief moment to marvel at his vast security measures and big screen spying machine on the wall she shook her head while smiling. Carrying her bag from within, being sure to close the passage door tightly behind her, she checked to be sure it wasn't visible. Then, heading back downstairs she strolled leisurely into the kitchen. Her bare feet slapped almost soundlessly against the cool ceramic tile as she walked. Getting herself a cup of black coffee she filched a cheese Danish from the box on the counter. Her stomach was a little upset again, but she figured it was probably because she needed to eat.

Taking up her laptop bag she shouldered the strap and walked quietly toward the front living room. She had a coffee mug in one hand and her Danish in the other. Leafing through Rafe's vast music collection Inara discovered, as she suspected, that he had several Karen Carpenter CD's. Selecting a couple to listen to, she tucked them under her arm and carried them along with her coffee and Danish down to the pool room. Once there, she set everything down and inserted a CD into the boom box she'd seen plugged in between the bathrooms. Setting up in what constituted as a deck chair, she propped her laptop on her lap and booted it up.

In the quiet of the pool room, Inara finished eating her Danish and drank her black coffee. Pausing for a brief re-fill a half hour later, this time she added mint and sugar. Setting back in the chair she sipped at her coffee, allowing the mint to soothe her increasingly upset stomach. Letting her imagination flow freely her fingers flew across the keyboard, barely pausing for obvious spelling corrections.

After a little over an hour, Inara's head fell against her chair. She stared at the inviting water within the pool. Inara realized no one was home and might never know. Guessing it would at least be another forty-five minutes before anyone would arrive home she finally broke down and shamelessly slid off her dress and undergarments. Glancing at the clock on the wall she noted it was just after ten thirty. Thinking she'd swim for maybe twenty minutes then get out Inara dove quickly into the water, relishing the feel of it slapping against her arms and legs. Careful to keep her head above the water most of the time, in order to prevent any possible accident, she swam a dozen lengths of the pool before finally pausing near the steps.

Submerging her head under the water briefly, she ran her hands across her face in order to pull her wet hair out of the way. The shorter hair was going to make swimming easier, she mused, and it was still considered a little long, though nowhere near as long as before. Peering up at the clock she noticed time had flown by, and it was already after eleven. Feeling the nauseous sensation in her gut increasing, she decided it was high time to get out of the pool anyway and get dressed. Quickly exiting the pool, she grabbed a towel from the rack near the bathrooms. Drying off completely she reached for her dress, sliding it on over her head. Bending forward, she was towel drying her hair when her eyes jerked towards the laptop sitting open on the chair.

Gasping audibly, a sudden surge of panic enveloped her. Her eyes flew open wide when she realized what she had done.

"No, no, no!" she wailed as her eyes filled with fear, knowing instantly what she would see when she turned around. Heart lodged in her throat, the terror overwhelming her. Inara's bare feet slipped on the damp tile beneath her, causing her to fall, smacking her hip hard against the floor.

It happened just as she'd written it.

Raising her head to the large dark figure looming before her she screamed with fright as the man lunged for her.

The sting of his fist against her left cheek barely caught her off guard, and her body drooped back to the floor. Struggling against him, she tried to shove at his arms to no avail, but he was too strong. Yanking her up from the ground Steven Simms held her by her wrists, laughing at her futile attempts to get loose.

Cackling like a man bent on revenge Simms pulled her toward him, delighting at hearing her squeal with fright. "Now lookie what I got here. Ain't one of the Blackthorne daughters, but I suspect you'll do, now won't ya?" he ground out. "Didn't know Lylia had a twin sister."

Knowing full well even before she said it, that it wouldn't do her any good, Inara spoke through chattering teeth. "Please don't do this Steven. You don't really want to do this. They'll be back from church. They'll be back any minute."

The words echoed within her head even as she spoke them. Like the movie reel in her mind, her reality was occurring just as she had begun writing her fantasy. But Inara hadn't gotten the chance to finish it. The ending had been left unwritten, waiting for her capable hands against the keyboard to complete it.

"Liar!" Steven Simms accused. Hauling back he smacked her across the face. The loud crack against her skin even louder than the first time he hit her. Blinking at the blinding pain streaking across the side of her head she groaned, choking on a sob. Her nightmare had been given reality and she feared she wouldn't survive it.

"See now, I know for a fact they never get home till close to noon. By then we'll be gone and it'll be too late." he grinned.

The rotting teeth and stench of alcohol on his breath made Inara feel woozy and she struggled to keep from passing out. Not really wanting to live the experience, she was almost more afraid to not know what his intentions were toward her. Though Inara suspected she already knew.

"Please Mr. Simms. I have three young children. I'm all they have left," she cried, even as he attempted to haul her over his shoulder. "Please don't do this to them."

"Please Mr. Simms. I have three young children." Steven mimicked. He laughed cruelly then began coughing. Spitting over his shoulder onto the pool room floor he got fed up with her struggles and hauled off and hit her again, knocking her out cold. Dropping her unceremoniously to the ground, he tied her hands and feet with fabric he tore from her skirts and then hefted her over his shoulder.

Groaning under the weight, he grumbled under his breath as he left the pool room and carried her down the back-patio deck. "Too bad you couldn't have been one of the lighter weight lady's. *Dang* your heavy girl, but that's all right. Ya' got the right parts. It's all that matters," he said gleefully. "'Twas awful kind of them Blackthorne's to leave the pool door open for me."

Hoisting her over the back of one of the two horses' he had tethered to the patio decking, Simms mounted the saddle of the other. Peering around him, then up at the darkening sky, Simms knew instantly he had to hurry. Heavy rain clouds were heading their way and he wanted to be undercover by then. The wind whipped around him frantically and he could feel a few drops of rain against his forearm.

Nickering the horses in motion he took off across the back lawn, racing both horses along at a quick pace, wanting to be clear of the brush before anyone could see he was there. Managing to make it to the path along the south facing portion of the ranch house, he suspected he'd managed a clean escape. He knew the ranch hands had their weekends off, so likely no one would be missing the horses until later in the day. Letting out a gleeful shout he kept a close eye on the horse with the cargo next to him. He didn't really care so much if she fell off, he just didn't want her dead. Not yet anyway.

Chapter 29

A sense of foreboding.

That's what Rafe was experiencing.

Ever since he left the house he'd had a knot in his gut, and it had stayed with him all through the church service. Hearing the winds outside picking up, he shifted where he stood, trying hard to pinpoint what it was that was bothering him, as he acknowledged the greetings of several of the elderly ladies in the church. Taking the extended hand of the widow Havish, as she expressed her appreciation for buying the stallion from her once again, Rafe gave her a courteous nod and shook her hand politely.

"He's no trouble at all Mrs. Havish. I think Redemption might work out just fine actually."

"It's Redemption now, is it?" the fifty-ish brunette with graying hair smiled back at him, attempting to be flirtatious as they spoke. "With him gone, I might actually get a chance to enjoy that pool my late husband put in two years ago. Even went out and got me a new bikini bathing suit."

Not really wanting the imagery of the bony, frail woman in a bikini in his head, Rafe shifted uncomfortably as he released her hand. "By all means, enjoy that pool while the summer lasts. Though I daresay, today doesn't appear to be the day for it." The whistle across the bell tower of the church, resting it from its normally silent state, caught his attention.

Feeling a hand on his shoulder he turned, grateful to see his son Dartanian had interrupted them. "I'm thinking we better get that bell locked down before things get too out of hand out there, and the rain starts pouring down."

"I'd wager you're right. If you'll excuse me Mrs. Havish."

"Widow Havish," she corrected him, smiling fondly as she waved. "I'll be seeing you, Rafe."

"Not if I can help it," he mumbled under his breath. He steered his son along next to him toward the stairs. "Thank you for the much-needed interruption."

"Don't thank me, thank Dante. He alerted me to your desperate desire to flee." Dartanian grinned widely next to him as he chuckled. His exceptionally good mood was clearly the result of Lylia's decision to be baptized. They had spent much of the night awake simply talking, so he'd been thoroughly surprised and pleased when she'd awakened him at sunrise and asked if he'd go with her to the church early.

"Its times like these when I am ever so grateful to God for blessing my children with discerning gifts." Rafe was forever being hit on by the many widows and unwed middle-aged single ladies of the church. Most of the time he didn't mind, but the Widow Havish had been getting more aggressive of late, than what he cared for.

Stopping before ascending the stairs Dartanian turned back suddenly, his perplexed gaze roaming back where he'd just come.

"What is it, son?" Rafe was getting an uneasy feeling from his son's behavior and intent stare at the Havish widow.

Eyebrows furrowed, Dartanian scratched at his forehead. "Something just now... Something I overheard Widow Havish say to you is eating at me. I feel like I forgot something really important."

Meeting them at the base of the stairs to the bell tower, Breydon pulled his tie loose. "You'd think after all these years I'd get used to one of these," he said off-handedly. "And you rarely if ever forget things, Dart. You have a memory like dad." Managing to get the tie off, he began folding it around one hand, as he loosened his collar with the other.

"Not true anymore. Dad's age is getting the better of him," Drinian joked. "He forgot just this morning he was supposed to lock up today when he offered to stay home with the widow Inara." He smirked with a wink then sipped at the Styrofoam cup of coffee in his hand. Gesturing towards the stairwell he continued. "I can take care of the bell if you'd like."

"By all means." Rafe waved him on. Becoming antsy he ran a hand across his freshly shaven face. His gut was telling him Dartanian was right. It seemed there something that had flown past his own memory.

"Anyone else get the feeling like Inara probably should have been here this morning to witness Lylia being baptized?" Breydon asked, catching a quick glance from everyone present.

"I had the same thought myself," Drinian said.

"There *is* something I'm forgetting. I'm sure of it." Dartanian was too distracted to pay attention to what was being said.

Intent on their own conversation the Blackthorne's were oblivious initially to the uproar within the throng of people in the fellowship hall. Their attention was soon gained by the child racing amongst the people, frantically searching for someone.

"Where are you?" A little boy called out suddenly as Lylia and Alaina came running into the hall with a distraught Lily at their side. Their worried gazes locked with the men from across the room. "Daddy ... Rafe, Dartanian! Dante, where are you?" Little Rafe screamed above the crowd, forcing people to move aside as he dashed one way, then another.

Concerned to see the boy in such hysterics Dartanian stepped promptly forward through the throng of people, quickly reaching his side. "Little Rafe calm down. What is it?"

"Help her," Little Rafe hollered. "Please," he begged. His little face distorted in fear as his eyes began to glaze. "The door, the door..." the boy panted, gulping as he tried to speak.

Taking the boy about his shoulders Rafe bent down before him. "What's wrong, son? What's this about a door?"

Little Rafe's pupils began to dilate as he began to shake. A soft moan escaped his lips. "Pool door."

"Something about a pool door?" Dartanian repeated, trying to understand. A faint memory of seeing Alaina come in through the kitchen patio door two days before glimmered into the forefront of his mind. Recalling suddenly the vague conversation they'd had about her leaving through the pool room doors for a walk when

Ricardo had arrived, his face registered understanding the same moment the boy began to wail.

"No! Mama!"

Little Rafe's ear-splitting scream silenced the crowd around them as they stared at him in shock.

"Oh no!" Rafe instantly realized what was happening.

"Inara!" Dartanian shouted, panic surging within him. Whatever was happening, was occurring as they spoke. The urgent need to return home seized them both.

"Dad! What's going on?" Breydon called as Rafe raced across the room with the boy in hand.

Passing little Rafe off to Lylia, he swiveled around, hollering back at his sons. "Back to the ranch! Everyone, now! Lylia, find Chase. The boys going into shock." He headed for the first exit he could find.

"What about the bell?" Drinian called.

"Forget the bell. Don't you get it? Simms has Inara!" Dartanian roared across the parting crowd.

His words gave them cause for momentum as they all raced after their father through the church. Struggling to keep up with him, they were met by Royce, Megorah and Crisalya near the church doors. The only one able to keep stride with Rafe was Dante as they reached the first vehicle.

"Is it my imagination or has that man got an inordinate amount of stamina for a sixty-year-old?" Pastor Drake could be overheard saying as the Blackthorne, Howard and Ryans' family members darted across the parking lot toward their vehicles.

Not bothering to wait on the rest of them, Rafe and Dante took the first vehicle out of the parking lot at a dangerous speed. Spinning their tires Rafe gunned the sport utility vehicle into traffic.

- - -

Arriving back at the ranch ahead of everyone Rafe and Dante screeched to a resounding halt near the walkway. Exiting the vehicle, not bothering to shut their doors they raced toward the house as Dartanian pulled up behind their vehicle. Slamming on the brakes he skidded to a halt in time to keep from hitting the vehicle in front of him.

"What are you trying to do? Kill us?" Megorah yelled at him as Dartanian hastily exited the jeep, leaving the vehicle running.

"Not now, Meg!" Dartanian hollered back, annoyed that he was having trouble keeping up with his dad and twin brother. Being the Sherriff, he figured he should be three lengths ahead of them rather than behind. Pounding up the porch stairs after them they ran through the house calling out for Inara.

Hearing the crooning voice of Karen Carpenter music coming from the pool room, Rafe skidded to a screeching halt near the double doors. Finding the pool room empty his eyes collided with the open laptop and torn brown fabric fragment lying on the floor near it. Picking up the swatch of light summer weight suede from the floor Rafe extended it toward Dante.

"Please, tell me that is not from her dress," he choked out, allowing the soft suede fabric to dangle from his fingertips. She'd looked so pretty in it, all dolled up and ready to go. Why didn't he just take her with him?

Wrestling with his conscience, he knew it was because his house was supposed to have been a fortress against predators. She should have been safe here; in his home, his domain. Surging with anger he swore aloud, awaiting impatiently his son's response.

Seeing the look of recognition on Dante's face, Rafe let out a strangled cry.

Knowing better than to get too close to his father, when he got in this raging state, Dante took several steps back. Reaching out with one arm he prevented his brother from getting any closer.

"Try and calm down, Dad. We don't know anything for sure yet."

"Her gift to know her child's to see," Rafe shouted. "The boy was screaming Dante! What do you think was happening here?" Eyes darkening from the crystal-clear blue from moments before Rafe felt the helpless panic within him. Where was she? Where would Simms take her? What was he doing to her now?

Pacing wildly, Rafe's dress shoe bumped the lounge chair and he began kicking at it angrily, taking his frustration out on the chair. The mangled mess of metal screeched across the tile floor into the pool, splashing noisily into the water. Clenching his fists at his side, his head twisted about the room. Thinking quickly he tried to determine where he wanted to start first.

Rafe! You must stay calm.

Warm air caressed his ear as if someone had exhaled a soft breath against his cheek. Rubbing his hands across his face he paced in agitation trying to push down the hysteria building within him. His mind shifted back over forty years to the day he'd arrived home from Colorado too late to save Sarah from being beaten nearly to death by his brother Rourke.

Not too late yet.

Read Rafe. Read, the gentle voice urged, regaining his attention.

Realizing what the Lord was trying to tell him and what the presence of the laptop meant he reached for it, snatching it up. Banging his hand against the mouse pad the black screen disappeared and a Word document opened up before him. Suspecting he knew what he was about to read Rafe paged back to the beginning of the chapter she'd been writing, his eyes skimming over the pages as he quickly read aloud. The rest of the family joined him in the pool room as her story came to a sudden jarring halt.

What she'd written so far had been upsetting. Seeing her last moments in the pool room, written out by her own hand, Rafe had trouble getting past where Simms had hit her the first time. She wrote that her character Christine had been bound by the shreds of her own skirts, then hauled over Simms' shoulders and carried from the house in an unconscious state. The horse's Simms stole had headed through the path south of the house, with her thrown over the back of a painted horse. From there it ended abruptly with Steven Simm's being unconcerned if she fell from the horse but that he didn't want her dead yet.

"Where's the rest? Why didn't you finish it, Inara?" Rafe punched at the keys on the keyboard. Snarling he let out a feral howl as he flung the laptop across the pool room with such force that it smashed against the smooth brick wall, clattering to the floor in pieces.

Dartanian and Dante waited with bated breath to see what their father would do. The last time he got the dangerous look in his eye that he had now, he had nearly killed a man who'd been abusing one of the waitresses at a local tavern. Normally their father abhorred such violent behavior, but when it came to the feminine gender he had a huge soft spot. He would quickly lose his temper if he deemed they were being poorly treated.

Thunder rumbled in the skies over the house, echoing in the pool room as the lights began flickering. Staring out the still open door of the pool room, that led out onto the back deck, Rafe watched as the rain began steadily streaming down from the skies overhead.

"I should have just let you arrest him, Dart," Rafe said harshly, the regret at his choice clear. "She would have been much safer if you had."

"But she gave us a clue to find her. He's taken her along the southern trail," Dante said.

"Yeah, but that could lead out to anywhere. It branches off in six directions." Breydon hated having to point out the obvious.

"We have to try and find her," Dartanian said firmly.

"I don't understand. What does Simms want with her exactly?" Hialey asked in confusion. "I mean, no offense intended Rafe, but his quarrel is with you. Why would he go after Inara?"

"Because she appeared to be a part of this household. Because she was a woman alone. And because he knew it was the one thing that would get under my skin the most." Leaving the pool room, he called back to anyone within earshot. "Get your dusters and hats. Anyone who's not pregnant and who is willing, I need you down at the stables. We ride south and cover all trails."

Chapter 30

Rafe didn't bother changing from his church clothes. Switching to his boots he tore off his tie and grabbed his Stetson. Punching his fists through the armholes of his all-weather duster coat, he ran the length of the yard toward the stables beating everyone there. Reaching the corral he ran into his new foreman, Teddy. Hastily explaining to him the situation, he began grabbing saddles and gear.

"You know I'll do what I can to help. But the men weren't expecting to be working today and most aren't even here right now." Teddy led Black Betsy back into her stall, opting for one of the painted horses instead, figuring one of them would be better if they had to head into mountain terrain.

"I'll take what help I can get. We think Simms headed south with her through one of the trails there," Rafe explained in a rush. They hurried to get horses saddled as Drinian, Hialey, and Royce arrived to assist. Following not far behind them Megorah, Breydon and Crisalya came into the stables dripping with water from the downpour.

"Drin, where is Dante?" Rafe called, not seeing him.

"He said he was going to the Arabian barn to pull Mocktail for you," Dartanian said, hurrying into the barn with Lylia in tow.

"No," Rafe said firmly. "I'll ride Redemption today or nothing at all."

"Are you sure that's wise?" Teddy could see the glint in Rafe's eyes and hesitated. "I don't mean to question you but you just broke him last night. Do you think he'll stay controllable in this weather?"

"Trust me. I *need* Redemption today." The knot in Rafe's gut churned uneasily and he knew he should have said something to them all sooner, but most importantly to Inara. "I'm heading to the Stallion barn to get him. Tell Dante he can ride Mocktail if he's already got him saddled," he called over to Teddy. Seeing that everyone had things under control, he rushed from the stable in search of his own horse.

Immediately drenched once again from the downpour, he ignored the splash of the water and the slight chill that came with it. The rain was coming down in torrents, and it was hard to see past arm's length for the sky had darkened ominously. Nearing the Stallion barn his feet sloshed in the muddy puddles already accumulating near the stable entrance.

Hearing someone coming up quickly behind him, he turned abruptly. Feeling something long and heavy slide from his coat pocket he attempted to grab for the item. Not quite quick enough the flashlight dropped toward the ground. A slender long-fingered hand snaked out suddenly, catching it before it hit the mud at his feet.

Deftly pulling himself back up from a hasty crouch, Brauman extended the flashlight he'd just caught back towards Rafe.

"Don't wanna lose your light, Sir," Brauman said. "You might need it in your darkest hour."

Struck by the young man's statement Rafe couldn't help but think he'd heard it before. A vague memory once again attempted to pull its way up into the forefront of his mind, but he shook it off. He didn't have time to live in the past when the present had Inara in danger.

Tipping his hat towards Rafe, the young ranch hand shouldered his rifle. "Happy to be of service if I can be," Brauman said as water dripped from his cowboy hat.

"You aren't drunk are you?"

"I don't drink, Sir."

Acknowledging the statement Rafe patted the young man's arm in appreciation. "Much obliged son. You can pair off with Teddy."

"Yes, Sir."

Meeting up with the rest of the family back near the main set of stables Rafe was surprised to see Lylia being helped up onto a chocolate brown mare by Hialey. Questioning whether her presence out in the weather was wise she huffed at him in aggravation.

"Meg, Cris, and Hialey are heading out to search, so why can't I? Besides, I'm not pregnant," she said haughtily, then added, "At least … not yet." Her eyes sparkled happily as Dartanian's head spun around at her. His face lit up as he grinned. Seeing her response and his son's reaction Rafe had the sense that a change had occurred within them both.

Knowing Lylia wasn't as experienced with the horses as the rest of them, Rafe was hesitant about allowing her out in such weather conditions. Grabbing the reins of her horse before she could, he cast a worried look towards Dartanian.

Catching his concerned look, Lylia took the reins out of his hands. "I *need* to help Rafe, *please*. If it wasn't for Inara I wouldn't even be here in Montana right now."

Both Rafe and Dartanian could see the determined look in her eye and the proud set of her jaw. Wearing a brown Stetson on her head with her pale blonde hair pulled back in a ponytail, he imagined Inara would look just as good astride such a horse. He regretted not letting her ride on one yet.

"All right. Don't wander from your husband's side, you hear me?" Rafe didn't like the notion of any of the women being out in the thunderstorm, but he recognized they didn't have much choice. Time was getting away from them. Inara had been gone from the protection of his home for nearly forty-five minutes already, and they had a lot of ground to cover.

Making sure everyone had cell phones, a walkie talkie, and flares for an emergency, Rafe insisted all present check in every ten minutes. Pairing everyone off, the twelve of them cantered until they reached the south side of the house. Lightning crackled in the sky as thunder boomed across the mountain peaks. The bright streaks lit the darkened sky briefly in its wake. Following the southern trail, until it forked off into three different directions, they dispersed off into groups of four. Further down through the trails the groups eventually split off again in pairs.

Ten minutes later everyone checked in. So far no signs could be found that would determine the direction Simms had taken. Another ten minutes went by before anyone was heard from again. By the next check-in, Rafe had heard from everyone accept Royce and Crisalya, who had taken the route just south of them.

The winds were fierce and the rain pelted against their coats, soaking them, regardless of their all-weather claims. Becoming concerned that they hadn't heard from Royce and his daughter, Rafe pulled the walkie talkie out again.

"Royce where are you? Why aren't you responding?" Getting only static, he was about to try again when he felt his phone vibrating in his coat. Grabbing for it, he turned to Dante as he answered, catching his gaze. "Yeah, Royce, why didn't you check in?"

Met with silence, Rafe could hear Crisalya in the background. She sounded like she was crying. "We think we know…" Royce's voice sounded strained through the phone, the sounds of the fierce winds and rain echoing through it were making it harder to hear.

"Know what Royce? What's going on with Cris?"

His son-in-law's response was muffled, but he was able to make out what he said. "The Divide, Rafe. Think about it. I'm betting Simms took Inara to The Divide. There's no other cover or shelter in this direction."

"Makes sense," Rafe agreed. The Divide was where the Blackthorne property and his old estranged friend Misham Howard's property intersected. He'd actually been having the same thought and wasn't surprised that Royce had come to the same conclusion. Misham Howard was Royce's father after all.

Over fifty years back, Rafe's own father Rathbourne Blackthorne had a small cabin constructed right on the dividing line of both their properties. That way anytime one family or another traveled back and forth between, they would have a safe haven to take shelter inside, in the event they were caught in a snowstorm.

Recalling that was where Crisalya had been trapped fifteen years ago after spraining her ankle, Rafe winced. He imagined with the storm that the memories were probably getting to her. Wishing he'd insisted all the women had stayed behind he sighed heavily, trying hard to focus on the most prevalent issue; finding Inara and getting her back alive and unharmed.

Passing the word on, they all agreed to head that direction. As Rafe and Dante were closest to the divide, he realized they should be able to see the cabin soon. In normal weather they'd be able to see the cabin clear as day when only within a few miles of it. Today, however, Rafe's eyes struggled to see through the torrential rain and darkened forest enshrouded by thunderclouds and shadows. The shadows were what had him the most worried, for he knew what might truly be lurking within them.

"We should almost be there," Dante called above the sound of the horse hooves plodding steadily through the thick underbrush.

Anxious to get there quickly Rafe worried at what he might find. Inara had written in her laptop that she'd been knocked unconscious and her skirts had been torn. She'd been alone now with the monster for easily over an hour. Half of that time likely spent at the cabin. Anything could have happened by now.

Rafe's blood began to boil at the notion of what Simms might have done to her already, and what he could be doing to her right now. Trying hard to have faith that God was protecting her he prayed fervently that he wasn't too late. Wishing once again he'd already given her what was hidden in his pocket, he swore when he saw her next, he would. It belonged to her, after all.

A brilliant flash of light blinded him briefly as he sped along the barely visible path. Rafe squeezed his eyes shut against the blinding light. When he opened his eyes, he thought he saw a small white bird cowering in a tree branch just above his head as he passed. Both hearing and feeling something plop down on the brim of his hat as he raced by, he reached up with one gloved hand. Assuming it was a small twig he pulled it off. Opening his hand in front of him, he peered down and was confused to find instead a sky-blue broken piece of crayon lying in the palm of his gloved hand. Tied to it with a piece of brown suede fabric was what appeared to be the black feather from a raven. Clasping the treasure tightly he peered back around at the branch he'd passed, only to see that the white bird was gone.

"Dad, was that a morning dove I just saw?" Dante called over to him in surprise. The direction of his gaze staring back the same way he was.

"When she sends a gift through the nigh'," Rafe repeated softly to himself, trying to understand the message. Carefully re-opening his gloved hand as he raced along, he stared back down at the items briefly. Comprehension instantly dawned on him. Exclaiming upon an agonized cry, his face registered shock at the realization of how appropriate it was he was riding a horse called Redemption today.

The name of sweet Sarah Ravena Croft had weighed upon his mind heavily ever since he learned Veta's daughter's name had been Sarah. At the moment Inara RavenCroft had given her name, Rafe had known that God had brought her to Montana for more than just Lylia. But until that moment he had not fully understood what God and Inara had been trying to tell him. He now realized she was present to help him atone for his indifferent behavior with Sarah over forty years before.

Being of similar minds at the time, Rafe and his brother Rourke had become interested in the same young woman for a brief time. The young woman in question had been Sarah Ravena Croft. Pretty and sweet with a gentle disposition, she had taken more of a shine to Rafe then she had with his brother. Even though they were identical in appearance their temperaments had been drastically different.

Since Rafe was first born in his family and would one day inherit the ranch as a result, he had been preoccupied with ranch business matters at the time. Though pleasant to spend time with, he found he had no real feelings towards Sarah beyond friendship. In the end, he made the mistake of turning a blind eye to Sarah's expressions of affection, and instead encouraged her to see his brother. By doing so he'd knowingly ignored his brother's previous aggressive tendencies and behavior toward women.

Rourke had been angry with their father Rathbourne and jealous of Rafe upon learning he would not inherit the ranch. Seeking revenge against him, Rourke convinced him that he was in love with her then pursued Sarah voraciously. Making her believe that he'd marry her if she gave into him, he ended up getting her pregnant. In the end, he'd had no real plans of marrying her at all, his intentions only to see how far he could provoke his brother.

Becoming enraged when Sarah informed their parents that he'd proposed and promised to marry her, Rourke had beaten her nearly to death, killing his own child in the process. Rafe's indifference towards her expression of love towards him had led her inevitably to his brother's arms instead, and her fate.

Upon his return with fresh horses from Colorado, Rafe learned of what Rourke had done. He'd sworn then he would never allow another woman to be harmed by a man in the name of vengeance ever again and had nearly killed his own brother in his attempts to teach him a lesson.

As far as Rafe was concerned women were never meant to be pawns in a man's war against each other.

A single shot rang out through the night air, startling Rafe from his reverie. His head jerked to his left. Above them on a rocky path was a lone horseman. Cocking back his rifle, the man astride it shouted out to Rafe above the sound of the wind and rain.

"Do you see the light?" Brauman gestured with his rifle in front of him. Rafe's head turned in the direction the man was pointing, unnerved once again by his words. Narrowing his gaze as he covered his eyes with his hands, he could barely make out a tiny flickering light in the distance. They were further from the cabin than he originally thought. Hearing terrifying screams coming from that direction, muffled by the sounds of thunder reverberating above them, he coerced Redemption into a dead run.

Snorting loudly Redemption's sides heaved from exertion. The closer they came to the divide the more terrifying the sight that befell him.

Snarling with rage Rafe surged forward astride Redemption, spurring the black stallion on with haste, leaving Dante in his wake. He'd be damned before he'd allow history to repeat itself.

It was time to right his wrong.

Eyes ablaze with righteous fury Rafe refused to allow his fear to overcome him. Surrendering it to God he pleaded for Inara's life and the strength to overcome Steven Simms while keeping a level head and not sinning against God.

- - -

Becoming aware of her surroundings, Inara moaned softly.

357

Thinking she was having one of her waking nightmares she lay motionless afraid to move.

Her eyes were only partially open but she could see him standing before her. Tall and dark, Steven Simms features were cast in shadows as they had been in her dreams for so many nights. Though only one of him this time she couldn't dispel the cloying chill that overcame her, lending her to believe there was an unnatural presence about him. His eyes had deepened to a murky black, which had her guessing that he wasn't completely in his right mind at the moment.

Murmuring unintelligibly Simms cackled as he paced the small room. He was unaware she had awoke yet. Inara quickly shifted her gaze down her front as she had so many times in her nightmares. Confused and frightened she realized that what in her dreams she'd thought was a shirt she was wearing; in fact, it was a torn dress. Bound with fabric from the skirts of that very dress, rather than ropes, she found she couldn't really move. Distressed at her revealing state, as the remaining skirt barely covered her to the top of her hips, she made the mistake of whimpering softly.

Catching on that she was awake Simms lunged toward her as he rambled, causing her to cry out in fright. Tears stung at her eyes and she stared back at him in fear. Crying softly she already knew what he intended to do to her for he'd stripped down to nothing but his dirty wet jeans and boots after taking the time to light a fire simply to warm the cabin.

"About time you woke," Simms swore at her, calling her all sorts of hateful names. Kicking off his boots he grabbed up the knife from the small stand near the bed while shooing at a black raven which had taken refuge within the cabin with them. The bird screeched at him angrily, its round black eyes circling the room as it took to flight. Its feathered wings flapped in a desperate attempt to give Simms a wide birth. Several feathers dislodged from its wings, one dropping within reach of Inara's bound hands.

Grinning at her cruelly he toyed with her by placing the knife close to her neck. "Slit this throat I could," he said gleefully, his voice sounding unnatural to her ears.

Closing her eyes Inara wept, praying for God's protection. She spoke aloud causing Simms to flinch away as though her prayers were making him extremely uncomfortable. Flicking the knife at the wooden headboard the metal made a sickening sound as it thumped into the wood, frightening her further. The sharp blade had embedded itself in the wood near her head.

He came at her with a bandana, intent to wrap it around her mouth, preventing her from further prayers or screams. Once he'd silenced her, Inara became hysterical when he rolled her onto her side for she was afraid of what he was about to do.

Unsure if Rafe had seen what she'd written on her laptop yet, she was worried it wouldn't be enough for him and his family to find her. She hadn't known what was to happen or even when until she began writing it on her laptop. Not realizing as her hands had tapped along the keyboard that she was, in fact, writing out what was about to happen to her, the revelation had come to her too late.

Wincing in pain and despair at the tight dirty bandana now tied roughly against her mouth, she tried hard not to panic. Taking several quick breaths in succession through her nose she managed to gain a small measure of calm. Surrendering her fate to God she prayed for peace and acceptance of His will as she watched the raven settle its perch on the sink near the opposite wall. The black bird eyed her warily as she stared at it, envious of its ability to flee whenever it chose.

Staring at the bird, Inara suddenly found herself recalling the words of a poem she'd written when she had been nine years old. It seemed a random thought initially until she recalled the poem had been about a horse called Redemption and a man astride its seat. She'd known even before that moment that her purpose in Montana was for more than just assisting Lylia with her faith. But she had not known to the full extent until then. Though she suspected the knowledge had been placed in the back of her mind for quite a long time. Inara had told Lylia she'd come for her, but it hadn't been entirely true.

Drifting back in time, she shut her eyes recalling the feel of the sky-blue crayon in her hand as she'd written the poem that spring day. It had been a school assignment she'd taken too far but in the end, had gotten an A for her grade. The scent of the crayons and colored pencils she'd used to draw the cover for her poem book enveloped her and she almost wished she were back in that school classroom. Inara opened her eyes and stared at the windowsill. A small spray of rainwater splashed across her cheek for the window had been left propped open. Thunder boomed across the heavens and a brilliant flash of lightning struck just outside the window, blinding her briefly, forcing her to close her eyes against its brilliance.

Eyes opening, Inara blinked suddenly in awe, when she realized what it was she was seeing huddling near the opening of the window. A small white bird rested on the sill as though taking cover from the storm. Within its small beak was an object but she didn't quite recognize what it was until the bird dropped it next to her cheek on the bed. Her hands were bound before her so Inara decided to take a chance. Reaching up cautiously she enclosed the pale blue crayon in her hand. Sobbing tears of joy Inara shook as she cried, accidentally breaking the crayon in two.

She recalled the picture of a horse and rider with the crystal-clear blue eyes she'd colored to go with the Redemption poem she had written. She'd forgotten all about it until then. Longing to see the poem book again and hold it in her hands, she prayed for God's forgiveness and the choice of her own she'd made out of fear so many years before. Seeing a small remnant of her torn dress had fallen from her bound wrists she took hold of the broken piece of crayon along with the raven's feather and tied the two items together with a shoddy knot. Gesturing toward the white dove still seated upon the windowsill she willed the bird to take her message to its intended recipient.

The white dove eyed her at first, its head tilting toward her as though inspecting her intently. Alighting from its perch the bird dove toward her outstretched hands, grasping the small package between its beak. Then it hopped back up to the windowsill and flew back out into the storm.

Feeling rough fingers struggling with the zipper on the back of her dress Inara's attention was drawn back to the moment. She realized it must be stuck for Simms was becoming enraged. He jerked her from her side onto her back and she could see the glint in his blackened eyes.

"That's all right. I'll just cut it off." He grinned, grabbing for her legs.

Narrowing her gaze upon him in anger, her tenacious spirit refused to let Simms win. Feeling warmth spread from her left shoulder through her chest and up to her head, her mind seemed to clear of all but one thought.

God was with her.

The relationship she'd been painstakingly attempting to develop with Him over the past six months would not be broken by the man before her. Her genuine desire to be one in spirit with Jesus would see her through whatever she had to endure; of that she was certain.

And that's when she heard it, the gentle calm voice upon the air.

Escape.

I am with thee.

Inara knew what she had to do. Continuing to hold tight to the remaining broken crayon piece in her hand, she felt Simms untie her legs. He crawled up on the small cot and yanked her legs apart. The moment he leaned in toward her she reached up unexpectedly with her bound wrists and thumped him hard against his chest. The momentum had been just enough and unexpected enough to knock him backwards. Struggling up off the cot Inara tumbled to the floor. She felt movement behind her as she attempted to rise up off the ground which only served to spark a surge of energy within.

"Come here! I ain't even gotten started with you yet!" Simms roared in outrage, attempting to grab for her as she came up off the floor.

Inara pummeled her tightly clasped and fisted hands into his stomach as hard as she could.

The split second she'd winded him was all she needed. The tiny one-room cabin was close quarters, and it was a short distance from the cot to the door. She was able to escape through it before he scrambled to his feet.

The cool slew of rain hit her the instant she fell through the door. Not stopping to look back Inara blindly sprinted through the rain as fast as she could. Frantic to get away and unwilling to let her fear get the better of her this time, she screamed as loud as she could through the bandana, desperate for someone to hear her. Attempting to pull it away from her mouth she gagged at the smell and taste. Wiping at her mouth she heard the thunder boom and reverberate across the heavens above her. Through the noise, as her bare feet slapped through the muddy saturated brush and across the forest floor, she heard the heart-stopping sound of someone coming up behind her once again. At the same time another faint noise, like the sharp rapport of a rifle blast, met her ears above the rain.

"Help me! God please!" Inara screamed out in terror and distress. Her bare feet created its own path across the uneven forest floor, catching on rocks and twigs, cutting and scraping them painfully. Trying hard to ignore the pain, she felt thick long blades of grass slap against her ankles, leaving paper-thin cuts in her skin. The thorn bushes snagged and tore at what was left of her skirts, tearing at the flesh on her legs.

Through it all, Inara surged forward, chest heaving with labored breaths from running as though hellhounds were nipping at her feet. A brilliant light, like the flash of a camera, struck nearby, causing her to squeal in alarm as she became disoriented. The rain continued to pelt down upon her, creating rivulets of water along her face arms and legs. She was quickly losing momentum for she was tiring fast; unused to such exertion.

"Please, God, bring me home." Her terror instilled within her a burst of energy at the sounds of thundering feet behind her. Pumping her short legs as quick as she could, she found she could barely breathe. Without warning a hand snaked out and forcefully grabbed her.

Spinning her about Simms yanked at her hard, causing her to slip and fall to the ground, jarring her even harder. Her body ached and her bottom lip stung where she bit it, the taste of blood on her tongue sending bile to her throat.

Growling Simms tackled her, grabbing her arms from behind. The motion pulled her bound hands towards her stomach underneath her, pinning her in place

"I got you now," Simms swore at her, forcing her onto her back as he sat on her.

Helpless, Inara screamed in blind panic, the terror within her welling uncontrollably as water poured over her face and into her mouth.

"Rafe!" She sobbed; no longer able to keep the fear completely at bay.

Inara struggled beneath Simms, kicking at him throughout his attempts to keep her pinned down. The sound of thunder pounded near her ears and the ground felt as though it moved beneath her. Her back was pressed hard up against several small rocks and they dug into her shoulder painfully. Jerking her arms back she flinched when Simms appeared ready to strike. Out of the corner of her eye, she could swear she saw a giant black shape moving towards them. The keening wail of what sounded like a ferocious dangerous animal the size of a bear rent the air and claimed her view.

The sudden jarring motion of Simms weight, lifting unexpectedly away from her had her rolling over on the ground. Startled, she barely registered the new onslaught of rain washing over her as the barrier Simms had made with his body had disappeared. Blinking in an attempt to see what was happening she tried to sit up. She raised her bound hands above her head in a futile attempt to protect herself from the water splashing down through the trees.

Gasping, she inhaled sharply. The noises assaulting her senses reminded her of grappling, growling animals in the middle of a strenuous fight. A sharp loud clap and a resounding thud left one large bare-chested figure unconscious upon the forest floor. Stumbling backwards the man now looming before her spun towards her as another reared up toward them on a horse.

Heavy snorting breaths at her side forced her gaze around as puffs of air brushed against her neck. Surprised to see the snout of a black stallion near her face she gave a startled cry.

"Inara!" Rafe had turned toward her, alarmed to see the state she was in. He staggered slightly, his chest heaving as he took several sharp breaths, attempting to regain his composure. Confident Simms was no longer an issue for the moment he ran towards her even as other riders joined them. Several figures dropped down from their mounts, calling out to them as they landed on the ground.

Wet and bedraggled, Inara's hair clung to her neck and face as she trembled. Engulfing her in his arms even as she cried in relief, Rafe could hear her soft sobs as she shook where she sat on the sodden wet forest floor.

"Inara, Honey, I've got you." Rafe's panic filled voice was hard to hear above the thunder. He held her tightly as she shook from the cold and fear. Her teeth chattered as she curled self-consciously toward him while trying to pull her torn wet skirts down. Rafe covered her as much as he could with his leather duster as a tiny figure strode up next to him with his Stetson in hand. It had flown off his head in the struggle with Simms.

"Here you go." Hialey shoved the wet hat back on Rafe's head. "You might want that on, heading back." Her slightly confused and amused gaze flitted between the two drenched figures huddled together on the ground.

More horses with riders appeared before their eyes. Nearly a dozen people circled them even as Dartanian could be seen wrestling a semi-unconscious Simms into handcuffs while reading him his Miranda rights.

"You're a real piece of work, Simms," Dartanian shouted, relieved they'd managed to find Inara hopefully in time. "Seriously, what were you thinking?"

Dante assisted his brother in hauling their former foreman up onto one of the horses. Slumped over the back of the horse, battered and bruised, the man looked much older than his fifty years.

"I gotta get you out of this rain, Honey," Rafe said close to her ear. The feel of his warm breath on her face and the warmth of his solid body next to her was comforting. "This rain is gonna make you sick before our wedding Tuesday afternoon, and we can't have that," he said aloud, eliciting several surprised looks his way from his children and their spouses.

Breathing heavily Inara gazed up into his handsome wet face. His kind, tender eyes met hers as a hopeful spark lit within her. "Our wedding?" she asked tentatively. "Are we getting married, Rafe?"

"Well, that depends."

"On what?"

"On whether you say yes." He struggled to untie her wrists as he spoke while still wearing gloves.

Trembling next to him Inara gave a strangled laugh. Reaching toward him once her hands were freed, she opened a fisted hand before him.

"Here's my answer." She hoped he'd gotten her message and understood its meaning. "What do you think?"

Staring down at her hand he beamed at her, his smile of recognition filling his eyes. Reaching one hand into his pocket he pulled out what was within, placing a crayon piece and an engagement ring into her hand next to the crayon she already had.

"Will you look at the broken crayons? When put back together they make one." He pointed to the two sky-blue pieces of crayon in her hand.

"Yes," Inara said happily above the rain. "Yes, yes they do, don't they?" Still crying she clung tightly to the broken crayon pieces and ring. "A dove brought forth shall burst to fly."

"I know," he said tenderly. "And 'during a time of memory its gift of peace...'"

"-Shall set her free."

Exhaling with a relieved sigh Rafe hefted up from the ground, taking her with him. "I think I'll take that as a resounding yes," he said firmly. Hiking the tattered dress down her legs further he gave the ranch hands next to him a dismissive look when they moved to assist him, then carried her toward the black stallion near them.

"Now ... how about that first ride, Inara, Honey?" Rafe asked, assisting her onto the back of the horse while attempting to keep from bumping the bloody scratches on her legs and feet. Swinging up behind her, Rafe pulled her close in the saddle. Covering her once again with his duster and wrapping her inside his coat and within his strong arms he then pried open her hand as everyone gaped at them in surprise.

"Now let's just take a second and see how this looks on you." He pulled the engagement ring from within and placed it on her bare ring finger.

"Looks awful g-good to me." Inara stammered, shivering from the cold wet rain. "And Rafe? Is this the horse? Are we riding astride Redemption?"

Grinning, Rafe responded as he prodded the horse along. "It sure does, Honey. And yes," he paused, emotion filling his voice as he spoke. "I found Redemption."

Giggling with delight as they road Redemption away, Rafe whispered close to Inara's ear. "You were always my first love and you are my last love. You're the choice I've made."

Sighing next to him, Inara closed her eyes and rested her head against his chest as they rode along. The secret message within his words was well received. She was grateful to God for the man sitting behind her and the Stetson on his head for cover.

Mounting his horse as he watched them plod away, Drinian stared after his dad and Inara in shock. "Is it my imagination or did dad just get engaged?"

"Nope. Nope, not your imagination," Breydon confirmed pulling up on his appaloosa next to him.

"Whoa! Talk about your short courtships," Hialey said dryly. She turned toward Breydon, then gestured toward the couple riding away. "And that man gave us a hard time over only dating for three months!" Even though it had been a short ride she was tired, wet, and slightly annoyed by the turn of events. She had a strong feeling there was more to that story than what anyone knew.

The rest sat staring briefly after them, too stunned to speak. After a moment the silence was broken by Dante. "I figured it out Thursday, and I'm still in shock." Turning towards Dartanian, who had grabbed one of the spare horse's Simms had ridden to the divide, he then said. "So, it turns out you're the oldest. You want the ranch house?"

"No," Dartanian said sharply. "Nope, nope, nope, Dante. It's all yours." His emphatic response had been automatic eliciting wild laughter from everyone present. He was more than just a little disinclined to be living in the same house with his father and his new fiancée - and soon wife - who was the same age as him.

"Probably just as well," Breydon said as everyone turned towards him. Shrugging he continued, "I imagine that would be awful awkward considering you were trying to convince her to have babies for you recently."

All groaning and grinning widely in unison they plodded forward as Teddy and Brauman exchanged wide-eyed looks. They held back a little way to give the Blackthorne family some room.

"You know what this means, right?" Breydon exclaimed suddenly.

"What are you on about, Brey?" Megorah asked crossly. Drenched and wet, all she wanted was to get home as quickly as possible. She was not entirely pleased to learn her sixty-year-old father was re-marrying but the situation had proved amusing. Distracted by an unsettling sensation she was experiencing Megorah glanced around at her family. Someone was thoroughly upset, frightened even, and she was having trouble discerning who it was.

"Meggie, I'm thirty-eight years old," Breydon cried in distress, regaining her attention.

"What's your point already?" Hialey asked, becoming exasperated as her smile spanned from ear to ear. She suspected she already knew.

"We're all about to gain a seven-year-old sister with our mother's name and twin five-year-old brothers by the name Rafe and Dartanian!" Breydon tried to sound disgusted even though his eyes were sparkling with mischief.

"Personally, I think one Dartanian in the family is enough." Drinian vented, clearly attempting to goad his brother.

"Would you just hush already?' Dartanian shot back. "Just be glad dad's done after only nine of us. Imagine if he were to have more."

Dante hollered across the spread of horses as they rode slowly back to the house. "You never know. There could be more."

Five horses halted abruptly as Dante's siblings stared in stark shock at his back. He continued to ride leisurely away, not once looking their way.

"Awe man! You don't really think..." Dartanian galloped closer towards his twin brother in an attempt to catch up.

Their eyes met. They stared back at each other.

"But the prophecy. Isn't it about Lylia and me?"

"Old and new numbers. There is a question there, now isn't there?" Without saying another word he continued forward.

Dartanian could be heard groaning in worry and dismay as he drooped against his horse, desperately wishing he had his paper with the prophecy written on it in front of him. He was almost glad he'd have to leave straight-away to haul the currently unconscious Stevens Simms off to jail. There would be less humiliation to suffer in Inara's and his father's presence for his behavior that way.

"Now that ... is one entertaining household," Teddy said aloud, wondering silently what they were all talking about prophecies for.

Turning towards his boss Brauman nodded his head in agreement. "Betting it's gonna get even more entertaining in about six to seven months."

Chapter 31

Late Sunday night.
June 14, 2015

While sitting on the couch with Inara that evening Rafe had fallen asleep. She was bundled up in blankets next to him and he took comfort in her presence at his side. The knowledge that she was finally safe, rested in the back of his mind as he dreamed of his late wife.

Rafe knew he was dreaming but he didn't want to wake up yet. The memory of that sunny spring day over forty years before played out in his mind and it was a very pleasant one.

Wearing her wedding dress Lilyandhi Blackthorne had been awfully beautiful that particular spring day. She had a lily flower tucked in her hair and she was wearing his mother's antique sapphire necklace about her slender neck.

Playing with the delicate teardrop sapphire pendant that dangled where the arrangement came to a V, he marveled once again at the tiny cross that had been carved out of its center. The scrolling ribbon-like quality of the setting was really unusual and it had been handset with sapphire gems.

They had been picnicking near the creek that afternoon and had fallen asleep under the shelter of his favorite tree. Waking in a lazy fashion they enjoyed resting together in each other's arms until he noticed a tear streak down her cheek. Sensing his new wife had awakened from a troubling dream he probed for her to share.

"Tell me your dream."

"No."

"Lilyandhi, I'm your husband now. Shouldn't I, of all people, know your dreams?" he'd asked playfully, wanting her to feel like she could talk to him about anything.

Fidgeting next to him she harrumphed softly then rolled away from him. Suddenly, she alighted from the ground. The long creamy ivory velvet skirts whirled about her as she spun in place. The dress really did look exquisite on her and her gloriously long dark hair spun with her.

"One day, Rafe Blackthorne, God will grant you a light in your darkest hour."

"You don't say?"

"Oh, yes," she exclaimed, her face expressive, alighting with mystery. "Will you choose to accept His gift when it finally reaches your doorstep?"

"That depends." His cheeks scrunched up as he grinned back at her, his amusement over her coy indirect questions and answers was obvious.

"On what?" Her steps faltered as she twirled. "Seriously, I'd like to know."

Rafe became thoughtful. "On two variables," he finally said. He leaned up against the tree and rested one arm on his bent knee.

"Which are?" she asked in a flirtatious manner. Batting her dark lashes at him her unusual pale blue eyes shined back at him, a distinguishing contrast to her tanned Mandan Indian skin.

"First of all, do I truly have a choice?" He stretched and yawned while rolling his shoulders.

"You told me once, that we always have a choice. It's why God granted us free will."

"Yes, and that's true. I still hold to that."

"So?"

"So, what?"

"Rafe, what's your answer?" she asked plaintively. "Will you accept the light in your darkest hour when it reaches your doorstep?"

Sighing in resignation, Rafe frowned slightly. "Well … how long must I wait for this 'light in the darkness'?" he mocked.

"I don't know. Maybe I just only know it's coming."

"Lilyandhi, where is this going?" He was becoming annoyed.

Giggling mischievously, even a little mysteriously Lilyandhi Blackthorne posed a question. "Answer me this and you get your answer. How long did Noah and his family seek refuge within the walls of the ark?"

"Forty days and forty nights," Rafe answered automatically. "You know that, Honey."

Frowning, she grimaced, looking confused. New to the Christian faith she was forever getting her stories mixed up. "Oh, no wait … that's not right." Her face became animated once again. "Wrong question. How long did God make the Israelites wait before they could see the promised land?"

Rafe hesitated, wondering suddenly if she was messing with him. "Forty years." Seeing her smiling brightly back at him he bowed his head in frustration and continued. "Lilyandhi, are you telling me I'm going to have to wait forty years for this 'light in the darkness'?"

"All good things come to those who wait." She grinned but then her expression became serious. Moving toward him she shyly wrapped her arms around him, resting her head against his chest then sighed sadly. She appeared troubled as she clung to him almost desperately.

Becoming concerned Rafe begged her this time. "Will you please tell me your dreams?"

Sighing again she pulled away. "I dreamed that one day you would have twelve children to call your own." Tears filling her eyes, she smiled weakly, almost anxiously back at him.

"Twelve children! Surely you jest."

"I would never make fun in such as this," she said, sounding almost hurt.

Laughing aloud he gave her a suspicious, disbelieving look, and asked in a teasing tone. "Are you telling me, you will one day bare twelve children for me?" His face became goofy at the notion.

Giggling nervously again, as she laid her hand upon her belly, she twirled away, avoiding his question. "Build me a home full of secrets within its walls," she demanded.

Barking out loud at her audacity, he laughed again good-naturedly. "We already have a home, silly. The ranch house of course."

Left to him by his father Rathbourne, when he returned home to Scotland with his brother, Rafe had lived alone there for several months. But now things had changed. He had a wife and soon a child to come.

"It won't be enough." She said playfully, swirling her skirts with her hands in front of her.

He decided to humor her. "Really? How big are we talking here?"

"Thirteen bedrooms," she said promptly.

Chuckling, he smiled at her, continuing to humor her as she teased. "And why so many rooms?"

"There were twelve disciples after all, and there should always be one, where the master of the house can lay down his head at night in peace. You know, where he can safely reflect upon Jesus."

"I see. Thirteen bedrooms, eh?" Smiling brightly his perfect white teeth shined in the sunlight.

"Trust me, Rafe." She twirled away again, skirts flying. "For one day, you will have many, many grandchildren as well. I promise you that." She sounded almost serious now.

"All I need from you," Rafe said as he reached out and ensnared her with his long strong arms. "Is a promise that you'll stay by my side until the day that I die."

Her face dropped suddenly and she became troubled. "I cannot promise you that. You know as well as I, that when God deems it's our time to go to Him, then it is our time, regardless of what anyone else might want."

Rafe's body trembled uneasily at her words and he experienced an unsettling sensation in his gut. Not ever wanting to imagine his wife leaving his side he attempted to shake off the feeling, then grinned.

"Twelve children of my own and many, many grandchildren you say?"

"Actually, I believe I said twelve children to *call* your own, silly. But then, what's it really matter? After all, I do often get my words mixed up, now don't I?"

"And I have to build a house with thirteen bedrooms?"

"And secrets within its walls," she insisted. She grinned mysteriously up at him. Twirling away, she called out to him, "As God said to Noah when He told him to build the ark, 'if you build it, they will come.'"

Marveling at her spirited, even whimsical personality, Rafe took two quick strides and playfully tackled her. He rolled along the grass on the ground with her as he tickled her mercilessly and she giggled hysterically. Their horseplay ended in a passionate and loving kiss.

"Oh, Lilyandhi. I love you so much." With a sigh, he gazed into her beautiful eyes so like his own. All of twenty, he was young and very much in love.

"Do you love me more than God?" she asked out of the blue, surprising him.

"No," he said firmly. "No one should ever love anything or anyone more than God, but I *can* promise you this. My love for you is infinite. I could never love another as I do you."

"The lines of infinity go both ways, Rafe." She spoke tenderly. "A person could find love again if he chose to be open to it."

Her response to his words had surprised him. Instead of insisting upon his undying love for all eternity, she had instead attempted to encourage him otherwise.

"I choose not to be," he insisted. "I will only ever love you."

"Please don't say that," Lilyandhi said quietly. Worry clouded her eyes and she sounded pained as she spoke.

"Why?" He raised up onto his elbows so he could look down upon her better. They still lay together in the grass, side by side, holding each other.

"Because, if you make that choice, it could ruin everything."

Becoming exasperated with his new bride, he bowed his head in frustration. "You're killing me, Lily of the Valley," he exclaimed, using his pet name for her. "I'm trying to be romantic here."

Laughing happily, Lilyandhi became serious once again as she toyed with the buttons on his white dress shirt. "My love, would you truly allow a choice you make to shake the foundation of God's grand plan?"

Surprised by her query, he stared down upon her, his eyes narrowing in consternation. He became both perplexed and troubled at her words.

"No, I would not want that burden upon my soul," he answered just as seriously. Running the back of his hand gently across her cheek, he wondered at what it was she had seen in that mind of hers as she'd dreamed. Clearly, it was more than what she was letting on.

"Then promise me, love," Lilyandhi pleaded. "Promise me, that when the light comes to your door, you will leave your heart open to it."

He kissed her tenderly then, realizing how truly serious she was being. "I promise. I will."

"Good. Listen to your wife for she knows much more than you might think. Heed her words even when what she says seems impossible and crazy."

Chuckling with humor he rolled her to her back, pinning her in the grass as he covered her small form with his large frame. The depths of his crystal-clear blue eyes grew dark, their color becoming a bright, almost sapphire blue.

"I always do."

Leaning forward as she giggled, he kissed her feverishly and tenderly wrapped her in his arms.

Waking slowly from the pleasant dream Rafe's eyelids flickered, registering the soft firelight coming from the warm hearth. The fire burned low, its embers appearing to be dwindling as he sat with Inara huddled quietly next to him. Her soft breathing was reassuring to him. His arm, still draped around her, was beginning to cramp so he adjusted it carefully, not wanting to wake her.

Peering down at Inara's sleeping form his late wife's words reverberated in his mind.

"One day, Rafe Blackthorne, God will grant you a light in your darkest hour."

Her words echoed within him. They were similar to the words spoken by his new ranch hand.

"Will you choose to accept His gift when it finally reaches your doorstep?"

Smiling at her words his eyes misted. He recalled when they woke together beside the creek that Lilyandhi had seemed so sad. He realized suddenly that she'd known. She'd known her life would be shortened by illness and that she wouldn't be the one he'd end his life with.

Wincing Rafe rested his head against the cushions of the couch. It pained him to come to the realization but he knew somehow she'd also known she'd been his second love and not his first.

His heart hurt for her.

He had never told Lilyandhi, not wanting to cause her pain. For that reason he'd hidden the secret away, covering it up with curtains in the art studio she'd never known he had.

Or had she?

"Build me a house filled with secrets."

"Lilyandhi … you little minx," Rafe murmured softly.

Feeling Inara's fingertips sliding across his belly and up his chest, he pulled her arm away in his hand. "I'm sorry. I didn't mean to wake you."

"You didn't. I've been awake for a little bit," Inara said quietly.

Peering down at her, Rafe became thoughtful. The poem book she'd shown him rested against her lap.

"I have to ask you something, and I'm afraid I need an honest answer."

Inara pulled herself up to a seated position next to him with her legs tucked underneath her. Her feet were wrapped with soft gauze in order to keep the antibiotic ointment from rubbing off. "If I am able to answer it, I will always be honest, though you may not like my response to your questions at times."

Acknowledging her response with an appreciative nod Rafe continued his inquiry carefully. "When you were talking with Lylia the other day, you mentioned you had been here in Montana once before and that you met one of us. Am I to presume it was me?"

Staring at her hands at first, she then looked bashfully back at him through her lashes. "It was you, yes. I was nineteen at the time and I had traveled here with the intent to move to Montana. I checked out the area and even found and put a deposit on an apartment. I'll give you one guess as to where and which one?"

Giving her a calculating look his eyes narrowed slightly. "Are we talking about the same apartment Lylia ended up renting?"

"Yes, which also happens to, interestingly enough, be the same one Veta rented from Drinian."

Rafe's gaze shifted to the fire. Learning that three of the future Blackthorne women had taken residence in the same location made him wonder if there might be significance to it for some reason, or if it was simply coincidence. Unable to ascertain, at that moment, what significance, if any, it might be, he shook his head and sighed softly. After a moment he spoke again.

"Inara, I am sorry but I do not recall ever having met you." He was clearly troubled by the notion of not remembering.

"You wouldn't; remember that is." She shook off his response with a nervous laugh and smile. "You were preoccupied with other matters at the time," she said after seeing his questioning glance.

Rafe prompted her when she didn't continue. "I would like to understand. Please explain."

Taking a deep breath she exhaled and began. "I was at the train station when I saw you. I was going to return to Michigan to get my things and come back here. You were standing on the platform near the train and there was a woman with very long dark hair standing near you with her back to me. You had just seen a short man wearing a polo shirt and dress slacks off onto the train and you appeared pretty distraught."

Thinking back over twenty years Rafe suddenly knew the moment Inara had been referring to. The last doctor that had seen Lilyandhi didn't like to fly. The man had just given them the bad news about his wife's failing health and that there was nothing more he could do. She passed away a month later.

"Inara, what happened? Why didn't you come back? What frightened you away so badly that it kept you from me for over twenty years?"

Closing her eyes Inara struggled to fight back the tears at the memory. Knowing he needed to hear the why, and understand the why, it was still painful for her to admit. She knew it would be difficult for him to hear.

"You have to understand, Rafe, when I saw you I became so excited. I'd been dreaming about you and drawing pictures of you for years. I was so in love with you already." Embarrassed, her voice became softer as she spoke. She was struggling to keep from crying. "So when I overheard what you said to Lilyandhi as I boarded the train, I was so hurt and frightened that your words were really true. I didn't…"

"Wait a minute. You're saying it was something *I* said that kept you from coming back?" He was more than a little disturbed to learn that he could be the reason for her absence in his life. Seeing her head bob up and down Rafe took her gently by the shoulders. "Inara, Honey, what could I have possibly said that frightened you so?"

"You said, and I quote, 'Lilyandhi my heart, my Lily of the Valley. My love for you is infinite and I will never love another for as long as I live.'" Her soft voice had a catch to it as she finally aired the words that she'd overheard, after so many years.

Grimacing, Rafe groaned in frustration. Resting his forehead against her shoulder he pulled her towards him, wrapping his arms around her shaking form as she cried. Tears streaked her cheeks and dripped into her hair.

"By the time I got back to Michigan, I had convinced myself there was no way you could ever fall in love with me. I wasn't much to look at even then so…"

"No! Don't do that. Don't ever do that with me." Rafe had become angry. "You are so beautiful, Inara. There is literally a light about you… You just have no idea!"

381

"But I am forever a mess," she countered, disbelieving him. "I haven't looked like Lylia does since I was sixteen years old! I likely never will again. Between having the kids and just generally not being able to take care of myself properly I have gained so much weight, and my hair is gone and…"

"Your hair?" Rafe was incredulous. "Inara, Honey, your hair is beautiful just as it is. It would be just as beautiful were you to allow your true color to grow back. It doesn't need to be down to your waist. As for the rest, I'll be more than pleased to show you how much I enjoy it tomorrow night." His grin held a spark of interest in his eye, causing her to blush prettily. Brushing a tear away from her cheek as she gazed back at him with dreamy eyes he smiled at her. "I will hear no more on this subject. Women seem to think they have to have a certain shape or size, or, color or length of hair in order to make themselves attractive to men. But for me, all I need is to see your heart and God's light in your eyes. Okay?"

Nodding back at him in understanding she wiped at her tear streaked face.

"As for what I said… I am so sorry, Inara. The timing there was just bad. I had just been given some really upsetting news from the doctor and I needed Lilyandhi to know…"

"It's okay, Rafe. I do understand now," she insisted. "I do. I just didn't back then. I didn't know what I know now and didn't fully realize that I even had this gift. Everything makes so much more sense now. I understand now that a person can find love more than once in their life. After all, I did."

"Yes. Yes, they can." Rafe could see her mind working overtime and could tell she had something eating at her but appeared afraid to ask him.

"What is it, my love?" Reaching out, he ran his hand through the length of her hair, enjoying the feel of the silken texture in his hand.

Screwing up the courage Inara finally spoke. "Is it true what you said on the way back?" She wasn't able to look him in the face. "You know, the same words repeated in my poem." She fidgeted with her fingers in her lap. The poem book she'd found in her bag slid from her lap to the floor. The word Redemption, scrolled out in crayon by a child's hand on the cover of the book was written above the picture of the horse and rider. It could be seen half peeking out from underneath the couch.

Knowing full well what she was referring to, Rafe took her by the arm and stood, helping her up from the couch. "Come. I have something to show you," he said as the book was accidentally bumped and slid further under the couch out of view.

Side by side they walked together up the stairs as he led her to his bedroom. Punching the code in his keypad he let her in, closing the door behind him. Gazing at him curiously she watched him walk away towards his bathroom and disappear. Seconds later he ducked his head around the doorframe back at her.

"Follow me," he encouraged then grinned devilishly. "I assure you I don't bite."

"You mean I actually get to see it?" Inara became giddy with excitement. She suspected she knew where he was taking her.

Rafe reached out to her and took her by the arm rather than her hand once again. Dragging her into the bathroom, he strode toward the sink and reached up at the ceiling. Removing a large ceiling panel he set it on the floor next to the sink then yanked on a chord that had fallen down from the large opening and was dangling above him. As he pulled on the chord, a set of wooden stairs folded down from the ceiling. Ascending the steps he helped her up through the ceiling passageway.

Emerging into a large open space Inara stared in awe and wonder at the sight before her. The expansive room appeared to extend the length of the house from his bedroom down to the space above his study. Finished off on one side, Rafe had built-in cabinets and drawers all along that wall and they were filled with a vast array of art supplies. Dozens of easels set about the room with canvas' in varying sizes propped up on them. Many were already completed but some were still waiting for the finishing touches.

All along the angled roof portion were a hundred or more paintings just waiting to be framed, hung, or simply found a home.

"This is amazing!" Inara's suspicions about where the many paintings in his home, and for that matter around town, had come from had been right. Slowly walking around the room she noted some were renderings of mountains or other forms of scenic views, and others were portraits of people and animals. Envious of his impressive skill with a paintbrush she was about to say as much when she halted before a copy of a painting she was quite familiar with.

"This is the Café Terrace by Vincent Van Gogh."

"Is it now?" Rafe was leaning against a nearby wall. He crossed his arms over his chest as he watched her. Enjoying the view of her dark blue eyes under the bright lights he waited to see if she'd figure it out.

"Wait a minute." She eyed the painting closely. Her brow furrowed then her eyes widened in dismay. "You? Did you paint this?"

Not saying a word he simply nodded.

"Geez, Rafe, this is an excellent forgery. Wow!"

Chuckling, he said, "I like to think of it as complimentary copying."

Inara appeared skeptical. "You could make a small fortune on your complimentary copying."

"High praise; I'll take it." Rafe grinned. "Only one problem, I have the habit of signing the wrong name and on the back of the canvas at that. It's automatic. I can't seem to help myself."

Flipping the painting over, she read the name aloud. "Vortigern Black. Oh, I like that name," she breathed, thinking it would make an excellent boys name. "Of course now, this doesn't really answer my question. Though I am ever so grateful to you for showing me this." She spun around, lifting her arms in an encompassing motion about the room.

Rafe stared at her without speaking. Rubbing his hands together anxiously he inhaled deeply. "Turn around," he said finally.

Perplexed, Inara did as told. Catching sight of a set of velvety navy-blue curtains in front of her she peered back at him in confusion.

"Open the curtain."

Pulling the curtains back she stood in stunned silence as she stared at the life-size painting before her eyes. Startled to find a meticulously rendered portrait of herself with medium length strawberry blonde hair in Lilyandhi's wedding dress she gaped at the beautifully painted portrait. Clasping a hand against her chest near her heart she peered wide-eyed up at Rafe as he came up quietly behind her. Her breath caught in her throat when he directed her gaze toward the bottom of the painting. The only painting in the studio signed by Rafe Blackthorne himself and the date listed for its rendering stunned her.

"Nineteen seventy-two. But, Rafe, this was dated three years before I was even born," she exclaimed in amazement.

"Yes. Yes, it was. You were always my first love, Inara. I've been waiting for the light in your heart for over forty years, Honey." Emotion charged his voice as he spoke and his eyes sparkled with moisture within. The desperate desire and need to have her in his life and as his wife overwhelmed him.

Leaning toward her, Rafe slowly slid his bare hand down her arm, the intent within his eye was clear. His fingertips grazed the sensitive skin at her wrist and her breathing instantly became ragged.

"Do you really think that's wise? You know, touching hands today?" Inara yelped as he moved to take her hand.

"Wise or not, it's long past overdue." His eyes flashed bright and clear blue, a warm glow emanating from them as he finally, after over forty years took her hand in his. The air within the room was suddenly charged with energy and everything around her seemed to fall away. The electric sensation rocketing from their joined hands sent them both into shivers.

"I'm gonna kiss you Inara," Rafe whispered, bending toward her.

Nodding mutual agreement she replied in a small voice. "Okay."

She was entranced by the light in his eyes.

Kissing her tentatively, softly, Rafe pulled her towards him their lips parting with a mutual desire to truly know each other as God had intended. He held her close then pulled unexpectedly away, inhaling deeply as he blinked in the bright lights of his hidden art studio.

"Now we really have got to get married," he said, struggling to reign in his need to be with her.

"Yes, yes." Inara stammered. "I think that would be wise."

Chapter 32

Wedding Day
Tuesday, June 16, 2015

Bathed in the glow of the soft, late Tuesday afternoon sunlight spilling forth through the crystalline windows of the church, the couple spoke their vows. With trembling hands, she reached out to him when the pastor prompted for the ring. Taking her hand into his for the first time since Sunday night, the sensation that shot through their hands as they touched overwhelmed them at its intensity.

Rafe's heart skipped a beat, while he drew a shaky breath, eyes locking with hers. He could see the same emotions; the same internal tumultuous experience mirrored in the reflection of the deep blue pools of iris's meeting his gaze.

Taking a tremulous breath, she held it as he slid the ring upon her finger, the padded tips of his fingers lingering at the feel of her skin below his. The light, floral scent of lavender ensnared his senses, bewitching him as his gaze lingered upon her sweet face before turning back to the pastor. At that moment, the instant before he had turned, poised as she was, prompted the image of the portrait he'd painted as he spoke his remaining vows.

Like a heart beating in an increasing rhythm, so too did his pulse quicken when the pastor announced them as husband and wife. Usually capable of dispassionate indifference and the exemplary composure required in order to reign over such a large household with great faith, Rafe found his demeanor cracking ever so briefly.

Turning back to the silent figure next to him the pastor encouraged him to kiss his bride. Rafe's eyes sparkled as they met her delightfully startled gaze. Chuckling softly within his throat, the smooth sound elicited an obvious shiver along her spine. He reached over and took her about the waist with his left hand. With a gentle pressure and light tap at her hip, he guided her up onto her tiptoes, as he bent toward her. His lips met hers upon a tremulous gasp from between hers, the sigh escaping her at their joined mouths, prompting a soft, barely audible groan and exhale of his own.

Rafe's right hand cradled her left cheek in a feather-light touch as they took pleasure in their very first kiss together as man and wife. Feeling a tap on the shoulder he ignored it initially, as he continued to enjoy with renewed vigor the feel of his wife's lips against his. Prompted once again for his attention by a firm thump on his back he finally stopped.

Peering almost irately back at his eldest son for the distraction, a hot flush surged at his neck at hearing giggles and whispers from the guests behind them in their pews. Grudgingly, and with regret, Rafe pulled away. Clearing his throat, he placed a slight amount of distance between them. Clasping Inara's hand within his, he peered down upon her tenderly, the excitement still prevalent in his darkening pale blue eyes.

Inara gazed back up at him as he flashed her an endearing grin; her heart fluttering as though to the soft beat of a butterflies wings. She had waited for this moment for so long and it had finally come.

Transfixed by his distinguishing visage, her gaze caught his profile as he peered out upon the church members seated in their pews. His pleasure at their union was evident in his expression for his eyes fairly sparkled with barely repressed joy. Inara had noticed, as she walked down the aisle, that he wasn't just wearing one of his suits but a tuxedo. She had wondered where he'd gotten one at the last minute. He'd looked so dashing, like her very own prince charming, and had been touched by his efforts to make the moment memorable for her with the church wedding rather than one at home.

Bending towards her Rafe whispered in her ear, causing her to shiver once again. "Let's greet everyone as we let them out of their pews first then head to the fellowship hall for the reception."

"There's a reception?" she asked in surprise.

Smiling tenderly at her once again he nodded in assent.

Inara licked her lips nervously and gave him a timid smile. Her hand holding the flowers shook slightly as she took the steps down the aisle to the first section of seats. She knew none of the people but addressed each one as though she had for a long time-grateful for their warm wishes.

As the evening wore on they partook of a meal together in the fellowship hall with his family and friends within the church. Inara had been stunned to see an Italian buffet displayed before them. Platters filled with lasagna, garlic bread with cheese, antipasto and salads rounded out the meal and a simple wedding cake was displayed in the corner of the room. Learning later in the evening that it was her favorite, chocolate with strawberry buttercream, Inara realized that Rafe had in fact completed reading most of her versions of book three. She had written of having the same wedding cake within one of her many stories.

Noting with amusement the many curious stares and questioning whispers over the broken crayon, small paintbrush and black horse figurine of Redemption displayed at the top of the cake, Inara smiled secretly. The gesture had been intentional and it touched her heart.

"You seem a bit surprised." He forked a piece of cake and offered her a bite. Accepting it gratefully Inara moaned with pleasure and licked her lips, sparking a twinkle in his eye.

"I am," she mumbled, covering her mouth as she chewed and swallowed. "Rafe, when did you have time to do all of this? And how?"

Chuckling he forked another bite. "You'd be amazed what a few phone calls can accomplish, especially among this throng of people. When they learned there was a Blackthorne wedding they all began chipping in straightway to pull it together."

"A Blackthorne wedding?" Inara emphasized. "Or Rafe Blackthorne's wedding?" Inara asked as she smiled brightly. "And how many broken-hearted embittered women do I need to watch out for exactly anyway?"

Chuckling, Rafe smiled openly, his ears turning pink with embarrassment. Pulling her close to him he planted a kiss against her cheek, lingering briefly. Patting her leg he cleared his throat as he stood and took her hand in his.

"Come Mrs. Blackthorne. Allow me to take you home."

His words made her shiver with pleasure. For so long she'd dreamed of hearing them, never believing it might ever be real.

"But, what about the cake?" she asked, sounding only slightly disappointed as he pulled her along.

"We'll have cake and champagne in our room." His voice dropping an octave as he spoke.

"All right." She grinned, her eyes lighting with mischief. "But only as long as I can have taco's for breakfast."

Laughing out loud Rafe ignored the many heads that turned their way at her request. "Taco's for breakfast it is." They walked side by side, waving goodbye to the people. Exiting the church Inara exclaimed in delight at the awaiting limousine which would drive them home. For the first time in her life, she felt at peace and it was an amazing feeling.

"Aren't we taking the children with us?" She could see little Rafe, Tanian and Lily playing with the rest of the kids as they drove by the church playground.

"No worries, Mrs. Blackthorne. Drinian promised to bring them home for us and put them to bed tonight. He said something about needing the practice of handling three at once."

"He does realize that handling three babies versus twin five-year-old's and a seven-year-old is a wholly different experience doesn't he?"

"I figured I would correct him on that tomorrow. I wasn't going to argue over freely offered babysitting services on my wedding night."

Giggling Inara beamed up at him. Resting her head against his shoulder, she snuggled up against his side.

"Just so you know. I'm in love you and have been for most of my life."

"Yes, my love. I know."

- - -

Late that evening, had Breydon taken the time to look out his window, he might have witnessed an extraordinary sight. Circling the ranch home, high in the heavens, were dozens of angels bathed in holy light. Hovering in place they had each taken up designated locations around the home. The light emanating from them created a circular barrier of sorts over and around the ranch house, ensuring the protection of those within its walls.

"The circle is now complete," Maleeka said while keeping a watchful eye out for the shadows that lurked at the edges.

"Yes, and just as God ordained," Woreash said.

The hour was quite late and most of the rooms appeared dark but for the flickering of candle flames or firelight easily observed through the windows. Even the lights from the playroom, where all the children had bunked together for the night, had been extinguished so as to allow for sleep. Soft plumes of smoke had the occasion to escape from the chimney above the Blackthorne patriarch's bedroom.

"He does seem quite obsessed with firelight," Maleeka noted, gaining his counterparts attention.

"He is? Or she is?" Woreash grinned, his brilliant grey eyes appearing almost silver under the star-laden sky. "Then again the Blackthorne men are well known for their romantic natures."

Chuckling humorlessly Maleeka scowled. "Regardless, I'm awful glad we managed to set this course aright. The troublesome three were becoming extremely tiresome in their attempts to derail this set of events. The demon Fallen seemed to take an annoying amount of pleasure at trying to set the ranch home ablaze with embers from one of its many hearths'."

"Ah, well, it will be quite some time before he'll get another chance at such a trick," Woreash said with satisfaction. "The troublesome three have become the troublesome two, at least for a short time." Having dispatched the demonic creature back to where he belonged himself, he knew it would simply be a matter of time before it would return. They never went away forever, for even their judgment would not come until the end.

"I am simply grateful we have finally reached this juncture in His plan. The decisions made by the humans within the past three days will provide the impetus for what is soon to come."

"Agreed."

Receiving the silent missive from the Lord both angels ceased their discussion. The heavens above them opened up with bright luminescent light. Separate shafts of light beamed down toward the Blackthorne ranch home, shining through the rooftops into several of the bedrooms. Watching with bated breath Woreash and Maleeka along with the many angels waited to see if God's brilliant white light would shine down on all the necessary rooms within. Circling the home in slow motion, the angels hummed as in a choir, anxious to see if all within had been touched by the events of the day. They all had their own personal task and a charge within one of the many rooms. Seeing the light had born down upon the Blackthorne patriarch's room first, Woreash and Maleeka turned toward each other briefly and smiled knowingly.

"He has been waiting over forty years after all," Maleeka whispered.

"Hhhmmm. Indeed," Woreash said with a sideways glance his way. Returning his attention to the ranch below, he noted beams of light touching down in the far northwest corner of the house and then again near the western center of the home. Moments later, not too surprisingly, another flash of light shined down southwest of the last.

"No real big surprise there. The light shines within that room just about every night." Maleeka commented dryly. The angel Rodrinus, who was the faithful companion to the youngest Blackthorne son, appeared troubled, however, as he circled along with the rest. Wondering at the consternation clear upon the angels face Maleeka was about to comment when another brilliant flash of light exploded with great force from the heavens. It soared toward the rooftop below disappearing through the ceiling of the last southwestern room of the house. Excited cries of glorious exclamations followed the wake of the light. The chorus of angels smiled happily, overjoyed that the last of the Blackthorne family members were now safely entrenched within the folds of the Lord's redeeming grace.

"And about time too, I would say," Woreash said with an approving nod toward the angel Marya, who was beaming over her charge. Her robes blazed higher and brighter. A pure white fire seemed to erupt from the tips of Marya's wings and the angel glowed ever brighter as the wings stretched and seemed to grow in size.

"It's so much easier for the demons to get in when they leave themselves open to them," Maleeka commented thoughtfully. "The human mind has enough to process and deal with. Add to that a demonic voice in their ear trying to sway their decisions and it can make choices that much more difficult for them to make." He was glad to see the woman had finally made her choice, and he knew the Lord was pleased.

The angels tarried longer; ever hopeful that two more beams of light would eventually find their way to the last couple rooms. After a while, as the hour grew late it became clear that no other lights would be seen. Frowning as the chorus of angels began disappearing one by one, Maleeka and Woreash turned to each other.

"It would seem more work is to be done," Maleeka said with disappointment.

"We knew this was likely even before the woman arrived. One is beginning to understand where her father's heart truly lay and the other…"

"The other is troubled by the past. For her, Sunday was an extremely painful reminder of her own poor judgment and choices."

Chapter 33

Saturday, June 29, 2015

Fourteen days later Rafe Blackthorne held a party on the lawn near his patio kitchen in order to celebrate his recent marriage and Inara's fortieth birthday. Feeling festive he invited the ranch hands and staff, much to his daughters' annoyance, as they had not anticipated such an immense gathering for the event.

That evening Teddy met on the porch of the bunkhouse with all the ranch hands, several with girlfriend's in tow, and they headed up toward the Blackthorne's back yard for the dinner. Unsure of what to expect, many joked along the way over their elderly employer and his young new bride in order to ease the tension. Their banter halted as they neared the porch, not wanting to offend or embarrass anyone.

Welcomed by Megorah and Crisalya looking harried but happy to see them, they were all instructed to dig in, to the buffet, and relax. The handlers and their lady friends were more than willing to oblige after seeing barbecue chicken and ribs with roasted red potato salad and coleslaw along the buffet. They helped themselves and even grabbed rolls and butter with their sodas.

Numerous tables and chairs had been set up on the lawn, laden with trays of fresh fruit. Finding a seat they watched and listened as a band was just starting their practice run while they finished setting up equipment on the hastily erected stage and dance floor.

The Blackthorne family members gradually found their way out to the buffet and tables, as the children were chased from the playroom for dinner.

Running late to her own birthday celebration, having been delayed by a wardrobe malfunction, Inara stepped out from the kitchen patio porch just as the band began playing her favorite song 'God Bless the Broken Road.' Catching Rafe's eye she laughed with delight when she realized he'd been waiting for her arrival for them to play their song.

Taking her hand as she stepped down barefooted from the porch Rafe chuckled while staring at her feet. "Why is it whenever I try taking you anywhere you're never wearing shoes?" he asked with a twinkle of humor in his eye.

"Honestly Rafe, if you want me to wear shoes then you need to actually take me to buy some," Inara said with a grimace of annoyance.

"I did." Pulling away he stared down at Inara with an amused frown on his face. "But I distinctly remember you telling me no one person really needs more than a couple of pairs of shoes. Yet you seem to avoid wearing any of the shoes I did buy."

"Yes, and if I could find those pairs of shoes amidst this vast house I would gladly wear them. Regardless, I feel at home when I am barefoot here."

Laughing heartily he pulled her toward the buffet table. They grabbed plates and began filling them. Noticing Inara was putting a lot of everything on her plate Rafe grinned back at her.

"Are you actually going to eat all that for once? Or are you just going to let it sit in front of you and stare at it all night?"

"I'll have no trouble eating it. Trust me," Inara insisted. "I can't help it, Rafe. I'm just so hungry lately."

"You and me both, Honey." Lylia met them at the table. Grabbing a plate she immediately began heaping it with food.

Shaking his head Rafe helped Inara find a seat near the stage and they spent the next few hours listening to music and making small talk with everyone. They watched the children eat then go play in the yard or on the playground. As the sun began setting in the sky the Blackthorne triplets began lighting the Tiki torches they'd set up earlier in the day around the gathering.

Starting a bonfire they brought out marshmallows, hot dogs and roasting sticks as well as Inara's birthday cake. Rafe presented her with a delicate pearl necklace as a birthday present, in addition to a new laptop.

"What do you think? Is it wise for me to continue writing?" Inara whispered, accepting her gifts gratefully.

Appearing thoughtful for a moment he finally responded. "I tend to think it's in all our best interest that you do."

Distracted by a commotion near the kitchen porch, the couple turned just in time to hear Hialey swearing angrily, as she banged through the kitchen patio doors.

"Don't see why I can't have it!" Hialey vented angrily. Spinning around suddenly as Royce stepped through the porch doors, she hollered up at him while shaking her tiny fists. "And if you'd have just made enough cake I wouldn't have to go after it in the first place."

"Hialey, you cannot eat their cake." Royce expounded in exasperation.

"I didn't get a piece of the birthday cake so why not?"

Pointing towards her as he shook his index finger at her, Royce argued as he scowled. "That's not true and you know it. I saw you go back twice for cake."

"Yeah, okay! But they were just little pieces." She wined as she pinched her forefinger and thumb in front of her face for emphasis. "Besides, what do they need it for anymore? They're already married. Who wants to eat it after it has been frozen for that long anyway?"

Exasperated and more than a little fed up with Hialey's antics from the night, Royce extended his arms above him then gestured toward her in agitation.

"Now hear this! You, Hialey Blackthorne, may not eat Rafe and Inara's one-year wedding cake. Leave it alone," he ordered before heading back into the kitchen.

Seeing Hialey huff indignantly, everyone watched as she crossed her arms and turned away. Her gaze caught Rafe's and she noted the hard set to his jaw.

Fidgeting suddenly, she flounced her loose orange and yellow flowered summer skirts then glanced away anxiously. Peering back at him she attempted to speak.

"Rafe, if I could just have…"

"No," Rafe said firmly as everyone present began to chuckle and laugh.

"Awe come on! You know what? *Fine!* Fine, fine, fine, fine, fine!" The crowd erupted in even further laughter as Hialey flounced away calling out as she went, "Bet that cake is nice and freezer burnt by the time it touches your lips in a year."

"Maybe I should go talk to her." Inara couldn't help but feel a little bad for her. She'd known Hialey would act this way, for she'd written about a situation quite similar in her story.

"You can try but it likely won't do any good. Once that girl gets an idea in her head she can't let it go."

"I know. I should at least try."

"Inara, Honey," Rafe called after her as she moved away in the direction Hialey went. He admired how beautiful she looked in the new sky-blue summer dress he'd bought her.

"Yes?"

"Be sure she finds the spare one-year cake I had made up, will you? It's in the fridge in the movie room."

Laughing out loud Inara followed after Hialey while shaking her head.

Watching the whole scene play out before him, Brauman shook his own head with amusement. Becoming tired due to the late hour and long day fixing fencing he yawned. He decided it was high time to head back to the bunkhouse for some much-needed shut-eye. Picking up the package set near his drink he grabbed his plastic cup and threw it away in the recycling bag. Strolling toward Rafe's table he dropped the package in front of him.

"What's this?" Rafe stared down at the small box the young handler had handed to him.

"Your wedding present," the young man said, as though the answer were obvious.

"Son, you already gave me the best gift you ever could by helping me find my new wife. Besides, I appreciate the gesture, but I have everything I need." Extending the box back toward the handler he shook it before him, encouraging him to take it back.

"With respect, Sir, no you don't."

Giving the young man an odd look, Rafe peered down at the box in his hand. It had been wrapped in a simple brown paper, quite similar to the sort most grocery stores used to use for grocery bags. Giving in to the inevitable, he unwrapped the small package before him and opened the lid of the box. Pulling the item out of the box he allowed it to rest in his hand.

Eyeing the item with a critical stare his facial features quickly changed as he recognized the item in question. Looking over at the man with a startled expression Rafe gaped at him. "Is this what I think it is?"

"Yes, Sir."

"Why are you giving this to me?" There was a note of concern in his tone, trepidation even as he attempted to lower it so no one could hear.

"Cause someday, she's gonna need it." The handler replied while gesturing toward Inara. She stood on the kitchen patio, listening to Hialey's animated speech over the cake.

"Who are you?" Rafe's words were crisp, holding a harshness in his tone. Eyes narrowing upon the young man, he gave him a calculating look as he attempted to size him up. He couldn't help but get the feeling like he was familiar to him somehow. Unable to put his finger on what made him seem familiar, he noted the man had soft brown eyes and brown hair.

Smiling grimly as he adjusted his hat he answered simply, "No one of consequence."

Gesturing toward the young man with the item in his hand, he queried further. He was suddenly suspicious and very worried. "How do *you* know?"

Watching the young man's response closely, Rafe observed his thoughtful expression, as though he were trying to determine the right choice of words. After a moment, the young man finally responded.

"Some know; and some see." The handler nodded his head toward Inara and the young blonde headed boy who'd run up to her from the playground, causing Rafe alarm. "And then there are some, Sir, who are what my father liked to call 'prophecy keepers.' They are extremely rare and few and far between."

"Prophecy keepers," Rafe exclaimed softly, stunned.

"Yes, Sir. Though personally, I prefer the term 'agent' or 'proxy'."

Rafe was aware that there were sometimes prophets among mankind, but he'd never encountered anyone like the man standing before him. Worried at what his presence meant upon his grounds, so near his home, he stared at him momentarily.

"Why are you here?" he asked sharply. The music from the band swelled in the background making it hard to hear.

The handler shrugged, as though the question were unimportant. "I'd wager a variable in His plan makes poor choices. Let's their emotions rule their life. I understand it's a rather unfortunate learned behavior from their mother, which tends to get them into a heap of trouble at times."

"Who?"

"Who else, Sir? My sister."

Surprised by Brauman's response, Rafe could see out of the corner of his eye that Hialey had managed to swipe the top of the cake from under Royce's nose and was now happily eating it in front of Inara, much to his annoyance.

"Who's your sister?" He asked uneasily. He noted once again the soft almond colored eyes and short brown hair plastered to his head as he took off his hat and held it with both hands in front of him.

"Miss Hialey, Sir." Brauman grinned, a look of pleasure on his face as he replied. "Of course, she doesn't know that. I think your about to get a shock, Sir." Brauman deferred his head toward the women on the porch. "Tread carefully." Placing his hat back on his head he touched his finger to its rim, nodded then sauntered away.

Stunned by the man's statement Rafe's attention was quickly drawn to the new scene now playing out on the porch. Lylia had come out to assist in trying to gain the cake back from Hialey just as Crisalya had grabbed several empty fruit platters from nearby tables to take inside. Turning towards the porch she was at the bottom of the porch steps when she looked up to see Inara and Lylia standing side by side on the porch. Crying out in alarm, Crisalya's eyes grew wide, and she dropped the platters to the ground.

"Oh, my gosh," she exclaimed while covering her mouth with her hands.

Taken aback by her unexpected behavior both Inara and Lylia exchanged glances then stared back at her. Her outburst had gained unwanted attention as people gawked at them.

"What? What is it?" Lylia was both confused and a little concerned at Crisalya's horrified, yet somehow joyful, reaction.

Pointing towards them as Hialey huddled over the one-year cake from several steps away, Crisalya exclaimed once again while laughing.

"You, you," she hollered exuberantly.

"You're causing a bit of a scene here. What are you going on about?" Inara asked quietly.

Stammering almost incoherently, as she jumped up and down with excitement, she finally blurted out. "You're pregnant!"

Doing a double take both women gaped at Hialey then turned to each other, their own eyes enlarging to the size of saucers.

"Wait a minute, Cris." Lylia finally regained her voice. "You said, and I quote, *you're* pregnant; that's all." She pointed towards herself then Inara in confusion. "Who were you referring to? Me ... or Inara?"

Somewhere Between
the Epilogue & the End

Hold...

...hold on. Just one second...

I need a ...
-A bit of a ...
-Just a swig more of ...
-Scotch.
You know – before I do my thing here.
Ahhhhh! That's b...(hiccup)...better.
No doubt you're sitting there thinking, "Why should I bother wasting my time listening to a narrator who sounds drunk and starts off a chapter by telling me to wait so he can suck down more scotch?"
Cause your time is precious, right?
And you've got better things you could be doing other than reading about some random narrator who doesn't have the decency to give you their full attention, especially when the person in question will only give you the cockamamie made up name of Vortigern Black.

Am I wrong, or am I right?

Here's the thing.

(Vortigern takes another gulp of alcohol.)

After reading through this story again and going back through all those booklets and notes of the original writer, I needed a little something to help me cope. Cause seriously, folks …

What have I done?

How could I have been so … (hiccup) … stupid?

Until now, I didn't fully understand. I mean, I knew... Because they told me if their secret got out it would be dangerous for them. But it didn't fully register completely what that meant until now.

People are ... k-killing people, to get their hands, on individuals who are gifted like the Blackthorne's and the RavenCroft's. Damien Biardon – or rather, Steven Adam Jameson was his real name, I guess – was murdered for it. Because that Phenom agent, Jericho Henley, wanted Ciara and her children.

The lengths the men from that organization will go to, certainly shocked the h...(hiccup)...eck out of me. My mind is still whirling with the reality of it.

(With a look of revulsion, he shivers and takes another hasty drink.)

I missed it all the first time 'round; the parts about Steven Adam Jameson. How could I have missed something so important?

(Vortigern shakes his head, looking desperate.)

Speed reading. That's how.

Geez! How could I have been so careless?

He's going to kill me when he finds out. Or worse.

(He starts hyperventilating.)

I've got to tell him; before it's too late. If it's not already.

The author tried to warn me. I should have listened to her. Somehow she knew I would regret putting this out there. Heaven only knows how many people might have gotten their hands and eyes on this stuff by now and figured it out.

I justified it, see? I told the author to write it up, put it out there as though it were fiction, and give that sanctimonious prick a good scare. Let him know he can't just disregard my needs like that, as if they were nothing and unworthy of his time. Who's going to know it was real anyway, right? There's a disclaimer at the front of the book after all. The one that says, any resemblance to actual events, locales, or persons...blah, blah, (hiccup) blah.

(Vortigern smacks his forehead with the glass and winces.)

But that's not all, because according to Ms. Christine, I've taken you as far as I can go with this tale, for the rest will have to play out from this point on. Or rather, the point from which time currently is progressing from at the time I stop narrating.

Which is now. Apparently. If that makes any sense.

(Hiccup)

Eh, never mind. Don't bother trying to figure all that out right now 'cause it'll just give you a headache. I know I have one.

You might have already figured this part out but, if I'm going to be honest here ... the An Unfortunate Lineage series technically was written by Angel Stryfe, a fictional – or maybe not so fictional – character within this collection of stories who, at this point, is now called Angela RavenCroft because she married Bastion, the RavenCroft patriarch.

Would you believe I managed to get my hands on everything she wrote?

I, along with the author, managed to read through all of it too.

(He makes shushing noises with a finger pressed against his lips, then downs the last of the Scotch in the glass.)

But then, you sort of knew that already didn't you? Cause I told you I was the thief in Total Kayos.

And when I say I've read it all, I mean every last page of every single novel whether completed, in the works or just started. As well as every last word of her notes. There was … (hiccup) … There was a lot.

That's why I missed it, see? 'Cause there was sooo much!

(Shoving the empty glass away, he picks up the bottle and takes a long drink)

In fact, I managed to finally finish it all a little bit ago. It's probably why … no, no … it's definitely why I started drinking his scotch.

I would have preferred rum, but that's all he had.

And it prompted the author's decision to finish this unfortunate family tale for you. Cause she found …

(Vortigern laughs bitterly, his brown eyes tearing up in distress. His laugh turns into a low agonizing moan.)

-She found what the ending is supposed to be. It blew both our minds!

(Puckering his lips he made explosion noises while jostling the scotch bottle in his hand.)

Why – you ask?

Because this isn't just a fictional story.

It's real.

-And, as it turns out, we're living through it as I speak.

Awe, geez.

(Vortigern can hear the steady clomp of booted feet down the hall. He begins to sweat. His hand shakes; the bottle clasped tightly within it.)

Here we go.

(The doorknob turns on the study door.)

I'm so screwed.

A man stepped into the study.

Their eyes found each other across the room.

Taking in the sight of the tall figure standing behind the desk with the Scotch bottle in hand; half poised in the air toward his lips as though he'd been drinking from the bottle, the crystal-clear blue eyes of the man who entered the study went instantly from confused to incensed in a manner of seconds. His body went rigid and his fists and jaw clenched ominously.

"How in the world did you get in here, and what possessed you to think I'd be okay with you drinking my prized Scotch from my own personal stash?"

Licking his lips nervously, the man who'd been calling himself Vortigern Black for the past six stories, closed his deep brown eyes then slowly opened them, preparing himself for the inevitable. Producing the key he'd found hidden in the door frame (*as he read he would per this short excerpt*) he proceeded to respond.

"K-key," he said with a terrified slurring stutter. "Was in the door frame."

Wide-eyed now, the other man jerked his head back toward the entrance of the door, then hastily checked his hiding spot near the hinge. Seeing a small slit of a hole where the key was supposed to be, his face registered shock. There was no way anyone could have known it was there unless they'd been told.

"How did you know where to look?"

Vortigern pointed toward the laptop, flash drive case, and stack of notebooks on the desk with one hand while extending the bottle of Scotch out to the man before him with the other.

"Trus' me. You're g-gonna wanna be d-drunk fer this ... Bastion."

A note from the Author

Dear Reader,

For your reading pleasure, the following is the poem from within Ciara Eve Biardon's book bag that she shared with Rafe after he found her and brought her home. Written at the age of nine it was bound by a child's hand and depicted the crayon and colored pencil drawing of a black stallion, listed as Redemption, with its rider. I hope you enjoy….

Redemption
A Poem by
Ciara Eve Kessler (maiden name)
Spring of 1984

Sitting astride Redemption the man came for her that fateful day. The skies were dark and the rain was fierce. No moon would light the paths way.

The man astride Redemption; a long-time faithful servant of God. He bore the burden of his service never once thinking it odd.

For the voice of God would be his friend long before he was even born, and his gift to "Know" a blessing, though his gift of "sight" he'd one day scorn.

His hair as black as the dark of night was just starting to show his age, and his eyes a pristine, crystal-clear blue, as bright as her colored page.

A duster he wore upon his back, a black Stetson upon his head. Dressed for church, yet wearing boots, he carried the ring for when they would wed.

Praying to God as he rode along, he hoped he wouldn't be too late. He'd always known this day would come. God had told him it would be his fate.

As a child, he had asked the Lord what His future plan was for him. The "voice" responded promptly. God's decision clearly not a whim.

"One day you will help fulfill my will," God had said in His reply, and then God told him of His plan, and he heaved a troubled sigh.

"As with Abram and Sarah, you will father children late in life. Though forty years you will have to wait, you'll take yourself a young wife."

The boy then asked, "Will I have a woman's love?" God said, "You will have three. Your first you won't know, the second's foretold, and the last will be set free."

Sitting astride Redemption the man could remember every word. Though now sixty years of age he looked forward to what he heard.

Recalling the rest of what God ordained the man hurried along his way. His focus on the light in the darkness, his own life he'd be willing to pay.

"Through a widow you'll find Redemption, and a troubled soul it will be. For though Redemption will have known death, a light in its eye you will see.

The horse's coat, black and sleek, will remind you of the one called Rohn. When your task's done, pass him on, for Redemption is not yours alone."

Sitting astride Redemption, he reminisced over the past forty years. The first he lost to the shadows, for her choices ruled her fears.

The second he lost to the Almighty, though he'd love her for all time. Nineteen years with her, not long enough, but they'd been truly sublime.

2

Sitting astride Redemption as he rode, the man called upon the Lord. His faith had led him to this day. He knew she would be his reward.

Begging that God would protect her and save her from his sins of the past, he swore his fealty to the Lord - that the gifted three would be his last.

So he sat astride Redemption, racing toward her that fateful day, and God revealed his memory, no longer holding it at bay.

Forty years before he met his second. Through their love, she bore him three. Six in total she'd given him, blessed with discerning gifts they would be.

But three years before he met his second, God came to him in a dream, bestowing visions of his first love, and it caused the man's eyes to gleam.

So poised before a canvas, he rendered her image with his own hand. Unaware he would need Redemption; of this he did not understand.

His first love was promised to him by the everlasting God above, but his sin of indifference had him seeking Redemption, not love.

So his first love became his third, and his Redemption was at hand. The light in his darkest hour found him again across the land.

Sitting astride Redemption the man surrendered his fear to God. Then he raced across his mountain, holding his flashlight like a rod.

A shot in the dark echoed throughout the shadow-laden forest, and then soon the Redemption beneath him would come to stand at rest.

Without Redemption, he'd have been too late, but he reached her before long. His own indifference had set their course on a path that had been wrong.

But her light guided him to her. He redeemed himself in God's eyes. And the man asked her to marry, for he knew this course would be wise.

Baring down along the dark path, Redemption would take them both home. Two long lost loves reunited. No longer would they be alone.

Redemption brought her to his arms when he surrendered to God his fear. So he held her tightly in the saddle and whispered against her ear.

Sitting astride Redemption, hand in hand before her his heart he laid, "You were always the first and you are the last. You're the choice I've made."

The meaning of the name Inara: Illuminating, Shining, Light and Radiance, Heaven Sent, Ray of Light, illumination, enlightenment, to bring light into darkness.

Thank you for taking the time to read my story. I truly hope you enjoyed it.

Please be sure to leave a review of Kayos Knows at amazon.com. I'd love to hear from you!

And now the finale. A looong time in the making.

Karisma Kayos: Out of Time
An Unfortunate Lineage Finale
Volume VII
By Delaine Christine

It's now available through Amazon.

Either way, I hope you're enjoying the series so far!

Delaine Christine

CHARACTER LIST OF SUSPECTS

Damien Biardon - (A.K.A. Steven Adam Jameson) - The husband of Ciara Biardon and father of her three children: (Little) Rafe, Tanian (Dartanian), and Lily (Lilyandhi) Biardon.

Ciara Biardon - The wife of Damien Biardon (A.K.A. Steven Adam Jameson) and mother to Lily, (Lilyandhi, 7), Rafe (5), and Tanian (5) Biardon. She is an aspiring author of a novel series.

Rathbourne Blackthorne - The former owner of The Blackthorne Horse Ranch. He is the father of Rafe, Rourke and Randulf (deceased) Blackthorne. He returned to Scotland with his son Rourke after his wife, Saphire, passed away in 1974. He still lives there with his unmarried son today.

Saphire Blackthorne - Is the deceased mother of the triplets Rafe, Rourke and Randulf (deceased) Blackthorne. She was a gypsy woman with unique and mesmerizing crystal-clear blue eyes. She was married to Rathbourne Blackthorne.

Rafe Blackthorne - The patriarch of the Blackthorne household and owner of The Blackthorne Horse Ranch in Kalispell, Montana. He was married to Lilyandhi Blackthorne (deceased.)

1

Lilyandhi Blackthorne - The deceased matriarch of the Blackthorne clan. She is the mother of Rafe Blackthorne's six children. Originally of Mandan Indian descent, she was the last of her particular tribe. She has maintained many of the journals left behind by her descendants and authored a few of her own.

Dante Blackthorne {A.K.A, Agent Franclin (Franc) Kastle} - Is the identical twin to Dartanian Blackthorne. He recently married Alaina Jordan (Astraia O'Kahner) and adopted her three children: Sayleena, Saruman and Storman Blackthorne (Jordan-Thatcher). They are currently expecting triplets.

Alaina Blackthorne {A.K.A, Alaina Jordan and Astraia Thatcher (O'Kahner)} - Widowed on April 19, 2015, she recently re-married to Dante Blackthorne. She is also the mother of his adopted children Sayleena (6), Saruman (4) and Storman (4) Blackthorne. She is currently expecting triplets fathered by Dante Blackthorne.

Drinian Blackthorne - The second born in the set of triplets within the Blackthorne clan. He is recently married to Veta Rohann and they are expecting triplets. A carpenter at heart, he owns and manages several rental properties.

Veta Blackthorne (Rohann) - Widowed in May of 2014, she is the new bride of Drinian Blackthorne. Recently wed, they appear to be expecting triplets as well. She had three children from a previous marriage: Casey (13), Aaron (13) and Sarah (8) but they are deceased.

Dartanian Blackthorne - The third son born in the set of triplets within the Blackthorne clan. He is an identical twin to Dante Blackthorne. The Sheriff of Breckenridge County, he is married to Lylia Blackthorne and father to her daughter Kayla.

Lylia Blackthorne - The wife of Dartanian Blackthorne, she has a daughter named Kayla (3) who is not Dartanian's biological daughter. She has a teaching degree and home schools most of the children at The Blackthorne Horse Ranch. Lylia's origins are unclear for it seems she was switched at birth.

Breydon Blackthorne - The fourth in the order of birth. He is the fraternal twin of Megorah Blackthorne (Ryans) and the prosecuting attorney for Breckenridge County. He is married to Hialey and is the adopted father of her two boys, Cody and Seth Blackthorne.

Hialey Blackthorne - The wife of Breydon Blackthorne. She owns an upscale lingerie shop called Hialey's Place. She has two children from a previous marriage, Cody (age 6) and Seth (age 4).

Megorah Ryans - The fifth child born in the Blackthorne family, she is the fraternal twin of Breydon Blackthorne. Megorah is married to Dr. Chase Ryans. They have three children together: Katana (12), Ethan (10) and Katie (8). She owns and manages The Ryans Real Estate and Rental Agency in Whitefish, Montana.

Dr. Chase Ryans - Owns a local family practice in Whitefish, Montana just north of The Blackthorne Ranch, but assists at the local hospital in the ER. He is married to Megorah (Blackthorne) Ryans and they have three children: Katana (12), Ethan (10) and Katie (8.)

Crisalya Howard - The baby of the Blackthorne family. She is an ER nurse, working in the local hospital along-side Dr. Chase Ryans. She also assists her husband, Royce Howard, at the popular local coffee house, The Coffee Haven. They have one son together, Aiden (2-1/2).

Royce Howard - The owner of a local coffee house and popular hang-out called The Coffee Haven. He is married to Crisalya (Blackthorne) Howard, the youngest of the Blackthorne clan. They have one son, Aiden (2-½).

Dylan O'Kahner (deceased) - He was married to Astraia Thatcher (O'Kahner). He is the biological father of Sayleena, Saruman and Storman O'Kahner (Jordan).

Woreash and Maleeka - These two angelic beings are merely two of God's many Holy Warriors. Their determination to see God's will through is fierce and unyielding.

Agent Jericho Henley - Is an agent who works for Homeland Security. Or does he?

Agent Ricardo Pegueros - Is an undercover CIA operative who partnered with Agent Franclin (Franc) Kastle, A.K.A. Dante Blackthorne on Alaina Blackthorne's case. He has a wife, Maria Pegueros, and a five-month-old son, Benito (Benni) Pegueros.

Kobi Radford - A drug lord who has a vast drug cartel spanning at least five different countries. He has a vendetta against Alaina Blackthorne and her three children because Alaina's former husband, Dylan O'Kahner killed his brother, Lionel Radford in Florida.

Author Delaine Christine

Photo by Rosemary MacDaniel

Who is this woman really?
Does anyone even know?
And what part of this here story
Is about her, do you suppose?

Much like the character Ciara,
an unnatural strawberry blonde,
she once visited Flathead Valley
a place of which she is very fond.

Though many years have gone by
since her eyes partook of mountains fair,
she still dreams of the double rainbow
she saw on her very last day there.

And though she often dreams of the day
she can go to Montana again,
'til that day comes, she'll write her stories
of gifted Blackthorne women and men.

For more about the series
and the author

vortigernblack.com

smashwords.com/profile/view
/DelaineChristine

Or to Contact the Author:
delainechristine15@gmail.com

www.ingramcontent.com/pod-product-compliance
Lightning Source LLC
Chambersburg PA
CBHW020503260626
47156CB00006B/1837